THE CRUEL GODS

THE THIRTEENTH HOUR

TRUDIE SKIES

fantasy author

TRUDIESKIES.COM

Cover design by James T. Egan, www.bookflydesign.com.

Map illustration by Soraya Corcoran, www.sorayacorcoran.com.

Edited by Nia Quinn, www.editor.niaquinn.com.

ISBN: 978-1-3999-0068-3 (paperback)

ISBN: 978-1-3999-0067-6 (ebook)

First paperback edition October 2021.

Content Warning

THE THIRTEENTH HOUR is an adult fantasy book that contains strong language throughout and content some readers may find distressing, including religious criticism, sexual themes, and scenes of abuse and torture.

For a full list of content warnings, please visit:

TrudieSkies.com/The-Cruel-Gods-Content-Warnings

For the apostates, the blasphemers, and the sinners.

Domain Map

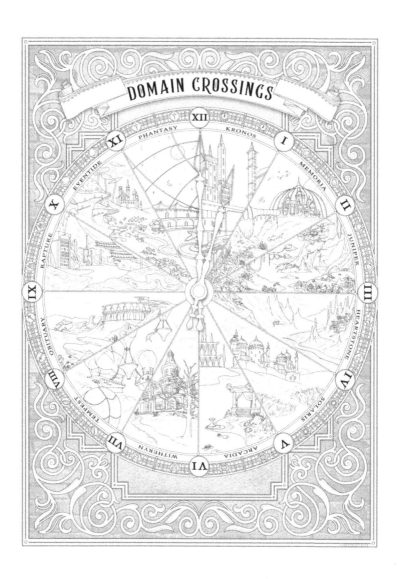

THE COVENANT OF MORTALS & GODS

We, the standing ambassadors of the twelve domains, do pledge to speak true as the holy voice of our patron gods. We ordain this Covenant as a record and warrant between mortals and immortals and agree to uphold its decrees in the eyes of our almighty gods, the faithful, and the Wardens who watch us.

The gods do pledge:

1. To create mortal life which obeys the laws of time.
2. To allow their mortals to exercise free will.
3. To provide a domain [hereby known as Chime] where mortals may seek life and liberty.
4. To bar non-mortal lives from entering this domain [Chime].
5. To allow mortals safe passage into their own domain.
6. To not interfere with the life or liberty of mortals belonging to other domains.

In turn, the mortals do pledge:

1. To honor their god and domain through factious worship and prayer.
2. To honor their god and domain by abstaining from sin.
3. To honor and respect the gods and mortals of other domains.
4. To honor and obey the ordinance of Chime.
5. To honor and obey the word of the Wardens.
6. To not commit the unforgivable sins of blasphemy and apostasy.
7. To bear a mark identifying citizenship to Chime and the twelve domains.

All mortals are made equal in the gods' eyes and shall be granted the same privileges and opportunities on Chime. Should a mortal fail to uphold these seven laws, or commit an unforgivable sin, their right to life and liberty within Chime is forfeit.

The Wardens do pledge to serve Chime and her mortals in accordance with these values and in honor of the gods and their mortal voices.

Signed by the twelve standing ambassadors in the eyes of our almighty gods, the faithful, and the Wardens who watch us.

The Unforgivable Sins

Blasphemy

To blaspheme: an impious utterance or action that besmirches one's patron god or the gods of other domains. To assume one's standing is above one's patron god.

Examples: curse words, disrespectful speech, or hateful imagery.

Apostasy

To reject the blessings and love of one's patron god.

To reject the laws of the Covenant.

To commit idolatry for another god or object in place of one's patron god.

To live a life of blasphemy and depravity.

PART ONE

1

Want to avoid your god's attention?
Then never pray.
Prayer is a direct line of communication between gods and their mortals.
By praying, you're shouting in your god's ear, "I'm here!"
Don't pray, not even in jest.
Without prayer, your existence will be another soul lost among thousands.
—Anonymous, *Godless flier on prayer*

TIME HAD RUN AWAY from me again, but I couldn't afford to let it escape, not today. It chastised me like an unruly student with every tick and tock. Even as a child, I could never be constrained by time, could never obey its laws or heed its lessons. Time had finally grown impatient with my attempts to catch up.

I stumbled on my way to the giant elevator that would take me topside. The elevator only operated twice per hour, and we were late—*I* was late. That was the downside to a city run by divine beings who could manipulate time. Everything ran like clockwork: The printing presses. The stock markets. The trams. The elevator.

Everything but me.

"I can't—can't believe we're chasing a *tram*," Dru whined as we scrambled for all we were worth over the train tracks. Her breathing rasped between a sigh and a wheeze. "We'll—We'll never make it."

"We will if you shut up and run," I spat.

"Of all the things I thought would go wrong, I never—never thought we'd miss the tram."

"Yes, you've mentioned that a few times already."

"Who—Who even does that?"

Dru should know you better by now, my inner voice berated. *Though if you'd left on time, you wouldn't be running through tunnels.*

Great, not even my own mind would shut up about the pissing tram. Too many lives were depending on the documents hidden inside my satchel, which now slammed into my hip with each harried step.

These documents were vital papers for refugees seeking a new home on Chime. Without these, they wouldn't be cleared to receive their passport and make the crossing. Then they'd be trapped inside my god's domain with no means of appeasing her greed.

When one's god demanded such heavy tithes of her own mortals and punished those who couldn't afford to pay, the poorest had no choice but to run, to seek the only city where not even the gods could tread.

And that's where my organization stepped in.

Too many mortals came to Chime seeking a means to pay the tithe, and most were desperate enough to enter workhouses to scrape together what they could. But we knew a better way. Out of our god's sight, they were out of her mind and free from her whims. Not even the gods bothered to track their many thousands of mortals, leaving such tasks for the Wardens—the gods' mortal eyes.

With these documents, we'd forge new identities that not even the Wardens could track.

Then our refugees would be forgotten.

But only if we smuggled them out before the next tithe count.

We'd hurried to get these documents signed, stamped, and sealed; all fake, of course, but navigating Chime's bureaucratic system had rushed us to the last ticking second.

And then I'd gone and missed the bloody tram!

My lungs heaved with the stale air that permeated the Undercity. Stumbling through the tunnels wasn't part of our grand operation, but when one worked for an organization that existed in the shadows, one improvised as best as one could.

One should move one's arse faster.

At least my Vesper eyes could navigate the tunnels better than Dru's Umber ones, though I kept glancing back to make sure I didn't lose her.

She trailed her palm against the pipes which ran along the walls as her guide. I knew darkness well, but she knew those pipes.

The soles of my flats struggled to gain traction on the grime and soot coating the gravel underneath, and the shawl wrapped around my neck flew behind me like a cloak. I'd be feeling the burn of my calves for days. But soon the tunnel opened into the cavernous Undercity station. The silvery-blue glare of the aether lamps lit our path, the only ward against the encroaching darkness.

And beneath sat our tram, snuggled into its bay and puffing out smug clouds of steam as commuters poured out onto the platform.

Dru bumped into me, and we both sagged against each other's shoulders to catch our breath. The two of us stood at the same height of six feet; standard size for a Vesper, though short for an Umber.

"I still can't—can't believe we chased the tram."

"Oh, give over. We made it in time, didn't we?"

"Did we? Kayl, look at the queue."

The usual mob of early morning workers crowded the Undercity platforms that spread out like spokes on a wheel. Most were Vesper, fellow members of my domain—all tall, dark, and broody—and they trudged past to catch a separate tram heading to the factories or warehouses built underground. Many more shuffled forward in one long tidy queue toward the great elevator.

My neck cracked as I traced the giant steel column up and up until it disappeared completely into the Undercity's plate ceiling, which blinked with a never-ending sky of aether lights shimmering like stars. Our only way topside.

And—shit, the queue was longer than I'd expected, but then I was never normally awake for the ten o'clock crossing.

That was the problem with living where natural light didn't find you. It was almost impossible to guess the time, let alone wake during civilized hours.

Dru doesn't have that problem.

Neither did the rest of the Undercity, it appeared. They depended on the elevator to lift them to a world with more light, only to continue their

3

daily drudgery stuffed in shops and offices. Better work, certainly. Topside, you could breathe fresh air, drink clean water, see with the power of the sun instead of the artificial lights that flickered threateningly, and escape the smog that stained everything it touched gray.

But work was still work, and every citizen of Chime belonged to a master. While our capitalist overlords forced us into servitude for bocs and the Wardens ruled the city with their ordinances, even they, and the rest of us mere mortals, were owned by our gods.

I wrapped my arm around Dru's solid bicep and dragged her into the tail end of the queue. It was like dragging a boulder. Not that I'd call her that. An Umber's physicality was as hardened and practical as their manners.

Among the line of Vesper, Dru's mossy-green skin contrasted with their dark blues, purples, and gray tones, and my indigo shade. While most Umber resembled walking stone, Dru took on the more natural aspects of her god. I loved the patterns of vined leaves that curled around her head instead of hair, and in place of her eyebrows, a line of golden daisies sprouted, though right now they drooped with dehydration and exhaustion. I'd made her run *hard* to catch that pissing tram.

"Stop your worrying, we'll make it." I nudged her playfully. "At least *you* don't sweat."

Dru wrinkled her nose, and the crystal freckles dotted across her cheeks caught the lamplight, sending a shimmer of rainbow across the drab green of her skin. "It's lucky for you I've got no sense of smell."

I made a show of sniffing my armpits and accidentally elbowed a Vesper man in front. His glare was a common sight for Chime's citizens.

Thou must not violate the sanctity of the queue, Kayl!

I flashed a grin and slid back into place, adjusting the shawl around my head to play my *oh so pious* act.

Like clockwork, the queue made its way forward with agonizing slowness, and I couldn't keep myself from tapping my foot and snapping the satchel's strap across my shoulder.

You're annoying Dru.

Indeed, Dru shot me her irritable *stop fidgeting* scowl. I didn't want to infect her with my nerves because then I'd have to admit it was my fault we'd missed the tram.

It was your fault.

Yes, but I wasn't going to admit it. The Godless would never let me run an operation like this again, and it had taken months to convince them they could trust me with *this* one.

I dipped my chin from the glare of the aether lamps hanging above the platform. They hummed with an annoying buzz that ached inside my head, and their light cast scattered silvery-blue wisps across the station. The vast majority of Undercity residents were Vesper, and we didn't need artificial lights to guide our way through the dark. Not when we could command darkness itself.

The lamps were for the rest of the sorry souls who graced the Undercity, and I stood on tiptoes to count them; a few red-skinned Ember who could summon flame if needed, and the perfectly shimmering silver of the Diviner station staff standing guard by the elevator.

A ripple of discontent passed through the queue as the Vesper jostled and attempted to straighten themselves. Someone was trying to cut in, earning tutting and jeers.

"Can you spare a few bocs? Please? Just a few spare bocs?" a woman's voice pleaded. "I need to pay the tithe. Please, anyone?"

"Probably gambled their last boc on Sinner's Row," the Vesper man before me muttered, his pointed ears twitching.

She could have lost her entire life's savings on Sinner's Row for all I knew, though for an Undercity resident, her life's savings likely didn't amount to much. "Dru," I whispered and nudged her. "Look."

The beggar was another Vesper. She wasn't outfitted in modest black and gray like the rest of us, but in a bright beige dress smudged with dirt that hung in flayed thread at the hem above her knee. Her dark blue legs were clearly visible, though she'd tried to hide her naked arms and shoulders with a tattered shawl.

The Undercity residents ignored her, because, dressed like that, they saw some whore straight from Sinner's Row.

I saw something much different. Desperation.

No Vesper would dare leave their home dressed immodestly enough to attract attention. Nor would any Vesper wear those colors—the colors of our greatest rivals, the Glimmer.

"She's from a workhouse," Dru whispered, agreeing with my suspicions.

Glimmer had been stealing Undercity residents for years now and forcing the poorest and most desperate among us into their workhouses. Refuges, the Glimmer called them—a hot meal, warm bed, and promised tithes for servitude to their golden god.

Forced idolatry, I called it.

To worship another god was akin to apostasy according to the Covenant, yet the Wardens turned a blind eye to the Glimmer's deeds. We Godless did not.

The Glimmer were the richest of the domains, and they lauded their position at the top of Chime's social hierarchy over the rest of us. They certainly hadn't gifted their generosity to this poor Vesper.

I opened up the satchel and rummaged for my purse. Shit, I must have left it behind. "Got any bocs?"

Dru patted her pinafore. "Donated what I had for the last pot."

Our pot was a collection of wages and donations the Godless pooled together for such situations that we kept secure back at our depot. Unregistered citizens of Chime—illegals, the Wardens called them—could avoid making the tithe, and so would our new batch of illegal refugees, thanks to our fake documentation.

While only the Vesper god required weekly tithes, other gods made equally outrageous demands. Mortals who failed to honor their gods were reported by the Wardens. Those unfortunate souls were then marched back to their domain to face the consequences—a flogging, perhaps, if their god was feeling particularly forgiving.

Normally we'd dole such tithe expenses out well in advance for those Vesper who needed them, but this Vesper woman... If she'd come from a workhouse, then chances were the Wardens would report her missing tithe. Then she'd be kissing her soul away.

She grew increasingly agitated as she fought her way through the queue. "Just a few bocs for the tithe, *please*!"

The Vesper grumbled and turned their backs from her pleading. I couldn't abandon this woman to her fate, but my satchel carried the documents needed to help a whole delegation of souls like hers—and if we missed the crossing, they'd come short for the tithe too and not live to see the next crossing. Or worse: the Glimmer would enslave our refugees in their workhouses with rubber-stamped authority.

There was no time to return to the depot now.

Pick a pocket.

I *could* slip my hand and steal a wallet or two, but this was the Undercity; everyone here suffered from the same struggles, and it wouldn't just be this woman desperate to make the tithe on time.

A dour-faced Diviner by the elevator held out his hand to stop the meandering woman. "You're holding up the queue, ma'am. Step aside."

"She's awaiting my tithe; I just need a few bocs—"

"Please step aside, ma'am, or we'll close the doors."

Even from my place in the queue, I could tell the elevator hadn't yet reached capacity, but if the station staff closed up early, then that would mean another half hour of waiting for the next lift. A half hour I could not spare on today of all days.

Both Dru and I were expected—for one, to hand over these documents for the crossing, and for two, we were both employed topside in a quaint little Glimmer teahouse. As much as I *loved* cream scones, my employment served one purpose: to spy on the Glimmer and discover exactly why the Wardens were happy to break the Covenant and allow one domain to enslave mortals of another in their workhouses.

My organization suspected foul play and corruption, and our seer had witnessed a deal taking place in Lady Mae's teahouse. Our seer's visions were haphazard and came in flashes—a place here, a time there—and only when the event drew closer would the visions clear and toll the bell of action. Those visions pointed to the same day our refugees made the crossing.

We simply could not miss the elevator.

The Vesper woman fell to her knees. "Please! You need to let me on!"

Shit.

The Diviner stepped back, aghast at the Vesper begging at his feet. "Close the doors!"

The last few stragglers hurried forward, and the queue lurched with a fevered desperation as the station staff began to slide the massive elevator doors closed.

"We're not going to make it," Dru said.

"Yes, I can see that."

"We can't miss the elevator—"

"I *know*." I patted my satchel, and the contents hidden inside. "Follow my lead."

The queuing Vesper grumbled and swore as I pushed my way past them, violating every unofficial city ordinance. "Hold the door!" I cried out. "Oh, please, hold the door!"

"There's a queue, ma'am. Wait for the next elevator."

Both Vesper and Diviner ignored the woman crying on the platform. No one would go near her, but she stood between me and that damn elevator.

I bobbed a desperate curtsy. "Oh, please, sir, this is my sister. She doesn't mean to be rude, sir, but she lost her savings to a pickpocket and can't make the tithe. Let me take her topside, sir, and we'll explain to the Wardens." I crouched and grabbed the woman's shoulders. "Don't pray," I whispered into her ear. "Pray and you're dead."

She glanced up, appalled that I'd suggest such a thing.

Great—the pious were always a liability.

The Diviner tapped his watch and scowled. "Look, lady, wait for the next elevator—"

"We cannot miss the crossing, sir, or my god, Valeria, will—she'll—" I wailed a sob.

Dru wrapped her arms around me and forced my head onto her shoulder. "There, there. These kind gentlemen are only doing their jobs, there's no need to cry. Valeria is forgiving. She might let you both back into Chime—"

I wailed louder and caught the expression of the Diviner. His silver skin and hair made him appear more machine than mortal, and from the few Diviner I'd come across, I knew they couldn't handle displays of emotion. Or indeed, any emotion. Now, his silver cheeks shone pink as he rapidly glanced between his watch and the grumbling crowd. For a moment I thought he'd touch me to verify my sob-story, but his lip curled with the disgust of a man who didn't want to go rummaging through the head of some crying woman.

The Vesper behind me jeered, unimpressed with my display, but the Diviner cared only for order. An angry crowd could be placated, but there was no chance he'd let the elevator go off schedule.

Mortals of the twelve domains were *supposed* to be made equal according to the Covenant, but when the Diviner literally controlled time, Chime's citizens obeyed their ordinances. What mortal could disobey the laws of time?

"Hold the door!" called another man, who came bounding across the platform.

"No more delays!" the Diviner shouted.

The stranger elbowed his way through the queue. "Excuse me, coming through." Another Diviner popped out between the taller Vesper and he flashed a badge—a brass *W*, the insignia of the Wardens.

Shit, running into a Warden was the last thing I needed.

"Sorry, chaps, can you hold the door for five?" the Warden asked.

"They're holding up the queue," the Diviner said with an air of indignation, and pointed at me.

"Then it's fortuitous that I'm here to resolve the matter. Would you?"

The Diviner tutted but nodded at his fellow station staff to hold the doors. They couldn't deny a Warden.

I pulled my shawl tighter around my face as the Warden approached. He stood five inches shorter than I, and while he hardly appeared threatening, I quickly scanned over his features to get his measure.

He wore a tan suit, but the shirt looked disheveled, his silver hair was a tousled mess, and stubble lined his face—though his skin was a shimmering pearl rather than pure silver, which made him appear more mortal than his counterparts. A pair of brass eyeglasses dangled precariously on his nose and did nothing to hide the tired dark circles under his silver eyes.

What was a Diviner Warden doing in the Undercity overnight? This one wasn't dressed in the usual black-and-bronze uniform issued to the Wardens, and Diviner weren't the type to seek pleasure on Sinner's Row.

Mortals from all domains served in the Wardens in one way or another, but Diviner were the worst. I wanted to catch Dru's eye, but she'd merged with the crowd. It didn't pay to act suspiciously around Wardens when they represented the gods' eyes. I tightened my fingers around the strap of the satchel instead, digging my fingernails into the leather.

"She's my sister," I blurted out, unsure what to say. "Someone stole her bocs and she's late for the tithe. We just need to get topside in time for the crossing, sir, and we'll be fine." I forced a smile.

Perhaps we could use this fool to get her tithe paid on time. No harm, no foul.

The Warden gave me a shrewd look, as though suspicious I'd scam him out of his wallet. Not a fool, then. There was something disconcertingly familiar about him. Had I seen his face somewhere? "Her name, please?"

Could I trust her not to contradict me? "She's shy, sir."

"So I see." He crouched down to the Vesper woman's eye level. "You've come from a workhouse, haven't you? Can you tell me which one?"

Shit. Had he come here to catch a runaway and send her back? I wouldn't put it past the Wardens to do the Glimmer's dirty work.

The woman shrank from his gaze. "They—They wouldn't let me go, but my Queen, she needs—she needs my tithe."

"It's quite all right." The Warden sounded kind for a Diviner, though based on the Vesper muttering and shaking their heads behind us, they didn't buy his act either. "I'll ensure you get to Eventide and we'll get your tithe paid on time. I need to ask you a few questions first."

"You—You won't take me back?"

"You have my word." His hand twitched by his side, as though fighting the urge to touch her.

"I don't believe you! I'm not going back; you can't make me!" The woman clasped her hands together in prayer. "My Queen! I'm sorry! Please save me, my Queen! I'm—"

She screamed, and her spine arched in a pained spasm.

The Warden and I both reached out to grab her at the same time. Bright silver light pulsed through the aether lamps, and a shrill screech tore through my head as though someone had whistled directly in my ear. I cringed from the sound, and my hand swiped through empty air as the Warden fell forward.

Get away from him.

I scrambled back from his touch—I couldn't risk brushing against a Diviner, not even accidentally. But he'd landed on the rags that had once belonged to the Vesper. She'd faded into nothing in a single heartbeat, leaving only her meager possessions and a mote of dust.

Our god had claimed her.

I didn't know whether to curse or cry. Hadn't I told her not to pray? Hadn't I bloody *told* her?

The Warden scooped up the woman's shawl with the reverence of a mortal who'd never witnessed death, yet his silver eyes told a tale of disappointing inevitability.

Around me, the Vesper bowed their heads and muttered quick prayers. Idiots, the lot of them. But when a god's power graced your presence, you bowed.

I supposed I should have, but I was one of the few Vesper who managed to avoid my god's attention. I was a mere speck of dirt in the grand scheme of my god's imagination. While mortals of the other domains may sneer at my lowly place here in the Undercity, at least my mind belonged to me.

And always would.

"You said she was your sister?" the Warden asked as he rose to his feet. "I'm sorry for your loss, but I'll need to ask you a few questions, if you don't mind."

Shit, shit, *shit*! If a Warden took me to his HQ, then it was all over. Everything!

One touch of his skin on mine and he'd see the past few hours of my morning. My pathetic crying display, my race to the elevator, missing the tram and chasing it along the tracks, which by city ordinance laws, was considered trespassing. Quickly getting dressed in the uniform I'd need to serve customers in Lady Mae's teahouse. And putting together documents to smuggle illegal refugees into the city.

Yes, it was that last memory which would get me thrown into the Warden's correctional facility. If he knew who he stood beside—what organization I worked for—then I wouldn't be leaving this platform as a free woman.

Perhaps this Diviner could act, but he'd never met *me*. "She was a friend to me, sir, like a sister." I gave my thigh a sharp pinch and forced a few tears out for effect. "But I need to get topside, sir, my mistress is waiting, and I can't afford to be late, or I'll—I'll end up in a workhouse, too. Please, sir, I can't miss—"

"Time!" the Diviner station staff yelled, making me jump.

Thank the gods for punctuality.

The Warden shot the station staff an exasperated look. "Yes, I am aware, thank you." His silver eyes returned to me. "Would you ride with me to the station? I promise I won't keep you long, but a mortal has died. It must be documented."

Curse the gods for bureaucracy. I dabbed my eyes with my shawl and bobbed a quick curtsy. I couldn't deny a Warden, either.

I followed him onto the elevator, the satchel clutched tight to my chest. More Vesper bounded on, and Dru squeezed in somewhere behind me. If I could at least pass my satchel to her, she'd deliver these documents safely, even if I were incarcerated.

The elevator was spacious enough to fit an entire tram carriage. Or about one hundred bodies, give or take. Right now, the early morning workers packed in tight enough to rub shoulders. Not ideal when so many pickpockets flitted among the Vesper, but when you needed to be at work on time, time did not care for comfort. Or little else.

The large metal doors clanged shut with an ominous thud, trapping me with my fate. Aether lamps flickered above, and the Warden took in a hitched breath.

My stomach lurched with the ground, and the familiar grinding of gears drowned out the hushed conversations around me. I swayed, careful to avoid brushing against the Warden, as the elevator finally rose up the shaft.

I didn't need a watch to know what time it was; nine thirty in the morning. Most businesses opened at ten, and the entire journey from the Undercity to topside would take twenty minutes, leaving me with little time to escape my new Warden friend, hand over my documents, and get to Lady Mae's.

But the plan was running smoothly, all things considered.

You're about to be arrested and tossed into the nearest correctional facility.

There was always that risk, no matter what I did. My organization called themselves Godless for a reason, and funnily enough, the Wardens didn't take kindly to apostates. We'd survived on borrowed time.

Though now my time was running out.

"I hate these things," the Warden muttered beside me.

"Elevators? Your domain invented them."

"So that all mortals may fly and embrace the sky," he quoted a legendary Zephyr engineer. "If all mortals were meant to embrace the sky, we'd all have wings."

I knew I shouldn't be making pleasant conversation with the enemy, but I couldn't let this opportunity slip. "Is that what brings a Diviner down to our level? Or were you checking the elevators ran on time?"

He tilted his head to better see me and a small smile curled his lips. "Not all Diviner pore over timetables. Some of us seek greater thrills."

"What thrills does a Diviner seek in the Undercity? Not a cat café, gods forbid." There were plenty of dangers buried underneath Chime for a Warden to hunt: beggars and thieves of the slums, corruption on Sinner's Row, tales of soul-sucking electrical monsters that supposedly stalked the tunnels, or, more likely, the rumors of a blasphemous cult of godless heathens committing apostasy in the shadows.

"A cat café? Goodness, I'm far too pure and innocent, and their tea is lousy. Hard water and all that." Again, that slight smile. "But no, my visit didn't bring me here for the tea." He bent his head close and his voice dropped to a barely audible whisper over the mechanical grunts and whirs of the elevator. "I don't suppose your friend spoke of her time inside the workhouse? Or you know of anyone who's been inside one? Perhaps you've heard rumors of Vesper going missing? Workers being snatched up or bribed with tithes?"

My heart gave a brief flutter; it was those rumors which inspired my operation this morning, and which resulted in the illegal paperwork resting in my satchel.

Glimmer had been stealing mortals from the Undercity for months—years, even—to serve in their workhouses. Why would the Wardens take an interest now? "Must be affecting a Glimmer's bottom line." The bitter quip came out before I could stop it, and the tips of my pointed ears warmed.

"Can't say I care much for the bottoms of Glimmer. Forgive me for prodding, but you're the only Vesper to indulge me. Hard to conduct an investigation when no one is willing to offer me the time of day."

"That's because we're smart enough not to indulge a Warden when an investigation is in play. It's almost nine-fifty, by the way. I thought you Diviner could tell the time?"

He turned to face me as the elevator slowed to a stop.

The plate rumbled underneath my feet and then the doors were being dragged open, the harsh clang signaling the end of our journey.

"Mind the gap!" the station staff called.

Bright lights blinded me for a moment, but I was soon swept away in the crowds pushing me forward, eager to get out of that stuffy dark box. Dru found my wrist and pulled me away before I got trampled, and we wove between the stomping feet.

I glanced over my shoulder and caught the eye of my talkative Warden. He too was being pulled away by the mob, though he tried to fight his way back to me. Why didn't he simply pause time and grab me? He could have.

Instead, he stared with a mournful pout, and I didn't know what to make of him.

He's a Diviner. They're dangerous.

I knew that, but there was something off about this one. Something less... orderly.

Dru dragged me ahead like some misbehaving student. "Are you mad? What were you doing talking to that Warden?"

"It's considered a social norm to reply when someone initiates small talk, Dru."

"Small talk is comparing types of tea."

"We *were* talking about tea—"

"And? Is that all the Warden wanted?"

I understood her fear all too well. "They're investigating the workhouses."

Dru almost tripped over her feet. "They are? That complicates things."

Indeed. We didn't need Wardens sniffing around the Undercity when so many other pieces were in play. But why would a Warden investigate at all?

If our seer's visions were correct, then the Wardens were throwing their support behind these workhouses. Did my inquisitive Warden know and was simply sniffing for leaks? Or could there be greater corruption within their ranks?

I'd have my answers when the clock struck ten tonight.

For now, I had to obey time's schedule or our Vesper refugees would be stolen by golden hands plucking them fresh off Chime's streets.

So many things could go wrong in the next twelve hours.

If I was a pious woman, I'd be praying.

But I was a Godless woman, and the gods left me to dictate my own fate.

2

Chime runs on Diviner power and logic.
When a mortal such as the Diviner can manipulate time, the rest of us
must obey. It is their bureaucracy which keeps the system running like
clockwork, regardless of whether that system works for the rest of us.
Don't let a Diviner touch you.
With one touch, they can see up to an hour of your past and immediate
future. They'll violate the sanctity of your mind to find any incriminating
actions or thoughts.
—Anonymous, *Godless flier on the Diviner*

WITH ONLY TEN MINUTES to spare, both time and the early morning crowds
worked against us. Dru and I squeezed past the queues and I almost collided
with a tram chugging by—and most definitely would have if Dru hadn't
yanked me back. The little wooden and brass carriage came to a halt further
on, and mortals from the various domains poured out, scattering across
Central Station.

Small Seren boys wove between the taller mortals, though with their
childlike cherub faces, it was hard to tell their age—they could have been
anything from thirteen to thirty. The soot-faced chimney sweeps whacked
mortals with their brooms, forcing them out of the way, while the
paperboys flew overhead to make their rounds, their wings a fluttering blur.

I ducked underneath them and skipped past a Vesper lad haggling with
an Ember street vendor selling freshly heated breakfast rolls and coffee from
a cart. The Ember occasionally sent ripples of flame over his goods to keep
them warm, while a Diviner stood in the queue and tapped his watch with
all the tuts he could muster.

That was what I loved about Chime: the hustle and bustle of mortals
from all twelve domains thrown together and forced to get along despite

our many differences. According to the Covenant, no domain overshadowed another. A hungry Vesper was no different from an Ember chef or an impatient Diviner.

Though the reality wasn't quite so balanced.

Dru tugged my attention away from the mouthwatering scents of baked bread and we marched across the cobblestones to our meeting place; a single wooden bench tucked around the corner of the station under an aether lamp that had seen better days.

A Vesper male slouched on the bench dressed in the casual shirt, slacks, and flat cap of a city slicker, though the hat did little to hide the long locks of black hair straggling down his back. He patted the satchel resting across his lap, filled with the latest broadsheets from the Courier—or should have been.

I knew what that satchel really contained—fliers printed with blasphemous propaganda. Who better to distribute them than a mortal who could hide within the shadows?

"What are two lovely ladies like yourselves doing loitering on the street corner?" he asked. "Don't you know all kinds of undesirables lurk here?"

"And you'd be loitering here waiting for such undesirables to come your way?"

"You must have me mistaken, ma'am. I'm but an innocent paperboy. I wouldn't hold such wanton desires." Malk's easygoing smile and brilliant blue eyes could win over any Vesper girl, yet I'd won him.

I slid onto the bench and gave him a playful shove.

Malk caught my hand and his lips pressed against my fingers, as smooth as butter. "Cutting it fine, aren't you? The Gate opens in five."

Dru leaned against the lamppost and crossed her arms. "We missed the tram."

"You did?"

Dru snorted. "Kayl did."

I rolled my eyes as I curled my hand around his, my stomach fluttering at the slight tingle of his touch. His skin was a darker midnight blue compared to my brighter indigo. I ached to feel the comfort of his lips once more; their shade a pure black to match mine. "We're here, aren't we? A Vesper woman died below. We think she came from a workhouse."

Malk's grip tightened. "Shit. Do you have any good news for me?"

"There was a Warden. They're investigating the workhouses."

"Sure, that's better. Wardens poking around our business is exactly what we need." He released my hand and removed his cap to run fingers through his thick strands.

"We're still on schedule." I opened my satchel and dug out the papers. "Don't look at them. Don't think about them."

"Relax." Malk shoved them into his own satchel. "I can't make the crossing until half past. There's a delegation of Glimmer passing through to Eventide. Nonessential travel is being delayed."

"*Into* Eventide?" Glimmer and Vesper were natural-born enemies—the dawn to our dusk. They wouldn't dare enter Eventide alone. A delegation certainly wasn't part of our intel, nor our seer's visions.

"I know, right? Chances are they'll be escorted by Wardens. Let's hope these copies get me past them or I'm thoroughly fucked, and not in a way I'd enjoy."

The clock struck ten.

I glanced to where I'd hurried from only moments before.

The clock tower dominated the skyline of Chime, connecting Central with the Golden City plate above and the Undercity below like one gigantic hourglass. Above us, the Golden City cast a shadow across Central, but at least the plate didn't cover everything unlike the Undercity, allowing the sun's light and warmth to reach us, albeit at an angle best enjoyed at dawn and dusk.

I'd always admired the clock tower. Not just for its sheer scale and impossible height, but there was something magical about it that drew my gaze. Like all things on Chime, the giant clockface always rang on time, and the vibrations of its bell could be felt even underground.

Two elevator shafts ran up and down the clock tower on either side. To the right, the metal elevator that led to the Undercity below, and to the left, the glass elevator that rose above the heights of Chime's Central Square into the skies, disappearing beyond the upper plate to the Golden City itself.

But that wasn't why Chime's citizens gathered around the clock tower.

Where Central Station's concourse had been built, the bottom half of the clock tower opened up into a wide arch hundreds of feet tall; large enough for an entire fleet of trams to pass through.

Through it, one could see another world. Twelve worlds, to be precise. At the turn of the hour, the Gate would shimmer and change to the next world, and then the next.

To cross through the Gate was to enter the realm of the gods. But to cross from those worlds *into* Chime was to escape their cruelties and their whims, for the gods couldn't leave their own domain, and Chime was ours.

Too many mortals sought freedom in Chime. Not all would find it.

On schedule, the Gate shimmered once more, changing from the red volcanic skies of the Ember domain to the permanent twilight of Eventide.

The domain of my god, Valeria. The home I'd never visit.

It was only through the Gate that I saw what other Vesper had described: rolling hills of bioluminescent mushrooms and a never-ending dusk.

"We're going to be late," Dru said.

I sighed and pulled myself from the bench. "She's right, we're expected." It wouldn't help our cause if we got fired now. "So what's today's performance?"

Malk rose and adjusted his satchel. "You know, the usual. I'm going to hit the jewelry stores and stare mournfully through windows as I contemplate which ridiculously expensive gemstone will win my lover's heart. The Diviner sure enjoy a good love story."

I placed my hand on his chest and reached up for a kiss. "Your lover could never be won with a pointless rock."

"I'm standing right here," Dru mumbled.

Malk's fingers traced the hem of my shawl, the tips lightly caressing my neck. "I'll need to thoroughly cleanse my thoughts," he murmured. "Seeing you in this uniform gives me all kinds of filthy ideas." He bit his lower lip.

I leaned closer. "I'll be wearing it when you return, so don't keep a lady waiting."

"You know, we could find a dark little alley together, right now. You and me, writhing in the shadows." His lips brushed close to my ear. "Give those Diviner a show they'll enjoy."

Just the thought warmed my stomach. "And dirty my skirts?"

"I'll dirty more than your skirts."

Dru scowled. "Again, I'm standing right here."

Malk grinned and kissed me full on the mouth. "I'll be back before you know it. The gods leave you to your fate."

"And yours," I whispered.

An ache tightened in my chest as Malk pulled himself from my embrace. "Keep her out of trouble, Dru."

Dru waved him off. "Don't I always?" She wrapped her arm around mine as Malk jogged behind a tram and disappeared into the crowds.

I couldn't chase after him or interfere until he returned from Eventide. He'd have to spend at least the next half hour channeling his thoughts into the persona of someone who wasn't about to commit crimes.

The Diviner Wardens didn't touch everyone who passed through the Gate, but they certainly preyed on the least reputable mortals—mortals from the domains at the bottom rung of Chime's social mobility, and that included the Vesper. Luckily for Malk, the Diviner didn't care to examine a mortal's past or future beyond a half-hour time slot, and certainly wouldn't linger on emotional memories.

It wasn't enough to simply clear one's mind. No, that would create suspicion. Instead, it was best to create an act—a persona—that a Diviner could well believe.

But when Malk passed through Eventide, he'd be stuck there until night. Twelve painfully slow hours where I'd never know if he'd been caught committing blasphemy by our god. One day he might never return.

Dru patted my arm. "He'll be fine. He's made the crossing before."

"He wasn't smuggling an entire group of Vesper refugees before." Nor did he need to contend with a Glimmer delegation. "So much could go wrong. We've seen it."

"Reve's visions don't always come to pass."

But I knew this one would.

Rows of tiny boutique town houses, salons, and souvenir gift shops lined the main road of Central Square. They stretched around the clock tower in a near-infinite circle, and nestled among them sat Lady Mae's teahouse.

A tiny bell rang above the café door as Dru and I stumbled inside.

The proprietor of this fine establishment stood with her arms crossed, a towel draped over her shoulder, her golden skin and hair a blazing dawn against the set pieces of fine ceramic teacups and pots. Her burning red eyes looked ready to send me up in smoke as I carefully squeezed my way past tables to the kitchen.

"You're late," the Glimmer snarled with barely repressed rage, and then fixed an exaggerated smile for a customer nearby who'd glanced up, startled.

I shrugged off my satchel as Dru ducked into the kitchen. "The tram didn't pull out on time, can you imagine?"

The Glimmer's carefully manicured eyebrow twitched. Her ire was fixed on me, and not Dru, because Dru was an Umber—a loyal, hardworking Umber who'd wash your feet and thank you for the opportunity—whereas I was a lowly Vesper, the shadow that crawled out of the Undercity to snatch your valuables when no one was looking.

What she didn't know was that my weeks spent slaving here were ending tonight.

The Glimmer—I forget her name, for I never cared to learn it—yanked off her towel with a whipcrack. "This will come out of your pay. Take off that ugly scarf and get to work."

From *my* pay, of course. Not Dru's. Not that it mattered—we both poured our wages into the Godless's pot.

I forced a placating curtsy and entered the kitchen, where I wafted away the steam. Dru had already rolled up her sleeves and began the arduous task of washing dishes. Our Ember chef slumped by the ovens as he summoned flame to grill cheese toasties. The poor boy's red skin looked washed out and anemic.

Our barista flitted about the kitchen, preparing brews of tea and coffee. At only four feet, it was sometimes hard to see the Seren beneath me, though those wings slapped across my thighs when I wasn't paying attention—they certainly weren't as delicate as they looked. Her pastel pink skin matched the awful décor of Lady Mae's, but she too looked tired, and dark circles made her usually youthful cherub face age a century.

Bloody gods, it was only ten past ten. This was going to be a long day.

I waved at them both with a cheery "Morning!" and grabbed my apron.

The Seren shoved a tray of cucumber sandwiches and a pot of steaming tea into my hands. "You're up, Vespie."

And so began another twelve-hour shift.

But I wasn't here just to earn a pittance.

Lady Mae's was one of many Glimmer-owned businesses feeding into the workhouses and actively profiting from them. Our seer's visions pointed to a deal going down today between these golden-arses and the Wardens. A deal which, if exposed, could affect public perception of both—and close these workhouses down for good.

Sadly, such visions couldn't provide enough clarity for *who* or *when*. In a twelve-hour shift, that would mean hundreds of customers. Hundreds of potentially corrupt Wardens.

And while I was playing hostess, Malk would bide his time in Eventide, collecting our refugees and preparing them for the crossing. Our seer's visions had warned it would go wrong, that our target would interfere, and our refugees would be stolen from under our noses. But as Dru had said, his visions didn't always come to pass.

At least we knew what to expect.

Balancing my tray, I navigated the tightly packed tables of the café and found my first customer of the day—another Glimmer dressed to the nines in a gorgeous low-cut red gown and matching ruby earrings.

She took her tea with a turned-up nose. "It really is generous of Lady Mae to offer employment to those less fortunate. You... don't handle the notes, do you?"

"Oh no, milady, we don't touch no bocs," I said with the Undercity lilt she expected.

"Very well. You may return to work."

They're only so stuck up because the sun shines out of their arse.

I smiled and sauntered back and forth from the kitchen as the tea began flowing.

All things considered, I didn't mind the work, even if my purpose was espionage rather than earning an honest wage. Though I doubted such work could make an honest woman out of me.

When Dru and I first started here weeks ago, I'd struggled to balance the various customers and their needs. There were too many variables to consider, too many mistakes. Each domain had their own dietary requirements, and though our pink Seren covered most of that, it was my job to take customer orders and ensure I didn't poison them or accidentally commit a hate crime.

Half the time I ran into the kitchen and forgot why I was there. Dru covered for me then and suggested writing everything down. That helped me find my rhythm.

I soon discovered that I could keep a fast pace between my tables so long as nothing distracted me or threw off my focus, and therein lay the challenge.

From Lady Mae's window, the Gate was clearly visible. I could see whenever the Gate changed from one colorful domain to another. Even if I averted my eyes, the dong of the clock tower rattled the cups; a god of its own who would not be ignored.

You've got me to keep you straight.

Yes, my inner mind noticed what I didn't, as stupid as that seemed, and I relied on that extra sense to spy on my patrons—the *actual* reason I worked here.

Though today, I gladly welcomed the distraction of work; the steam of honeyed tea, the clink of spoons on saucers, the calm and polite chatter of the patrons, the ache of my feet as I danced with my trays.

You're too distracted, idiot. You've forgotten the Mesmer.

Shit, I had.

A Mesmer sat in the corner staring at a decorative plate hanging from the wall, their head tilted, mouth ajar. They could have been contemplating the secrets of the universe or just admiring the pattern for all I knew. The Mesmer were dreamers who often fell asleep into their cups. Good customer service meant making sure they woke in time for their crossing at the eleventh hour.

I whipped out my notepad. "May I take your order?" The Mesmer rarely held gender; thus, I skipped my usual honorific titles. This one wore a tight black suit and their skin was a dark purple to rival the Vesper, only their skin rippled with the patterns of a nebulous star.

"Would you like something caffeinated?" I prompted again. Mesmer liked sweet things. Candy, cakes. "We also serve fruit teas."

The Mesmer slowly lowered their gaze and stared with fathomless black eyes speckled with starlight. "Tea." I wasn't sure if that was a proclamation or a question. "Is that why we're here?"

"Yes, this is a café."

My Glimmer boss scowled at me from across the room as she chatted with another customer.

"I'll tell you what, I'll get you something that'll perk you right up. The crossing to Phantasy is opening shortly."

"The Gate," the Mesmer murmured. "Is that why we're here?"

Gods, I had no idea, but I knew for sure that a Mesmer wouldn't be organized enough to serve the Wardens. "I'll get you a nice coffee." I skipped to the kitchen and rang the order in. "Mesmer order up! Extra cream, extra sugar, and, uh, an extra shot of something strong. Dru, can you walk them over to the Gate when the clock strikes?"

Dru scowled over her shoulder from her position by the sink, her green hands covered in suds. "Why do I have to do it?"

"Because you understand them, and if I go, I'll get distracted on the way and end up at a candy store."

Dru tutted but waved me off with a soapy dishcloth.

The next hour came and went in a blur of teacups, and then the clock struck midday. The Gate's portal changed from the Mesmer's starry skies to dull gray buildings. Kronos, the domain of the Diviner. Not just masters of time, but masters of bureaucracy.

Masters of boring.

Other than Glimmer, the Diviner were the most frequent visitors to Lady Mae's, and I needed to be careful when moving around them. Thankfully, it was considered socially unacceptable for a Diviner to touch someone without their consent, but that didn't always stop them. It certainly didn't stop Diviner Wardens.

The afternoon dragged on as the Gate cycled through the various domains—Memoria, Juniper, and then at three, the Umber's mountainous home world came into view.

"Do you miss Heartstone?" I asked Dru in the kitchen. The café traffic had died off, and I helped her dry cups while leaning against the counter to rest my poor feet.

Dru glanced at her worn hands, rough from overwork. "Sometimes," she admitted. "But the work there is more backbreaking than here."

I glanced over to where the Ember boy had fallen asleep over the cooling stove, his face smudged with soot. "You didn't need to take this job, you know. It's not like you'll be spying on anyone from here."

Dru cracked her knuckles. "I'm your backup for when it all goes wrong."

"*If* it goes wrong."

"Definitely when."

"I appreciate your faith in me." We were a team, of course, but no one trusted me to handle myself.

That's because they know what you're like.

Which was? Resourceful? Adaptable?

The café's bell rang. I tossed my dirty rag onto the counter. "Well, these customers won't serve themselves." Though gods, I wished they would.

As the afternoon wore on, the Gate changed to the Glimmer domain of Solaris at four, followed by Arcadia, the Seren's paradise islands, at five.

Our barista stared mournfully out of the window at the palm trees visible through the Gate. So many mortals spoke of their domains with a wistfulness, but I couldn't relate. Outside of Chime, the gods ruled their domains, and their mortals were troublesome flies that meant little to them. Buzz in the wrong manner and you were liable to get swatted.

25

The Wardens may run Chime like gods, but at least they didn't wield the same power.

At six, the sun began to descend in time with the opening of Witheryn. Night fell on Chime as the Gate passed through Tempest and Obituary.

Then the bell chimed nine, and the Ember domain of Rapture returned once more.

Only one hour until Malk's return.

Late-night stragglers came into the café for an apéritif, but I found myself impatiently glancing out to the clock tower and the hand that crept closer to ten. I'd wanted this day to go by quickly, but as the time neared, I couldn't keep myself from wringing my apron.

Among our clientele, I'd not noticed anyone out of the ordinary.

No secret Warden deals.

Had the visions been correct?

The tiny bell rang, and a Diviner stepped inside. At first, I worried it was the Warden from this morning, but no, this Diviner's hair was a rarer bronze instead of silver and he dressed like a gentleman with an impeccable striped suit, groomed to perfection. He sat beside the window and gazed out to the Gate across the street.

There was something about his facial features I recognized but couldn't quite place.

I approached his table with my rehearsed pleasantries. "Good evening, sir. It's a fine night for a pot of tea, or perhaps something stronger?"

He glanced up, and his eyes unnerved me. They were a startling brass, as smooth as metal. Combined with his silver skin, he appeared even more mechanical than the usual Diviner. "Coffee. One pot, no milk, no sugar." He pulled out the latest Chime Courier broadsheet from inside his inner jacket pocket and turned his back by way of dismissal.

Rude.

Yes, but that was a Diviner for you. I rang in his order and busied myself cleaning the nearby tables with an eye on him. There was nothing suspicious about his manner; mortals came and read the broadsheets all day long while nursing a cup. Even at this late hour. I angled myself to get a good look at the Courier's headline: *Construction Begins on Clock Tower Reinforcement.*

Nothing interesting, then.

Another Diviner stepped inside the café, this one an older gentleman dressed in tweed and carrying a briefcase tucked under his arm. Sweat flushed his silver brow. He sat at the same table as my bronze-haired guest. "Good evening, Your Ex—*sir.*"

The bronze-haired Diviner glanced up from the Courier with a mild air of irritation. "You're tardy, Doctor."

The doctor placed his briefcase flat on the table. "Apologies. I needed to go over our schematics one more time. I gather your meeting with the press went well?" He nodded to the Courier broadsheet.

"Construction will cause only minimal disruption to the station's traffic—daily crossings will remain unaffected, with any luck. Once the Glimmer come through with their new batch of workers, they'll begin work immediately."

My ears pricked up, and I began cleaning another table nearby.

"Are you quite sure we can trust them with such a delicate endeavor?" The doctor flipped open his briefcase and knocked over the mug. "Oh, deary me." Coffee splashed across the table and ran down the side.

I reached for my dishcloth. "It's all right, sir, I'll clean—"

The tick-tock of the café's clock suddenly stopped.

All around me, the air seemed to pause. I held my breath and stared outside. The usual late-night shoppers and bar-trawlers had stopped mid-walk, and beyond them, even the shimmer of the Gate had become one solid picture.

I didn't dare glance at the patrons behind me, but I knew what I'd see—them frozen in place, suspended like I should have been, yet my fingers tightened around the dishcloth, and the silence built in my ears like an awful pressure, ready to pop.

Then the chatter started again, only it sounded distorted, wrong. The mortals outside walked backwards. The hands of the clock tower went counterclockwise.

And the usual tick-tock became a tock-*tick.*

I bit my lip as the spilled coffee moved up the table and into the mug, and then the mug flipped back into position, righting itself as though it had never been knocked over.

The café remained in suspended animation, yet the two Diviner did not.

"How clumsy of you, Doctor." The bronze-haired Diviner folded his broadsheet and finished his coffee. "Nervous, are we? Do you need time away?"

The doctor fidgeted in his seat. "No, no. You can depend on me."

"I'm glad to hear it. But you needn't fret. Gloria herself will oversee the operation, and her compatriots will keep the Vesper in line. Once the Glimmer have no further use for them, we'll ensure no knowledge returns to Valeria. With your updated schematics, we can begin testing them."

Testing them? For what? Whatever they were discussing sounded far more sinister than simply locking Vesper inside a workhouse.

The evidence lay inside the doctor's briefcase, but I couldn't snatch it while the world stood still and I too stood here awkwardly.

Why hadn't I paused alongside the rest of the café's patrons?

Worse, forcing myself still like a statue had made my nose terribly itchy.

"What of the aether creatures?" the doctor asked. "Are you certain they won't target the Glimmer?"

"You've seen the reports. Moving our operations from Diviner technicians will keep them safe, and then we'll confirm if it's our mortals being targeted."

My nose twitched, forcing my jaw to scrunch with it.

The doctor's silver eyes made contact with mine and they opened wide. "That Vesper server—she moved."

"What?"

"Her face, it—it moved."

Shit!

The bronze-haired Diviner leaped from his seat, knocking the chair back with a crash. The air returned to normal. Mortals strode past the window as the gods intended.

I stepped back, and the dishcloth fell from my grasp.

"Who are you? What did you see?" the Diviner demanded.

What had I seen? A Diviner using his power? They could control pockets of time, but I shouldn't have been able to see it in action, should I? Was it because I was standing so close that I wasn't caught in his power like the others?

Run. He's no ordinary Diviner. Get out of here now.

The Diviner's eyes narrowed. "Why were you watching me?"

I put on my best demure smile and fluttered my eyelashes. "Not watching you, sir! Forgive my rude manners, I saw the headline of the Courier and—"

"How long have you worked here?"

My heart sped up.

He knows what you are.

My Glimmer boss came rushing over. "Is there a problem with her service, sir?"

The Diviner straightened the collar of his shirt. "How long has this Vesper been in your employ?"

The Glimmer scowled. "Her? I hired her a few weeks ago. Came from one of the Undercity workhouses on promotion. Is there a problem?"

The way the Diviner's brass eyes roamed over me, as though studying every intimate detail for truths and lies, roiled my stomach. "Give me your arm."

A command I didn't have to obey. "Who are you to make demands? You're no Warden, and I know my rights. I *work* here."

The Diviner sighed. "You can give me your arm now, girl, or I can call in the Wardens and they'll storm this little teahouse and arrest everyone in it. Your choice."

"Oh, for goodness' sakes, give him your arm!" The Glimmer grabbed my wrist.

I tried to pry her free, but something tugged in my palm, as though my hand were a hook and it had snagged onto her skin. The tug burned—not with pain, but with the throbbing buildup of pleasure before the release of an orgasm.

What in god's name?

The sensation quivered up my arm as my indigo flesh turned pure gold to match the Glimmer's.

She shrieked and jerked as a static jolt snapped from my touch. The Glimmer fell and crashed onto a table, sending a teapot flying.

The doctor backed away from me, the briefcase clutched to his chest as he gaped in pure horror. "She's—She's one of them!"

Time slowed around me once more. The teapot glided past me as though enjoying its descent to its inevitable doom.

Run, you idiot. Run!

Blinding light burst from my skin, and the two Diviner shrank from its haze. Though for reasons I couldn't explain, I could see through the light as clear as a Vesper could navigate shadow.

I ran to the café entrance as the brass-eyed Diviner stalked after me, his eyes shielded with his folded broadsheet, though now the annoyance across his face held a sliver of fear. "What *are* you?"

I yanked the door open, which thankfully hadn't been caught in the Diviner's power, and dove outside into the cool evening air.

The city seemed to speed up all at once as it caught up to present time. Crowds of mortals still filled the streets at this time of night, and I flung myself between them, ripping off my apron and tossing it aside as I tried to blend in.

I ran headfirst into another Vesper and grabbed hold of his arm to steady myself. That same tugging sensation burned in my palm and I yanked my hand free. The Vesper threw me a glare and shoved past me.

"Excuse me, sir." I caught a glimpse of my hands and examined them. They'd returned to their indigo, but I could have sworn they'd turned gold. Was I losing my mind?

What the shit had happened in there? What had I *done*?

Aether lamps lit up Central Square with a screeching buzz that made me wince. A quick glance over my shoulder proved I'd lost the bronze-haired Diviner, but my nerves were suitably frayed.

I'd left Dru behind, and the Diviner could have gone back to question her and the rest of the café's employees.

The clock tower rang out, signaling half past the hour.

Malk would be returning with our Vesper refugees from Eventide in only thirty minutes, and I'd gone and blown a signal to every Warden in Central Square.

III

The Wardens' first responsibility is to uphold the Covenant.
All mortals are made equal, though they vary between the twelve domains
in ability and temperament. A Seren does not match the height of a
Glimmer, thus we cannot build doors with only a Seren in mind.
How, then, can one maintain equality when faced with these inequalities?
First, when disputes arise between separate domains, you must be the voice
that binds them.
—E. Karendar, *Warden Handbook Volume I*

THE TRAM WAS THIRTEEN seconds late.

I snapped shut my fob watch and shoved it into my pocket as the tram pulled up smoothly, unaware of its own tardiness, though likely the driver was a flustered mess. Thirteen seconds late? I'd be hanging myself from the beams.

All right, Quen, there's no need for such dramatics.

I hopped into the carriage alongside a few other patrons—a Seren, two Glimmer—and found a spare seat near the window.

At this time of night, the tram was almost full. Rapture's crossing would close soon, with Eventide due to open shortly, and that always attracted the drug peddlers. I leaned my arm against the back cushion and watched the tower blocks of home disappear in a slow rumble forward.

I'd been a flustered mess all day, and the late tram was only one rung on the rope of a disorganized and frayed chaos. My entire routine had gone off track. I'd normally start the day like clockwork—a fresh cup of tea, two bourbon biscuits, the latest Courier broadsheet, and the sight of Obituary turning to Rapture on the Gate.

But at nine this morning, I'd found myself rushing for the Undercity elevator. I'd not intended to spend the night underground, but that's where my visions took me.

In my line of work, every ticking second mattered.

I pulled the note from my pocket; *9:39 p.m. Lady Mae's café, Central Station. Ember Male.*

I'd already lost one mortal today. My nerves couldn't stand to lose another.

The tram pulled into its next stop and more squeezed on, taking all available seats except the one next to me. The carriage could only hold a maximum capacity of eighty, yet we'd gone beyond that, with more struggling to keep balance as they stood.

An entire section had been taken up by Umber and Leander alone. The heavy stone bodies of the Umber required some accommodation, though the Leander's muscular lion form didn't need to take up an entire row of seats. They just liked to spread their legs and flick their tail at any passersby. They deserved a tut, at the very least.

A Seren clung onto the center pole. Her smaller body was more vulnerable when surrounded by so many taller mortals, and she constantly glanced over her shoulder to make sure her wings weren't brushing against anything. She could have used those wings to fly rather than get the tram, but at almost ten at night, the tram was the safer option.

I patted the seat beside me. "There's space."

The Seren shot me a glare and turned away.

Of course no one would want to sit beside a Diviner. If I so much as grazed my hand against hers, I'd see her entire past and future to come. Or so she believed.

My domain perpetuated the stereotypes because they were an antisocial lot who thought making eye contact on public transport was the height of indecency. Saints forbid anyone would start a conversation! They'd be locked away for the good of society.

Blast it, I *liked* conversing.

The half-past bell snapped my attention to the window.

"Central Station, this is Central Station," announced the driver. "The time is nine thirty. This is your last call for Rapture. Eventide will open in thirty minutes. To repeat, this is your last call for Rapture."

On cue, the tram's denizens rushed for the sliding doors and joined the Central crowds. I shoved my hands into my pockets and followed at a brisk pace.

Even this late at night, travelers passed through Central Station. The Gate dominated Central's skyline, and Rapture's volcanic atmosphere cast an eerie red glow across the square. I'd never been fond of Rapture, and they weren't fond of me, either. Diviner were banned from their gambling halls and casinos, so what else was there to do?

As I made my way to the station, I noticed what the crowds likely didn't.

There were more Wardens on patrol. Their dark uniforms blended in with the crowds, but each of the station exits, even the emergency ones, had at least two Wardens on watch.

Security never needed to be this tight.

What had I missed?

Traffic was still entering the station and filtering out onto the main concourse, but I avoided the station altogether. That wasn't why I was here.

Instead, my path diverted in the opposite direction to the teahouses and bars that encircled the clock tower. Only they remained open at this hour, with the stores selling the usual bric-a-brac now closed.

On the way, a flier fluttering on a lamppost caught my eye. A Godless flier. One of many which consistently made their appearance across Central.

This one depicted a crude drawing of the Glimmer god, Gildola, spanking a Diviner over her lap as golden notes poured from his pockets. I couldn't fault the art, though the artist would face time in a correctional facility if ever caught. I ripped it down and shoved it into my inner jacket pocket. Where *did* these blasted things keep coming from?

A mystery to ponder another time.

I glanced around the area, but knew I'd not find any Godless foolish enough to be loitering on street corners. The Wardens had been hunting them for years with little success, and our dossier on their organization remained embarrassingly thin. I'd personally been assigned to deal with such heathens, but Chime had far greater problems than a few distasteful fliers.

I jogged over the tram line and crossed the square. It didn't take long to find Lady Mae's. Two Diviner Wardens were standing outside on schedule.

"Evening, chaps. Having a spot of bother, are we? Mind if I go in?" I flashed my badge.

"Did Ambassador Karendar send for you, sir?"

My heart skipped a beat. "The ambassador is here?"

"At the station—there was an incident, and we thought it best to move him to safety."

That would explain the number of Wardens, though my visions had brought me *here*—not the station. "What incident?"

The two Diviner shared uneasy glances. "There was an attack on the ambassador's life. The café's owner stepped in and was killed. The suspect fled before we could arrive, though we're not sure of her domain—His Excellency reported both a Vesper and Glimmer woman. There're three witnesses inside; two of the café's staff, a Seren and Ember, and a customer who got into a spat with the Ember. They're both wounded."

Holy saints. None of these events had appeared in my visions or notes, and Father wasn't one to withhold His visions, especially not where our ambassador was concerned. "Did you call a Necro for the wounded?"

One of the Diviner shrugged. "None on call, sir. His Excellency told us not to bother. We'll, uh, leave you to sort them out."

The two Diviner stepped aside, allowing me into Lady Mae's.

I'd not frequented this establishment before as far as I could remember, though the gaudy porcelain wares covering the walls were distinctly Glimmer. One of the tables had been snapped in half, and a shattered teapot littered the floor.

A spat indeed.

At first glance I didn't notice any abandoned clothes inferring a mortal death, but the Wardens could well have taken evidence for further investigation.

Who would dare threaten the Diviner ambassador's life? Though what had brought him to a Glimmer café in the first place?

A Seren leaned by the kitchen door, swaying unsteadily on her feet, her mascara smudged from tears. "They're back here," she said with a muffled sob.

The unprofessional in me wanted to stomp outside and berate my colleagues for leaving a traumatized Seren alone, though I supposed we Diviner were useless at comfort. We needed an Umber's touch. "Thank you. Take a seat and try to make yourself comfortable. I'll be with you shortly."

The Seren dabbed her eyes with a serviette and climbed onto the nearest chair.

I stepped through to the kitchen and my nose instantly rebelled at the scent of burned flesh. My gaze fell upon the Ember.

A male, less than sixteen years judging by the short length of the horns protruding from his head. He sat leaning against an oven with his knees tucked against his chest, his body quivering as he rocked back and forth.

The entire left side of his face had been burned off.

Blood trickled from where his left eye dangled out of place, though his cheek was a patchwork of pulpy red flesh and white bone. Saints, it was a miracle the poor boy still lived. I fell to my knees beside him and resisted the urge to touch him.

I knew what I'd see if I did.

"Pray to Edana," I urged. "Ask her to heal you. Please. Pray to her."

There was nothing I could do to help the boy, not without a Necro healer on hand, and based on my note, he wouldn't last the next few minutes.

But his god could save him. They held that power.

The boy's lips parted in a wheeze. "She—She doesn't... want to."

He sucked in one last rattling breath and then his body disappeared in the blink of an eye. His clothes collapsed into an empty pile on the tiled floor.

I sat there staring at his threadbare boots. The soles had worn until holes poked through the leather.

The time: 9:39 exactly.

I wanted to scream, but at who? Edana? She could have saved the boy's life, but chose not to.

My Warden colleagues? For not caring to summon a Necro?

No mortal needed to die like this.

"What a useless sap," came a female voice from behind me. "I advised Lady Mae not to rely on hired help from the Undercity, and look what it has cost her. Such a pity the management ran this café into the ground, but what does one expect when one hires Vesper and Ember?"

I slowly stood and turned.

A Glimmer. Of course.

It was always a sodding Glimmer.

The Glimmer leaned against the kitchen counter dressed in Golden City finery of a red minidress, showing far more flashy skin and jewelry than was appropriate for this level. Especially this late into the evening. She, too, had suffered burns across her face and neck, though not as severe as the Ember's.

In a contest of skill, the Glimmer's sunlight could burn as deadly as an Ember's flame, as it so clearly had.

Before my eyes, her skin glowed gold as her wounds patched themselves together. The burn marks faded until they'd fully healed.

Edana didn't care for her mortals, but Gildola did.

I squeezed my hands behind my back to keep my ire in check. "A friend of Lady Mae's, I presume? If you don't mind, I have some quest—"

"I was drinking chamomile tea when the attack took place. Karendar knows the details." She smoothed her dress and then helped herself to tea, seemingly oblivious to the mortal who'd died in her presence.

Who she'd helped murder.

"And the Ember boy?"

"He tried to run when the Wardens showed up. I stopped him from leaving, and he attacked me. Me! Can you believe the gall of it?" She sipped from her cup, and the saucer rattled in her grip. "I acted in self-defense."

"You should have left him for the Wardens."

She placed her cup down with a loud crack. "Is that how you speak to citizens performing a public duty?"

"It's not your place to police other mortals, my lady—"

"*My* place?" She snorted. "That Ember was clearly an illegal—"

"Clearly, since Lady Mae seemed inclined to break labor laws by hiring a child as part of her staff." And paying him a pittance for the privilege. "A mortal has died, my lady. This cannot go undocumented."

"Then report me and see where it gets you."

The Glimmer flashed a smug smirk. She knew there was little I could do except file the paperwork that would likely go ignored. When the gods encouraged their mortals to ignore the tenets of the Covenant and act self-righteous, then how could one govern fairly?

One of the Diviner Wardens popped their head into the kitchen. "Sir? Ambassador Karendar has called for you."

What a fine mess this evening was turning into. "I need to finish questioning—"

"We'll finish up, sir. His Excellency insists on your presence."

I didn't trust them to file the correct paperwork, and truly, I wanted to continue my questioning. This Ember boy could have come from a workhouse, but without evidence, I couldn't get a warrant to investigate my suspicions that mortals were being abused there.

But duty called, and I needed out of this blasted kitchen. "Right you are."

I strode across the square over to the station and entered via the public waiting area. Few sat on the benches waiting for Eventide, though the tourist information and currency exchange remained open twenty-four hours.

Even the cozy café continued to serve their bland, overpriced teas and coffees.

A few stragglers ran ahead to catch the Rapture crossing and were caught at the barrier. No one could cross without flashing their passport, and a few burly-looking Umber Wardens were on hand to arrest anyone that tried.

I made my way to the private waiting rooms and station offices and nodded a greeting to the Diviner Warden on watch outside.

"His Excellency is waiting in the dawn suite," the Diviner announced.

I nodded again and slipped inside. At almost ten at night, I wasn't expecting many to be inside the private lounge, least of all for an Eventide crossing. Sure enough, it was empty. The soft sofa cushions had already been cleaned and plumped for tomorrow.

And that's what I couldn't fathom.

What would bring the ambassador here this late?

I followed the corridor along to the dawn suite, so named for its gaudy brass furnishings and orange checkered drapes and cushions. Popular with the Glimmer, I was sure.

More Diviner stood on guard, and I found the ambassador pacing inside. He wasn't wearing his usual regal tabard, but was instead dressed in a gray pinstripe suit. A jacket had been discarded onto one of the nearby couches, next to a half-empty cup of coffee.

The effect made him appear almost normal.

But there was nothing normal about Elijah Karendar.

His pacing stopped, and he snapped gleaming bronze eyes in my direction. "Quentin."

I swallowed the bubble caught in my throat. The veneer of calm I'd been cultivating slipped in his presence, and I approached with my head bowed, then dropped to one knee. "Your Excellency." My breath rasped.

"Up. This isn't a social call." Elijah snapped his fingers and the few Diviner vacated the dawn suite, leaving us alone.

I stood and forced a smile. "It never is."

He didn't return the courtesy. "What I say does not leave this room. Approximately twenty minutes ago, there was an attack on a Glimmer-owned café across the square—and its owner was killed. Shortly after, one of the station staff discovered a body near the maintenance shaft of the clock tower. A Diviner mechanic."

"Unconscious?"

"No. Dead. The body was intact when I arrived, and it's still intact now, though we've since moved it from public view."

A body? My head started reeling. "But that... That's not possible." Mortal bodies decayed almost instantaneously upon death as their souls returned to their god. They rarely lingered, and never for this long.

"I want you to examine it."

Examine it. Damn it, I knew what he was really asking of me. "I doubt my power will work on a—on dead tissue. You should ask a Necro to—"

"A Necro has already examined the body and reported their findings. I want *you* to examine it."

The hard edge in his eyes brooked no argument, and I held no power to refuse him. "Where?"

Elijah led me out into the corridor, but instead of diverting to the public waiting rooms, we went through a staff-only maintenance door into a kitchen.

Two Diviner stood beside a tea trolley, but its contents had been replaced with a sprawling body, its limbs dangling over the side uselessly.

A body. An actual body.

Unnaturally warped by its stillness.

The tips of my fingers trembled slightly as I approached. Both Diviner stepped outside, giving me space, though I could sense Elijah's stare boring into the back of my neck. It took all of my strength to focus on the scene before me.

A male, early twenties. He was dressed in a set of maintenance overalls and oil stained his smock and hands. His lips were a dull gray. His hair a tousled white.

But his eyes...

Saints. He had no eyes.

There was no blood. No signs of cutting or struggle. Nothing. Just two dark, empty sockets where his eyes should have been. I pressed a fist to my lips and swallowed bile.

"They found him this way," Elijah said behind me. "Check his neck."

I tentatively reached for the body's collar and pulled it aside. Red marks in the shape of a handprint had been burned into his flesh. The mark of a Glimmer? Or an Ember?

"What was his name? Do you know?"

"It hardly matters."

"His body shouldn't *be* here; it should have dematerialized—"

"*Quentin.*" Elijah's voice snapped with the force of a single command.

Only he, ambassador to our Father, knew what ability I possessed—an ability no other Diviner held or knew of. And I, his lowly servant, had no choice but to act as he wished. I sucked in a breath and pressed my palm to the dead Diviner's forehead.

And his final dying memory bloomed in my mind's eye.

I'd pulled the short straw again. Electrics were always buzzin' around the maintenance shaft, and I hated that place. Too dark, and it didn't smell right. Not like cogs and oil were supposed to smell. More like rotten eggs.

But if the buzzin' knocked out the lights, I needed to fix it before the next elevator run. Station master would dock my pay if he caught me slacking again. I grabbed my utility belt, torch, and picked up some spare bulbs on the way. The upper levels were noisy with the Rapture traffic, and all I could hear was them stomping their feet and jeering. Wish I was with 'em, but they'd never let a Diviner take a shot at poker.

My torch passed over the upper shaft and something flashed back.

There it was again; a silvery-blue spark.

Not another electrical leak? Aether was bleeding out of these pipes, and they'd need more than a screwdriver and hammer to patch.

Another spark flashed and blinded me for a second. I blinked the silver and blue dots away, but the colors glowed, as though someone had switched on the light.

This wasn't just a spark, but a complete malfunction.

I slowed time around me so I could pinpoint the damage among the flashing lights, but my power didn't have any effect. The spark grew, spasming as it stretched and contorted, like it was growing limbs, and the silvery-blue hue shimmered through a whole rainbow of colors.

Eh? This wasn't how aether worked!

"Hey!" I yelled behind me. "If this is a prank, it's not a very good one—"

The spark flared. Something grabbed my neck. I screamed as the touch burned, and tried to pull free, to slow it down, but the light—

I gasped as I yanked my hand free and stumbled back.

I knew those colors. Those sparks.

I'd seen them in my own visions.

Elijah was by my side in an instant. "What did you see?"

Darkness. Nothing but an endless vastness of time where nothing existed and nothing was born. This vision appeared unusually hazy, as though his soul had left behind a faded print. But I knew what I'd seen. What I'd felt. "An electrical malfunction—aether." But that wasn't any normal aether reaction that I knew of. Aether energy powered lanterns and trams. It didn't *attack*. "Or some creature made from aether. Its shape looked... mortal."

"Aether? Not an attack from an Ember?"

That had been my first thought, too, but this poor soul's last few moments were unfortunately distinct. I pulled a handkerchief from my pocket and wiped my smudged spectacles. The brass handles shook in my grip. "No, I saw no one, only the glow of aether."

"What else?"

"He'd tried to slow this creature, whatever it was, but his power held no effect." I'd witnessed nothing like it. Even aether obeyed the laws of time. My gaze was drawn to the body's empty eye sockets. "I don't understand. Even death via an aether malfunction wouldn't have left his body behind, but I... I felt no life in him. No soul. Nothing." Why hadn't his body faded back to Father? To our god?

Elijah rubbed a hand across his jaw. "The Necro came to the same conclusion. He couldn't find any signs of life. The Glimmer from the café died in the same way—Ambassador Gloria has yet to be informed."

"What in god's name does this mean?"

"Quentin."

"Sorry," I mumbled. I shouldn't blaspheme, but this whole scenario was *exactly* like my visions. After this night, I'd need more than a stiff cup of tea.

"This is the fifth one."

I stared. "What?"

"The fifth body. In the past few weeks, we've come across more. All Diviner, save Lady Mae. All found in the exact same way; eyes missing, burn marks on their neck or arm. And... It gets worse."

"How could it possibly be worse?"

"These souls have not returned to Father."

My stomach churned. That was why the body hadn't faded. If our souls weren't returning to our god, then what became of them? Was this creature literally devouring them?

Our mortal souls were owned by our god. It was the gods who animated us, gave us life and purpose, and sent us out into the domains so that we may live and experience it in their image, only to return to them at death with those memories.

Nothing could stop that natural order.

"Why am I only hearing of this now?" My status among the Wardens meant I should have been alerted to this from the start.

Elijah paced again. "Because the implications are far too great. Finding one body is a tragedy. Finding two with the same manner of execution is a coincidence. But three? Four? Five? That's a pattern I cannot afford to ignore. Someone—or some*thing*—is targeting Diviner. Taking our souls, our connection to Father. I want you on this, active immediately."

Trust him to care for the political ramifications before the loss of life. "I'm tied up investigating abuse within the workhouses—"

"The workhouses aren't my concern. Our mortals are."

"And Lady Mae? There may be a connection between these attacks—"

"*I* was their target. Lady Mae unfortunately got in their way. Forget the workhouses. This is your priority, do you understand?"

I bit the inside of my cheek. "Yes, Your Excellency."

"Good. I'll have someone send over the files. I also have a suspect. You said that our power didn't affect this creature?"

"That's right."

"I stopped off at a café tonight for a quick coffee before my work brought me here. You know I like to stay sharp." A slight smile graced his lips. "There was a female server there—a Vesper—aged mid-twenties. I knocked over my cup and she witnessed me use my power. And when I tried to question her, my power held no effect on her at all, and she tried to attack me." His throat bobbed. "That's why I came here tonight, to lock the station down and find her, and then I stumbled onto another attack."

Tonight was turning into a series of impossible events. Only a Diviner could witness the power of another Diviner. Certainly not a Vesper. "You believe this Vesper may be responsible for these deaths?"

"I'm taking no chances."

"Perhaps this Vesper is connected to the workhouses." I hurried on before he could object. "If she worked at Lady Mae's. What's happening in the Undercity is no coincidence."

Elijah frowned. "Then show me what you've seen."

My heart sped up as he approached me with his hands raised. I'd wronged him, as I always wronged him, and this was the price; to sift through my mind and explore my sins. I flinched as his fingers traced my neck for my pulse. His power could have reached me from any touch, yet he liked to press down on the beat of my veins, to feel the flutter flow through them and know exactly what power he held over me.

His breath blew over my cheek, so tender it could have been a kiss. "Show me."

And then he was digging into my mind.

I clenched my eyes shut as the flashes of my day rushed by in reverse. The Ember boy. Riding the tram here. My evening meal, cold and discarded as I pored over reports. Soaking naked with primrose lotion after my sojourn to the Undercity.

He lingered on that memory. On my nakedness, helplessly suspended for his own amusement. To trawl through my memories, my thoughts, my past, to see everything I'd been and everything I could become; it was a violation.

But he'd always enjoyed violating me.

44

The memories moved on to my quiet desperation as I searched the morning crowds for the Vesper I'd encountered on the Undercity platform. She'd been the only Vesper to even speak to me during my investigation, and I'd wanted to question her a little further, but the crowds had swept her away—though I suspect she'd been willingly swept with them.

The memories ran down the Undercity elevator and then paused at another mortal dying at my feet.

"That's her," Elijah breathed with a hint of bitter coffee, and he released me.

I rubbed my neck where his warm touch lingered. "Her?"

"The Vesper you conversed with on the elevator this morning; she's the same woman from the café." The bronze of his eyes flared. "Find this woman. Use whatever resources you can, but *find* her."

The intensity of his gaze made my heart flutter anew. I didn't believe in coincidences.

A Vesper with the ability to resist time.

Creatures made of aether that could steal the souls of Diviner from our god.

The same creature in the visions I'd witnessed of my own future death.

If I followed this case, I'd be following the timeline to my doom, and not just mortal death, it seemed—my very soul was at stake.

The clock struck ten and the vibrations of the clock tower rattled the body still sprawled on the tea cart. Eventide had now opened.

Didn't time come for us all, in the end?

"It will be done, Your Excellency."

45

4

Do your hands regularly crack through work?
You feel you owe your love and labor to your god, but Unghard does not
afford you rest.
Why do you toil, Umber?
You were built with the strength of a mountain and the gentle heart of a
flower. You were not built to serve others, to slave away in workhouses.
There is no sin in selfishness.
What reward awaits you at the end of your mortal life?
—Anonymous, *Godless flier on the Umber*

WARDENS SWARMED THE ENTRANCE to Lady Mae's.

Shit, shit, *shit*!

More of them mingled with the evening crowds of Central and loitered beside the station's many exits. Many were dressed in plain clothes, but I could spot a Warden anywhere; it was the way they walked and carried their posture that made them stand out.

So many. Just who *was* that Diviner from the café? Certainly no ordinary citizen, to summon such a massive force with a single command. I'd recognized his likeness, but from where?

You've seen his picture in the broadsheet.

Had I? I couldn't even remember. Had he recognized me? I'd committed so many sins, I may have left a trace somewhere, despite how careful the Godless were. But no. My gut told me he didn't know what organization I came from. Just the fact I'd seen his power work when no mortal should—resisted it, even—had raised his suspicion enough to send the Wardens after me.

And you turned gold.

Yes, and that, which I couldn't explain either. The Glimmer must have used her power on me in some new, unforeseen way I'd worry about later.

Though now the Diviner would have passed on an image of my likeness to the Wardens currently searching Central Station. I may not have been recognized before, but I certainly would be now. My days of spying for the Godless could well be over.

Focus, idiot.

Right. The Gate. Malk and the refugees. And shit, Dru could still be trapped inside the café. No doubt the Diviner Wardens would examine everyone's recent past. But the Gate was about to switch to Eventide, and Malk would be waiting. Our seer's vision was still in play, and things were already going wrong right on schedule.

He'd said whoever I met at the café would intercept our refugees. I wasn't expecting it to be as simple as the Wardens arresting everyone. With so many Wardens swarming the station, we wouldn't be able to stop them.

I was physically torn between rescuing Dru and sneaking to the Gate, but I knew Dru was resourceful enough to take care of herself. Malk, however, had no warning of the Wardens about to pounce him.

Stick to the shadows.

I did so. Aether lamps lit Central Square but couldn't burn away every shred of night. I moved to the outer edges of the station and let darkness pool around my fingers, expanding my own shadow to merge with what already existed naturally without arousing suspicion.

To the outside eye, I wouldn't be seen. Another Vesper would notice me, but we didn't tattle on our own.

The ten o'clock bell rang, rattling me out of my bones. The red glow of Rapture changed to purple—the evening skies of Eventide. I slowly inched my way around the outer station wall and peered through one of the paned windows.

And waited.

Something bumped into me, and I almost screamed. I spun around, only to be confronted by a harried-looking Dru. The yellow daisies on her head had wilted to one side.

"Is that you?" Dru whispered.

I expanded my cocoon of shadow to envelope her so she could see me. "How did you find me?"

"Where else would I find you?" Dru checked over her shoulder, but no one spotted us. "What in the twelve gods did you do? I heard you run out and the next thing we were raided by Diviner Wardens! I barely slipped out the back."

"I didn't *do* anything!" I struggled to keep my voice quiet.

"Kayl, have you seen how many Wardens are out there?"

"Yes, I've noticed—"

"Then what did you *do*?"

I threw up my hands in exasperation and then quickly shoved them down again as the shadows followed and flickered around me. "There was a Diviner. He knocked over his coffee and—have you ever seen a Diviner actually use their power?"

"The effects of it?"

"No, I mean, actually in use? Where you can see the world slow and then go in reverse?"

Dru stared at me as if I'd gone mad, which I probably had. "Is this a joke? Because it's a poor time for one—"

"I'm being serious. I saw a Diviner use his power, and he saw me watching him, so he tried to question me. That's when I ran."

"And this Diviner ordered an entire warehouse full of Wardens to lock down the station?"

"Apparently so. I think he was the one from Reve's visions. There was another Diviner, and they were talking about the workhouses. Reve was right. They are colluding with the Glimmer." And my idiot self had forgotten to grab the briefcase as proof.

"We need to get back to base and inform the others." Dru turned to the window. "Look. Is that...?"

I followed her gaze. Figures were emerging through the Gate from Eventide, but certainly not the faces I'd expected. An entire group of Glimmer.

The delegation that Malk had warned about.

And walking among their group were Vesper. An unbroken line of Vesper. Nervous-looking Vesper in patchwork rags whose eyes darted around the chaos of Chime as though seeing it for the first time. Each one clung to a sack at their hip or over their shoulder, their only meager possessions.

"The refugees," Dru gasped.

Yes, they'd been taken by the Glimmer, but... "Where's Malk?" I couldn't see him among the refugees, and he hadn't crossed yet. My heart began to pound.

What if he'd been caught?

By the Glimmer? The Wardens?

And they knew he was one of the Godless? An apostate? A blasphemer?

Or worse... what if our god had sensed him stalking in her domain?

Apostasy was a crime worth death, and not a pleasant one. Malk could be hanging from his neck, his body flayed and—

Stop panicking and look.

I sucked in a breath.

The Wardens of the station had pulled the Glimmer and our refugees to one side and were speaking with the Glimmer.

"They're questioning them," Dru whispered.

Sure enough, the Glimmer produced papers, and the Wardens began checking the passport tattoo of each of the Vesper standing there. Some flashed lanterns in the eyes of the Vesper, making them recoil.

"What are they doing to them?" Dru said, appalled.

I swallowed a lump in my throat. "They're looking for me."

Shit.

I recognized one of the Wardens among them—the Diviner with eyeglasses from the elevator this morning. He, too, spoke with the Glimmer, though he at least had the good grace to appear uneasy about it.

More Vesper stragglers came through from Eventide and were examined in the same way, as well as any Vesper attempting to make the crossing. There weren't many for the evening crossing, so it wouldn't impact their travel times, but it still made my stomach roll.

And then Malk rippled through the Gate, and my heart almost leaped from my throat.

The Wardens immediately jumped him and dragged him to one side. Malk made a good show of being outraged as the Wardens checked his passport, flashed a light in his face, and then roughly grabbed his wrist.

They were examining his past. I could only hope they found nothing incriminating.

Minutes flew by as I watched, and I went to tug my satchel, only to remember I'd left it at the café. Thank god I'd given my documents to Malk this morning. They wouldn't find anything of interest among my personal effects.

The bell chimed quarter past the hour when the Diviner yanked his hand free and then demanded Malk empty his pockets. He did so, revealing a wrapped package of tiny purple and pink mushrooms.

"Mushrooms?" Dru asked.

"That's his back-up plan." Because getting caught smuggling illegal hallucinogenic mushrooms into Chime was a lesser crime than being caught smuggling Godless refugees. The Wardens would have suspected him for something—he had that sort of face, a troublesome one—and now he'd deflected their suspicion.

As I expected, the Warden confiscated Malk's mushrooms and shoved him on his way. They had more important things to concern themselves with tonight—namely finding me—than dealing with some rogue mushroom smuggler. That, and the Glimmer were kicking up a fuss, because of course they were.

"Come on," I whispered to Dru.

We abandoned our spot by the window and edged away from the station altogether to our meeting place on the bench. None of the station staff had noticed the bulb of the aether lamp go out weeks ago, and the shadows gave us some privacy.

It also gave a splendid view of the Gate and the Glimmer still arguing.

I let my shadows pool around the bench as Malk approached casually, as though taking a nightly stroll, and then he slipped under the cover of shadow beside me.

Malk instantly grabbed my hip and pulled me in for a quick kiss. "Everything's gone wrong," he said with a muffled gasp.

Dru flopped onto the bench. "Tell us something we don't know."

"Are you hurt?" I asked. "What happened on Eventide?"

Malk released me and rubbed his wrist where his passport had been tattooed; two semicircles that represented Chime and the Golden City, and a pattern of twelve circles around that. Only one circle had been colored in—the purple orb beside the tenth hour for Eventide. The rest were blank. "I never made it to the refugees. Those damn Wardens and Valeria's guards escorted the delegation to the refugees before I could get to them. I couldn't even smuggle myself into their group because the Glimmer spent the entire time questioning them. I had to lie low for twelve pissing hours. And as you see, the Glimmer brought them through." He waved a defeated hand toward the Gate.

I rubbed my left wrist where my own passport had been permanently tattooed. "Why would Valeria hand over her own mortals?"

"The Glimmer brought chests of gold across. You know Valeria loves her treasure."

Our god had a reputation for hoarding trinkets, right down to the crippling tithes she demanded. But to hand over her own mortals in exchange for gold?

And why would a Glimmer pay for Vesper? They despised us.

"All that effort just to staff their workhouses? Why bother?" Dru asked the question I pondered. "They could snatch any desperate mortal off the streets."

"The real question," Malk said as he rubbed the black stubble on his chin. "Is how they knew the refugees would be there packed and waiting at exactly that time."

"What are you suggesting?" I asked. "That someone from our side leaked the information?"

"That's exactly what I'm suggesting. For all I know, I could have been walking into an elaborate trap."

It couldn't be anyone within our organization. This intel had traded hands straight from the highest source; the Vesper ambassador, Valeria's mortal voice. If anyone knew of this Glimmer delegation, it would be him. "I'll speak with Varen when we get back, but what's our next step? There's no way we'll get on the elevator without the Wardens checking us."

Malk cocked his head. "Why *are* there so many Wardens? What did you do?"

"I didn't do anything—"

"She attracted the attention of some high-level Diviner and now they're trying to find her," Dru explained.

I shot her a scowl. "Yes, thank you, Dru."

Malk frowned. "What do you mean, attracted their attention?"

"Look, we don't have time to go over it now, but I'm a wanted woman. I won't make it to the elevator."

"Shit," Malk muttered and ran both hands through his shaggy hair.

Dru sat up. "We'll stay at the safe house—"

"*No,*" Malk and I snapped at the same time. Our safe house was an apartment a few blocks over here on topside, owned by the Godless's leader. It wasn't a terrible place, but I held no desire to remain here when our friends waited below.

"You think I spent twelve hours hiding in a muddy ditch just to let those Glimmer get away?" Malk pointed at the Gate. "If we follow, we may stand a chance of intercepting them."

"Fine," Dru sighed. "I'll get on the elevator, then—"

"No," I said. "They may recognize you from the café. Don't risk it."

"They might not even get on our elevator," Dru muttered.

The Undercity workhouses were the only place the Glimmer would take a group of vagabond Vesper.

Sure enough, I could see from our vantage point that the Wardens had finished their questioning and the Glimmer, along with the terrified Vesper, now queued up for the Undercity elevator. That's where we would have been taking them, but I doubted the Glimmer were merely escorting them to the Grayford slums.

They owned workhouses underground. Factories and workshops that always turned over labor. And while they'd deny it, I'd long suspected they had a few hands in businesses on Sinner's Row, too.

With the fake documentation we'd so painstakingly put together, we'd aimed to divert these refugees to our base and give them a new life, hidden from Chime's bureaucracy, from the Wardens' purview and our god's eye. We'd have smuggled them into the Undercity with the pretense of marching them off to a workhouse to earn their tithes, but now they'd be doing so for real, under a Glimmer's golden whip.

Whatever the Glimmer wanted with these Vesper, it wasn't in their best interest.

Tests. That's what the Diviner had said. But testing for *what*?

"What now?" Dru said. "We can't get *on* the elevator—we can't even get in the station!"

Ride the service elevator down.

That could actually work. "You ever broke into the storage elevator, Dru?"

Dru stared at me. "You've got to be joking."

Malk's lips widened into that troublesome smile that never failed to make my pulse quicken. "I've broken at least five ordinances today, what's one more?"

"Why do I listen to either of you," Dru whined.

Oh, Dru, she should have known better where Vesper were concerned. We just *loved* shoving our noses where they didn't belong.

Malk let shadow flow from his palms and then led the way around the back of Central Station and the clock tower. The hands rested at twenty past ten, which meant we had little time to act.

While the public-facing elevators at the front of the station had a large inner car that could carry groups of mortals together, attached behind them was a secondary storage elevator that would make the drop at the same time.

This carried cargo; various wares headed for the factories and warehouses below, or goods and carriages for the Golden City above.

My intention was to sneak in with the cargo bound for the Undercity and ride it down. The entrance to the loading bay was hidden from public view, and while Wardens patrolled here too, security would be lax tonight. Or so I hoped.

We slipped past the metal gate of the storage yard, using the cover of shadow to remain undetected, and ducked behind a stack of large crates.

Umber maintenance staff were loading the last few crates into the elevator, the doors still wide open, but a group of Diviner Wardens were standing watch, looking thoroughly bored.

We'd never get past them.

"Shit," Malk groaned.

"What if we smuggled ourselves into the crates?" I whispered.

"Wouldn't work," Dru whispered back. "They inspect the crates."

She was right. As the Umber went to shove another crate on, one of the Wardens insisted on opening it up and peeking inside.

"There'll be an opening for the maintenance shaft," Malk said. "Find that and we can ride the elevator down on top of it."

"Do you know how dangerous that is?" Dru asked. "The amount of steam and aether needed to run this elevator is immense. Do you want to get fried by a loose wire?"

"Come on, Dru. You know these station hands aren't gonna let loose wires fly around. There'd be public outcry."

"You've apprenticed with the steamworks, you know how they work." I nudged her.

"It's precisely *because* I've apprenticed with them that I know what they get away with," Dru muttered.

"It's not like we have a choice."

"We *could* stay at the safe house—"

"You think the Wardens will give up their search for me at dawn? We need to get back to the depot. And I need to speak with Varen."

Dru glanced up to the sky and mumbled something incoherent. "Fine. There's a panel round the side. We might be able to squeeze in."

"Then hurry," Malk urged. He spread his shadow over Dru and let her weave between the crates as we followed in a slow zigzag. The Wardens were too busy inspecting the crates to notice the shadows spread and elongate beside the station's inner wall.

A toolkit marked where a square panel had already been pried open on the shaft. Someone had been doing maintenance here and had abandoned it in a rush.

Dru grabbed the edge of the panel and bent it open further with her brute force. She waved us into a tight, dark space.

Darkness was no problem for Malk and I as we squeezed inside the elevator shaft on to what appeared to be a thin maintenance platform. The bangs and clanks of the station staff loading the last of their crates vibrated beneath me, and from further beyond, the elevator wobbled with the march of footsteps entering the public elevator. Above us, the air hummed with the faint buzz of aether.

Dru squeezed in beside us, forcing our shoulders to rub against each other. "What now?" She glanced around. "I can't see anything. Is there a ladder?"

"Not that I can see."

"Then how do we get on it?"

"When the elevator goes down, we'll jump on."

Dru's mouth gaped open. "Are you serious?" She turned to Malk, but couldn't see him in the dark, and addressed a pipe instead. "Is she serious?"

"Where's your sense of adventure?"

"Back on Heartstone where it belongs!"

The half-past bell rang and a gasping hiss sounded above us. Pressure from the steam pipes moved the churning cogs and the elevator slowly edged down.

I gave Dru's arm a reassuring pat. "Get ready."

"I hate you."

"I'll go first and catch you," Malk said. "Can't have an Umber landing hard on this thing, you might dent it."

Dru scowled. "I hate you, too."

The elevator picked up speed as Malk leaped first and scrambled over the top of the elevator. He waited until he was almost equal to the platform's edge and held out his hand. "Now!"

"Don't scream." I gave Dru a shove forward.

Dru stumbled and fell on top of Malk, knocking him down onto the top of the elevator with a loud *thunk*. Hopefully the grinding clanks of the elevator's gears masked the sound.

Your turn. Jump.

Their sprawling bodies were in the way of my landing!

The elevator was picking up more speed. If I didn't jump now, I'd either miss my shot, or I'd break something.

Where's the fun without a little risk?

Indeed. I went for it.

The drop was further than I thought, and hot air fluttered through my hair as I fell.

Malk rolled away in time as I hit the elevator. He half caught me, breaking my fall, but not in time to save my shin as it bashed against hard metal. I sank down with a yelp.

Malk shuffled beside me. "Are you all right?"

I rubbed my shin and winced. Only bruised. "I'll live."

"For now," Dru muttered. She was clinging onto a metal railing for dear life.

The elevator rattled down at a casual pace. I leaned on Malk's shoulder as he wrapped his arms around me, holding me tight. The steam hissed and puffed above us, making the air stuffy and uncomfortably hot with the taste of oil, but it was still breathable.

We sat in the dark, but passed points along the way down marked by glowing aether lights. I tried not to stare at them. The further down we went, the brighter the lights flashed with their menacing silvery-blue. Their hum grew louder and a pounding headache throbbed in my forehead.

Aether lights always had this effect on me if I stayed in their presence too long, as though I was allergic to them. But who suffered an electrical allergy?

Look up. See the stars.

I glanced up. The aether lights continued to blink, but something tugged in the depths of my soul, some strange yearning to go up and explore the inner workings of the clock tower and discover what secrets it held.

"Why were the Wardens searching for you?" Malk asked, bringing me out of my thoughts.

"It's best if I explain back at base." I leaned my head against his chest. "I was worried sick, you know."

He kissed my forehead. "You always worry."

"Because what if you make the crossing and never come back?"

"I'll always make it back."

"How can you know that for sure?"

"Because you'll be waiting for me. And I'm not going to risk getting on your bad side." His grin flashed in the dark.

I lightly slapped his thigh. I wished I possessed his bravado.

The steam hissed with angry disapproval and the elevator slowed.

Malk stretched to his feet and peered over the elevator's edge as it came to a clanking halt. "There's a platform below. You should be able to climb down, Dru."

Dru scrambled to the edge with a moan.

Malk went next and held his arms out to catch me. I readied the jump, but a bright light in the corner of my eye caught my attention.

An aether lamp had suddenly flickered into life. The silvery-blue glow seemed to pulsate, as though growing larger and stretching out into star-shaped patterns. I stared at it, mesmerized by its dancing contortions, and the gentle hum turned to a buzzing shriek.

One of us.

One of what?

Pain lanced through my forehead like a hot knife. I grabbed my head with both hands as the buzzing shredded through my mind.

I opened my eyes to an explosion of colors, so many of them, all twinkling and bright and dotting my vision in painful splotches.

I stumbled with a scream and fell off the elevator.

Malk caught me, and his brow furrowed in concern. "What happened? Did you hit something?"

The throbbing pain lessened, and I stood on shaking legs. "Did you see the colors?"

"What colors?"

"Hey, we've got to go," Dru said with urgency. She'd already pried off the panel leading out to the Undercity.

Malk dragged me outside. We sprinted to the tram platform and crouched beside a carriage. Two Wardens—an Umber and a Glimmer—came running to the panel as the Glimmer summoned a beam of sunlight from her palm and wielded it like a lantern.

Shit, my screaming must have alerted them, and Dru hadn't had time to replace the panel.

Now the Wardens knew we were down here.

"We can't stay here," Dru whispered.

"I'm not letting the Glimmer get away with our refugees!" Malk hissed.

The Glimmer Warden shone her light near our hiding spot. Vesper shadow didn't work against their power, and if we remained here, they'd find us in a heartbeat.

Slowly, we peeled away from our hiding spot and stalked behind the cover of the Undercity tram. More Umber Wardens searched the tram carriages.

Thank the gods they didn't have a Diviner with them, or we'd be truly fucked.

It was hard to see from our vantage point underneath the trams, but the telltale golden glow told us which tram the Glimmer and our Vesper refugees had boarded.

"We can't go after them," I said. "There's too many Wardens."

Malk ran a hand through his hair. This was my fault, I knew. If I hadn't screamed, I wouldn't have drawn them to us. "What now? We walk back to Grayford and sit on our arses as they take more Vesper for their gods-damn workhouses?"

I patted his arm. "We'll speak with Varen. He can help—"

"We can't keep relying on Varen. Sooner or later, we're going to get him killed."

A part of me knew that; he took a considerable risk to help us.

But the Vesper ambassador was one of the few friends we had.

5

New to Chime and can't find lodgings or a hot meal?
Lost your wages in Sinner's Row?
Workhouses won't take you?
Head to Grayford!
We're home to those who aren't welcome topside. Ember, Fauna, Umber,
Vesper—all are welcome! Take the Undercity tram from Platform Four
and head for the soup kitchen.
You needn't bring any bocs, just the clothes on your back.
We're not a workhouse, however we'll gladly accept any donations.
—Anonymous, *flier on the Undercity*

IT WAS ALMOST MIDNIGHT by the time we made it to Grayford.

With the Wardens swarming the Undercity station and inspecting each tram, we'd had no choice but to duck into the tunnels and return the old-fashioned way: by foot.

It took near enough an hour of dejected lumbering along the tracks and my feet were screaming by the end, but at least the tunnels were dark—and safe. Only once did a tram come rattling past, and we'd hidden in Malk's shadows.

We'd emerged from the tunnel with caution, but thankfully, no Wardens were waiting at the other end. Instead, we were greeted with the morose notes of a hurdy-gurdy.

Even this late, the slums were alive with the bustle of open-air cooking and trade. Time held little meaning underground, and the Vesper kept a late schedule along with the other degenerate domains who'd been forced to call Grayford home.

Roasting chestnuts on an open grill caught the attention of my nose. I patted my pinafore and remembered I'd forgotten my damn purse. "Malk, got any bocs?"

"You think I can keep buying snacks on my wage? You're the one earning tips."

"The only tips I ever earned were to get a new job." And, sadly, I'd now need one. "What happened to your tips from delivering the Courier?"

"I spent them all on your gaping appetite."

I fluttered my eyelashes. "The way to a woman's heart is through her stomach."

Malk rolled his eyes, but pulled out a few notes from his pocket.

The Ember chestnut-roaster was one of many food stalls that lined Grayford's Main Street. A few years ago, this street had been barren. The stall owners didn't realize *who* had supported them with such generous donations.

If it wasn't for the Godless, many of these mortals wouldn't have work or meaning beyond their god's whims.

But there was always more work to do. More improvements to be made. Dru scooped up litter along the worn cobblestones and shoved it into her pockets.

"You can take one night off, you know," I said with my mouth full.

She gave me a disgusted look. "Laziness is a sin."

For an Umber, sure. I popped open another chestnut, making sure I didn't drop the shell. Otherwise, Dru *would* have something to say about it.

We passed more rickety huts draped in cloth canopies. Their chefs were a mixture of Vesper and Ember; roasted mushrooms and stuffed peppers from the Vesper, and baked goods and grilled delights from the Ember. The scents of spicy vegetable skewers, grilled cheese, and freshly baked bread buns complemented each other.

I knew my mind should have been on our failed operation instead of food, but I needed something to make this day worthwhile.

You'll take any excuse to eat.

Such was a lady's prerogative. Besides, once we got back to the depot, I doubted my appetite would last.

We passed under the oil lamps which dangled across Main Street and entered the main square where the tram terminus resided. Gray brick buildings surrounded the platform; the rest of Grayford's businesses and homes.

The plaster had worn from them years ago, and while there wasn't much we could do about the smoggy air which dirtied the streets, we'd helped repair the broken windows and repainted the square so that Grayford appeared less drab.

A couple of rats scurried past my feet, and I almost dropped my chestnuts. "Watch where you're going!"

One rat paused and wiggled its nose. "Sorry, miss! Can we have one?"

Cheeky scamp! In their animal form, I couldn't tell which of the Fauna these were.

Dru swiped my bag of chestnuts and tossed a nut each for their grubby little paws. One instantly transformed into a red-furred fox and they bounded through the streets giggling, the nuts clasped in their teeth.

I snatched my chestnuts back. "You could have said *please*."

Dru rolled her eyes and pointed across the square. "Varen's in."

A much larger town house in a considerably better state of repair towered over the square. Varen's place. An aether lamp burned in the upper window, signaling that he was indeed in residence.

Malk helped himself to a chestnut. "Varen can wait. Harmony won't."

He's right, you know. Stop dragging your feet.

I wasn't dragging them; I was just bone-tired, and the last thing I needed was our boss berating me for everything that had gone wrong today.

Though both Malk and Dru were itching to get back. We needed to formulate a plan to recover our refugees, after all. And I at least had something to report.

Our echoing footsteps took us along the rusted railway to the great trash piles of metal parts, stainless steel panels, tram cogs and gears, and many other technological treasures that had once attracted residents to these slums.

I'd spent many an afternoon scavenging through these heaps.

The train tracks disappeared into the abandoned depot, home to the worst sinners of Chime's civilized society; apostates, blasphemers, heretics and heathens.

My family.

A Seren waited at the depot entrance, her arms crossed, and a worried scowl planted across her childlike face. She'd dyed her curly locks a subtle auburn to contrast her lilac skin, and wore a smart casual cream blouse and black trousers—the effect of which made her appear closer to her actual age of forty. Her one wing, a soft wispy-white, quivered.

"About time," Harmony snapped.

"We had to walk back," Malk explained. "Wardens on the trams. You don't look too surprised."

Indeed, we should have returned much earlier with a group of new Vesper.

"Reve saw a vision of you fucking up." Harmony's harsh diamond-shaped pupils lingered on me. How could such pretty eyes hold such scorn? "Get inside and report."

Malk strode in with his chin held high as Dru and I slunk after him. It was all right for him; he'd had twelve hours of sleeping in fields when we'd been on our feet all day. The flowers on Dru's head had wilted further. Poor girl looked as exhausted as I felt.

I sighed with relief as I stepped inside the one place in Chime where I was free to be myself. I wanted nothing more than to run up the metal stairs of the hangar to my room and strip out of my modest clothing. But Harmony's temper wouldn't wait.

Instead, I tossed my shawl onto a coat hook and made my way across the platform to our meeting area—a solitary tram abandoned years ago, which we'd turned into a private lounge.

This entire hangar had once been a maintenance depot for cleaning and repairing tram carriages, but we'd converted it into a cozy sanctuary with armchairs draped in blankets and tables covered in scattered mugs, books, and playing cards. All scavenged.

The large windowed archways had since been covered in thick curtains for privacy, though like Grayford's square, we'd painted over the chipped brick walls and lit them with dangling oil lamps. Dru took a moment to check on the planters by the windowsill, full of thriving vegetables and flowers thanks to her Umber's touch.

We'd all worked together to make this depot our home.

The ceiling rattled with the tremors of the midnight hour striking the clock tower. Above us, another tram carriage dangled from a hook in the ceiling. It swayed, causing a few dust motes to rain down. My own private room. For some reason, the other Godless rarely stepped inside.

Because no one else is crazy enough to sleep inside a precariously hanging tram.

Or adventurous enough, I'd say.

The inviting orange glow of oil lamps beamed from the windows of our lounge, welcoming us. This tram was lodged tight and safe in its own bay. Harmony hopped in first, and I ducked in last, following Malk and Dru. The inner carriage was stuffed full of cushions along the renovated bench, and a table had been built around the tram's center pole. The three others who made up the rest of our team were already sitting around it.

Sinder's Ember skin glowed a bright red underneath the lamps dangling across the top railing, and he perked up from his slouching when we entered. "Who took them?"

Malk plopped himself on the edge of the bench and crossed his leg over his knee. "Glimmer, who else?"

Sinder's lips formed a thin line. He turned to Vincent beside him. "Called it."

Vincent shared the same grimace, and the lamps gave his Necro-white skin a healthy pallor. "It was hardly in question."

Harmony sat at the head of the table as our leader. "Yes, and I'd like to find out why. Grab a seat, you two. I'll try to keep this short."

Dru flopped onto a pile of cushions next to Reve, our Mesmer seer, who still wore his nightgown from this morning. Though Mesmer often forwent gender, Reve took on the persona of a young boy. He sat as still as a statue, though his dark skin flickered with the speckled dots of stars.

Those intense eyes bore into me for a moment, and then returned to staring at the framed placard hanging above the lounge, containing a single note from our organization's mystery benefactor. A note which had inspired and birthed the Godless.

"Chime needs godless heathens.

May the gods leave you to your fate."

Our organization existed thanks to Reve's visions and our benefactor's intel, though none of us knew the identity of our mysterious benefactor, not even Reve.

Sinder shuffled aside to make space and patted the cushion beside him. "You look exhausted, darling. Come sit with us."

I gave him a grateful smile and squeezed between him and Vincent.

Immediately, Sinder's hands were massaging my shoulders with his soothing touch. His hands shimmered with the warmth of his power—not enough to burn or hurt, but it felt *good*. These skills could make him the finest masseur on Sinner's Row.

"Are you going to do me next?" Malk smirked.

"Only if you ask nicely," Sinder responded with a purr.

"He doesn't need it," I said with a slight moan. "He spent all day sleeping in a ditch."

"It was a particularly uncomfortable ditch."

"Can we focus?" Harmony said with a slight flare of her nostrils.

Sinder's hands slipped from my shoulder and I mourned their absence. Cool air radiated from Vincent's skin beside me in contrast to Sinder's heat.

The two of them were complete opposites, yet each intimidating in their own way; Sinder dressed in outrageous corsets and skirts which put my outfits to shame, and much of his red skin had been inked over in black tattoos of flames and the word *sinner* across his collarbone, though this was partially hidden by a silk scarf around his neck. The silver piercings in his horns only added to his 'don't touch me' vibe.

And though Vincent appeared a proper gentleman at first glance, with his smart attire, combed white hair, and stylish cane, those who spotted his pale face, bloodshot eyes, and deadly fangs soon skittered away. His usually dry lips were plump from a fresh feed. Knowing what he drank to sustain himself didn't bother me like it should.

We were all sinners here, and I wrapped my arms around them both.

"Well?" Harmony demanded.

Malk sat up and recounted his day from his encounter with the Glimmer to returning to Chime. Beside me, Sinder fidgeted whenever the Glimmer were mentioned. He had more reason to hate the Glimmer than any of us. Even speaking their name was enough to raise his anxiety. I bumped my elbow into his, and he gave me a strained smile.

Harmony listened as she jotted down notes. "So they've taken the Vesper to one of their workhouses. It shouldn't be too difficult to find which one. But what are they working on that requires a donation of gold to Valeria?"

"Varen should have known," Vincent said in that calm and eloquent voice of his. "He's Valeria's mortal eyes. How did he not hear of a Glimmer delegation heading for Eventide?"

"At the very least, someone from Varen's staff must have leaked this information," Harmony said. "Kayl, he'll be coming to question you shortly since you brought Wardens down on our heads. I want you to prod him then."

"Wardens came here?" I asked, alarmed.

"Varen sent them packing, but it's not the last we'll hear of them. Can you explain to me what in god's name you did to summon them?"

All eyes turned to me.

"Why do you assume it was something *I* did?"

"She offended some well-off Diviner in Lady Mae's and ran," Dru said with a yawn.

"*Dru!* I did not offend him—at least not deliberately—"

"Kayl," Harmony warned. "Was it him? The saboteur Reve's vision warned of?"

I didn't want to explain what had really happened, lest the rest of the Godless believe I was finally going crazy. Not that Dru believed me, anyway. "I don't know. He was just another customer reading the broadsheet, but he—he thought I was suspicious for some reason. It's done now, what does it matter?"

"It matters because it took us *months* to get you both in that position. A prime location right next to the Gate, serving some of Chime's most prominent members?"

"Such a shame I'll no longer be wasting my time bending over backwards serving tea for Glimmer, or Dru slaving away—"

"You blew it, Kayl."

Harmony's words hung in the air. I knew she needed to be harsh. She had so many of us to protect, so many threads in play, but...

She's right. You done goofed.

This had been my chance to prove myself among the Godless, and I'd blown it.

"This wasn't her fault, Harm." Malk broke the silence. "She caught the eye of a Diviner. That could have happened at any time. She got out of there and we got back here in one piece. Things could have turned out much worse."

"Things could have turned out much better. The Glimmer—"

"Wasn't our fault either. We didn't see it coming." His gaze flickered to Reve, who remained characteristically silent. "We move forward."

"We move forward," Vincent agreed.

"We fuck up some Glimmer," Sinder added.

"Right, we move forward." Harmony visibly deflated in her seat. "We need information on what these Glimmer are doing with the Vesper. Neither Kayl nor Dru can return topside for the foreseeable future. The Wardens won't give up their search easily. And we can't risk Malk by sending him back and forth to Eventide each time. But I *do* have some news of my own." Harmony pulled the latest Courier broadsheet from her handbag, spreading it out across the table. "Today's headline. Notice anything?"

I peered over the table with the others, except Reve, who was staring at the wall. I'd already seen this—*Construction Begins on Clock Tower Reinforcement.*

"They're doing maintenance, so what?" Sinder shrugged.

Harmony tapped the paper with a perfectly manicured nail. "The real story is never in the headlines. Want to know why they're doing such heavy maintenance? Because there's aether leaking everywhere."

That wasn't news to the residents of the Undercity. Aether sparks and other electrical disturbances were becoming more frequent. I'd suffered migraines as proof. "We know this."

"*We* know this. The Wardens are carrying on like everything's fine. I oversaw a report on the leaks this morning and was ready to print it when a Diviner Warden turned up and forced us to stop the presses early. Our morning editions got pulped."

"So they're censoring work on the tower? Not exactly a thrilling headline," Malk said. "What's the real story?"

A gleam shone in Harmony's eye. "These aether leaks are killing Diviner. At least four so far."

That elicited an audible gasp.

Malk leaned closer with his hands clasped. "Only Diviner? No one else?"

"So I overheard."

I wrung my hands in my lap. "You beat my brow for summoning the Wardens when they were more likely investigating these deaths and assumed me to be some saboteur?"

Harmony sat back with a smug smirk. "I 'beat your brow' because you need reminding of the consequences of your actions. But yes, it's likely they called in the guard because they saw your face and thought you were a saboteur. It's an easy mistake to make."

Sinder tutted. "That's a bitch move, Harm."

"Being a bitch is why I'm in charge of keeping you heathens alive." Harmony winked at me.

For a moment, I stared at her—at this tiny Seren with her single frail wing. Dru was our literal muscle, but most assumed Malk ran the Godless. He possessed the intimidating height, the power to command shadows, the grumpy charm and endearing scowl, and no one could best him in a knife fight.

Yet our dear leader was the least intimidating among us; sweet, innocent Harmony, copywriter for the Courier by day, treasonous plotter by night. I stifled a giggle.

I understood why Harmony beat my brow as much as she did. The rest of the Godless knew my nature; reckless, prone to distraction and wanton acts of danger, and completely scatterbrained. Only my inner voice kept me straight.

Someone has to. You're getting distracted even now, you dumb arse.

Shit, I was.

"That's why the Glimmer are taking Vesper," Malk was saying. "I'll bet you the Glimmer have some sort of contract with the Wardens to work on their pet maintenance project. Why risk Diviner lives when they can risk Vesper?"

"That's right," I blurted out as I suddenly remembered. "The Diviner from Lady Mae's—he said something about the Glimmer's contract with them, and that some woman, Glenys, or Glory—"

Gloria.

"Gloria, that's it. She'd be overseeing the whole operation."

"Gloria?" Sinder frowned. "Are you sure? That's the Glimmer ambassador."

Shit, she was? I wasn't the best with names.

"That would explain why they'd go to this trouble to cover it up," Harmony mused. "Wardens hiring Glimmer is no story; Diviner ingenuity and Glimmer gold make for a powerful partnership. But bribing Valeria for workhouse slaves to protect Diviner lives? That's breaking the Covenant."

"The Diviner mentioned something about testing the Vesper," I added as I squirmed in my seat. "Could they be testing them against these aether leaks?"

"Has our benefactor not left any intel on this?" Vincent asked.

Harmony tapped her nails on the table. "None. Last note I received from them was regarding the Glimmer workhouses weeks ago, but we can't afford to keep waiting for their intel, or Varen's. We need to find out what's really going on and get proof. We need to get inside those workhouses."

Sinder leaned back with his arms crossed. "You step foot in those workhouses and you aren't coming out."

"He's right, Harm," Malk said. "It's too dangerous—"

"Send me," I said. "They want Vesper, don't they? I'm the obvious choice."

"The obvious choice," Harmony repeated with her brows raised. "To send you straight into the arms of the Wardens?"

"It's not like I can leave for topside anytime soon, can I? The Wardens won't search for me hiding inside one of their own workhouses. And Vincent can alter my face, change a few details here and there to mask me."

Vincent bowed his head. "That, I can do."

"I'm a worker. Send me instead," Dru said.

"They want Vesper, Dru—"

"No offense, but you're adept at finding trouble."

"Trouble finds me, that's the problem, and there's a lot of it going around." I turned to Harmony. "I'll slink in with them, act the part of a scared and starving Vesper, and find whatever intel I can. Then I'll get out of there. You know this makes sense. I won't blow it."

"And just how do we get you out?" Sinder snapped. His usual calm had quickly deteriorated and his skin was rippling with repressed flame. "Do you know how tightly locked up the Glimmer keep their workhouses? What if they drag you to Solaris?"

"If there's one thing I can do right, it's run. I managed tonight among an entire team of Wardens."

"Barely," Dru muttered under her breath.

Sinder's fiery gaze smoldered with doubt.

"Send me," Malk declared. "I've got the background of an illegal-mushroom seller. The Glimmer would lap me up, and if Kayl goes, there could be Diviner who grab her, and then she'll expose—"

"It has to be Kayl," Reve said with the booming voice of an adult, so at odds with his younger body.

We all turned to stare at Reve, even Dru, who'd been half-asleep.

Reve's eyes had turned a solid black, as dark as the void. Silence gripped the air as we waited for him to continue his vision.

"It has to be Kayl," he repeated. "I see her there. I see where her path leads. The clock of fate is ticking for her." His dark eyes turned to me. "Tick. Tock. Tick. *Tock.*"

I glanced at Malk, who looked uneasy. "Then... I'll go with her as backup."

Harmony folded the broadsheet. "We have a plan."

Sinder threw up his hands. "It's a stupid plan, as you'll find out when you're locked inside one of their prayer rooms and forced to sing hymns. Fuck it, I'm going for a smoke." He pushed past my knee and yanked open the tram door, his finger already flickering, ready to light up a cigar. Vincent shrugged an apology and went after him.

Harmony grabbed her handbag. "Kayl, speak with Varen. Let's see if he can find out which workhouse we need to smuggle you into. I'll make sure he knows you're here. The rest of you, get some sleep and be on your guard."

Dru helped guide Reve from the carriage, though the poor boy looked confused by everything, leaving me with Malk.

I slipped beside him and wrapped my arm around his. "Alone at last."

"I don't like this plan."

"Reve's already seen it."

"Which makes me like it even less. When have Reve's visions ever brought us good news?"

"It's thanks to Reve's visions that we're still here."

"I suppose."

"Then stop being so grumpy." I reached up to kiss him.

He returned the kiss with hungry fervor. And then his hands were in my hair as his lips trailed down to my neck.

"We won't be able to do this in the Glimmer workhouse," he breathed against my ear. The slight touch of his teeth grazed against my pulse and heat spasmed through me, as though he'd burned me with aether.

I tilted my head back, opening myself to the exploratory kisses tracing along my collarbone. At the same time, his warm hands moved to my hips and tugged on my pinafore.

"This was all I could think about in that damn ditch. This gods-forsaken skirt. What you look like under it. Taste like."

"Such sinful thoughts."

"I almost stroked myself blind thinking of you."

I blinked at him. "You spent the entire day wanking off in a ditch while I worked myself to the bone fretting you'd been caught?"

"You worry too much—"

"*Malk—*"

He licked the sweat from my neck and I groaned.

Gods, his touch *was* aether.

His lips battled me with the energy of a starving man at a meal, and his groin pressed against my leg, hot and *firm*. It was always like this after he returned from making the crossing to Eventide, as though he needed it—needed me—to wash over the experience with something pure. Something that was just us.

Two Vesper writhing in the dark.

Someone tapped on the tram window.

Stop snogging. You have company.

Malk leaned his forehead against mine and sighed. "Shit."

I pushed him back with my finger pressed against his lip. "Later."

The lust in his eyes made me want to grab him again, but he pulled away from me, awkwardly adjusted his slacks, and then slid open the carriage door. "She's all yours."

I straightened my pinafore and hair as an older Vesper replaced Malk, his long black hair tied into a topknot and tinged with gray streaks to match his dark-gray skin.

Varen wasn't dressed in the formal amethyst tabard of his office, but instead wore the shirt and slacks of the Undercity. He could have passed for any of the Vesper of Grayford, but even they knew to bow in recognition of the man they affectionately referred to as the Gray Lord. For Varen spent his days acting on behalf of our god as her mortal voice, but at night he served his mortals right here under the heart of Chime, which included passing on whatever intel he could to a bunch of heathens in defiance of the god who owned his soul.

And for that, I loved him.

Varen took a seat beside me with his disarming smile. "Am I interrupting anything?"

"Oh no, Malk and I were just chatting."

"Okay, good." He paused, and then his smile twisted into a frown. "Why did an entire legion of Wardens march through my town?"

I tucked my hands into my lap. Varen was rarely an angry sort, but his disappointment could bite as hard. "Diviner have been murdered topside, so Harmony says. I think I was mistaken for some sort of saboteur."

"Mistaken?" His breath blew out in disbelief. "I had Wardens pounding at my door over a simple case of mistaken identity? No, you forget who I am and where my place is. Do you have any idea of who you confronted in Lady Mae's? Any inkling at all?"

An uneasy feeling roiled through me. "I recognized his face."

"As you should. That was Elijah Karendar, ambassador to the Diviner."

My jaw dropped. The Diviner ambassador? He was the most powerful Diviner in Chime, second only to his maker, and the closest Chime had to a god. "But—he was dressed in civilian clothing! How was I to know?"

"What did you do to him?" The seriousness in Varen's voice made my stomach lurch.

"I..." I couldn't keep the truth from Varen. Not Varen. "He used his Diviner power, and I saw it."

Varen's brow furrowed. "Saw it?"

"I saw it work, saw him slow and reverse time. And when he noticed, he tried to question me. Tried to slow time so he could stop me. But it had no effect on me at all, and I ran from the café. And that's when the Wardens came swarming out of nowhere." Which made complete sense now that I knew he was the gods-damn ambassador! "I didn't attack him; I didn't even *insult* him."

"And what of Lady Mae? The Wardens say you killed her."

"She's dead?" Gods. I hated the woman, but I'd never wished her dead. Harmony would need to know. "She tried to grab me and fell against the table. I—I didn't kill her! She must have banged her head. Varen, I didn't know—"

72

"I believe you. I hate that I believe you, but I do." Varen tugged at the thin black beard dangling from his chin. "This... This could change everything." His shrewd eyes turned to me. "Forget the Glimmer. Who else have you told about your encounter with Karendar?"

"Dru, but she didn't believe me."

"Good. Don't tell anyone else. I sent the Wardens off to bring the proper paperwork before they storm Grayford, but they'll be back come morning. You need to lie low. You've put the absolute fear of their god in them."

"We need to find our Vesper. The Glimmer interfered with our plans. They've taken them to some workhouse—"

"So Harmony informed me."

"Someone knew about the meet. Someone from your house. Why is Valeria handing over Vesper in exchange for gold? You must have known."

He rolled his shoulders and neck, easing out the creaks I knew he suffered from the thick ridges splayed down his spine. "Valeria is like most gods; prone to irrational whims. I assure you, I wouldn't have gone to the trouble of stamping your refugees' documents if I'd known. The Glimmer must have sent their own ambassador to meet with her, because nothing came through me, and Valeria gave me no sign. You understand I took great personal risk to deliver this intel. I take great personal risk speaking to you now—"

"We're all taking risks."

"Are they worth it? I've always believed in you and your Godless, but remember what I said all those years ago? They'd have a home here so long as their actions never impacted the Vesper. With a Glimmer dead and Wardens marching over Grayford again, you're reaching that line."

"The Glimmer are taking Vesper, just like they took Elvira. We want them back."

"I don't want to lose another Elvira."

I understood his fears, what we all stood to lose—without Grayford, mortals would have no place to hide from the workhouses or Wardens, and no place to hide from their gods.

Years ago, Malk's mother had escaped Eventide for a better life and found shelter under Varen's wing. She'd found me, too, and was the closest I'd ever have to a mother. Elvira had fed and clothed me with her own bocs, even though she didn't have to.

Then one day she'd vanished; taken by the Glimmer to slave away in their workhouses. We'd all been devastated by her disappearance.

Varen had loved Elvira. I'd seen it, even if he'd never said the words.

When Elvira had escaped the workhouse and came back to us, Wardens had dragged her away, never to be seen again.

That's when Malk and I had decided that the gods and their Wardens weren't worth our worship and servitude. That's when we'd formed the Godless.

"With your help, we'll find out which workhouse the Glimmer have taken them to and try to get them out. Or at the very least, find out what they and the Wardens are using the Vesper for and put a stop to it."

"With my help? If Valeria sanctioned this, then there's little I can do—"

"The Wardens are breaking the very Covenant they swore to uphold; even us heathens can see that."

Varen drew in a breath. "I can't keep doing these favors for you. You've been lucky, but your luck will only run for so long."

"Then make this your last favor. For old time's sake. For me. For Malk. For Elvira. For every Vesper who ever sought shelter at your door."

We'd all suffered under the gods, and none more than Varen. He rubbed his neck and sighed. "For Elvira. For you. And for the sins of my past and the sins yet to come."

VI

*The vast majority of Chime's Vesper make their home in the Undercity
slums colloquially known as 'Grayford' – though few are aware that these
slums are owned by Ambassador Varen, Valeria's mortal voice.
The Vesper are a pious, if not grumpy, lot, though their affinity for darkness
stands opposite the Glimmer's love of sunlight. Vesper feel most comfortable
in dark areas, hence the Undercity. Their ability to manipulate shadow
makes them adept pickpockets. They often come into conflict with Wardens
due to their pilfering fingers or illegal mushroom dealings.
As Valeria's mortals, they are expected to make a regular tithe and also
cover their mortal bodies as to not distract from her beauty. Anything less is
sinful in Valeria's eyes.*
—Q. Corinth, *Warden Dossier on the Vesper*

THE GATE CHANGED FROM the warm orange hues of Obituary's desert to the
blazing red of Rapture's volcano. I picked up my tea and took a satisfyingly
hot sip.

My morning routine returned at last.

Only not.

I'd barely slept a wink, and the cup trembled slightly, sloshing the black
dregs with the tides of Arcadia's summer isles. This return to normality was
meant to center me, but the clock on the mantelpiece blasted my ears with
nine harsh bells. Each a throb in my temples.

Fate was coming for me with every tick and tock.

I placed my cup aside and gathered the collection of folders and papers
on my desk, the Courier broadsheet discarded elsewhere. There'd be time
for small comforts later, with any luck, but I needed to go over these before
Eventide opened in the next hour. I flipped open the first; details of those
employed at Lady Mae's café within the past six months.

Mostly Vesper. A few Umber. The Ember boy who'd died at my feet.

Undercity residents. Illegals, by the looks of them.

One of Elijah's men had handed these over last night. We'd gone long into the early hours questioning the Glimmer with their new collection of Vesper—fresh for a grueling life in one of their workhouses—as well as any Vesper in the vicinity. Only later had I learned that the Undercity shaft had been tampered with, and my intrepid quarry had ridden the blasted service elevator down. I could hardly believe the audacity!

The station staff were *not* impressed.

I leaned back in my chair, my eyes glossing over the city skyline below my apartment and to the hands of the clock tower counting away the minutes.

So many of Elijah's assignments over the years had felt like a punishment, but this... I couldn't tell if it was a gift or a curse. A creature made of pure aether that could steal the souls of Diviner? Specifically targeting us? A truly terrifying tale to be dismissed as fantasy and speculation. Yet I'd seen it—felt it—through the death of another.

A Vesper woman who could see Diviner power in action, and not just see it, but avoid it like some sort of magical immunity? Again, this belonged to the realms of fantasy.

Nothing about this case made logical sense.

And that was why Elijah had assigned it to me.

So many of my brethren couldn't imagine possibilities beyond the laws and logic of nature. But I... *I* could think in the realms of the impossible. Because I'd lived it.

The woman, then. Unknown name, unknown birth, quite clearly an illegal Chime resident to navigate it with such ease, and quite clearly from the Undercity, given we'd almost rubbed shoulders on the elevator. I should have been suspicious then; Vesper were rarely chatty with Diviner, especially ones with my reputation.

But a Vesper did not possess the ability to see Diviner power work. Or shouldn't.

Though there was something about this Vesper that didn't shout *murderer*. No, she didn't seem like the murdering type.

Yet she'd apparently killed a Glimmer and then run. I remained skeptical.

I picked up the first note. The Wardens had taken the logical action and headed for the Grayford slums, home to a large quantity of Chime's poorest Vesper, among other less-reputable mortals. And rather predictably, Ambassador Varen had denied them entry, sending them back for the proper documentation. A wise man who knew the only thing that could defeat a Diviner was damnable paperwork.

That documentation sat in my folder. I held in a sigh. I'd be taking another trip down the elevator, and I so hated those things.

I'd already passed on my suggestion to search Sinner's Row. So kind of Elijah to leave Grayford for me.

Perhaps I'd visit the steamworks after. Creatures born of aether made no sense, but the engineers there would at least understand how aether worked.

I gulped the rest of my tea and shuddered at the residual bitterness. Where I was headed, the tea was much worse.

The tea they'd offered me was serviceable at best. Light on the milk, as I'd requested, but also heavy with sugar, which I'd *not* requested. They likely added it to mask the metallic taste of hardened, unfiltered water so common underground. If they planned to poison me, I supposed the attempt was subtle enough.

Things could have been worse. They could have offered me coffee.

I sat in the reception area of Varen's office in Grayford. Varen wasn't the only ambassador to make his home in the Undercity—the Ember ambassador ran the entire stretch of Sinner's Row and was a most entertaining host—but Varen was the only ambassador who seemed to live among and truly care for his mortals.

He'd always been my favorite.

The room was well-decorated with floral wallpaper and an antique oak-and-brass desk. Certainly, from the inside, I'd almost forgotten I sat in the slums. But outside, Grayford remained as dilapidated as ever. A mishmash of broken homes. Dark eyes staring from behind cracked walls, watching me cautiously as I intruded into their world.

The most desperate souls always found their way to the Undercity eventually, and then they'd see for themselves that the promise of Chime wasn't all polished brass and gilded sanctuary, but rusting ruins and rotting greed.

Stepping into Grayford always filled me with a deep melancholy that not even a good cup of tea could placate.

"His Excellency will see you now," the Vesper receptionist announced.

I placed my cup down and stretched to my feet. "Wonderful."

The receptionist guided me through to a private study and clicked the door shut behind her, leaving me with the harsh glare of Ambassador Varen.

I immediately dipped to one knee and bowed my head. "Your Excellency."

"Quentin Corinth." The ambassador's voice held no welcome or patience, clearly unimpressed with my attempts at flattery. "Of all the Wardens Karendar could have sent, he sent *you*?"

I stood and pushed my spectacles up my nose. "A pleasure as always, Varen."

He sneered. "Address me with the proper respect, Corinth."

This was starting off well. "Apologies, Your Excellency. You understand why I'm here? I filed the required paperwork with your staff." In fact, I saw it discarded on the good ambassador's desk, unopened next to a stack of passport applications and crossing approvals for visitors from other domains.

Varen strode around his large, ornate desk and sat, leaning back to get a good measure of me as I observed him in turn.

Time had not been kind. Wrinkles stretched from his eyes and across his forehead, and his black hair held more silver these days. He wore a dark purple tabard over black robes, the official wardrobe of his office, though not even the thick robes could hide the bony remnants of wings which had once protruded from his spine. A gift from Valeria before she had unceremoniously ripped them off.

I'd often wondered why Varen would continue to serve her, but did any of us really have a choice when the gods picked their favorites? Despite Varen's wounds, he *was* her favorite. Or else he wouldn't be sitting in this room.

Valeria had at least adorned her pet with treasures befitting his rank. A silver chain dangled from his neck holding a crescent moon; the symbol of the Vesper. More silver rings adorned each finger, some embedded with sapphires and diamonds.

All the wealth of his god.

His entire study dripped with the same decadence, and I wondered how many of Grayford's poor had stepped foot inside to see it. The dark purple drapes blocked out most of the window's light, and only orange oil lamps kept the shadows at bay. It was a dark room, deliberately designed to intimidate me.

He hadn't asked me to sit. He wouldn't.

While he may command the power of darkness, that meant nothing to a man who commanded time. I could have hummed a merry tune, but that would get me thrown out of Grayford a lot quicker.

Instead, I placed my hands casually into my pockets and rubbed a thumb over the fob watch resting inside, as patient as I.

Varen maintained his stare. "Your presence here is an insult to me and the mortals of Grayford. Ambassador Karendar cannot force his way into my jurisdiction to harass my town. Your behavior and that of your Wardens is unacceptable. If you continue to push, then this matter *will* be brought to Valeria."

Involving the gods in the mortal disputes of Chime was a worst-case scenario, and Varen knew it. They didn't understand, nor care, for the well-being of other domains, which was why each employed a mortal ambassador to handle delicate mortal interests, and why we Wardens maintained a careful balance with our ordinances.

It wasn't like Varen to go straight for the jugular—something must have him rattled. "Diviner have been murdered, Your Excellency—"

"And Vesper have been disappearing from the streets, but I didn't see Karendar sending you to discuss *that*."

"On the contrary, the missing Vesper are part of my investigation."

Varen snorted a laugh. "That proves how much the Wardens care for my domain. Do they honestly believe my mortals would cooperate with the likes of you?"

"Ambassador Karendar sent me because he knows I'll be subtle about it."

"Subtle." Varen shook his head. "That's what you call barging into my office and demanding an audience with this?" He lifted the unopened folder and flung it across the room. Papers came loose and flapped listlessly to the ground. "I grant you no ground to terrorize my mortals."

Such dramatics. "Your Excellency, we merely wish to find one Vesper for questioning. The Wardens have no intention of razing Grayford or rounding up every Vesper who ever stepped foot in Chime—but failure to assist our search will reflect on the Council's relationship with Eventide."

One Vesper. One woman. It shouldn't be this difficult.

Varen's nostrils flared. "There are thousands of Vesper in Chime alone."

"You have records, I assume?"

"My staff and I lack the time needed to scour through thousands of records. None of which includes illegals that slip through the cracks, which this girl likely is—"

"You're not keeping track of them, Ambassador?"

"Don't test me, Corinth."

"Work with me and give me something, and I'll be out of your domain, never to step foot here again. It's all there in my file." I nodded to the discarded paperwork on the floor. "One Vesper woman. Aged mid-twenties, about six-foot, indigo skin, short black hair. Didn't get a good look at her eyes or passport."

Varen waved a dismissive hand at me. "That description could apply to any number of Vesper—"

"Worked for the past three weeks at Lady Mae's, a Glimmer-owned café within view of the Gate, which sells a variety of teas and cream cakes. Went by the name of *Yuda Mann*." So obviously fake I was surprised even the Glimmer fell for it. "When questioned, Lady Mae's associates informed us that this 'Yuda Mann' had been forwarded a recommendation that came from this house itself." I strode to his desk and placed both palms on the surface, leaning over as close as I dared. "Do you care to explain that?"

For a heartbeat, I slowed a bubble of time around the desk, my hands pressing down on the wood so he wouldn't see my fingers twitch.

And there, in the darkness of his pupils, flashed a look of panic. It blinked away as quickly as it came and I would have missed it hadn't I taken the time to appreciate it.

I raised my hands and allowed time to catch up. He hadn't noticed this tiny fluctuation in time, and for that I was grateful. At least *he* wasn't one of the soul-sucking aether monsters I've been sent to hunt, though now my suspicions had been confirmed.

The good ambassador was hiding something.

Varen crossed his arms, the picture of nonchalance. "Are you accusing me or my staff of enabling criminal behavior?"

"Or you've been played, Your Excellency. Which is it?"

"Played?" He scoffed. "Hardly. There are hundreds of Vesper employed topside in places like Lady Mae's. Part of my commitment to my domain is to help them seek employment with references from this house. We inspect the backgrounds of those we put forward, and I do not recall a Vesper of your description, nor any reference to Lady Mae's. It's possible the recommendation may have been counterfeit."

"You're telling me you've never put forth a Vesper for Lady Mae's?"

"Never. But I'm not surprised someone would go to such extreme measures to find work. What choice do my mortals have when opportunities are so few and far between? I'd say this girl, whoever she is, is built of a resourcefulness few possess. She worked there for weeks, you say? And there were no problems with her work? Then what was her crime?"

"If you'd read the report—"

"I read Karendar's report. A Diviner turns up dead. Such a loss. And you instantly blame a Vesper who happened to be in the wrong place at the wrong time. Do you see why we don't trust your domain?"

"And Lady Mae? Would you not consider her death worth investigation? Though your mortals have never cared much for Glimmer, have they, Ambassador?"

"From reading the report, Lady Mae fell onto a table and cracked her head. A tragic accident that you again seek to pin on Vesper. Predictable, really."

Elijah had left out details regarding Lady Mae's death and the woman's strange immunity to our Diviner power. It was bad enough Diviner were turning up dead; the last thing we wanted was for anyone to know that Diviner power could be resisted.

"Quite a coincidence that our eyewitnesses caught this Yuda Mann running from the scene of her death. All I'm asking is for your cooperation."

Varen tugged at his beard and sighed with real exasperation. "I don't know what to tell you. If this girl is an illegal, I won't be able to trace her, but you can inform Karendar that I and my staff will hold an inspection within Grayford. We'll launch our own investigation, if only to discover how someone was able to counterfeit our work orders. I don't want the Council holding this over our heads. If you care for us as you so claim, then you won't drag the Vesper into this mess."

They were empty platitudes which wouldn't get me anywhere. "You keep an ear to Grayford's streets. You must know where your illegals congregate?"

"If you're intent on finding them, then search Sinner's Row. That's where they go to find work and shelter when they're desperate, and where they're likely to find the means to counterfeit work orders." He rose from his chair. "Are we done?"

I wasn't going to get much more from him. I bowed my head. "Thank you for your time, Your Excellency. I will inform Ambassador Karendar of your cooperation."

Varen's mouth formed a tight line as I directed myself from his office.

Well, the tea and hospitality had been terrible as always, but it hadn't been a wasted venture.

For one, I'd learned for certain that Varen knew my quarry.

For two, I'd learned where she was hiding—the Glimmer workhouses.

A Vesper would never lose any opportunity to criticize their greatest rivals, and while Varen had tried to steer me to the more obvious answer of Sinner's Row, he'd not once mentioned the workhouses, the one place where Glimmer actually *did* take advantage of illegals coming to Chime. I'd questioned an entire group of them last night coming from Eventide.

My trip to the steamworks would have to wait. I couldn't sit on this.

Ah, the good ambassador misunderstood my intentions. Nothing motivated social justice more than guilt, and I held plenty of that. The mortals of Grayford hated me for good reason, but Elijah Karendar had sent the best Warden for this case.

Because among the Diviner, only I gave a damn about the Vesper.

7

What is sin?
The Covenant makes many references to sin but defers to each god.
The Glimmer refer to sin as distractions that separate a mortal from their
god, because one's mind and prayers should be focused at all times.
Each domain has their own separate definition of sin. What one god finds
sinful, another will encourage. How can one win against such hypocrisy?
Learn the sins of your domain, no matter how asinine they may seem.
Practice abstinence by day. Then at night, sin to your heart's content where
the prying eyes of the Wardens cannot judge.
—Anonymous, *Godless flier on sin*

"GOOD MORNING, KAYL. PLEASE make yourself comfortable."

Vincent welcomed me inside his parlor. I scooted my behind onto one of the two beds and let my legs dangle off the end.

The chandelier rattled above me in a soft melody at the turn of the hour, and the silvery-blue light cast scattered shadows across Vincent's storage cabinets, containing supplies from medicinal mushrooms to murky green potions. We'd scavenged the chandelier, and it certainly brought an extra layer of class to Vincent's office, though I found the faint hum grating. I much preferred oil lamps, since aether needed a connection to Grayford's generator over at Varen's place.

I supposed a medical room needed the extra light. None of the factory bays underneath the main hangar that we'd converted into rooms held windows.

"How's Sinder?" I asked. He'd been avoiding me since our meeting the other night.

"He's worried for you. You know this mission brings back memories for him."

"I don't want Vesper to suffer the same fate."

"He understands that. Give him time, he'll come around. Now, let's talk about you and your needs."

Vincent clasped his hands in his lap. As the only Necro in Grayford, Vincent's skills and supplies were often in demand; not only to patch up scrapes and injuries, but to tailor the appearance of those wanted by the Wardens, and to touch up their fake passports.

Without Vincent, we'd never have helped as many mortals as we had.

And now it was my turn to seek his expertise.

"How do we do this? I lie back and you make me beautiful?"

Vincent smiled—a subtle, restrained one that hid his fangs. "I'd needn't trouble myself, then?"

Smooth.

Smooth indeed. Among the Godless, Vincent stood out as the most handsome. His porcelain skin had been carved into perfect symmetry, though the aether lights masked the prominent blue veins I could normally see. His fashion style bested us too, dressed as he was in an impeccable black suit with his slick white hair combed back.

But even his charm held subtleties. Vincent sat on a stool a good arm's length away from me, his body tensed but relaxed—like a predator trying to convince its prey he could be trusted. Every movement Vincent made was with the same consideration; slow, deliberate.

It saddened me to see him leash himself this way, but I understood why he did it. A monster hid underneath his beauty, and it was that side of the Necro mortals feared.

Necro, Ember, Fauna, Vesper; we were the undesirable mortals. The sinners. Those who wouldn't play by the rules of civilized society, though the Wardens had no choice but to allow us into Chime in order to keep all twelve gods happy.

If the Glimmer had their way, they'd decide who passed for civilized. It was their influence which forced us to wallow in the Undercity, tucked away and out of sight.

But they used us when they wanted us. For their factories and workhouses, or in the Necro's case, for their glamorous beauty parlors.

Just as the gods used us.

"Before you start, there's something I need to ask of you… and you can't tell the others."

He raised a perfectly plucked eyebrow. "You have my discretion."

I let out a breath. "For as long as I can remember, I've always been… uncomfortable around aether. I don't know what it is, the brightness? The spark? The weird buzzing it gives off? Regardless, whenever I'm near it, it gives me headaches." I massaged my temples. "And the headaches have been growing worse."

"Describe them to me."

I went over the symptoms; the sharp pains sometimes accompanied with nausea, dizziness, colorful dots that blurred my vision. And how last time in the elevator I'd almost hallucinated and passed out. "I've dealt with them for this long, but now they're becoming a liability. I can't have a moment like that again and risk jeopardizing this mission. Is there anything I can do to stop it?"

Vincent stood slowly and held his hands over my forehead. "May I?"

Don't let him inside.

"Go ahead."

His cool fingers pressed on both sides of my forehead, his touch as cold as ice. I shuddered slightly.

"Would you like me to fetch Sinder and warm them?" he asked.

"No, it's fine. Soothing, even." Not quite a lie. The cold eased my aches.

His fingers massaged my forehead in circular motions. "Migraines can be caused by bright lights or sounds, though I've not heard of anyone reacting to aether in this way. I wonder. You said they were getting worse?"

"Mm, yes, these past few months."

"When the aether leaks started?"

Could that be possible?

"Let me examine deeper," he said, and then Vincent's fingers slipped *into* my skin.

It was a startling tingling sensation, like an itch I couldn't scratch because it came from beneath my skin, and I clenched my fists to resist fidgeting.

"Do you see anything?" I asked.

"You have a delicious-looking brain."

"*What?*"

His cool breath huffed across me in a slight chuckle. "Joking. Brains aren't to my taste. Though no, I see nothing out of the ordinary. Let me flash you with aether. Try not to move, I don't want to give you an aneurysm."

He kept one hand pressed to my skull, and flicked on an aether lamp on the bedside table, pointing the bright glare directly at me.

A screech tore through my mind, and I cringed at the sharp pain behind my eyes.

It hurts, get him out, get him out—

"Stop!" I yelled and tried to turn away.

He immediately pulled back and twisted the light to one side. I rubbed the blotches of color from my eyes.

"Are you okay?" Vincent lowered his hands as though afraid to touch me.

"I'm sorry. It wasn't you, I just—"

"I felt something move inside you."

My stare met his. "What do you mean?" Shit, I wasn't pregnant, was I? But that couldn't be possible; mortals needed the blessing of their god before they could merge their life's essence into a new one, and Malk and I would never seek permission for that.

"I don't know. Your body, it... reacted to the aether. Like a shield. It blocked me out."

Of course I did, he was digging too deep looking for me.

I swallowed a breath. "Looking for what?"

"Pardon?" Vincent asked.

I shook my head and blinked away the dots. "I'm sorry, I'm confusing myself." Or my imagination was finally running away from me. "I get these thoughts, sometimes, like they're mine but not quite mine."

Because they're mine, dumb arse.

Gods. "Am I going mad?"

"Only your god can answer that."

If a Necro couldn't fix me, then I was truly doomed. "What do I do? Avoid aether?"

"If possible. And hope the Wardens can fix their aether leaks."

"You won't tell anyone, will you?"

He smiled with genuine charm, showing a slight fang. "You have my discretion as always."

I'd picked a fine time for losing my mind.

I returned to my room to get changed into the ragged shirt, slacks, and shawl the Vesper mushroom farmers wore on Eventide. My face still tingled from where Vincent had worked his magic. We'd agreed to a few subtle cosmetic changes, nothing that would bring attention to my face; the opposite, really.

The tram carriage that made up my room swayed as Malk jumped in. "What have you done to your nose?" He gasped with mock shock. "It's huge!"

I sat on the bench and pulled on my boots. "It's only temporary."

"Just as well. How am I supposed to kiss you?" Malk wore a matching farmer's garb and stood awkwardly in the entrance, not wanting to step in further, and not wanting to lean on anything either.

He'd always complained my room was a death trap and refused to sleep with me here overnight, or do other more pleasurable things, but that was fine with me.

My room was mine, and I'd decorated it as such.

"You're playing the part of my brother. The Glimmer wouldn't approve of the incestuous kisses you have in mind." I finished my laces before taking a final glance around my room. I wouldn't be returning here for a while, days perhaps.

To some, my dangling hovel of tranquility resembled the trash heaps outside. I'd piled cushions at the far end to serve as my bed and created a fort of drapes, bunting, and baubles for privacy. My clothes hung from the upper railing like curtains, and I'd decorated the driver's dashboard in all manner of trinkets, or junk as Dru would say, that I'd scavenged. Small pretty things that had caught my eye. My personal treasure trove.

Malk pulled me up into his embrace, his blue eyes burning with lust. "I have more than incestuous kisses in mind." He leaned in and began nibbling my ear.

I groaned at his touch.

"Oh, the Glimmer are going to have their hands full with you two," Dru called from outside. "You know you're supposed to be siblings? And keeping a low profile? Nothing will attract their attention quicker than two Vesper committing sins."

Malk pulled away with a sigh. "To them, we're nothing *but* sin."

"I can be pure," I said.

Dru snorted. "It's time, so finish your sinning and get down there." She left us for a moment of privacy.

I ran a fingernail along a loose thread of Malk's shirt. "This will be dangerous. We're heading into the heart of a Glimmer workhouse. We may never escape it."

We'd all seen Sinder's scars; both emotional and physical.

And we were willingly walking into that.

Malk took my hand with both of his and kissed my knuckles with such tenderness, it made my chest ache. "I'm not scared of them. But I am scared of what they'll do to the Vesper if we don't get them out of there."

That's what I loved about Malk. He'd witnessed his father's torture and death, his mother forced inside a workhouse only to escape and be dragged away by Wardens, experienced childhood under a cruel and pitiless god; and he didn't shy from it.

I reached up to kiss him and my nose jabbed him in the cheek. "Shit!"

He laughed and tweaked it. "We'll get this fixed when we're done. Shall we?" He offered his arm.

It was time to go save our mortals.

The workhouses of the Undercity were located on another tram line, separate from Grayford. We'd made our way here on foot, and waited for a tram of Vesper to turn up fresh from the ten o'clock Eventide crossing, to merge with their group.

The Glimmer, it seemed, had a need for more workers. Bad for the Vesper, but it worked in our favor. Thanks to Varen's intel and Harmony's talent for counterfeiting documents, we'd slip right on in.

Malk, Dru, and I crouched by the platform and waited for the tram to pull in. There were so many workhouses belonging to the various domains, we still weren't sure which one they'd take us to.

"That's them," Dru whispered as a tram containing the golden glow of Glimmer pulled into the station.

My heart fluttered. I grabbed Dru in a quick hug. "Keep an eye on Sinder for me."

Dru squeezed me back, and almost popped one of my ribs. "I will. Remember—find whatever intel you can and get out. No heroics from either of you, right? I'll be waiting for your signal. And *please* be careful."

Malk slapped Dru on the shoulder. "I'll keep her out of trouble, I promise."

"You better. The gods leave you to your fate."

We had no more time to waste.

The Glimmer led a small procession of skulking Vesper from the tram. Once they stepped off the platform, Malk and I slipped among them. Dressed like them, we'd hopefully pass as them, and I slouched my shoulders to mimic their mannerisms. Malk at least had grown up on Eventide and knew their ways and slang, but I was a fabulous actress and would pick it up quickly.

I didn't dare glance back to Dru. She'd be following us at a safe distance and keeping watch for our signal once we entered the workhouse. Many Umber made up the workforce of the Undercity in factories and warehouses, so Dru wouldn't be completely out of place. Neither Harmony nor Vincent could help here, and Reve would be safer back at base where he'd pass on any visions of our success or failure. Sinder... His powers to summon flame would have been useful, but we'd never get him within five feet of a workhouse without him suffering a literal meltdown. None of us would put him through that.

It was down to Malk and I.

Two Vesper stalking in the dark.

He brushed my hand briefly, and I bit back a smile. With him by my side, we could handle anything.

The Vesper trudged forward. None of them dared whisper a sound. There were eleven of them, and three Glimmer handlers that urged us forward to our new home.

Aether lamps lit our path along the wide and dusty streets. I averted my eyes from their oppressive glow, but they weren't all that seemed oppressive. Rows of towering dull-gray buildings dominated the Undercity skyline on either side, their brickwork stained with soot. Smoke puffed from stacked chimneys. It was their smog that coated the streets in a thin layer of grime and made the air taste like ash.

What a depressing heap.

I couldn't agree more.

Many of the factories and workhouses here were Diviner or Glimmer-owned, often employing the lesser domains to create products for contracts held by the more aristocratic ones. The Umber were natural-born workers and had whole swathes dedicated to their employ, because no one enjoyed work more than an Umber, or so the saying went.

The work we were destined for would be more important than an assembly line of canned goods or sewing fabrics. This contract had come from the Wardens themselves.

We walked for what felt like miles before we stopped outside brass gates. They screeched open, and the Glimmer hurried us into a courtyard of what appeared to be a stately home plucked from the Golden City and dropped right here. Not a warehouse or factory. Its walls were painted a bright white, untouched by the Undercity smog, and even the glass windows were clean.

The estate's double doors opened, and a Glimmer stepped out wearing a matron's dress, apron, and bonnet. "Welcome to your new home. Come. We will bathe you, feed you, and help you find suitable work. All paid for with blessings to the great shining one, Gildola, the goddess of radiance."

"With blessings," the Glimmer handlers murmured.

Shit, this wasn't a workhouse at all. It was a correctional facility.

You're walking into a trap.

Most likely, but this was the easiest way to find our refugees and discover exactly what these Glimmer were up to.

That was the plan; infiltrate the workhouse, gain intel on this contract between the Glimmer and Wardens, do a headcount of just how many Vesper were locked inside, and look for ways of smuggling them out.

Against a whole workhouse of Glimmer, we'd likely not smuggle many—if any. But information we could use. Perhaps not to save these sorry souls, but to prevent more from ever being taken. And Chime's citizens needed to know what shady deals were happening underneath their feet. Even the other domains would balk at the Glimmer disregarding the Covenant, and then the Wardens would have to come clean.

Besides, Harmony was right; we couldn't keep waiting for our mystery benefactor to grace us with their intel. After years of benefiting from their bocs and dossiers, we still didn't know who they were, or what agenda they served.

We needed to take this into our own hands.

"Please submit your papers before you enter," the matron said.

I did so, and they must have been satisfactory, as they were soon tucked away. At least we'd passed the first test, and the Glimmer hadn't been paying enough attention to notice two extra Vesper among their new workers. I resisted the urge to glance at Malk as our handlers escorted us inside the estate.

Upon entering, I cringed at the harsh glare of their oil lamps. These weren't aether, thank the gods, but their orange glow shone unnaturally bright. Nor did they leave a single shred of shadow, as though Gildola herself graced us with her presence.

Once my eyes adjusted, I was again surprised by the extravagant furnishings. A wide staircase led to an upper balcony, where a fresco on the domed ceiling depicted a naked, sunlit Gildola in all her glory against the backdrop of Solaris—the golden city of their domain. Similar paintings and decorative vases filled the entrance hall in a glittering and gaudy museum of actual junk.

It was a home for Glimmer, not Vesper.

Our handlers split us into two groups—male and female. I glanced mournfully at Malk as he was led away—as mournfully as a sister could for her brother—and followed one of the Glimmer with two other Vesper women into a brightly lit corridor. There were no shadows here to lurk in, and no sign of the other Vesper.

Where were they hiding them?

"Before we can house you, each of you must be questioned," our handler explained. "A test of faith, and to determine your suitability for our cause." We stopped outside of a double door. "Who would like to go first?"

The two other Vesper stared at their feet. I wanted this over with. "I'll go."

"Very good." The Glimmer opened the doors. "Please, step inside, and don't be afraid. We mean you no harm."

Somehow, those words didn't fill me with confidence. I stepped inside, and the door clicked shut behind me.

I'm not sure what I'd imagined, but it wasn't *this*.

A gray sheet draped the entire room, from the ceiling, down the walls, and across the floor. At first, I thought it must be a padded cell, and I turned to run. But a single Glimmer sat on a couch with her leg crossed over her knee and a clipboard in her hand. She pointed her pen at a small round stool, also covered in a gray sheet.

"Sit." It wasn't an offer, but a command.

Something crunched under my boots—dirt, perhaps—and I sat tentatively with my hands in my lap. A single chandelier lit the room with that same golden glow, though it could have come from the Glimmer herself for all I knew.

The Glimmer flipped through various sheets on her clipboard. "And you are?"

Malk and I had rehearsed our backgrounds on the walk to the tram station as Dru questioned us to ensure we left no gaps. "Anne Arkey. I came with my brother—"

"Yes, your brother." The Glimmer scribbled down a note. "Mushroom farmers, yes?"

"Yes, that's—"

"Do you know why you have been chosen, Anne?"

Chosen? "I—I don't, your ladyship."

"Please. Just 'my lady' will suffice. You have been chosen because my god, the blessed Gildola, loves you. She so loves you that she asked my domain to go to great personal expense and sacrifice to help you. To save you. Isn't that wonderful?"

Shit. This truly was a correctional facility, all sanctioned by the Wardens.

Five years ago, Sinder had stumbled into Grayford after escaping the clutches of a Glimmer workhouse with Malk's mother, Elvira, who'd disappeared long ago. Her return had shocked us both, though not as much as the news she'd brought with her.

All that time we'd believed her dead, she'd been trapped inside a workhouse no different from this. Only, the workhouse had been a front for more nefarious deeds; a correctional facility to 'cure' the sinners of sin, the blasphemers of blasphemy, the apostates of their apostasy.

We'd been trying to get them closed down ever since.

The Wardens turned a blind eye and were content to run their own state-sanctioned correctional facilities. But surely even they must realize that a god could punish their own mortals as they saw fit, but couldn't punish the mortals of other domains? It didn't just break the Covenant; it pissed on it.

The fact that Valeria herself had given her blessing to allow Glimmer to torture Vesper made the Covenant pointless. So much for life and liberty.

And so the Godless acted to protect the gods' mortals, even if the Wardens wouldn't.

"Forgive me, my lady. What does it mean to save us?"

"It means we will offer you food and housing and the blessings of Gildola, if you swear to serve her will. But we can only accept acolytes who are willing to purge their impurities and pledge themselves to her light."

Gildola so loves you, she wants you to kiss her arse and thank her for the privilege.

Well, that wasn't going to happen. "How can one purge their impurities, my lady? I thought your mortals taught that all were tainted by sin?"

"Where did you hear that?"

Shit.

You heard it from a sermon at Meridian Park.

"A sermon," I hurried. "One of your priests spoke of sin at Meridian Park. I vaguely remember it."

"You've made the crossing before? Show me your arm."

Damn it. I rolled up my sleeve, exposing the tattoo that clearly showed my clearance for Chime and Eventide. "My brother and I passed through once, to sell—"

"To sell mushrooms, I see. Well, you are correct, Anne. Mortals are not born with sin. We are the perfect vessel for our god, even Vesper. But the temptations of a mortal existence create sin. Do you know what sin is? It is the actions which seek to separate us from the loving embrace of our god. By indulging in acts of sin, there is less room in our hearts, minds, and souls for the love we must hold dear for our god. And this path is the seed which nurtures blasphemy, which then leads to apostasy. The greatest sin of all."

I tried not to fidget in my seat.

If she knew which organization I represented, we would not be having this conversation.

"If you have lived and breathed, then you have indulged in sin," the Glimmer continued. "It cannot be helped. But my domain seeks to purge sin, to train against temptation and create the purest relationship between mortal and god. I will test you now, and you must answer my questions honestly. Are you prepared?"

I had no idea what I was preparing for. "Yes, my lady."

The Glimmer tapped her lip with the tip of her pen. "Have you ever fornicated with another male or female?"

What was this? Asinine purity questions? "Never."

"Performed a lewd sexual act on another male or female?"

Many times. "No."

"Exposed yourself to another male or female?"

"Only when bathing."

The Glimmer frowned and scribbled down a note. "Have you ever drunk alcohol?"

"No."

"Taken illegal substances, including mushrooms?"

I had to admit to that one, lest she think I was the purest Vesper in Chime. "A few times, but only a few, and I regret it, my lady."

Another scratch on her notepad. "Don't worry, my dear, we can purge these deficiencies. Valeria demands a tithe from her mortals, does she not? Have you always paid it on time?"

Pfft, hardly. "We try."

"And how often do you pray to her?"

Never. Not once in my entire mortal life.

The Glimmer must have caught my reaction, for she leaned forward. "You can be honest with me, Anne. Do you love your god?"

It's a trick question.

Of course it was, and there was no right answer. Say yes, and I fail the Glimmer's test and reject her god for my own. Say no, and I admit to the greatest sin of them all.

Look at the walls.

They were gray, but among the gray were smatterings of dirt.

Not dirt. Ash.

The crunching beneath my feet...

Shit.

These gray sheets were to protect the furnishings; to quickly mop up the remnants of Vesper who failed the Glimmer's test. Because here, in this room, that Glimmer held the power of the sun. She could scatter my ashes with a single concentrated blast, and my shadows would not be enough to hide or protect me.

I suddenly wanted to be sick.

Was this what fate awaited the Vesper refugees?

Gods. Malk was in danger, too.

"Do you love your god?" the Glimmer prodded, her shoulders tense, awaiting my answer.

If I was going to die in this gods-forsaken room, then I'd die being who I'd always been.

A Godless.

"I hate her." The words came out with ease. "I hate what she is, what power she has, that she owns my soul but cares not for it." I sucked in a breath, surprised at the depth of my scorn. "Valeria is not and will never be my god."

I glanced up and expected to be met with a look of sheer horror.

Instead, the Glimmer smirked. "I believe we have a place for you in our home, Anne Arkey."

8

All that glitters is not gold.
The Glimmer may bask in sunlight, but do not fall for their piety.
They'll lock you in their workhouse and work you to exhaustion while
preaching their god's doctrine. Why do the Wardens allow them to terrorize
mortals of other domains?
Because the Glimmer have the Diviner's ear.
It's their gold which runs Chime.
Why else was the Golden City named in their honor?
—Anonymous, *Godless flier on the Glimmer*

THE GLIMMER LED ME out into the main foyer as the remaining Vesper were questioned. From there, I was whisked away into a bathing chamber where another Glimmer and a female Necro waited.

"Strip," the Glimmer ordered. "And submit yourself to a physical examination."

I was a prisoner of their order now and didn't have a choice. Personally, I didn't care much for modesty, but revealing too much skin was considered a sin in my god's eyes, and so I clutched my shawl tight around my shoulders in mock horror. "You wish for me to undress in front of another?"

The Glimmer forced an impatient smile. "To ensure you are healthy and whole. So many of Valeria's subjects come to us damaged. You are in our care now."

Damaged. Such an ugly word. It was no secret that the Vesper god liked to smite her own subjects, though I had to wonder why Valeria would allow her mortals to be used and abused by Glimmer. Our mortal souls still belonged to her and would return to her at death. Even from this deep underground.

I unbuckled my boots and began to unpeel the layers of clothing. The Glimmer averted her eyes in some parody of privacy, but the Necro woman did not. In fact, her eyes bulged out of their sockets and her lecherous stare lingered on places I'd rather they didn't. She, like Vincent, possessed unnaturally perfect porcelain skin and looked a beautiful sight next to the golden Glimmer.

But unlike Vincent, this Necro made no attempt to hide her more predatory nature. She didn't seem to notice my discomfort as she reached out to touch me.

I recoiled.

"Let her examine you," the Glimmer ordered.

I held out my left arm, displaying my passport tattoo. The Necro grabbed it, her grip frozen and strong. Goosebumps immediately popped up along my arm and sent a shiver down my spine.

"Your nose is wrong," the Necro said with a raspy voice.

"I broke it as a child. It never quite healed right."

Her hand dropped from my wrist. "Turn around."

The thought of turning my back on a Necro filled me with revulsion, but I bit my tongue and did so. Her cold hands rested on my lower spine and then slowly skimmed up until they cupped my shoulders. She stood so close to me now, holding me intimately, like a lover—like Malk would— and a pang of unease curdled in my stomach.

Malk was either trapped in this mansion as I was, being poked and prodded in the same manner, or he was a smear across the walls. I needed to get out of here and find him, and that was the only reason I'd endured the indignities they'd so far flung at me. Obedience meant this would be over with soon.

"You are a fine specimen," the Necro leered.

I spun around, ripping myself from her touch, and stared into her bloodshot eyes. The Necro licked her lips, her tongue flopping out the side as though it had grown and she couldn't contain it.

She'd eat you if the Glimmer wasn't there.

I didn't doubt it, and hastily stepped back.

"You may bathe," the Glimmer said.

I washed in a small pool of lukewarm water. The Glimmer and Necro watched, not giving me any privacy as I quickly went about my business. When done and dried, the Glimmer presented me with a familiar beige dress. Where had I seen this before?

The dead Vesper a few days ago.

Gods. I almost dropped the horrid thing. That Vesper from the Undercity platform had been wearing this exact dress—had died in it. This design would leave my neck, arms, and legs bare, which is exactly what the Glimmer wanted. To their god, a feminine body was the height of worship, and they took every excuse to display their golden skin and perfect curves, right down to the silhouette-shaping dresses they wore.

But for Vesper, this was the height of indecency, and by forcing us to wear it, the Glimmer knew it was a form of torture on its own. They wanted us to sin.

I slid into flat shoes and followed the Glimmer to the foyer once more as the chime of the hallway clock struck midday.

"Are you hungry, Anne?"

In truth, I was famished. "A little, my lady."

"I'm afraid our new acolytes are not permitted to lunch with us until you have been taught the proper prayers to her sacred holiness, Gildola. We'll begin your instruction within our study."

We climbed the staircase. "How long will instruction last?"

The Glimmer chuckled. "Oh, my dear, instruction never ends."

I swallowed an uncomfortable lump in my throat. "Then how will I earn my keep?" What became of the Vesper refugees? Of Malk? "And what of my brother?"

The Glimmer stopped beside a window on the top-floor balcony and pointed outside.

I followed her gaze. A line of Vesper men dressed in beige slacks were being led to another building hidden behind this estate. That appeared more like a factory with smoke puffing out of a stacked chimney and aether lamps blaring from the soot-stained windows. Among the Vesper I spotted the swaying rhythm of damp, loose hair. Malk. Even from the back, I'd recognize his swagger. "What are you doing with them?"

The Glimmer gestured for me to follow her and we continued along the upper hallway. "One of the simplest ways to defeat sin is to distract our minds with work. The Umber know this well, which is why they toil as they do. Though alas, the Ember reject work in exchange for pleasures of the flesh. You will be put to work that is best suited to you."

"Then why aren't I with them?"

"Because you are a woman, Anne, and your body was not meant for such debasement. It is the male body that was built to labor, and their labors will bring them closer to enlightenment. Did you ever wonder why Glimmer are women? Because women birth light and life. We are Gildola's daughters and we honor her by honoring our own mortal bodies."

They honor their mortal bodies by never enjoying them. These Glimmer don't know what pleasures they're missing.

True, despite showing off their fancy clothes and golden skin, the Glimmer were known for their prudish ways, and that was one reason why they disliked the Vesper; they considered us as promiscuous as the Ember.

You and Malk are proof.

I blushed at my own sinful thoughts. Five years ago, we'd created the Godless to stand against these gods-cursed workhouses-cum-correctional facilities. That was when we'd lost Elvira to the Wardens, and when we'd decided to take a stand and make a difference.

In our shared rage and mourning, Malk and I had kissed for the first time.

We'd gone from our first kiss to our first fuck in the space of an hour.

And we'd been at it ever since.

Gods, if the Glimmer separated us for more than a day, we'd both be scratching up the walls. I'd need their sermons to tame my sins then.

"What will my brother be working on?" I asked as we reached a door.

The Glimmer paused outside it and raised a brow. "You ask many questions, Anne. Did you know curiosity is a sin?"

Of course it was. Staring lustfully at a cream cake was also a sin to these mortals. "Forgive me, my lady, I seek to learn."

"And you will have your answers." The Glimmer opened the door and ushered me inside.

Amethyst eyes blinked up at me. Six other Vesper women of varying ages kneeled atop cushions on the floor of a brightly lit study. On a couch before them sat another Glimmer, cradling a large tome in her lap. More books filled shelves on the walls, and a stained glass window depicting Gildola shone a blazing collection of red and orange hues into the room.

"We are reading from the Book of Dawn," the seated Glimmer announced. "Please sit and join us."

Great. They were going to bore me to death.

I took the cushion nearest the door and sat awkwardly. The door clicked shut by another Glimmer in the corner and I blinked at the long, thin cane tucked under her arm.

Shit. What had I walked into?

The Glimmer at the front cleared her throat. "Before we begin our reading, please undo the cords of your robe at the back and lower it down your shoulders. We don't need to see your breasts, just your back, please."

I frantically glanced at the Vesper in the room, but they didn't look surprised or cowed. They willingly exposed their backs, and the sight of them made me want to scream.

Each back was etched with a crisscross of scars and raw lesions.

I should have known this. I'd seen Sinder's scars.

I knew this was how the Glimmer taught their sermons.

He'd warned me not to come here.

And I was completely at their mercy.

If this was how Gildola honored her daughters, then name me a man and I'd go labor with them! The Glimmer's obsession with sin was borderline obscene. The Wardens didn't care, so long as the Glimmer quite literally whipped up a workforce to maintain their clock tower while keeping Chime's more troublesome mortals under control.

You need to get out of here.

But how?

The Glimmer with the cane stood over me. "Lower your robe."

What choice did I have? In a mansion full of Glimmer, I wouldn't even be able to call my shadows to sneak out, let alone run. I fumbled at the cords and exposed my back.

The Glimmer with the tome began reading an extract—something about sacred light, I wasn't paying attention. I *did* need to get out of this room; I'd found the Vesper refugees, all right, though I still wasn't sure what they were forcing Malk into making. The Godless needed to know the Glimmer were up to their usual tricks, though I couldn't return without knowing how this fit with the aether leaks and dead Diviner.

In short, I wasn't going to find answers here. I needed to get inside their factory.

"Excuse me," I interrupted. "Is there a washroom—"

Pain lanced across my back with a harsh *crack*.

I fell forward onto my palms and choked a gasp. A burning sensation throbbed across my tender skin and I blinked away tears.

How dare she!

The Glimmer cradling her book scowled. "You are not to speak—"

"I need to piss!" I blurted out and flinched as the other raised her cane.

The Glimmer wrinkled her nose. "Hold it in until commanded otherwise—"

"Please, my lady, I can't." I brought tears to my eyes, which was easy enough thanks to the stinging on my back. "I don't—I don't want to shame myself."

"Very well." The Glimmer rolled her eyes. "See to your needs, but when you return, we shall speak of your attitude."

I bowed my head in gratitude and quickly covered my back.

Mortals were made in the image of their god, and from what I'd learned of the Glimmer, Gildola was nothing more than a spiteful bitch.

Say that out loud.

I'd be painting the walls with my ashes in a heartbeat.

Another Glimmer escorted me downstairs to a washroom and locked me inside. There'd be no escaping that way, but the room did at least have a small window.

I skimmed the edges for a latch. Locked. I grinned. They'd made me strip and bathe, but should have checked my ears. I pulled out a single lockpick stuck to the inner crevice of my elongated point. The metal blended in well with my skin.

They expected you to be as dumb as you look.

Why were my inner thoughts always so rude?

It was Malk who'd taught me how to pick locks, and thanks to his patience, I quickly popped open this one, tucking the pick back against my ear. The moment I squeezed through the gap, I'd be in trouble. They'd know I'd run. And they'd find me.

But not if I found Malk first.

I lifted myself out of the window and dropped silently into a crouch. I'd emerged out into the estate's courtyard, but this wasn't as well-lit as the mansion, giving me ample shadow as cover. A carriage had since pulled into the yard; the fancy sort that belonged to the Golden City. What guests were the Glimmer entertaining?

Two Glimmer stood guard by the gate. Not even shadows would be enough to sneak by them, but I had Dru for my escape plan. A place like this would receive frequent deliveries, and the Glimmer wouldn't blink at an Umber coming through with two Vesper-sized crates of supplies.

All I'd need to do was cast an elaborate series of signals on the estate walls to catch her attention, and she'd do the rest. Dru knew my signals well. Shadow puppetry was a common hobby among Vesper children, and I'd perfected the art into my own miniature plays.

My shadows wrapped around me like a cloak as I made my way around the outer edges of the building. Raised voices came from beyond an open window, and I risked a peek.

"A mortal has died, and yet you waste my time by demanding an audience?" said a Glimmer in a tight-fitting red dress, who leaned on the edge of a sturdy marble desk. "What do you expect to find here?"

"With all due respect, it is the nature of this death which prompts my investigation. I've filed the required paperwork with your staff," said a male who stood out of view.

I recognized his voice. The Diviner Warden with the eyeglasses. What in god's name was he doing here?

Twice now I'd encountered this idiot. First on the elevator before my shift at Lady Mae's, and then again that night he'd been questioning the

Glimmer. He'd mentioned he was investigating the workhouses, but I hadn't believed him. Or was it me he searched for?

"The incident took place in Lady Mae's, may light rest her soul. What grounds do you have for searching this estate? Karendar could not have agreed to this."

"It is no coincidence that a Glimmer was targeted by a Vesper. I have reason to suspect the perpetrator may be hiding within this very workhouse."

Shit! The Wardens *were* looking for me. They still believed I'd killed Lady Mae.

Gods. I'd forgotten all about my Glimmer ex-boss.

The Wardens certainly hadn't.

But what reason did he have to suspect me of being here? Had someone leaked our intel?

The Glimmer tapped her nails against the desk in an impatient staccato. "The work we do here is nothing like your correctional facilities, as you should well know. We open our home to the misfortunate. They are quite happy to receive our services in exchange for their own. Valeria herself agreed to this trade—"

"A Vesper broke out of this workhouse and died on the Undercity platform only a few days ago, Your Excellency."

Oh *shit*.

This wasn't just any Glimmer, but the ambassador herself.

You need to get out of here.

Not without Malk, and not without what I came for.

I ducked from the windowsill and left the Warden and ambassador to their argument—I doubted they'd reveal any additional information of use. Breaking into the ambassador's office could have uncovered some incriminating evidence, but not while they remained inside.

The entire mansion was off-limits while Glimmer stalked the halls. Not even my shadows would help me. But the factory behind... that was where I'd find answers.

Aether lamps created pools of light in the courtyard between the mansion and the factory, but there remained enough shadow for me to skirt the edges. Two more Glimmer stood guard by the main factory door. I wouldn't be able to sneak past these—they'd notice my moving shadows.

I waited until their attention wandered and then slipped from the shadows and approached with my chin dipped and my hands clasped demurely.

One of the Glimmer glowered. "What do you want? The factory isn't for women."

I bobbed a curtsy. "My lady, Her Excellency sent me to tell you a Warden is here to inspect the factory. A Diviner from Ambassador Karendar's office. I'm to assist."

The two Glimmer exchanged a glance. None of what I'd said was a lie, and the scenario sounded plausible enough.

"Fine," the grumpy Glimmer said. "Wait inside."

I forced another curtsy and pushed through the double doors.

The factory rang with the chaos of creation; hammers banging, steam hissing, and a conveyor belt of nuts and bolts churning through the main shop floor. Vesper made up the bulk of the workforce, though some Ember were scattered between them. All of this commotion focused on large metal plating the size of a tram carriage. Truly, if I'd just walked in here, I'd assume nothing suspicious.

You did just walk in here.

Yes, but I knew what I meant. I scanned the many tired faces stained with sweat and oil. All men, but not a single sign of Malk.

A set of metal stairs led to platforms above, where Glimmer watched over their workers with tight frowns and a cane in their hands. I pretended I held a purpose and strode for another set of double doors where there'd be fewer prying eyes, with any luck.

The buzz of aether screeched in my ears before I noticed the lamps flickering overhead. I'd entered some sort of maintenance tunnel. I didn't want to get lost or trapped here, but I needed answers. I needed Malk.

My path took me down a metal staircase and the screech of aether grew worse.

This place is death. Turn back. Turn back!

The hairs on my bare arms stood to attention. What in god's name were the Glimmer doing down here?

I chewed my tongue and pushed forward, though the aether in the air roiled through my stomach, making my legs heavy and weak. I gripped the handrail with a shaking hand. Sweat gathered under my armpits.

Whatever they were doing cost considerable aether.

The stairs stopped at another dimly lit tunnel. And at the end of that was a single metal door with a tiny square window. Colorful lights flashed behind it.

I'd seen those same colors in the Undercity elevator.

Pure aether.

Don't go any further.

I needed to. Dull pain throbbed in my head, but I forced a laborious step forward, then another. Every nerve and muscle fought against me reaching that damn door.

While I knew I should listen to instinct, the fear which slithered down my spine only moved me onwards. I needed to know what lay ahead.

My breath came in ragged rasps, but I made it to the door and slumped against its cool metal. Lights flashed through the window, and I cringed.

The silvery-blue hues of aether filled the room. No, not quite. It focused on a blurred shape I could barely make out for all the light.

A man.

It was the outline of a man!

What gods-forsaken shit was this?

Get out of here!

Panic flooded my blood. I listened to instinct now as my body seemed to act of its own accord. My feet ran with harsh slaps, and I was scrambling up the stairs before I even knew what I was doing.

Voices shouted, and golden light filled the tunnel behind me.

Shit, I'd been spotted.

I burst through the double doors onto the factory floor and startled a group of Glimmer, who swung their attention to me.

Use your shadow. Aim for their eyes and run.

I threw my hand up and aimed my shadow at the nearest Glimmer's face. She snarled and staggered back, temporarily blinded.

Golden sunlight burst around me. I shielded my eyes and staggered forward, raising my shadows to fight off the Glimmer, but their light was too strong. It burned *everywhere* with a horrid sizzling sound. Summoning my shadows was only pointing a target at myself as I ran for the exit.

"Stop her!" yelled one of the Glimmer.

I burst outside into the main courtyard.

And straight into the Diviner Warden.

"You!" he exclaimed, his silver eyes wide with shock.

I skittered back and searched frantically for a way out. More Glimmer came tumbling out the estate, blocking the driveway surrounding the mansion between where I stood and the gate.

Shit, I was trapped.

Gods-damn it, what was the point of Reve's vision if it was going to end like this?

If I'd be caught, only to lead the Wardens to my friends and family?

What was the pissing *point*?

The bells of the mansion's clock rang in my ears.

"The clock of fate is ticking for her."

Tick.

Tock.

Damn that Mesmer! Reve had never said my fate would be favorable.

Nor had he said it would cause our destruction.

"Arrest her!" yelled the Glimmer ambassador as she came stomping across the gravel and shoved her mortals aside. "She's infiltrated this workhouse to attack me!"

I pointed a damning finger at the ambassador. "You're the one torturing Vesper and Ember with your correctional facilities and forcing them to perform sermons to *your* god! And bribing Valeria with gold—how does that not break the Covenant? What do the Wardens have to say about that?"

The Diviner looked baffled, but soon regained his composure. "This matter is now under the purview of the Wardens."

He raised his hands and the tick and tock of the clock drew out into one long drone.

The entire courtyard slowed to a stop.

The Glimmer didn't move, their breath and blinks frozen in time, as the Warden casually prowled toward me.

Run, Kayl. Run!

I summoned balls of shadow in my fists and crouched, ready to launch into a sprint, when I caught his gaze.

His eyes widened again. "You truly are immune."

Then he leaped for me.

I tried to barge past, but he snagged hold of my arm.

Stop him.

I grabbed his wrist and tried to pry him free. An odd tingling sensation tickled my palm again, like when I'd touched my Glimmer ex-boss. It spasmed up my arm, turning my indigo skin into a silvery-blue.

I yanked my hand free and stared at it.

Diviner silver.

The Warden looked just as shocked. "What are you?"

Shit, I didn't know! I didn't know what I was!

The Glimmer remained frozen in place, and I could *feel* it—ripples of time swimming in the surrounding air. Without even looking at a clock, I knew the exact time—12:37—and this awareness felt as natural as breathing. Like I'd been born this way.

This was a dream, a nightmare, it had to be.

The buzzing of the aether lamps screeched. Flashes of silvery-blue blurred in my vision. Each flash sent a spasm of pain across my forehead.

And each came with an image burning into my mind.

A tram crashing into another, exploding with fire as mortals screamed and ran.

Glimmer falling from the great glass elevator of the sky.

Blood splattering the streets of Central Square. Mortal bodies. Gods, so many bodies collapsing and then fading to nothing.

Sparks of aether bursting from the clock tower.

Chaos, utter chaos.

As the clock struck thirteen.

Pressure built in my head as though my brain was about to burst through my skull. It sent agony pulsing down my neck with the touch of electrifying aether. I fell to my knees and grabbed my head, squeezing with both hands. "Make it stop!" Tears ran down my cheeks. "Please, make it *stop*!"

I stood on shaking legs, but I wasn't aware of asking my limbs to move. My palms opened, but I wasn't doing that, either. Gods. I wasn't in control of my body! I tried to scream, but my mouth wouldn't open and words wouldn't come.

Calm now, sister, the voice inside me crooned. *I'll save us both.*

Time suddenly sped up as aether exploded from the lamps, knocking me down hard, and plunged everything into silent darkness.

IX

The Covenant exists not only as a code of conduct for mortal behavior, but as a series of laws that must be obeyed. Should a mortal be in breach of these laws, then the Wardens are ordained to detain and question them. Our correctional facility exists for detention of such unlawful mortals, including those who are a danger to themselves or others. For those who commit the unconscionable sins of blasphemy or apostasy, our facility is also designed to reeducate and rehabilitate mortals back into society where possible. These rehabilitation programs reinforce the values of the Covenant and are run with the blessing of the twelve ambassadors.

For each transgression, a Warden must contact the ambassador of the mortal's domain. It is the right of each ambassador to sentence their mortals as their god deems fit.

—E. Karendar, *Warden Dossier on the HQ Correctional Facility*

ONE OF THE LOWER-RANKED Wardens, a Seren admin with peach skin and matching wings, brought me a cup of tea.

"Bless you," I said as I cradled the steaming cup and turned to the two-way mirror. I needed something strong after what I'd witnessed this afternoon.

The woman, Anne Arkey, or so she'd claimed to be, was still sleeping on a bench as one of our Necro examined her. I'd gone hunting for a Vesper and somehow ended up with a Diviner, and I still couldn't believe my eyes, even after thoroughly cleaning my spectacles until they damn near snapped. She'd stood there right in front of me, all indigo skin and righteous anger. My powers hadn't worked on her at all, hadn't even slowed her, and we'd scuffled in my desperation to grab her.

Then she'd touched me.

And her entire complexion had changed, morphing into the shimmering silver common to my domain. She'd remained in that state after the aether lamps had blown out and she'd fallen unconscious in the middle of the Glimmer's Undercity estate.

The Glimmer were confused, and I'd made up some lie to cover both myself and Anne's sudden transformation, but Ambassador Gloria was no fool.

What a political nightmare this was turning into.

I'd commandeered a Glimmer carriage and brought Anne and her Vesper companion to Warden HQ. He was locked securely away in a cell further down the hall, and I'd question him shortly before Elijah arrived. But first, I watched and waited to see if my intrepid quarry would awaken.

Was she truly a Diviner? I didn't even know anymore. It *was* her, despite the modifications a Necro had obviously made to her face, and our Necro carefully removed those, returning her back to factory settings, as it were.

Yet she remained a Diviner, or a woman trapped in the body of one.

A woman who'd been a Vesper only hours ago.

Not even my Academy education could have prepared me for this, but my tutors did say I had an aptitude for puzzles.

The Necro finished his examination and stepped into the observation room as I sipped my tea. "Besides a few structural changes to her face, we've found no other physical tampering," the Necro said. "Her physiology is that of a Diviner."

"A Necro couldn't paint her skin? Give her the look of a Vesper?"

"We are skilled, sir, but we cannot change the appearance of a mortal from one domain to another."

Blast it. It wasn't a disguise, then. But I knew what I'd seen. Or was I finally losing my senses? I placed my tea aside, finding that my desire for it had absconded. "And you're certain she's not a Fauna?" They had the ability to shape-shift from one animal form to another; an animal, yes, but could their chameleon powers apply to the various domains?

"Certain, sir."

I was grasping at straws. "Any other abnormalities?"

"Her passport tattoo is fake. A well-done fake. Whoever painted it is knowledgeable about Warden techniques. And she has a recent mark across her back. From a cane or whip."

Damn those Glimmer. "Heal that up, will you? Anything else?" I added, as the Necro looked confused. Nervous, even.

"I cannot explain it. But... there are two energies inside her body. Two life essences. I—I've never seen a body contain two, but it may explain her appearance." The Necro rubbed his perfectly pale jaw.

I reached for my tea again. "Two life essences? Are you speaking of souls? This woman possesses *two* souls?"

"Only her god would know for certain."

I took a scalding swig and gasped as tea burned my throat. A woman with two souls? Impossible.

But it could explain why she'd changed, if one soul was Vesper, and the other a Diviner. Mortals from my domain were losing their souls—having them ripped away from our Father. Could one of these lost Diviner souls have become trapped inside her, somehow?

It was the only explanation I had. I abandoned the rest of my tea and stood. "Alert me as soon as she wakes." I had another Vesper to question.

The halls of the Warden HQ were painted a bland gray with no other decoration. I'd always found them oppressive and daunting. This section of HQ—the correctional facility—housed criminals until they could be processed and either rehabilitated back into Chime's society or exiled to their respective domains. The higher-ups didn't like us describing the rooms as cells, but that's what they were.

I hated these halls. Hated being here. Each footstep echoed against the pristine tiles and then vanished altogether, as though even sound was snatched and locked away.

Returning to this place was a reminder of my own shortcomings.

Umber and Leander Wardens manned the various cells, with a few Fauna guard dogs patrolling the corridors, though Fauna lacked the discipline for much else. Umber were deliberately chosen for their ability to look and act tough, and their calm nature made them natural mediators in situations Diviner would rather avoid. Most of these cells were occupied by Ember and Vesper, and an Umber could placate most of them. Their stony flesh could even withstand an Ember's enraged fire, if it came down to it.

A Leander sneered at me as I strode past, their fangs raised in a leering grin. Of the twelve domains, the Leander stood out as the most intimidating. Their athletic bodies were that of an upright lion, their teeth and claws sharp as a razor's point, though their thick manes left fur everywhere.

Personally, I cared little for the Leander's aggressive instincts, nor did they care much for Warden authority, yet a few of them ended up in our ranks.

The Wardens needed to represent all domains, after all.

I found my guest already waiting for me in one of the facility's interrogation rooms, or as the Wardens liked to call them, 'reflection chambers.' I nodded to the Umber standing guard, a mortal cut from beige sandstone with tiny succulents for eyebrows, and stepped inside.

The silvery-blue glare of an aether lamp burned above, its harsh light designed to counter any shadows a Vesper might summon. This particular Vesper sat on a chair with his hands chained across a table, twisted at an angle so that his wrists were palm up for a Diviner's touch. His feet would also be chained. They'd be no running from here, though he'd be foolish to try, regardless.

He didn't strike me as a fool.

This Vesper was much taller than I, with the slim build of shadow itself. His skin was a deep navy blue, and his black hair draped down his back, casting his cheekbones in shade. Those sapphire eyes glowered as I took a seat opposite.

If looks could kill, my soul would be floating back to Father posthaste.

"What have you done with her?" he demanded with a snarl.

Right, then, straight down to business. "She's unconscious but unharmed. We have no intention of causing either of you discomfort—"

"What a crock of shit. You've every intention of throwing us to our doom. That's what you Wardens do; you swear to care for the citizens of Chime, but when the domains get rowdy, you cart us off to our deaths and wash your hands of it. Do you know what gods like Valeria do to their mortals?" He chuckled a bitter laugh. "Of course you do."

I sat opposite him. "What's your name, please?" He hadn't revealed anything; no name, no intent, nothing.

"I'm not telling you shit."

"It's in your best interests, and that of your friend's, to answer my questions."

"We Vesper have a quaint saying for Wardens who ask questions—go fuck yourself."

Such dramatics. "Why were you inside a Glimmer estate?"

"Visiting for tea and cream scones, same as you."

I tilted my head to one side. "You were searching for Vesper refugees."

"Would there be any point denying it? You're going to rifle through my brain and see for yourself. Vesper are being dragged into Glimmer workhouses, tortured into worshipping their golden god. You know, the same old shit. And where were *you*, Corinth? Shooting up more Vesper?"

Ah. I should have known he'd recognize my profile. We weren't going to get anywhere like this. "I'm going to take a look inside your memories."

His eyes narrowed but he said nothing.

I strode to his side. "If it makes you feel any better, I don't enjoy doing this."

He glared up at me. "It doesn't."

I truly didn't enjoy this aspect of my Diviner power and tried my damnedest to avoid brushing up against others, whether accidentally or otherwise. Least of all because my version of the gift was twisted in a way it wasn't for my brethren.

My first touch of a mortal's heartbeat showed me their death.

It always came as a shock, no matter how I braced for it, because my second gift was to feel it as though the death was my own. *Your empathy is a curse*, Elijah once told me. Only he and Father knew of my particular talent, and it was this talent which endeared me to the Wardens. The idea was I could save lives, prevent murders, if I knew how a mortal might die.

The reality was more... traumatic.

I pressed the tips of my fingers into the Vesper's wrist and searched for his heartbeat, sorry for what fate I'd find.

Color drained from the hills and the sky. It was all turning gray!

I could feel it slipping away.

Gods, no.

It was all slipping away.

And she stood there, her entire being encased in glowing swirls of silver and blue and pink, the last vestiges of color in the entire world.

She was a goddess.

My goddess.

"Malk!" she screamed.

I reached out to touch her, one final touch, the words slipping from my tongue.

"Kay—"

I swallowed a gasp, but kept my fingers firmly pressed against his pulse.

His death came soon, and it mirrored my own.

A creature made from pure aether.

I could never tell him. Who would want to know the nature and time of their own demise? It certainly hadn't helped my fate. In this, we had something in common.

Focus, Quen.

Images flashed through my mind's eye as I traveled through the Vesper's—Malkavaan's—memories in reverse. It wasn't his memories that interested me, but through him, there was a chance I'd discover more about the impossible woman sleeping only a few corridors down.

The images flashed by quickly; the Glimmer estate, an illegal jaunt through the Undercity's tunnels, Grayford, and—oh.

Oh no.

Malkavaan belonged to the Godless. They both did.

Well, that explained a few things.

The world of the Godless bloomed inside my mind as though I'd been a loyal member of their organization myself.

The abandoned tram depot of Grayford. That was where the Godless made their home. I'd long suspected they were hidden there, and not in Sinner's Row, as my Warden colleagues believed.

Each of the Godless's profiles flashed by with incriminating clearness.

Their leader, a Seren who worked for the Chime Courier. No wonder they knew of events they shouldn't have. That was where they gleaned their information, and likely where they gained the means to print their fliers.

An Umber. How odd. I'd never have taken them for the blasphemous type.

An Ember. There was something distinctly familiar about them.

A Necro, and again, something familiar that I couldn't quite place.

Even a Mesmer. All part of the Godless team.

And Ambassador Varen. My dear ambassador. I'd held an inkling that he was sympathetic to the Godless cause, and this certainly confirmed that he and my quarry were indeed allies.

The entire operation of the Godless unraveled in my mind, and there was enough damning evidence here to destroy their organization for good. This I hadn't wanted to see.

I'd been tasked by Elijah to find and destroy them long ago. They were apostates. Blasphemers. Their filthy fliers vandalized the walls of Central with such despicable propaganda. Only they dared question the rule of the gods and we Wardens who helped maintain such rule. Only the Godless dared point out Chime's obvious inequalities.

All mortals were born equal under the Covenant. It was blasphemy to consider otherwise. But when Diviner and Glimmer held the most influence over Chime, then truths became heretical lies.

Truth was, the Godless weren't a violent group, and their protests had improved lives among the Vesper and poorest of Chime. If anything, Chime needed a few Godless heathens to upset the status quo. To actually make the Covenant worth something.

When Elijah came for my memories later, he'd see all of this too, and then the Godless and Varen's treachery would end. The Glimmer would continue to stuff their workhouses full of desperate Vesper, and the Wardens wouldn't care to stop them.

Unless I wiped this evidence clean from my mind first.

Malkavaan's memories continued to move through his past. And then...

Kayl. An interesting name, but in Malkavaan's memories she was clearly a Vesper.

And... *Goodness me.*

Copious amounts of coitus burned my mind's eye. The pair of them were keen lovers, and there were reams and reams of such memories and lustful thoughts flowing through Malkavaan's history. I tried to skip past them as quickly as I could. To sift through his memories was violation enough, but I held no intention of desecrating his most intimate and private ones.

A sharp pain built in my forehead.

Diviner power held its limits. Most only searched the first hour or so of a mortal's recent memories. To push beyond that was too difficult, and it *hurt*.

But I needed to push. I needed to discover what she was.

I chewed the inside of my cheek and went back weeks. Months. Years.

Five years ago, when the Grayford Incident occurred.

And they'd shared their first kiss.

It stirred memories of my own first kiss, devastating in its way, and I swept it aside.

Beyond that, Malkavaan and Kayl had been close. Raised together under Varen's tutelage. No wonder he cared for them.

Then there'd been an older Vesper woman in Malkavaan's life. His mother, Elvira. Taken away by Wardens during the Grayford Incident, never to be seen again, judging by his memories. Odd. There was something familiar about the woman, too, but I couldn't place her either. Perhaps her facial features simply resembled Malkavaan's.

She'd escaped from one of the workhouses. No wonder Malkavaan and the Godless held such a burning hatred for them.

But before then, this Elvira had stumbled upon a young Kayl in the Undercity; lost, hungry, and scared.

An abandoned child. But still a Vesper.

Elvira had taken in the younger Kayl and raised her like a daughter.

And that's where Malkavaan Byvich's memories of my quarry began.

I held no desire to see what pain remained in Malkavaan's childhood, and let go of his wrist, returning to reality. Something wet dripped from my nose, and I pulled out a handkerchief to dab the flow with shaking fingers. Blood.

I'd pushed myself beyond my limits.

Malkavaan leered at me. "See anything you like in there?"

I sank into my chair and tried to hide the wave of dizziness that came over me. Malkavaan's memories gave me everything I needed to see of Kayl's life, and yet they answered few of my questions. She'd been a Vesper the entire time Malkavaan had known her, and I was fortunate they'd been close enough to grant me that insight, but there'd been no signs of her experiencing a fateful encounter with a Diviner soul.

Nor any mention of her, or her Godless compatriots, conspiring to assassinate Elijah, as he'd wrongly assumed.

It made no sense.

From what I witnessed of her, of the Godless themselves, she wasn't a murderer, and their methods weren't violent.

Whoever—whatever—was targeting the Diviner, it wasn't Kayl. She was as much a victim in this as we were, regardless of what power she now possessed.

I needed to convince Elijah of that.

Someone tapped on the room's two-way mirror. News at last.

"What'll happen to us?" Malkavaan called as I headed for the door.

I glanced over my shoulder. What could I tell him that he didn't already know? "I'm sorry." I closed the door behind me.

The Seren who'd brought my tea waited outside. "His Excellency, Ambassador Varen, is here. He's demanding to speak with you."

What wonderful timing. I hadn't summoned him, but news traveled fast. "Good. Fetch some tea for the ambassador, something strong." I had the feeling he'd need it. "Have you received word from Ambassador Karendar?"

"No, sir. He's currently on business in Kronos."

Good. If Elijah was stuck in Kronos, he wouldn't be returning until the midnight crossing. That gave me plenty of time to write up a suitable report, then visit my Amnae friend and wipe any damning memories before Elijah could rifle through them. I wouldn't be able to exonerate Malkavaan Byvich—Elijah would notice if my memories left unexplained gaps. But I could at least protect the rest of their organization, and then some part of the Godless would survive.

Saints. If Elijah ever discovered how many memories I'd destroyed before our meetings, well... I couldn't risk dwelling on the consequences.

"Can you fetch some water for the Vesper here? Make him comfortable, please." It was highly likely Elijah would order Malkavaan off to Eventide, but that didn't mean I'd let him suffer in the meantime.

"Certainly, sir. Uh, sir? You have blood on you."

"Yes, I'm aware, thank you."

I strode along the hall and broke into a run when I found the good ambassador barging into Kayl's cell. "Stop!"

I and another Warden—the sandstone Umber—tumbled in after him.

"What is this?" Varen exclaimed as the sleeping Kayl woke with a start.

"Varen!" she cried out, and grabbed his hand.

Varen yanked his hand back, recoiling as I gawked.

Her silver skin rippled back into the indigo shade of a Vesper. As though the past few hours had all been some terrible hallucination.

"Restrain her!" I ordered the Umber. "Everyone else, out!"

The ambassador complied and followed me into the observation room where two fresh teas waited on a table. We both watched through the two-way mirror as the Umber struggled to place Kayl in restraints, and a Leander came rushing in to assist. I couldn't hear her yells from inside this room, but the mirror shook slightly as she thrashed in their hands.

Even with her build, the Leander overwhelmed her, though she'd left the sorry sod with a red eye that would soon swell.

Rather him than me.

"What have you done to her?" Varen turned on me with a glare as equally poisonous as Malkavaan's. Saints preserve us. There must be something in the Grayford water.

I became keenly aware of how much taller—and stronger—the good ambassador was compared to myself. In a pinch, I could slow any opponent to escape an attack, but I'd used too much of my power exploring Malkavaan's memories to put up an effective defense. The ambassador could pummel me into the wall and looked as if he was about to.

I pushed my spectacles up my nose. "You recognize her then."

A flash of annoyance crossed Varen's features. "I have no idea who this woman is, but she's one of my mortals, and therefore—"

"Please don't lie to me, Your Excellency. She called you by name. And we have another of her compatriots here. A strapping fellow by the name of Malkavaan Byvich. Know him?"

"You've questioned this man?"

"I've searched his memories, yes." I stared at the ambassador over the rim of my spectacles and waited for the mask to drop.

It fell with a sigh as Varen ran a hand down the full length of his face. "Whatever you've seen is not the full truth. Malkavaan and his kind—they blackmailed me. Turned my generosity against me to take advantage of my position in Grayford."

A convenient lie. He didn't realize how far back I'd gone in Malkavaan's mind. Varen held affection for these Vesper, like that of a paternal figure, but that didn't interest me. "They were both found breaking into a Glimmer estate. This has repercussions—"

"And they will be brought before Valeria to face them."

"Not so fast. I no longer need to question the male, but this woman is a suspect in an ongoing case—"

"They are Vesper." Varen's nostrils flared. "Which means they belong to me and my god. You cannot deny her will—"

"This matter belongs to the Wardens. When this woman has been questioned, she will be sentenced in accordance with the Covenant." I glanced through the mirror. The Umber Warden had successfully restrained Kayl into a chair and was now placing reinforced gloves onto her hands. Smart man.

"You cannot shut me out of this, Corinth—"

"On Ambassador Karendar's orders, I can. I'll send for you when we are done."

Varen stomped from the room, slamming the door behind him and rattling the neglected cups of tea. I supposed there'd be time for tea later.

This truly *was* becoming a political quagmire. I sighed and cleaned my spectacles. Yes, I would need to give my memories a thorough cleanse soon as well. I relished making work for myself, didn't I?

I turned to the two-way mirror. The Vesper woman glared right at me.

My god. Her eyes.

They were a silvery-blue. Like pure aether.

Heat rose to my cheeks, and I swallowed a dry lump. There was no chance she'd be able to see me through the mirror, but who knew what her powers could do?

I straightened my spectacles and shoved my hands into my pockets, rubbing a soothing thumb over the marred brass of my fob watch.

It was time to question the impossible woman.

10

Illegals are not bound by the same constitutional rights of the Covenant as other mortals. Thus, illegals can be deported to their domain without representation.
To avoid this fate, we recommend you take the following steps:
Seek housing and work in the Undercity. Avoid the workhouses.
Avoid the prying eyes of the Wardens.
Arrange for a fake passport tattoo for Chime and your home domain, but no other as this will arouse suspicion.
Use Necro parlors within Sinner's Row for passport adjustments.
Children are rare in Chime. Hide them at all costs.
Never pray. Prayer will alert your god to your existence.
Avoid the temples. The domain ambassadors frequent these.
—Anonymous, *Godless flier on illegals*

I KEPT SQUEEZING MY eyes closed, hoping this was all some sick nightmare, and I'd awaken in Malk's arms back in the depot.

But when I opened them again, the shrill aether of the lamp above stung, and my limbs were still strapped to a chair. They'd even put gloves on my hands for some gods-forsaken reason.

Because I'd touched a Diviner and somehow my skin had changed to his.

And when Varen had barged in here, I'd touched him and returned to the body of a Vesper. None of these things I could explain.

They fear you.

And that was the other thing.

This... voice inside of my head. It spoke to me. It had taken over my body and caused whatever interference had destroyed the aether bulbs in the Glimmer estate. I'd woken up here with this voice talking to me as though it wasn't part of me at all!

I am part of you, idiot. Though if you hadn't fainted, I could have helped us escape. Good job getting us both caught.

Gods.

I truly was going mad, and Malk and Dru and Harmony and the rest of them weren't here to witness it. I may well never see any of them again.

My body trembled and I could barely hold myself together. If not for these straps holding me firmly in place, I'd be pounding the walls. I hadn't cried in months, but I was one more revelation away from a breakdown.

I knew where I was—locked inside the Wardens' correctional facility— and what was about to happen to me.

They may not know *who* I was, but one touch of a Diviner, and they'd soon find out.

Mortals like me... We didn't earn happy endings. Forgetting all the petty sins I was sure the Glimmer would punish me for, I'd committed far worse crimes.

Blasphemy. Oh yes, lots of that. From our fliers to our protests, and sabotage designed to disrupt Chime's carefully balanced society. We'd spread our glorious propaganda all across Central without being discovered.

And apostasy. The worst sin of them all.

Not all domains got along, and while their petty arguments bordered on blaspheming one another, such blasphemy was at least understandable.

But apostasy... To most denizens of Chime, it was obscene to imagine a life without one's god. To deny that god your love and devotion. It was the gods who made us, who birthed our souls and shaped a physical body so we may live. They were our parents. Our reason for existence. Why would anyone reject a parent? Hate those who'd created them?

Because we saw the truth; the gods were cruel.

They owned us. They dictated who we were, how we were meant to live. They'd given us free will and punished us for using it. They toyed with our lives because to them, we were little more than simple playthings. Pets.

Chime was the only place in the entire universe where the gods couldn't tread. A godless city that gave rise to godless mortals.

Or so it could have been.

The door to my cell opened and in stepped the Diviner Warden who'd caught me. He sat at the opposite end of the table between us, his hands clasped together, and observed me over the top of his eyeglasses.

The gods aren't so perfect if they made a flawed mortal who needed four eyes.

I ignored the voice in my head and my gaze dropped to the Warden's waistcoat. A few droplets of blood stained it. His? Some other poor soul's?

The Warden seemed oblivious to it. "Anne Arkey. Also known as *Yuda Mann* and Kayl. Though I'm afraid I'm not acquainted with your last name. Or your many other false identities."

Shit, he knew my name. Who had he learned it from? Varen? "I don't have one."

"Ah. An illegal, then."

An illegal. The name the Wardens gave to those who'd been born on Chime but never registered. By law, all births were registered by each domain ambassador, and they kept a record of their god's mortals. When appropriate, those mortals would then make the crossing and meet their god.

I'd done none of those things. At my request, Varen had never registered me.

There were hundreds more like me hidden in the Undercity. Thousands, even.

"I'm Quentin," the Warden said. "But please, call me Quen. It's a pleasure to finally have this opportunity to converse." He pulled a flier out of his pocket and laid it flat on the table. "I believe this is one of yours."

It was one of our Godless fliers; an image of Gildola's golden eye and the words *'Who owns your thoughts?'*

Who indeed. This flier was crinkled and worn, as though the Warden had been carrying it for months. "Are you aware it's a crime to be carrying such blasphemous propaganda? I should alert a Warden at once."

"I'll send for one. There's plenty of them here."

And with that, ice filled my veins. He knew what I was. There was no point in pretense. "So, what now, Quinn?"

"Quen, if you please."

"What now, *Quen*? You interrogate me, explore my memories for information on the Godless?" I almost choked on that word. Because I'd got myself caught, this Diviner would now rummage through my mind and pull out whatever he needed to destroy the Godless.

I'd fucked up once more, and now my friends, the mortals I'd named my family, would pay the price.

He'd see where we made our base. Our members: Dru, Harmony, Sinder, Vincent, Reve. They were all in danger.

Malk too, if he had gotten away. I had to hope he and Dru had escaped, had rushed back to Grayford... Because soon, the Wardens would march on the slums once more, arrest our mortals and illegal refugees, and bring them here for processing. Just as they'd done five damn years ago.

Just as they'd taken Elvira, and neither I nor Malk had ever seen her again.

Not even Varen could help us, because they'd see the connection I shared with the man I thought of as my father. And his life would be forfeit, too.

Then they'd be exiled from Chime. Carted off to face their god.

I'd heard enough horror stories to know none of us would be treated kindly. "Do you know what our gods will do to us?" I squeezed back tears as I forced the words out. "Do you know why we hide from them? Let me tell you our stories." He was going to see them in my mind, regardless. "Our leader, a Seren; her lover was killed by her god for failing to provide an adequate tribute. She was forced to watch her lover be ripped apart, limb by limb. And then when she mourned the love of her life, she too was punished by association—Serenity ripped off one of her wings. Can you imagine that, Quen? A Seren who can't fly?"

Quen's already pale face blanched. "Well, I—"

"Our Ember was used and abused by his god. Treated like a plaything, and then discarded when Edana grew tired of him. She sent him to one of the Glimmer workhouses where they tortured him for the sins his own god had encouraged! He still bears the scars."

Quen opened his mouth, but I cut him off. "Our Mesmer is plagued with never-ending nightmares. His screams wake me at night. Our Necro only ever wanted to use his skills to heal, but his god forced him into performing dissections on mortals from other domains while they were still alive! Do you understand the trauma the gods inflict on their mortals? On other mortals? Do any of them even care? Do *you*?"

"The Wardens care. We work with the ambassadors of each domain to provide a civilized and independent life here on Chime."

I couldn't keep the derisive snort from ripping out of my throat. "You say you care, but you're more than willing to cart us off to our gods should we step out of line. And then you conveniently forget we were ever your responsibility to begin with."

"Chime is served by functional laws and regulations, otherwise the entire system would be thrown into chaos and more mortals would suffer the consequences. It is only those mortals who forgo the system, who undermine the Covenant, that we exile for the greater good."

Such pretty rehearsed words. I could have pulled them straight from a Warden handbook. "These are mortals who have been failed by *your* system. When it's the likes of Glimmer and Diviner who kick Vesper down to the Undercity, I'd say your system doesn't work. And that's why the Godless exist—and will always exist. We'll care for them even if you do not. Even if you destroy us. We'll return stronger than ever."

Quen grimaced. "I agree with you."

That I wasn't expecting. "What?"

"I agree that our systems are flawed. Balancing the needs of twelve individual domains is no simple task, especially with twelve gods breathing down our necks. Do you have any understanding of what's needed to placate the whims of twelve all-powerful gods? They despise each other. They despise their own mortals sometimes. And they despise the Wardens for interfering. Chime is a safe space from that chaos.

"You Godless see yourself as mortals standing against the gods, but it's us Wardens who do the heavy lifting, the bowing and scraping necessary to keep Chime afloat and prevent the domains from warring with one another. Yes, the Vesper have it rough, I won't deny that, but they're alive at least—"

"At *least*? You said you were investigating the workhouses, so you must believe that the practices which go on are harmful at best and abusive at worst. By forcing a mortal to study sermons of another god, they're committing apostasy! Where does that fit into your Covenant?"

"I'll admit the Glimmer have crossed lines, but if Valeria herself gives consent, then they are still acting within the Covenant's laws whether you or I agree or not. Regardless, my interest in the Godless and your irresponsible beliefs is not why you're here in this room."

Irresponsible?

He's a Diviner. Were you expecting someone who wasn't a sanctimonious arse?

"Why else would I be here, if not for my blatant blasphemy and apostasy?"

Quen leaned across the table, the aether light catching his eyeglasses. "There is the matter of Lady Mae's death, not to mention your particular talents. I can't say I've met any Vesper who could magically turn into a Diviner and back again. Nor a Vesper who, for reasons unexplained, is somehow immune to time. Yes, I'd say that interests me far more."

Shit. I hadn't dreamed it after all.

This Warden was proof.

"Let's start at the beginning." Quen's silver eyes studied me over the rim of his eyeglasses. "You were seen at Lady Mae's café three days ago on the eve of her death—"

"I didn't kill Lady Mae. She tried to grab me and then she fell against a table and must have cracked open her head."

"You served as her employee for quite some weeks. Any Vesper in your position would have been tempted to shove a Glimmer to her death—"

"I did *not* kill her!"

"Eyewitnesses saw you running from the scene."

What in god's name could I say? I had no defense.

Though if I could go back in time, perhaps I *would* murder Lady Mae for all the pissing hassle she'd put me through.

"On that night, you served a Diviner who tried to question you," Quen continued. "Do you remember what happened?"

Of course I did. "Your Diviner friend was rude, so I finished work early. Though perhaps you should ask what a prominent ambassador was doing drinking coffee in a public café with Glimmer?"

"It's not against the Covenant for a man to order coffee."

"For any man, sure. But for the Diviner ambassador to dine with the owners of workhouses who'd just bribed a god with gold at ten o'clock at night? In civilian clothing? Rather suspicious, don't you think?"

"I'd say a Godless spying on the Diviner ambassador is far more suspicious. And please, I'll be asking the questions if you don't mind, or we'll both be stuck in this room for an eternity. Trust me, eternity is an awfully long time. Speaking of time, the ambassador tried to slow you down. His powers didn't affect you."

"Perhaps Diviner men suffer from impotency. It happens to the best of us."

A slight smile graced Quen's lips. "Shortly after, we found a body in Central Station. A Diviner. Dead." The smile vanished. "Would you know anything about that?"

"I would not."

"And then earlier this day, I found you skulking in Ambassador Gloria's estate. I can assume why you were there. I also tried to slow you with no effect."

"Then you need the same Necro doctor as your friend."

"Were you aware of time changing around you?"

Yes. Painfully aware.

But I couldn't explain any of it.

"How do you change form?" Quen asked.

"I... I don't know. It's never happened to me before. Whatever answers you're seeking, I don't have them."

Quen stood with a heavy sigh and strode to my side. I knew what he was about to do, and I yanked at my restraints, but they held me tight. I was completely at his mercy.

"I'm going to touch you, but it won't hurt. I want to see what's inside your mind."

I didn't want him in my mind!

I clenched my eyes shut and thought about cream scones and blueberry pancakes, anything but the Godless.

His fingers pressed onto my wrist and I sucked in a breath. I counted the seconds as they passed into minutes.

"That's odd," he murmured at last.

I opened one eye and looked at him. Even seated, he stood at my level. "What is?"

"I can't feel anything."

"Thank the gods, I'm already dead."

"No, I can feel your pulse." He moved to my other side and touched my wrist there. "Nothing. Forgive me, but I'll have to touch your neck." His fingers slid to my throat and found my pulse, now beating erratically.

After another minute, Quen stepped back, his brow furrowed in exasperation. "You *are* a puzzle."

I scowled. "I'm glad I entertain you."

He rubbed his jaw and I swore I could see the cogs turning in those silver eyes of his. "Have you ever noticed anything odd about yourself in comparison to other Vesper? Any strange feelings? Happenings? Thoughts?"

Oh gods, so many. "Nope, never."

"Nothing at all?"

"Not a thing."

Quen turned to the mirror and snapped his fingers at the aether lamp dangling from the ceiling.

It suddenly buzzed and light filled the room as though a Glimmer had burst inside. The light blinded me. I couldn't shield my eyes, but I ducked my head.

The buzzing turned into a grating screech that scratched the inside of my skull.

It hurts, tell him to stop, tell him it hurts!

"Stop it!" I yelled with a gasp.

The light dimmed and I blinked away dots to see Quen crouched beside me, examining my eyes. "You react to aether. I realized after our meeting in Gloria's estate." He straightened up. "It bothers you, doesn't it? Aether? What else are you lying about?"

"I haven't lied—"

"You've always had this reaction, haven't you? Ever since you were a child. You've never been able to withstand aether. Interesting."

"You saw my memories?"

"No. Your Vesper friend. You downplayed these headaches in his presence, but he noticed."

Malk. Gods no, they had Malk. And they'd already torn through his memories.

Then this was it. The end of the Godless.

The end of everything I loved.

Someone knocked on the door and called for Quen's attention. "I'll be right out." He turned back to me, his expression pensive. "You may not realize it, but you are no ordinary Vesper. I must speak with my superior, but I'll return to ensure your comforts are met." He scooped up the Godless flier and tucked it into his jacket, then turned to leave.

"What will you do with me?"

He either didn't hear the question or ignored it as the door closed behind him.

I rested my head against the chair's backrest and took in mouthfuls of air. The room had grown stuffy, and the aether light, though now dim, still hummed like a maddening itch at the back of my brain.

Why did aether bother me as much as it did?

Because you're made of aether.

I wasn't in the mood to deal with my thoughts running rampant. The Wardens held Malk prisoner, and I wasn't faring much better. As apostates, the sentence would be clear; a trip to Eventide, unless Quen and his kind kept me trapped here and ran tests to find out exactly what was wrong with me.

I might never see Malk again.

The thought filled me with gut-wrenching despair.

I wasn't sure how much time had passed when the door opened again. There was no sense of time in this place—not that I ever possessed any sense of time—nor did the little cell I found myself in contain a clock. I felt oddly relieved to see Quen enter. The rest of the Wardens wore blank faces, as though they'd trained the emotion right out of them. For a Diviner, Quen was certainly expressive.

Though the expression he wore when he entered did not look good, and my relief was short-lived.

He sat at the table. "You'll be kept here for the remainder of the night. I'm afraid we cannot remove your restraints. Given the dead Diviner and Lady Mae, plus your remarkable abilities, it's not a risk we can take. I'll assign a female Warden to attend to your needs."

"You can't keep me here—I know my rights!" At least if I returned to Varen, he could smuggle Malk and I out to safety. "The Covenant states I must be returned to Ambassador Varen for judgement—"

"Unless a mortal is deemed a threat to the safety of Chime. However, as an illegal, I'm afraid your rights are rather limited. A mortal cannot play by the rules of the Covenant if they never pledged allegiance to it."

An icy dread uncoiled in my stomach. "Then what happens to me?"

"Tomorrow, you and the other Vesper will be escorted to Eventide. Ambassador Varen has already made the ten o'clock crossing tonight, and with his confirmation tomorrow, we shall follow."

The heat drained from my skin.

Tomorrow I'd be meeting my god for the first and last time.

11

Mortals are only permitted to make the crossing from their domain into Chime with valid passport identification. This is a mark which is permanently embedded in one's skin by a qualified Necro practitioner as employed by the Wardens.
Please bear in mind the following:
Travel into Chime requires the blessing of your domain ambassador.
By default, you will be granted the stamp for your domain.
A background check is required for access to the Golden City elevator.
Access to the Undercity elevator is permitted for all.
Travel to additional domains is at the behest of individual domain ambassadors and can be revoked at any time. This too requires a stamp.
—E. Karendar, *Warden Handbook on Passport Identification*

THEY CAME FOR ME early.

I didn't sleep a wink all night. How could I? Knowing that Malk and I would be carted off to Eventide to our inevitable death? Quen didn't visit me again, but a peach-skinned Seren offered me food and drink. I turned her down until the morning, when I eventually relented and indulged in a simple cheese and watercress sandwich with a cup of tea.

If I was going to face my doom, I should at least be prepared for it.

The Wardens insisted I change out of the gaudy beige Glimmer dress into something more appropriate, offering me the plain black tunic, slacks, and boots of a Warden uniform. It lacked the bronze-lined jacket they all wore, but covered my bare skin.

They at least offered me more privacy than the Glimmer, and I could piss and change in peace. But as soon as I was done, they slapped those ridiculous gloves back on and chained my wrists. It wasn't like I was going to murder them and break out of Warden HQ. Sadly, they possessed more sense than the Glimmer and had confiscated my lockpicks.

All too soon, the Wardens came for me. They escorted me through their dull gray corridors and shoved me inside a waiting carriage without a chance to grab my bearings.

Time had finally run out on me.

"Good morning, Kayl," said Quen, who sat in the carriage on a bench opposite me. He appeared refreshed in a clean tan suit with the Courier broadsheet stretched across his knee. We could have been off for a fun jaunt across Chime to the local café for tea and scones based on his cheerful welcome.

I sat stiffly on the cushion; my manacled wrists tucked into my lap. "You're to be my escort then?" I glanced at the window, but curtains had been pulled across it. "Where's Malk—the other Vesper?"

"I thought it best if you both traveled in separate carriages. We'll take a brief detour around the block to attract less attention and then meet at the Gate." He pulled out a pocket watch. "Time to get moving." He tucked the watch away and banged on the carriage roof.

With a lurch, the wheels churned forward.

I'd never been inside a carriage like this, but it resembled the ones that sometimes passed through Central Station carrying residents from the nicer parts of town; all wood and brass and powered by an aether engine and driver—I could sense the aether humming around me. Only the richest could afford the carriage fare; everyone else took the tram. I wasn't quite sure how riding in a fancy carriage didn't attract attention, but I supposed it wasn't appropriate to drag prisoners onto a tram.

And that's what I was. A prisoner being sentenced.

Would Harmony, Dru, and the others know? Would they devise a plan to rescue us? Surely Reve must have seen us in one of his visions, or Varen would have informed the Godless of our fate.

Quen lifted the broadsheet and began reading the headlines. His nonchalance grated on me.

"Are you often this cheerful when you sentence mortals to their deaths?" I snapped.

He stared over the top of his eyeglasses. "You're traveling under Warden protection—"

"Which means nothing when you leave us in Eventide and exit through the Gate. You'll be leaving us to die, and a quick death is the best we can hope for. Are you aware of how Valeria treats her mortals? Shall I tell you another story?"

"Does it have a happy ending? I just ate."

"You don't care at all."

He lowered his broadsheet with a sigh. "You are under *my* protection."

"You think your Diviner powers will work on a god?"

"No, but my charm will."

"You're an actual idiot."

He flashed a smile. "Wonderful, we're already getting along splendidly."

Meeting a god could be fun. I don't understand why you're so worried.

Don't get me started on you! I yelled into my own bloody mind. "So you're not leaving me in Eventide?"

"Let's see now; a woman with the ability to shape-shift and evade time." He cocked his head. "What do you think?"

"This is a *test*? And Malk—my Vesper friend? What of him?"

Quen grimaced. "His fate depends on your willingness to cooperate and your ambassador's ability to grovel." He returned to his broadsheet. "I simply ask that you trust me."

Gods. We were doomed. Absolutely doomed. "She killed his father. Valeria. She'd tortured and killed him because he couldn't make the tithe, and when Malk's mother smuggled him into Chime, the Glimmer stole her—"

"I've witnessed your friend's memories."

"And yet you still don't care."

Quen remained silent, and he averted his stare from mine.

Good. Let him wallow in uncomfortable guilt.

The carriage rumbled on. I had no idea which part of Central we were in, but I heard the bell ring across the city. "What time is it?"

"Half nine," Quen said without glancing up.

I flexed my fingers in my lap and felt my palms sweating in the tight leather gloves. Only a half hour until the Eventide Gate opened. If I started crying now, would the Diviner care? Or would he tut and return to whatever article was more fascinating than my certain death?

The carriage came to a sudden stop. Quen folded the broadsheet and left it on the cushion as he stood, his head not even reaching the carriage's roof. "Let's go."

Gods, no, I didn't want to go! My heart was hammering in my chest.

I barely noticed as Quen took my arm and guided me down the steps out into Central Station. We'd arrived at the back where the storage crates were, away from the public queues. Another carriage had already parked, and I frantically searched for Malk.

Quen tugged me inside to the private waiting room. I almost cried out.

Malk stood there, both his wrists *and* ankles chained up. His blue eyes widened at my approach and I read the fear, the despair, and regret burning there. He too had been forced to dress in Warden clothes, and he was chaperoned by not one Warden, but two massive Umber: one with gray stone skin and the other with a sandstone complexion.

If any of the Godless needed such heavy security, it was Malk.

I wanted to run to him, but Quen stopped us at an unbearable distance. He nodded as one of the station staff, another Diviner, approached.

"The public crossing has been delayed on your command, Master Corinth," the Diviner said.

Master Corinth?

I shot a sharp look at Quen, and then to Malk, whose mouth formed a grim line.

"Quentin Corinth," I whispered.

Quen stiffened next to me as Malk nodded.

Shit. I hadn't made the connection until now.

Quentin Corinth. Vesper killer. The Dark Warden cursed with death.

That was a name I'd never forget.

Five years ago, he'd been involved in a botched Warden raid on Grayford seeking Sinder, Elvira, and a runaway Glimmer from one of their workhouses. It was Corinth who'd launched a trigger-happy attack and shot two Vesper along with Sinder. The Vesper had died instantly, returned to their maker, and Sinder would have joined them if not for Vincent.

Then the Wardens had swooped into Grayford and rounded up entire families of illegals, including Malk's mother, pinning the blame on *them*.

A minor scandal in Chime, all things considered, but the Undercity never forgot the Dark Warden's name, nor did any Vesper.

It was Quentin Corinth who'd inspired the Godless.

And he expected me to *trust* him?

The quarter-to bell rang. Quen pulled me along, and the Wardens dragging Malk followed. If the Godless were going to launch a rescue attempt, now would be the time.

But as I stepped outside into the main station, my heart sank.

Wardens were everywhere.

The public queues had been cordoned off, leaving me and Malk surrounded by an entire circle of protection. There was no chance we'd fight our way out of this, nor would Harmony be able to trick her way in.

No, in this Malk and I were alone.

Two Vesper awaiting our fate.

The red glare of Rapture burned angrily upon us as Quen marched us across the concourse to the Gate.

"No more calls for Rapture!" one of the Diviner station staff yelled and blew on a whistle. "I repeat, no more calls for Rapture! Public traffic for Eventide will depart at quarter past ten."

I'd never been this close to the Gate before, and it truly was huge; bigger than the Glimmer estate by far. The entire station had been built around it and the clock tower above. From where I stood, I couldn't see the queues, but the Wardens ran the station like they did everything in Chime—with organized precision. There were queues for foot traffic and carriages both coming in and out, though one didn't need a ticket. Only a passport.

We stepped right up to the barrier, which had been lowered in front of the Gate in preparation for the crossover. A precaution, so I'd heard, to stop travelers from racing through and colliding with one another, or worse—to stop travelers from losing a limb or head if they should enter the Gate as it changed.

Even the concrete floor had been painted with arrows and directional signs for travel, and we kept to the left lane.

Buzzing filled my ears, and I became painfully aware of the aether swirling not only in the portal to Rapture, but from the Gate itself. The clock tower loomed above us, sitting atop the Gate, though the dark brass of the tower was masked by the many cogs and gears which made up the arch of the Gate. All Diviner ingenuity.

I cringed from the silvery-blue aether swirling around the edges. The amount needed to power the clock tower and Gate was unfathomable.

What would it take to make it stop?

Stop it? Why would anyone want to? The Gate had operated since the dawn of time.

It was ancient. Wonderful.

I was utterly terrified of it.

My heart clashed with an entire marching band as the hands of fate counted down the seconds until the Gate turned. I stared into the heart of it; at the shimmering transparent ripples. I could see the volcanic skyline and vibrant casinos of Rapture on the other side, as though gazing at a reflection in the water. Mortals wandered by, their shapes distorting through the portal, but no one could cross now.

The clock tower struck ten.

And the bell tolled my end.

The portal shimmered and the red glare of Rapture vanished, as though someone had swept their hand through a puddle, wiping it away, to be replaced with the sky at dusk.

Eventide.

I'd grown up hearing so many tales of my domain, and each one had convinced me to never dare step foot on Valeria's land.

Yet here I was.

The portal rippled, and a man stepped through. Varen. He wore his official ambassador's tabard and avoided my eye. "The way is clear. Valeria is expecting you." He strode through, and Quen tugged on my arm.

I pulled back. "Shit, I can't do this," I whispered. "I can't—"

"Is this your first time crossing?"

"I'm an illegal, what do you bloody think?"

"Take a deep breath and walk as you normally would. The crossing doesn't hurt."

I dug my heels into the ground and found my strength outmatched Quen's. "I won't."

Quen sucked in an exasperated breath. "Do you want your friend to cross alone?"

Malk. They'd already dragged him through.

No matter what happened, I wouldn't leave him.

I closed my eyes and stepped through to my fate.

Quen was right. It hadn't hurt. It tingled.

Stepping through the Gate was like leaving a warm and bustling kitchen for the open air of a café dining hall. The noise of Chime had been sucked away in an instant, leaving me with a cooling breeze and the distant sound of hooting.

Instead of town houses, coffee shops, and tourist traps made from brick and brass, I was surrounded by a forest of tall mushrooms. And beyond that, the sky glowed with the purples and blues of early evening, despite the fact it was still morning back on Chime.

It reminded me of Meridian Park at night, but with more mushrooms and fewer Leander joggers running past.

But it didn't feel like home.

"Over here," Varen called. He gestured to a small wooden hut that served as the station on Eventide. A tiny, modest thing compared to Central Station. It was manned by Vesper Wardens, I noted, and stocked with wooden carriages which had no roof. Vesper milled around it; some who looked agitated by our presence, and others who looked agitated at being made to wait before they could cross into Chime.

Quen guided me around to one of the carriages. "We'll be traveling on these. Valeria's castle is a little far away on foot."

And then my heart plummeted, remembering the real reason I was here.

Again, Quen helped me up, and we rode separately as Malk, his Umber handlers, and Varen entered another carriage. I hated to be separated from both Malk and Varen, but at least they were together.

I'd wanted to get Varen's attention, to just *see* him, but he'd completely avoided looking in my direction, as though I were a complete stranger. Self-preservation? Or guilt?

I'd always hoped, if it came down to it, that Varen would be on my side. That he'd use his position as ambassador to keep me safe, or the Godless's mystery benefactor would at last reveal themselves and save the organization they'd invested so much of their bocs into. But no savior came to my rescue.

Varen understood the cruel whims of his god. That was one reason why he risked associating with the Godless, to help us undermine her in the few petty ways that he could. I thought he believed in us. In me.

Now I wasn't so sure.

Unlike the fancy carriages on Chime, this one was powered by a steam engine and operated by a Vesper driver dressed in tweed. The carriage jerked and spluttered as it positioned itself on a muddy drive.

And then we were off.

Wind blew in my face as the little engine chugged away. The roads here were bumpier and much more treacherous than Chime's, and it delighted me to see Quen clasp on to his seat for dear life as he bounced all over the place.

This is fun.

Yes, riding to my death was *so* much fun.

Eventide's landscape opened up to wide lavender fields and quaint farmhouses built inside giant treelike mushrooms. I'd always known Valeria's mortals held a penchant for mushrooms, but seeing it with my own eyes brought their tales to life.

The trees were made from a variety of mushrooms; some tall and droopy, others with thick toadstools and dull gray caps that loomed over the fields like giant umbrellas. The many homes we passed were made from red-and-white spotted caps draped in linen, and the foliage along the roadside was a mix of colorful and glowing toadstools, chanterelle, and puffballs.

The beautiful, the deadly, and the rotten.

Many more mushrooms grew in organized lines on the farmers' fields; the basic white buttons that were imported to Chime and cooked in toasties, soups, and stews, and the more extravagant oyster, morel, and truffles that the Golden City dined on. And, I'm sure, hidden away from public view were the less wholesome varieties banned from public consumption in Chime. Some that could make you view the world like a Mesmer. And others that could choke the life from you.

It wasn't all mushrooms; I spotted gourds and pumpkins too, some of which had been carved into ridiculous faces and lit with a candle inside like a lamp.

Though all the mortals we passed working the fields were Vesper.

Eventide didn't receive many visitors from the other domains, it seemed.

"So this is your first time in Eventide," Quen said, his teeth chattering slightly.

"How can you tell?"

"Your eyes are only marginally bulging from their sockets."

"That's the fear of knowing I'm about to be ripped in half."

Quen opened his mouth to say something and then frowned as the carriage slowed.

Were we at our destination already?

No. The road had widened to accommodate a line of monuments on either side. There were hundreds of them; each either a statue of a woman holding a bowl, or stone plinths etched with words so worn I couldn't tell what they warned of as we passed.

Each monument had been draped in wreaths or silk shawls, and the bowls were full of coins and gemstones, silver, gold, and more besides. Other objects were carefully placed at their feet: silver, pottery, knives, jewelry, baked goods, large pumpkins.

Tributes. Tithes.

So many of them.

"What stops them from being stolen?" I asked aloud and then wished I hadn't.

Spaces had been left between the monuments for tall poles, and swinging from those were metal cages.

Gods.

I bit my lip as the carriage lumbered past them at an agonizingly slow speed. Each cage was occupied with a Vesper man, woman, or child. They'd been stripped naked and left there. Many sported bruises and cuts, and they were hunched over, contorted into twisted shapes in order to fit within the cages that were too small to stand or move in.

Their dark eyes were open, watching in silence as we passed.

Shit. They were still alive.

I glanced at Quen, whose pearly face had paled. "Is this *your* first time in Eventide?"

"No," he said, so quietly I barely heard him over the rattle of the carriage.

"You've seen this before?"

His throat bobbed. "No. These were... empty."

That made it so much better. "Then what is this? A welcoming banner?"

He averted his eyes.

That's exactly what this was.

I glanced toward Malk's carriage a little way behind. Both Varen and the Wardens avoided looking at the caged Vesper, but Malk was staring at them, his expression hard and unreadable.

His father had been placed in one of these cages to die.

The thought of Malk being placed inside one, too...

Gods, I was going to be sick.

I sank into my seat, trying to make myself as small as possible. "You realize Malk and I will be placed into one of these, assuming our souls aren't ripped from our bodies outright."

Quen grimaced. There wasn't any point in trying to get through to him, but I couldn't leash my tongue and let it go.

I shook my shackles in the direction of the tributes. "Are your eyes so damaged that you can't *see*, Quen? Or does this come back to the truth—Wardens don't care what happens to mortals outside of Chime?" The evidence was dangling before us in these cages. "How many mortals have you damned?"

"I won't deny the gods can be hasty in their emotions—"

"*Hasty?*"

"But they are still gods."

And thus the Wardens were utterly useless in their presence. Malk and I would have to survive without his help. "You didn't have to bring us here." A sob caught in my throat. "Turn the carriage around. Take us back."

The grips of his knuckles turned white. "You know I can't."

"Then why pretend otherwise? Why act like this means nothing to you?"

"Do you want me to be honest?"

"Shit, Quen, I'm not a child. I'm Godless." Quen cringed at the word, and I was sure I saw the carriage driver wince. "I know how this goes."

Quen pushed his eyeglasses up his nose. "Then I won't lie. My superior wants you both here, and I cannot deny him. Nor, as a Warden, can I deny the Covenant. But I can bend it. I don't take pleasure from this work, but I do it because *this* is the only way I can make a difference. This is the only power I have."

"And how do you intend to use your power?"

"To keep you both alive."

I didn't believe a single word he said.

"You don't trust me." Quen cleared his throat. "I wouldn't either. But if you want your Vesper friend to remain whole, you'll do as I say. Do you understand the etiquette of meeting with a god?"

The Wardens at their HQ had rattled off a list of instructions, though I'd ignored them. Varen had taught me all I needed to know about the gods and the lives of the rich and famous of Chime. Besides, nearly everyone had read *The Traveler's Handbook to Chime and Beyond,* which covered such things, albeit from a Warden's biased perspective.

While Malk had come from Eventide with a farmer's swagger and twang, I'd grown up in the city with the street skills needed for urban survival. Both of us understood our god's cruelty, though Varen had raised us with that knowledge in mind.

Don't piss on them. Gods don't like that, my inner voice said.

Thank you for the advice. "I'm not a complete fool."

"Good." Quen looked visibly relieved.

The lines of monuments, tributes, and cages seemed to stretch for an eternity, and I struggled to pull my gaze from them. Then the wide-open fields turned into thick forests of mushrooms again, and a dark blot rose between them.

A castle. A gigantic dark purple castle, like something from a nightmare.

Its towers and turrets were twisted with sharp points, as though the castle itself was a sleek obsidian knife of many ends.

This was home to Valeria. God of dusk and despair.

Shadowy figures waited outside the castle gates, and I swallowed a scream as the shadows faded and revealed grotesque gargoyles with massive black wings. Winged Twilights, the Vesper called them. Immortals. Valeria's own personal guard.

The Winged Twilights moved aside as the carriage parked. Their eyes were a pure onyx and watched with a still curiosity as Quen reached for my arm.

My legs were shaking so badly I almost fell down the steps.

Malk's carriage pulled in behind me and they practically hauled him from the carriage. He jostled in the Warden's grip and came bounding for me.

I gasped as Malk shoved Quen aside and grabbed my gloved hand with his. "I love you with everything I am."

Then he lurched forward and kissed me.

One last desperate touch.

I tried to deepen the kiss, to grab onto him and never let go, but the Wardens pulled us apart. I cried out as the sandstone Umber punched Malk in the stomach, sending him to his knees.

Tears burned in my eyes. "Stop it!"

"That's enough," Quen ordered.

The Umber relented and grabbed Malk by his arms, lifting him to his feet.

Quen strode to Malk and stared up at him; comically so, since Malk was a head taller. "Try a stunt like that again, and neither of you will leave this castle. Understand?"

Malk glared at him with such loathing, I could feel the heat from where I stood. "Enjoy killing Vesper, don't you, Corinth? Like the sight of us dangling in cages? Do you get off on watching us suffer?"

The Umber's nostrils snorted, but Quen raised his hand in warning. "You have every right to hate me, Malkavaan Byvich, but your hate won't serve you now. My advice? Keep your tongue inside your mouth and don't flap it."

Malk scowled and turned his head away.

The Winged Twilights looked on, as though curious or amused by our interaction, I couldn't tell. Varen approached them and bowed with the reverence reserved for the residents of the Golden City, not these stone aberrations.

"Inform my Queen that we have arrived."

"She knows," one of the gargoyles said with a deep, gravelly voice.

"Well then." Quen adjusted his eyeglasses. "We mustn't keep her waiting."

Panic rose in my chest.

It was time to meet my maker.

XII

While Wardens may have purview to travel between domains, Warden presence can sometimes be considered unwelcome. Should you encounter an issue with a mortal, contact the domain's ambassador foremost. Should you be required to venture into a domain, bear in mind the following guidance:
Do not interact with the local mortals.
Similarly, do not touch or ingest the local flora or any beverages.
If a visit requires a tithe or tribute, see the Warden treasury.
Should you meet with a god, consult your handbook on god etiquette. It is considered grossly offensive to ignore their summons.
It is advised you conduct your business within the hour and leave the domain before the turn of the crossing.
Wardens hold priority for all domain crossings.
—Q. Corinth, *Warden Handbook on Dealing with Domains*

I HATED IT HERE.

Hated this castle. This domain. The mortals were nice enough, I supposed, though all doom and gloom, and there was the matter of them hating *me*.

I hated that Elijah had ordered me here, despite understanding the necessity.

I hated the hate that burned in Kayl and Malkavaan's eyes.

I hated that I sympathized.

Empathy was a curse.

Eventide was certainly one of my least favorite domains, right down there with the jungles of Juniper, another place that appeared picturesque from the outside, but venture too far in, and you'd soon find the rot spreading wide.

That's what so many of these gods were.

Captivating in their beauty. Rotten underneath.

And now I'd have to thoroughly flay myself for indulging such blasphemous thoughts. *Damn it, Quen.*

We followed the Winged Twilights into Valeria's castle; an oppressive and bleak building made from darkest obsidian, which seemed to close in the further I ventured. My arm was wrapped around Kayl's, half dragging her inside like a ball and chain attached to my ankle. I'd tried to be nonchalant, to not terrify the poor woman, but why had I bothered? Of course she was terrified. She knew exactly where I was leading her.

"How many mortals have you damned?"

More than I could remember.

I'd met with Elijah the night before and gone over what I'd discovered of Kayl and her peculiar abilities. Regardless of Elijah's suspicions concerning Kayl, he'd asked me to damn the male. Malkavaan was Godless after all, and this was what the Wardens were sworn to do; protect the rest of Chime's sensibilities from his kind.

He'd denied his god. While it was a gross simplification, we mortals were the property of our patron god.

And I was merely returning Valeria's lost property like a good custodian.

We walked along the main hallway of the castle and our footsteps echoed off the stone, the only sound in the uncomfortable silence that clung to each surface like the Vesper's own shadows. Moths fluttered by braziers containing alternating blue and purple flames which lit our path, though they seemed to create more darkness than they eradicated. Black drapes hung over the open windows, stirring with a light breeze, and in the darkness, I caught flashes of sapphire and amethyst eyes. Valeria's Vesper servants lurking within.

Above, bats made their home in the castle rafters and would occasionally flitter across the space. Kayl jolted beside me as one flew overhead.

"Bats," I whispered. "They won't harm you."

"Everything in here will harm me," she whispered back, the tremor in her voice clear.

I could offer little comfort. "When we enter the grand hall, stay behind me. Don't move, don't speak, but keep your eyes on the dais." To turn away was deemed a great offense in Valeria's court; she needed attention on her at all times. "This is my show, and I can't have you ruining it."

"Every play needs a foil."

"Are there many plays in the Undercity?"

"Tragedies, certainly. So what am I? A stock character in your life?"

"Right now, you're the villain. I'm serious, Kayl." She really had no idea how dangerous she was, nor did she know she was about to become the starring act. "Do as I say."

"Have it your way, then."

We'd almost reached the towering double doors of the grand hall. Four more Winged Twilights stood guard, their stony faces watching on with apparent disinterest. Each carried a scepter with two sharp points in the shape of a crescent moon—Valeria's crest. Blood dripped from the tips. They'd been used recently.

The Winged Twilights sniffed the air and their dark gaze landed on Kayl. She tensed.

"Don't look at them."

"How can I not?" she whispered. "I'm going to shit myself."

I forced a smile. "Please don't."

The Winged Twilights didn't bother checking us for weapons—they trusted Varen to handle that duty, at least—and the double doors opened with a thunderclap. Varen stepped through first. Kayl sucked in a breath as I made us follow second, with the two Umber Wardens and Malkavaan behind.

The grand hall earned its name for its sheer size.

Like everything else in this cursed castle, the walls were a shimmering purple obsidian that sparkled with starlight the longer you gazed at it. The floors were made with perfectly shining tiles that reflected the evening sky above, for there was no ceiling, and the true beauty of dusk's colors was on display.

Lines of naked Vesper males and females kneeled on the ground between us and the dais, their spines curved in a permanent kowtow with their buttocks perked up in greeting.

Nothing shocked me anymore. I'd seen far worse in Rapture.

Varen led us between them, and my eyes finally rested on the dais.

Piles of gold and silver coins were littered around the steps in such large heaps, one could swim in them. Among them were various treasures and jewels; pendants, brass candlesticks, diamond-encrusted mirrors, even decorative spoons. An entire trove of wealth that could pay for Chime's upkeep for a millennium.

These were Valeria's tithes; trinkets and relics that she demanded from her mortals in exchange for their existence.

I knew what happened to mortals who couldn't pay an adequate tithe.

They ended up in cages, battered, bruised, and broken.

Or they ran and hid in the Undercity like Malkavaan and his mother.

Atop the grotesque pile of wealth sprawled the queen of it all.

The god of dusk.

Valeria took the form of a mortal female. Though, like a Necro, there was something not quite natural about the perfection she chose to display. She towered above her subjects at nine feet in height, and her long, lithe figure was barely covered in a thin black gown which did little to hide the mound of her sex, or the shape of her breasts. Her skin was the midnight blue of most Vesper, her hair a thick black that coiled down to her shoulders. Her face too was sculpted like a statue, with high cheekbones and plump puckered lips painted in silver.

More silver glittered across her body: three pendants dangled from her neck, each the shape of the moon in various forms, and her arms and wrists were wrapped in silver bangles. Each finger also bore a silver ring. She liked her silver, did Valeria.

No wonder she enjoyed the company of Diviner.

The Glimmer described Valeria as sin incarnate, and it was difficult to disagree with their assessment. She certainly rivaled the Ember god for wanton sin.

That was Valeria, really. Breathtakingly beautiful, and all for show. She thrived on the attention of mortals and demanded their absolute worship. Even her throne was surrounded in tall mirrors so she could preen herself.

And yet she'd sold her mortals to the Glimmer. While Valeria thrived on attention, she cared more for her treasures than her own mortals' lives.

I stopped before the dais and released Kayl from my grip as Varen strode up the steps between the piles of gold. He kneeled before his god and took her bare foot, cradling it with the tenderness of a lover.

"My Queen." His lips pressed to her flesh with such obscene eagerness, I almost gagged.

"My dearest Varen." Valeria's voice carried like an echo. Feminine, but distorted, as though speaking nowhere and everywhere at once. "You've brought me guests." Her eyes landed on mine and I swallowed a lump. To stare into her eyes was to stare at the night sky; a maddening void of stars that rivaled the Mesmer. "Quentin Corinth. You've not entered my domain in some time. I was beginning to think you'd forgotten me."

I flourished a bow. "Never, dark lady. You know how the Wardens like to keep a gentleman occupied. I come bearing gifts." I pulled a parcel from my inner jacket pocket and unwrapped an intricate necklace, holding it up for Valeria to inspect. "Made of white gold and pearls from Memoria." It was worth my entire apartment back on Chime, and then some. Luckily for me, the Wardens' treasury held a budget for such bribes when it came to dealing with the gods.

Valeria dismissed it with a delicate wave of her hand. "A worthy item, but I already grow bored. What else have you brought me?"

It was Varen's turn, and he strode to where the Wardens held Malkavaan. "We return to you Malkavaan Byvich, my Queen. An illegal we recovered from Chime—"

"Byvich? Step forth."

The Wardens removed Malkavaan's shackles and shoved him forward. He staggered a step closer to the dais, sweat already beading on his brow despite the perpetually cool evening.

Valeria ran her finger idly through the air and a cut sliced across Malkavaan's cheek with agonizing slowness. To his credit, Malkavaan stood strong and defiant, even as his legs shook and his blood dripped onto his Warden-issued shirt.

"I remember your father. Honest man. Not honest enough. He hid your existence from me. I would have taken your life as his tithe, but he chose instead to give his own. Though he didn't last long in my cage, did he?" Valeria glanced at one of her Winged Twilights with a look of adoration, as though admiring the antics of a beloved pet, and the gargoyle hacked a laugh in response, like that of a choking Amnae.

"What did you do to my mother?" Malkavaan asked. His words were quiet. Seething with the anger and rage he'd carried for his brief mortal life.

Valeria regarded him with the contempt she saved for her lowliest mortals. "I created your mother. Elvira. She was mine to do with as I wished. She made such a pleasing sound when I crushed her ribcage. I reanimated her body just to hear it again."

Malkavaan stared at her, and I saw the fear slip, replaced with a mask of bitter hatred.

I'd not thought him a fool when we first met, but I could see my earlier assessment was mistaken. Shadows burst from his skin, and he leaped at Valeria.

The god didn't move. She didn't have to. Neither did her Winged Twilights. Varen at least attempted to tackle Malkavaan, to prove his foolish loyalty with some unnecessary modicum of honor, and it *was* unnecessary.

With a wave of Valeria's hand, Malkavaan crumpled to the floor.

Screams tore from his throat as his limbs contorted and cracked in unnatural spasms.

Valeria cackled. "I love when they struggle. It makes them far more entertaining to break—"

"Stop it, you vile bitch!" Kayl screamed.

I grabbed her arm to hold her in place, though at this point, the gesture meant nothing.

Malkavaan's spasms stopped, and he rolled onto his side with rasping breaths. Forgotten.

Valeria's eyes turned to Kayl, the sneer of her lips curling into a snarl. "What is this creature?" she demanded.

My heart skipped a beat.

Now the *real* show began.

"Another illegal we found on Chime, dark lady—"

"I do not recall this one." Valeria rose from her throne, the pendants and bangles of silver clinking into place, and she thrust her fist out, as though reaching to crush Kayl's heart.

Kayl stepped back, bumping into me, but that was more from fright than from whatever Valeria was attempting to do. I resisted the urge to smirk.

Valeria yanked her hand back and bared her teeth in a furious roar. "What Diviner trickery is this?"

I blinked my eyelashes in feigned confusion. "She is Vesper, dark lady—"

"She is no mortal of mine!"

And there it was; confirmation at last of what both I and Elijah had suspected.

Kayl was no Vesper.

So now the question remained—*what* was she?

But first, I needed to deal with this quandary, for an angry god was not a pleasant one. "Are you certain, dark lady? This girl is quite clearly a Vesper—"

"Do not condescend to me, Quentin Corinth! What is this mortal? Which domain seeks to undermine mine with such a farce?" She snapped a glare at Varen. "What do you know of this? Speak!"

Varen bobbed a series of ridiculous bows, looking bewildered. "I—I have no idea, my Queen, this is the first I've heard—"

"The Wardens don't know what she is, dark lady." There you go, Ambassador, I'll save you a flogging. "I was rather hoping you might."

Kayl glanced at me, her own expression a mixture of fear, anger, and... curiosity.

She didn't know what she was. None of us did.

But by my god, I'd find out.

Valeria returned to her throne and tucked her hand under her chin. "You come to me for answers, but none has ever dared take the form of my mortals. Are there other such creatures as this one?"

"Not that we know of. She has taken the visage of a Vesper and believes herself to be one; a most cunning deception, I'm sure you'll agree, but neither she, nor we, know who or what she is."

A dark glint flashed in Valeria's eyes. "Leave her with me and my Twilights will rip the answers from her."

Kayl flinched.

"That won't be necessary," I hurried on. "The Wardens will handle this matter—"

"I want answers, Quentin Corinth. Another domain is exerting its power over mine, and I will not stand for it. Gildola, most likely, that treacherous cunt. I gave her leave to take my mortals, and she twists them against me."

I doubted the Glimmer had this sort of power. "If another domain is targeting Eventide, then we will investigate with your cooperation." And we would. That was part of the Covenant—to maintain the balance of the gods. *If* another god was using Kayl to overthrow that balance, then we'd put an end to it. "But you know I cannot speak details of an ongoing investigation, regardless of whether another domain was involved—"

"You would deny me?"

"By my oaths, dark lady, I'd have no choice."

Her nostrils flared. Angering a god was never a wise idea, and Varen grimaced in my direction. He opened his mouth to speak and quickly closed it again. At least they both understood that killing a Warden would cause greater problems.

For that was the joy of not only being a Warden, but also a Diviner. When your patron god controlled time itself, even the other domains hesitated when it came to crushing the skulls of time's messengers. "If the other gods knew of this girl"—and really, I hated to refer to Kayl in such diminutive terms, but that was what Valeria wanted—"there would be outcry. I'm taking great liberties in bringing this matter to you, dark lady, and I do so to warn you. However... if we were to come to some sort of agreement, shall we say, I'd be willing to pass on certain details to your ambassador."

Varen looked appalled at the very thought.

Valeria leaned back against her throne. "Name your price."

"Release Malkavaan Byvich."

All heads turned to me, including the poor boy still groaning on the floor.

"You covet Vesper flesh?" Valeria swept her hand to where the many naked Vesper remained bowed on the floor. "I could give you any number."

"What can I say; I'm a man of impeccable taste. But no, dark lady. The Wardens require Byvich's return to our correctional facility. By understanding illegal minds such as his, we can develop techniques to counter sin." A lie, but a necessary one.

Though no doubt Elijah *would* be interested in such research.

"Then we'll strike a bargain. You deliver me the truth of this creature, inform me of which domain seeks to attack mine, and I'll give you this boy."

"That's hardly a fair bargain—"

"Oh, I think it's a fine incentive." She rose from her throne once more and strode with feline grace to Malkavaan squirming on the floor. With a flick of her fingers, his limbs contorted, but this time she'd reanimated his body like a puppet, forcing him to stand and then magically float a few feet off the ground until they were eye level. His body hung helplessly in the air, his arms rigid at his sides, his eyes wide with fear. She ran a finger along his jaw. "This one owes me a lifetime of tithes. It will give me great pleasure to take what is owed."

Kayl jerked forward, and I grabbed her arm before she could do something truly foolish. "Don't," I whispered.

Valeria must have heard, for she smirked in my direction.

"We have an agreement," I said. "So long as he is left untouched."

Valeria's finger dropped from Malkavaan's jaw with a playful sigh. "You spoil my fun, Quentin Corinth, but you have my word. He will remain in my domain untouched until you call to collect him. Call soon, I already grow bored." She returned to her throne, her fingers skimming through the piles of coins with a subtle clink. "See our guests out, Varen."

I didn't hesitate. I marched Kayl out of the grand hall, the two Umber Wardens and Varen at my heels.

"I can't leave him," Kayl whispered. "Please, I can't—"

"This is the best I can do for him," I whispered back. "Trust me. Varen will watch over him, and we'll return for him, I promise you. Now *please* let us get out of here."

Kayl looked ready to yank from my grip and dash back, but her throat bobbed and she nodded.

I didn't dare breathe a sigh of relief until we reached the carriages still waiting outside. The Winged Twilights remained on guard, and would likely follow us until we abandoned Eventide entirely.

Varen strode up to my nose and snarled, and for a heartbeat I thought he was going to slap me to the ground. "You could have informed me of your intentions instead of making me look the fool."

I took off my spectacles and rubbed them clean of his saliva. "And spoil the surprise?"

"What about Malk?" Kayl asked, her voice hoarse. "Please, Varen—"

"You've both put me in an impossible position." Varen scowled. "Is that what you wanted, Corinth? To force me to play spy for you? And just what is wrong with her?" His glare turned to Kayl, who visibly recoiled.

Now the ambassador was playing the prat. "We don't know. Diviners have died, Your Excellency. This is now a Warden investigation, and since she is no longer classed as a Vesper under your own god's eye, she will remain in my custody."

Kayl's scowl matched Varen's; I'd deal with her after.

Varen threw his hands up. "Do what you will." He stomped off to the castle.

"What of Malk—Malkavaan?" Kayl called.

Varen glared over his shoulder. "Valeria will keep her word."

We'd have to hope so. I pulled out my fob watch. "Quarter to eleven. We best leave now if we want to make the crossing back to Chime." I didn't fancy returning to Valeria's castle and Varen's hospitality for another twelve hours if we missed it. Eventide tea tasted far too musty for my liking, as though mixed with soil and their rotten mushrooms.

"It took almost half an hour to get here. We'll never make it."

I took her arm and guided her to the carriage. "You forget I control time." I gestured for the driver to scoot out and helped Kayl up to the driver's seat, slipping in next to her. I grasped for the various levers and contraptions.

"You know how to operate this thing?" Kayl said, disbelieving.

Honestly, her lack of faith hurt. "I'm an Academy-trained engineer. Yes, I know how to operate it." With the press of a button and the yank of a lever, the steam engine puffed into life and we jerked forward. The carriage rattled as we hurtled away from Valeria's castle and down the uneven dirt roads. "Would you believe that I once trained as a tram driver?" I called over the noise. "In another life, I'm happily operating one of Chime's trams."

Kayl gritted her teeth as she bounced up and down. "That's nice. Honestly, Quen, just what the *shit*?"

Alas, she wasn't interested in my bumbling tram-driving career. *"Why did you become a Warden, Quen?"* she could have asked. *"For precious moments like these,"* I'd answer.

I held out my spare hand as though operating an invisible lever and allowed my power to flow around us. A bubble of time enveloped the carriage. We still moved at normal speed, but I'd slowed the outer layer. Anyone glancing in our direction would see a blur racing past.

Now we'd make it to the Gate in time.

Kayl glanced around us, staring openmouthed as we passed the world in slow motion. "You've slowed time."

"Yes, and you can see it. How convenient." Slowing time held another advantage; it would muffle the world around us, including the little steam engine, allowing us to converse freely and privately. "I asked you to trust me. I know your Vesper friend isn't quite with us, but I did the best I could for him."

"Did you know Valeria held no power over me? Or am I lucky that my limbs are still in the right place?" There was an edge to her tone, and her gloved fists were clasped in her lap, still chained.

"I had my suspicions—"

"You gambled with my *life* against a god. An actual god."

"Yes, it was a gamble, and I won't apologize." Because the alternative, which I couldn't admit out loud, was that Valeria kept them both, and the Wardens washed their hands of the whole affair. Really, this was quite clever of me; Valeria wouldn't turn down an opportunity to gain an advantage over the other domains, nor would she care for Malkavaan's fate or whatever I wanted him for. "Though you called her a *vile bitch*—a gross breach of etiquette, by the way. This makes us even."

She snorted in disbelief. "What now? How do I get Malk back?"

"We solve the mystery of you." Because that was what she was. A mystery. An abnormality. No one in the twelve domains held her powers, though I knew she was mortal, at least, or else she wouldn't have been able to make the crossing. "Diviner are turning up dead with their souls ripped from their bodies—"

"I haven't killed anyone—"

"You killed Lady Mae. You may not realize it, but you somehow took her soul. She didn't die from a simple head injury."

Kayl openly stared at me, her silvery-blue eyes full of genuine surprise. "How—How could I have? Whatever I did, it wasn't me! I'm not killing Diviner!"

"I know. But this, and your inexplicable ability to switch your persona, means there is unfortunately a connection between you and whatever creature is targeting Diviner. I intend to discover the truth with your assistance."

"*My* assistance?"

I met her raised eyebrow with my own. "You want your lover back, don't you?"

"You're so certain Valeria will hand him over? Or your Wardens? And what then?"

"Once this investigation is over, the two of you can skip off with your merry band of heathens and retire to Arcadia. It matters not to me. My priority is the dead Diviner; anything beyond that is mere bureaucracy."

"Warden business is hardly my business. You were investigating the Glimmer workhouses, weren't you?"

"I can't comment on an ongoing case—"

"They're connected with these aether creatures. I don't know how, but they are." She gave me a cool look. "So if you want my assistance, you'll tell me everything you know about the workhouses. You'll help me shut them down."

Even as a Warden, I didn't exactly wield that level of power. I doubted the Glimmer would dare involve themselves in a conspiracy to murder Diviner, especially not under Elijah's watch, but I wanted those blasted workhouses gone, too. If our investigation uncovered some means to close them for good, I'd gladly take it. "Agreed."

She didn't look convinced. "You're really willing to dirty your reputation and work alongside an apostate?"

"I'd say my reputation is dirtied enough, wouldn't you?"

She frowned at that. "You're not going to lock me up in your HQ? Perform tests?"

That was the official Warden response. Elijah had left me with strict orders to bring her to Kronos for questioning, and if I ignored the twelve o'clock crossing, I was effectively disobeying his command.

But I didn't see how torturing her for answers would reveal any. I was still a high-ranking Warden; I could pull this off. Elijah wouldn't be pleased, but my methods hadn't failed him yet. "We're all seeking answers. Don't you want to know what you are?"

She leaned her head back and stared at the swirling Eventide skies. "I always thought of myself as a Vesper. I don't know what I am now."

"You're a Godless without a god. But we'll find yours."

One of the twelve gods would be responsible for her.

The question was finding out which one.

Oh, the question of Kayl's existence held so many political ramifications, and we Wardens needed to get this under control, and fast.

If another god was manipulating Kayl to attack Eventide, or for any other reason, then we needed to nip it in the bud before the domains warred.

If she *was* related to these aether leaks, we needed to contain that, too.

And if Chime's citizens learned of a creature that could tear a mortal's soul from their god, then there'd be mass panic and riots on the streets.

Not to mention it was Diviner law that ran the universe. If the other domains learned of a power that could resist time, then... I didn't even want to consider it.

Anarchy. Chaos. A city that no longer needed time, or logic, or Warden rule.

The Covenant would be nothing but a sheet of paper, then.

Eventide's Gate came into view with five minutes still on the clock. We'd stride into Chime comfortably. I slowed the carriage while allowing time to catch up. Vesper loitered around the station, though a flash of my badge would get us past them.

I pulled a key from my pocket. "I'm trusting you now. Please don't steal my soul and run for the Gate." I unlocked the chains from her wrists.

She immediately pulled off the gloves and flung them from the carriage. "I'm not your pet or your science experiment, Quen. If I agree to help you, then we do this as partners." She held out her hand. A challenge.

I did so love a challenge. I grabbed her palm with a firm grip.

She remained in her Vesper form, and I retained my soul. Interesting.

These next few days were going to prove entertaining, if nothing else.

Though a strong part of me wondered just what trouble I was going to find myself in.

"Partners, then."

PART TWO

13

WHEN QUEN SUGGESTED WE return to his apartment to make plans, a part of me had thrilled at the idea of taking the great glass elevator up to the Golden City and finally seeing how the other half of Chime lived.

But as it happened, Quen didn't own property in the Golden City, and instead lived in one of the Tower View Apartments; the tall blocks overlooking Central Square and the Gate. We'd caught the tram there, and as we neared the towers, I had to wonder what in god's name I was doing.

The clock tower rang quarter past twelve as I stepped off the tram. Only this morning had I crossed over to a world I'd never wanted to see and somehow survived the experience. Only this morning had I confronted a god and lived to tell the tale. Only this morning had I lost Malk and agreed to partner with the Dark Warden of all mortals in order to get him back.

Time flies when you're having fun, my mind said.

None of that was fun. Not a single part.

Not even the part where you called Valeria a vile bitch?

Not even my mind was going to let that go, was it?

The various blocks of Tower View were divided by domain and affluence. Harmony owned an apartment in City Rise we'd often used as a safe house. The thought of her and the rest of the Godless made my heart ache.

Naturally, Quen led me to the most extravagant of the towers—the Silver Suite. Home to Glimmer and Diviner. This was a gated community of Central's richest residents; either those who wanted to be closer to the Gate for travel or business purposes, or those who weren't quite rich enough to live in the Golden City. I wasn't sure where Quen fit.

Two Diviner stood by the gate and gave me curious looks as Quen hurried me inside. I suspected they didn't get many Vesper passing by, but I was still dressed in my Warden's attire; presumably they thought I was here on business.

I wasn't sure I wanted to be here anymore.

"This way." Quen ushered me into the foyer of the Silver Suite. I could see how it had earned its name.

The inner foyer shone with so much silver it hurt my eyes. Truly, I thought Valeria was bad, but silver covered everything here, from the trim of the wooden furnishing, to the levers and handles of the brass elevator. Even the walls were a light cream with silver drapes.

A Glimmer sat at the reception desk, her golden skin standing out like a lamp among the sea of silver. Her perfect customer service mask slipped as she laid eyes on me. I gave her a cheerful wave as I followed Quen to the elevator.

"Entertain many guests, do you?" I asked.

Quen pushed the button for the thirteenth floor. "Would you believe me if I said no?"

Actually, yes, but I wasn't going to say that out loud.

The elevator buzzed to life, and I cringed at the aether lights above. It lurched worse than the Undercity elevator ever did, and my stomach clenched when it stopped with a little *ping*.

Out we stepped into a carpeted hall of dull gray in contrast to the cream walls. We strode past a plethora of paintings, each depicting various locations in Chime, including Central Station and Meridian Park, and past many seemingly identical wooden doors. We stopped outside one such door—303.

Quen pushed it open and beckoned me inside. "Here we are."

I wasn't sure what I was expecting a Diviner apartment to look like. Plain like the Warden HQ? Covered in silver like the foyer? Perhaps decorated in walls of brass gears and cogs and ticking clocks, which they adored so much?

Certainly neat and orderly like Diviner were.

What I stepped into was the complete opposite.

Stacks of books and papers lined the entranceway, making it resemble a paper-based version of the trash heaps in Grayford. "I thought you Diviner were supposed to be organized?"

"We are. This is an organized sort of chaos. I know where everything is. You can leave your shoes there."

I searched for space but didn't see any. "Where?"

"Anywhere." He kicked off his shoes into a pile of what appeared to be early editions of the Chime Courier and wandered along the hallway.

I left my boots and carefully picked my way past the papers along the smooth wooden flooring. Quen led me under an arch to his main living room.

I whistled out loud.

Glass stretched across the entire far wall, from floor to ceiling. From our height on the thirteenth floor, I was eye level with the face of Chime's clock tower. Gods, I'd never been this high before, nor seen the clockface this close up. I glanced down and swayed with dizziness.

Central Station sprawled beneath me, and I was gifted with an excellent view of the Gate, now set to Kronos, the Diviner home world.

Quen stepped beside me. "Magnificent, isn't it?"

"Is this why you don't live with your domain in the Golden City?"

"It's one reason." He turned to his couch and began shuffling papers aside. They truly covered every single surface, including the dining table beside the window. I snatched a quick glance and wished I hadn't; one was a file on my employment at Lady Mae's.

Quen had done his homework.

Wooden furniture with brass handles completed the cozy little room, though it looked more antique than ornate compared to the Glimmer mansion. Bookshelves filled the far corner next to a small wooden desk and a quaint reading nook, both covered in papers and files. A piano sat in the other corner, also covered.

"Do you play?" I gestured to the piano.

Quen scooped up papers from the couch and deposited them unceremoniously on the floor. "No, not me. Can't remember where I got that from, honestly. I suppose it brings the room together. Here." He thumped the couch's cushion, and a layer of dust bloomed in the air. "Make yourself at home. I'll need to prepare the spare room, but it should suit your needs."

"My needs? Quen, I'm not staying here." Not when I needed to get back to the depot and ensure Dru, Harmony, and the rest of the Godless were safe and sound; and to report on Malk's disappearance, though they likely knew already.

"Of course you are. Did you think you could go swanning off to the Undercity and then meet up for tea whenever you felt like it?"

I put my hands on my hips. "You agreed this is a partnership."

"A partnership with *some* caveats."

I was going to snap his eyeglasses in half. "*What* caveats?"

"You are still a member of the Godless. Not to mention a dangerous, unknown entity. I can offer you some freedom under my protection, but my protection only stretches so far. It's either this, or you spend your nights in a Warden-sanctioned cell. I can assure you I am far better company."

"So I'm your prisoner?"

"Such a dismal word. I like to think of you as my guest."

He's the enemy. We shouldn't be here.

I knew that, but what choice did I have? Quen was my only chance of getting Malk back in one piece, if at all.

"I thought we could begin with some questions," Quen said. "Spend a few hours going over your history, your personality, your idiosyncrasies."

"I said I wasn't your science experiment—"

"This isn't science, it's more... philosophy. You're clearly not a Vesper, but one of the gods must hold a claim to your soul. Only by uncovering that can we get to the bottom of your unique abilities. In short, I need to understand *who* you are if I am to understand *what* you are."

That sounded like experimentation to me. "You're asking me to strip myself bare in front of you."

"Not bare, you can keep your clothes on." He grabbed a pen and notepad and leaned on the edge of an armchair, his pen poised for action. "To begin, tell me about your childhood."

"Gods, Quen." I wanted to grab his pen and shove it up his arse. "I've just come back from the shittiest morning of my life, and you want me to answer inane questions about my *childhood*? I'm gods-damn tired. I'm hungry. I've been forced to endure actual mental trauma by you dragging me all the way to Eventide so you could quite literally gamble on my *life,* only to discover Valeria isn't my god. I might not even have a god. My entire existence is a lie!" My hands were shaking again, and I couldn't stop imagining those horrid gloves pressing into my skin, or the chains around my wrists. I'd been utterly helpless and at Quen's mercy, and I distinctly hated the feeling. "And the only man I have ever loved is being held at the mercy of that—that—"

Vile bitch?

You're not helping!

"I'm sorry." Quen put his pen and notepad aside. "You're right. This is no way to treat a guest. If you'd sooner rest, I can sort out the guest room now, or we can order some food in? There's a concierge service downstairs. Let me find the menu." He began awkwardly searching among his pile of papers.

I pinched the bridge of my nose. Quen's enthusiasm was grating, but needed. The sooner we solved this riddle, the sooner we'd get Malk back. I didn't trust Valeria to treat him with kindness, even with Varen watching over him. What power did Varen have over his own god? None. And the way he'd slobbered over her feet and then glared at me... It was like I didn't know him. Like those years of him teaching me meant nothing.

I knew it was an act for our survival—hadn't he taught me how to adapt in any situation? But his act had been too real. Too convincing.

As much as I hated this, I needed Quen, and I needed this distraction to keep myself from dwelling and sinking into further madness. "No, it's fine. It's—It's best I answer your questions now and we formulate a plan. Let's get it over with."

Quen glanced up. "All right. Tell you what; you make yourself comfortable and I'll go brew us a pot of tea."

The Diviner answer to everything.

Right now, a cup of tea was exactly what I needed.

I curled up on the couch as Quen returned with a tray: one pot, two cups, a bowl of sugar cubes, and a large plate filled with a towering assortment of biscuits.

The man knew how to impress me.

I snatched a custard cream as he poured steaming tea.

"One lump or two?" he asked, scooping cubes with a spoon.

"Three, please."

His brow raised. "Sweet tooth, hrm? That's very Mesmer."

I stuck out my tongue and grabbed another biscuit.

Quen sank into his armchair with his foot crossed over his knee. His big toe stuck out of a hole in the sock. With his eyeglasses perched precariously on the tip of his nose, a pen tucked behind his ear, and another pen in his hand as he balanced his notepad, he looked ridiculous, and not like the Dark Warden known for spreading death wherever he stepped.

"So, Kayl," he began. "I'm going to ask you a series of questions, and I want you to be entirely honest with me. And I mean *honest*, no matter how embarrassing or awkward the answer. If you lie or withhold any information, even if you deem it irrelevant, then you'll only hold back my investigation. I promise when this is all over, I'll have my mind wiped completely clean of your deepest, darkest secrets so I can't later blackmail you."

"Wait, you can wipe your own memories?"

"I know an Amnae who can—"

"But why?" Why would anyone want an Amnae digging into their mind and removing parts of it?

"Have you ever read a good book that you wished you could read over again and again? That's one reason. But I digress. Tell me about your childhood."

"Can't you go through my memories yourself?"

"As you witnessed back in Warden HQ, my Diviner abilities don't work on you. We'll need to do this the hard way."

I sighed. What was there to tell? "I grew up in Grayford with Malk. It was his mother, Elvira, who took me in when I was thirteen and raised us together until the Glimmer stole her for their workhouse. Malk and I depended on each other to survive." That was how we'd grown so close. He'd resented me back then, when we were two young Vesper struggling on scraps, but we'd had no choice but to rely on each other. And the rest was history.

"And before you met Malkavaan? What do you remember of that?"

What *did* I remember? "I was alone. Hungry. And I hated the aether lights." Even back then, they'd annoyed me.

"You don't remember any parents? Or how you came to be in the Undercity?"

"No."

He scribbled a note. "Not all mortals are born. Some are made, like the Mesmer. But a god wouldn't be able to conjure a mortal outside of their domain. You ended up in Chime somehow."

"Refugees smuggle into Chime all the time."

"You would know. So you possess the body of a Vesper, and you've always believed yourself to be a Vesper. Perhaps this was a survival mechanism on your part to adapt to your surroundings in Grayford, though I saw you summon shadow at the Glimmer estate, so you possess their abilities, too. Can you change form at will?"

I'd not thought about it, and now that I did, I had no idea. "I could try, but I might stain your couch with the strain."

"And you've never transformed before? You've lived however many years and never once accidentally touched someone?"

I *had* thought about that, and while there were times I'd playfully flirted with Sinder and Vincent, or hugged Dru and Harmony, or snogged horny Ember girls in my teenage years, I'd never touched them in the way I touched Malk. Perhaps I'd remained a Vesper because of our connection. "Twenty-six years, and no, I think I'd know if this had happened to me before now."

"I wonder if the increasing aether leaks triggered your abilities," Quen mused, more to himself. He put his notepad down. "I'm going to regret this, but I want you to touch me."

"Excuse me?"

He rolled up his sleeves, exposing the colorful circles of his passport tattoo—all the circles had been filled, marking him as well traveled. "You transformed into a Diviner after you touched me, yes? So do it again. Right now."

My heart raced as I sat up. "Are you serious?"

"Everything I do is serious." He held out his arm.

"What if I accidentally steal your soul?"

He wore a wry smile. "Try not to."

Great, I was going to murder Quen in his own home and then the concierge service would call the Wardens and that would be the end of everything.

One less Diviner is no loss.

Was that really what I thought?

I tentatively touched Quen's arm with my fingers. Nothing.

"Grab it," he ordered.

"Don't tempt me." I slid my hand around his wrist and felt foolish for doing so, but then a tingle danced in my palm, followed by a tugging sensation. I wanted to pull back, but some compulsion tightened my grip, and the tingling grew into an itch.

Buzzing filled my ears like the aether lamps, but there were no lamps lit.

"Shit!" I yanked my hand free and examined it.

My skin had turned an odd silvery-blue color with flecks of pink; almost the opposite shade to Quen's pearly-silver. I turned over my wrist. My fake passport tattoo hadn't changed; that was Necro craftsmanship for you.

Quen was staring at me openmouthed. He pulled a handkerchief from his pocket and cleaned his eyeglasses, then pushed them back up. "What do you feel? Any different?"

"No, I..." I caught my reflection in the glass window. My face wasn't Vesper anymore. Even my pointed ears had shrunk. "How in god's name is this possible?"

He took my wrist and felt for my pulse. "Still nothing. I was hoping I'd feel some sort of connection now we share domains, but no. See if you can slow time."

"Just how do I do that?"

"It comes naturally to all Diviner. Hold out your hand as though gripping an invisible lever and slowly pull it back."

I imagined I was controlling the gears of a carriage, as he'd done on Eventide. My breathing slowed, and the air seemed to slow with me. We both turned to face the clock tower. The hands weren't moving at all.

"Gods." I shook my hands, and the effect dropped away, returning us to normal time, or what passed as normal for a Diviner.

Quen was still staring at me. "Remarkable." His silver eyes roamed over my face, my arms, taking in every part of me in intimate detail. And then he frowned. "Ah."

I flumped onto the couch. "Ah?"

"You're a woman."

"You've only just noticed?"

A pink tinge bloomed on his cheeks. I didn't think it was possible for Quentin Corinth to feel embarrassment. "There are very few female Diviner, just as there are no male Glimmer. I'm afraid I've made things rather awkward for you. You'll stand out in a crowd."

"So we kidnap another Vesper. There's bound to be one or two working for your concierge."

"Actually, I was planning on hiring you a maid."

"Hiring *me* a maid?"

"If you're going to be staying here, you'll need someone to care for your needs, buy you clothes—"

"How needy do you think I am?"

He waved me off and took a gulp from his tea. "Let's get back on topic. My question now is, can you take the persona of other domains? We need a willing volunteer."

"A maid."

"Essentially. I need to know if your abilities are locked to certain domains. However, we cannot go about kidnapping mortals from the domains and risk their gods discovering you."

"Wouldn't that be the quickest way of finding out what I am? Go on a round trip to each domain, speak with the gods. You're well acquainted with them, aren't you?"

Quen winced. "Alerting the gods and domains of your existence would cause no end of issues. No, it's best we keep you away from prying eyes. At least until we discover what you are, and who is responsible for the deaths of the Diviner."

"I'm your dirty little secret."

"A female Diviner in my apartment? The rumors will soon fly." He snapped a bourbon biscuit in half. "When you were held at Warden HQ, I had a Necro examine you. He noticed some strange energies in you... like a twin soul."

A twin soul?

He means me.

I gripped the edges of the couch cushion. Quen was rambling on about *energy* this and *soul* that, but I couldn't concentrate on his words. "How— How could I have a twin soul?"

"That's the part I'm not sure of. Diviner have been losing their souls; it's possible one of these stray souls entered you without your knowledge and this is how you gained such impossible abilities."

I'm not a Diviner. Who'd want to be one of them?

Gods. This couldn't be happening. *You are my thoughts!* The proof that I was finally losing my mind, but still me, my innermost self.

So you think.

"Are you all right?" Quen asked.

I was gripping the cushion so tightly it was about to burst; or I was. "Quen. I hear voices. In my head." He wanted me to embarrass myself with my honesty, so there I went, admitting the one truth I couldn't even tell Malk. "I don't think they're my thoughts."

Quen leaped off the armchair, almost knocking over his cup, and crouched in front of me. "How long have you heard these voices?"

I swallowed a lump in my throat. "My entire life."

It wasn't a lie.

I'd assumed this voice to be me, my inner self. It had always chattered away with me as though we were old friends, and memories came back to me; times when I'd talk to myself when no one was around, or even argued with myself sometimes. Times when I'd doubt myself, but then my mind would convince me of the correct course of action.

And I *did* remember a time before I met Malk and Elvira, when my imaginary friend kept me company when all was dark...

Except my imaginary friend had been real all this time.

Real and trapped inside my mind.

Perhaps your body is trapped in my brain.

Shit. Shit. Shit.

"What are you?" I whispered.

Your twin soul. Wasn't that obvious?

I swallowed a scream. "*Quen.*"

Quen took my head in both hands. I may have balked at the intimacy of his touch if I wasn't going insane, but Quen might be the only mortal I could trust to understand this.

"It's not unusual for a god to communicate with their mortals telepathically," he said, as he examined my eyes. "Father—my god, Dor—will sometimes speak this way. Though most choose to be mute. When you pray, does this voice answer?"

"I'm Godless, I've never prayed. And I'm not about to start."

"Praying to your god would be the quickest way to discover who they are—"

"*No*, Quen."

"Right, fine. Have you ever had visions?"

I had witnessed *something* after I'd touched Quen at the Glimmer estate—images of Chime's destruction—though if I was going to start experiencing visions of the future, I'd sooner the Godless learned of them first. "Why visons?"

"That's synonymous with the Mesmer. You do have quite the sweet tooth."

Because everyone knew the Mesmer gorged themselves on candy for some gods-forsaken reason. "Do you think I'm so spacey that I'm a Mesmer? Actually, don't answer that." I knew what Dru and Harmony would say; I *was* scatterbrained. But I was nothing like Reve. I wasn't haunted by visions or nightmares. I barely remembered my dreams.

I'm no god, but I'm flattered the Diviner thinks so.

Then what are you? I asked.

I'm whatever you are, silly.

Gods, I was getting nowhere fast. "This... voice, it's answering my thoughts, but I don't know what it is, and it won't tell me."

Quen still held my head. "Perhaps it will answer me. Hello, random soul trapped inside my good friend here. Do you have a name?"

You named me Jinx.

I had? *I don't remember that.*

Just as I named you Kayl.

You named me?

I needed to name you something. You were lost and sad. You cried for our mother.

Our mother? *Elvira?*

No. The mother who made us.

I broke from Quen's hold and launched myself across the room to pace. My mind was reeling, literally it seemed, and tea wasn't enough to fix this. I needed to get out of this place, to head to Sinner's Row and get absolutely fucked in more ways than one.

I needed Malk.

You don't need him. You have me.

"Shut up!" I screamed.

Quen walked into my path and grabbed my shoulders, stopping me. "Calm down—"

"Calm down?" I screeched. "I have a—a *thing* inside my head! And you're telling me to calm down? How does this fit into your theories, Quen? How does it *fit*?"

"I'll be honest; I have no idea. But we'll figure it out, I promise you. I have a contact at the Academy, an Amnae professor named Walter. He's more well versed in matters of souls and memories than I. With his help, we can look into your past and unlock what memories you may be missing. Now, sit down and have a cup of tea."

I did so, lifting a fresh cup with trembling fingers. "Do—Do you have a bath, or—"

"The washroom has a shower. Have a soak, calm yourself, and I'll send off a telegram. We can visit Walter first thing tomorrow."

I nodded. Quen left me to go speak with the tower's reception desk as I stared outside his window at the clock tower. The Gate had since changed to Memoria, the underwater home of the Amnae. I'd never actually met one because they didn't grace the Undercity, but I'd take all the help I could get.

Just what was I?

Truly Godless? Or was there a god waiting out there for me?

I was almost too scared to find out.

But for Malk... I would.

14

LOOKING FOR WORK?
WANT TO EARN TEN BOCS AN HOUR WITH BREAKS?
Then avoid the Golden City.
Most Golden City and Central businesses are owned by Glimmer who run
them like workhouses.
You may think you've escaped drudgery from the Undercity or Sinner's
Row, but there's no freedom under a Glimmer employer.
—Anonymous, *Godless flier on finding work*

STEAMING WATER SPLASHED DOWN my face, and I used my new power to slow its flow and appreciate it. Hot water was a rare luxury in the Undercity, and this was my third hop inside Quen's tub since I set foot in his apartment yesterday.

The first time, I'd needed to scrub away the mental trauma of the day. I'd cranked the shower's pressure to maximum and allowed the tinny sounds to drown out my sobs and wash away the images doomed to haunt me until the end of time: the Vesper hanging in cages, Malk's screams as his limbs snapped and spasmed, Valeria's dark eyes as she reached out to crush the life from me.

I let those images go along with my sorrow, and they swirled down the drain.

Moping about Malk's fate wasn't going to save him.

My second foray into this tub was to cleanse myself physically and to get to know the soul inside my head—Jinx, I'd apparently called it. A good hot soak eased my muscles and removed years of Undercity grime from underneath my fingernails and embedded in my scalp. While I washed away the years, I reflected on the times I'd shared with myself—with this voice—and where my thoughts ended and Jinx's began.

"What are you?" I'd asked. "Are you male? Female? Neither?"

I'm whatever you are, only smarter and with more charisma. If I had my own body, I'm sure I'd be better-looking, too. Shame we're stuck inside yours.

"So how does this work? You just... float inside my consciousness?"

That's one way of looking at it. I see everything you do, feel everything you feel, tolerate whatever silly thoughts pass through your mind—

"Tolerate?"

You think a lot of twaddle for someone with two minds.

"And we're stuck together? There's no way you could, say, get your own body?"

Your body is *my body, but you do the heavy lifting. While you lug that fat arse of ours around, I'm free to do the heavy thinking. One of us needs to pay attention to things.*

My twin soul had a biting sense of humor, it seemed.

I'll freely admit that my third splash inside the tub this morning was merely for pleasure. Quen's washroom stocked an entire jar of lotion that I took full advantage of. I'd never have taken him for the type.

I wrapped myself in his cream silk robe and strode out of the washroom. Quen sat at the dining table, where an entire breakfast buffet had been laid out: a pot of tea, toasted teacakes with clotted cream and jam, poached eggs, portobello mushrooms, cherry tomatoes on the vine, hash browns, a bowl of baked beans, and slices of toast with pats of butter already melting.

He truly did know how to impress me.

Quen lowered the early edition of the Chime Courier. "Good morn—" His eyes dipped down to my legs. The robe was so short, it barely covered my thighs. He cleared his throat and his gaze snapped back to the Courier. "Good morning. Help yourself."

I bit back a smirk and slid into the dining chair opposite. "See anything nice?"

"What?"

"In the Courier."

"Oh. The, uh, usual. Did you want to read?" He folded the Courier and slid it across the table, his silver eyes scanning my face as though he wasn't quite sure what to do with me.

He wants to fuck you, Jinx said.

How vulgar of you. Of course he doesn't. He's clearly never seen a woman this close before. Many Diviner were supposedly asexual. Supposedly.

You think he puts on an impressive spread for just anyone?

Given the state of his apartment, it was highly unlikely, but I didn't feel any guilt for the expense Quen wasted on me.

Yesterday afternoon, we'd ordered in an impressive amount of food via his concierge service. Their menu covered the dietary needs for each domain, including kelp salad popular with the Amnae, sweet potato curry beloved by the Ember, pancakes and maple syrup favored by the Mesmer, a traditional Seren apple pie, a bowl of actual solid pebbles indulged in by the Umber, and the various nuts and seeds of the Zephyr, for a start.

Quen encouraged me to try a bite from each to see if any drew my attention, and I certainly made an attempt. I almost chipped a tooth on the Umber pebbles, though I balked at the meat skewers. Meat wasn't common in Chime, and only the Fauna and Leander held a taste for it. I'd half expected Quen to offer me a glass of blood and declare me a Necro.

I couldn't help but think he was bribing me with food to keep me happy, or to ensure I wouldn't run away to Grayford. Or perhaps it was guilt for putting me through such an intense interrogation. He'd spent hours grilling me—and Jinx—with various questions and personality tests, and I'd only left him with more questions.

I wasn't a Vesper. That much was obvious when Valeria failed to exert her power over me. I wasn't Diviner either, as Quen had prayed to his god and confirmed that Dor held no knowledge of my existence.

The Fauna could change shape much like I, but their forms were limited to those of animals, or humanoid-animals, and they could perform such changes without the need to touch another to do so, which I couldn't.

The Necro could alter their own skin and physiology, and suffered a roaring hunger as a result. But I actually had warm blood in my veins and my hunger was for cake, not flesh or blood.

We could safely rule out the Amnae, Leander, Seren, Umber, and Zephyr; I looked and acted nothing like them.

I most definitely was *not* a Glimmer, despite my female body and dislike of modesty, to which Quen agreed. A Glimmer wouldn't contain as many blasphemous thoughts as I did.

Though he'd entertained the idea that I could be Ember, especially after questioning my sex life—an awkward part of our questioning we'd hurried past.

But no, it seemed the closest domain that matched was the Mesmer, and as to that I wasn't convinced. They shared a connection with other minds, as I appeared to, but they certainly didn't fuck like I did.

I grabbed a teacake and opened up the Courier as Quen poured tea and nibbled on a bourbon biscuit. The morning view of Chime still stole my breath away. At nine o'clock, the Rapture Gate cast its red glow over Central Station. Eventide would open soon. I'd not be looking then.

All things considered, I was handling everything remarkably well.

You hardly slept, and you cried in the shower, Jinx said.

Yes, but all things considered.

The bell to Quen's apartment rang. "Ah, that'll be your new maid, and excellent timing, too. We can't have you visiting the Academy in my dressing robe." He left me to my second teacake and the Courier headlines.

It was the usual shit. News of the Wardens' plans to reinforce the clock tower, a minor scandal involving an Ember—always an Ember—celebrity gossip of a Seren revealing their latest art pieces, and Leander dominating the sports pages.

And there, tucked under an advert for Vesper pharmaceutical mushrooms: "We're coming for you, Kay?"

A coded message from Harmony.

The Godless were coming for me.

"And here we are," Quen was saying, as he escorted an Umber into the living room. "Kayl, this is—"

"Dru!" I said out loud, and scrambled from my chair.

Shit. I'd just blown her cover.

"Short for Drusilla," Dru quickly added. Her Umber eyes were bulging out of their sockets as they took in the sight of me—half-naked, sitting in a Diviner Warden's apartment eating teacakes. What must she think?

And you look like a Diviner.

Oh yes, there was that.

"You know each other?" Quen asked.

Dru bobbed a quick curtsy. "We bumped into each other in a laundromat once, sir. I'd never forget a face like hers."

I forced a smile. "Quite."

"Well, that *is* interesting," Quen mused. "Considering Kayl's face must have appeared completely different as a Vesper." His shrewd look turned from me to Dru. "There's no need for dramatics. I know who and what you are, Druzy Smith. Why else would I hire you?"

The golden flowers on Dru's head wilted, and fear rippled across her stony features.

I crossed my arms. "When you said you were hiring a maid—"

"I needed someone both of us could trust. And, by the way, Miss Smith, the speed with which your organization filled my application was rather suspicious. If you wish to remain in my employ and steal whatever secrets you will, then I'd only ask you act with more subtlety in future." Quen glanced at the window. "We'll need to leave in an hour for our meeting with Walter. Please don't dally."

"If you'll excuse us." I wrapped my arm around Dru's and dragged her into the guest room, which had temporarily become mine. Its small box shape contained a single bed, dresser, wardrobe, and a less impressive view of Chime's other tower blocks. Unlike the rest of Quen's apartment, this room was organized and clean—exactly what I expected of a Diviner.

And that was why I couldn't sleep. It was *too* orderly, and I missed the precarious swing of my old tram room back in the depot.

Dru closed the door behind me and leaned against it. "Kayl, I love you and I'm glad you're safe, but what is going on with you? Just—*how?*" she spluttered and gestured at me.

I sank onto the edge of the bed. "Malk's trapped in Eventide."

"Okay. We know that. We had eyes watching you enter and then arrive here. He's the same Warden from the elevator, isn't he? We thought he'd kidnapped you." I could hear the sense of betrayal wobble in her voice. "Why are you dining with a Warden?"

I sat Dru next to me and tried to explain everything that had happened since Malk and I entered the Glimmer estate, though my poor tired mind kept wandering off on tangents and needed to be yanked back on track. I described my newfound abilities, but kept Jinx to myself—no point in revealing that particular insanity yet.

Dru listened patiently. I'd wanted to grab her in a crushing hug and apologize for everything, but she truly looked hurt, confused, and scared. Of me.

"He knows we're Godless," Dru said, wringing her hands. "We need to get you out of here and back to the depot. If we can get you outside—"

"I can't."

"Can't? Or won't?"

Last night when I couldn't sleep, I'd considered sneaking out of here and hiding in Harmony's safe house only a few blocks away. Quen wouldn't be able to find me then, and the Godless would have recovered me quickly enough. Only Quen had turned me into a pissing Diviner, which meant I'd stand out for miles.

And I didn't want to return to Grayford, not yet.

"Quen is my only chance of getting Malk back—"

"*Quen*, is it?" Dru's eyes narrowed. "Do you know who he is? Quentin Corinth, killer of Vesper? The Dark Warden?"

"Yes, Dru, I know." Not that she'd recognized him on the elevator, either. "But look at me." I raised my silvery hands. "I need him to figure out what *I* am."

"Are you still one of us?"

Her doubt stung. "Always."

Quen rapped on the door from outside. "Time, ladies."

Time was always escaping me. "Listen, I *need* to follow this lead. You know we can't rescue Malk without help, and what better help than a Warden? A Diviner? I'm not letting Malk rot in Eventide. And Quen needs me as much as I need him, to discover who is behind these Diviner deaths."

"We're worried for you. Sinder is beside himself thinking it's his fault he didn't help with the Glimmer estate mission, and Reve's nightmares have gotten worse since you left—"

"Tell Sinder none of this is his fault and that I love him and miss him. Tell them all I'm doing this for Malk. And while you're here playing the part of my maid, think of what leads the Godless could find. He was investigating the Glimmer workhouses, Dru. We can't pass up this opportunity!" With the number of papers and files piled in Quen's apartment, Dru would certainly find something of interest. Not to mention the potential espionage by placing Godless in a Warden apartment. Really, I'd given Harmony a gift.

Not even the Godless's mystery benefactor could get us *this* level of intel.

And I wanted Dru here with me. Needed her. Even if I didn't quite understand Quen's intentions.

"I still don't trust Corinth. You've heard the stories; death follows him everywhere."

"You don't have to trust him." Though trouble certainly followed *me*. I stood up from the bed. "Now please tell me you've brought me something suitable to wear."

Dru rolled her eyes, more her old self, and she helped me dress in a smart, casual ensemble comprising a cream shirt, tan trousers, flats, and a tan jacket. I matched Quen's own tan suit, I realized, and perhaps that was deliberate.

Though now I was no longer owned by a Vesper god, and therefore technically no longer a Vesper, it meant I was free to dress how I wished. No more hiding my face behind a shawl. No more restrictive leggings or hot, itchy shirts to preserve my modesty.

And I'd actually be able to paint my nails and lips without needing to scrub them clean before stepping out of the depot.

Perhaps on our trip to the Golden City, I could convince Quen to stop off at a boutique.

Quen waited for me, leaning on the edge of his armchair and tapping his fob watch. "Are you always this tardy?"

"Get used to it," Dru mumbled.

He tucked his watch away and gave a little shake of his head. "Since we're now running behind schedule, I'll forego the pleasantries; Kayl, I want you to touch Miss Smith and take on her persona."

Dru recoiled. "You want to what?"

"You want two Umber maids?" I asked. "That's a little greedy, don't you think?"

Quen's lip quirked. "For the Silver Suite? There was one other reason I hired you, Miss Smith. I'm not sure how Kayl has explained the situation to you, but she can wear the persona, the visage if you will, of other domains. Unfortunately, wearing the mask of a female Diviner would only draw attention, especially in the Golden City. As an Umber, it wouldn't be odd for Kayl to be seen acting as my assistant."

I raised my brow. "Your assistant." I couldn't fault his logic, though he seemed to be forgetting we were meant to be partners.

"If you would kindly transform?" Quen said, peering over the rims of his eyeglasses.

Because 'transforming' was such a simple matter. I approached Dru, and she hesitantly stepped back. "I'm not going to hurt you, or steal your soul, or any of that."

"You're going to steal my soul?" Dru squeaked.

"*Not* steal your soul. Please trust me and give me your hand."

"Why am I always getting dragged into these impossible situations," Dru muttered, but she held out her hand.

I took her wrist with a firm grip. Instantly, I felt the tug. A tingling sensation rippled under my skin, and I pulled away quickly. Something tickled the back of my neck, and I reached round to tug at my hair. Only it wasn't my hair, but leaves. A whole cluster of them.

Dru was staring at me. "What. The. *Shit*."

Wowee. That's the first time Dru's ever sworn.

Jinx was right, I'd never heard Dru curse in her life. I glanced at my hands. They didn't feel any different, but the skin had turned a grayish blue with a stony texture to it, like the gravel around Meridian Park. I turned to the window and caught my reflection. Tiny flowers sprouted from my brow; three daisies on each side; blue and pink petals.

Quen eagerly skipped off to his kitchen and returned with a pot containing mint. The leaves had wilted, as though it hadn't been adequately watered in weeks. "Touch it. Make it grow."

His giddiness was infectious, though I was painfully aware of Dru's judging eyes watching my every interaction with him. I casually ran my fingers along the mint's stem, coaxing it. The wilted leaves perked up, responding to my touch.

Dru was shaking now. "Are you serious? Are you both serious?"

Quen seemed to remember her then. "Please don't faint, Miss Smith. I don't possess the muscle mass to catch you."

"Rude," I chided. "Aren't we supposed to be *catching* an elevator?"

"Ah, yes. Quite right. Miss Smith, if you could clear up breakfast? There are some leftover pebbles in the upper kitchen cupboard if you'd like to help yourself. We'll be back by lunch, if all goes well."

Dru sank into the dining chair, her mouth still gaping open with the look of a mortal who'd been slapped by their god. I didn't want to leave her alone in such shock.

She'll be fine. She knows you're crazy.

I'd given up hoping I was normal.

Quen offered me his arm. "Time won't wait."

I brushed past him and glanced over my shoulder. "No, it won't."

We needed to stop by Central Station's passport office first; I lacked the golden semicircle in my tattoo to grant access to the Golden City. The Necro who took my arm inked it with painstaking slowness and spoke with a low groan. Honestly, I was worried he'd die during the procedure. Quen tutted and tapped his foot, watching over my shoulder.

"I thought you Diviner were supposed to be patient," I said.

"Diviner are uniquely attuned to time, which means we are therefore painfully aware of when others waste it."

When we were done, Quen whisked me into the queue for the great glass elevator. I could barely hold my excitement. Quen rolled his eyes.

I twirled the vines of leaves stretching down my neck and I couldn't keep myself from touching my own petals.

A Glimmer standing in the queue gave me a disgusted look.

Offer her your flower. See if she takes it.

An Umber's flowers were supposed to be a sacred, personal relic offered only to close friends and loved ones. They held no such sentiment for me, though I supposed if Malk were here, I'd be plucking them for him. Maybe I'd give one to Dru as a peace offering.

Quen elbowed me. "Stop playing with yourself, we're in public."

I tried to smooth my daisies out, but they stuck out however they wanted. "Did you want one?" I offered to a Glimmer standing close by.

The Glimmer looked appalled.

Quen smiled through gritted teeth. "Please behave."

No promises.

On that, we agreed.

The elevator doors opened up, and I tried to hide my surprise. It appeared about the same size as the Undercity elevator, but the inner design was more gold than brass, and cushioned seats of various sizes were nailed to the floor.

One of the Diviner station staff checked my passport and welcomed me in. "Mind the gap, ma'am, and have a pleasant afternoon."

Certainly more pomp and politeness than the Undercity.

This queue wasn't a crowded mob that needed to squeeze together in order to fit inside. Instead, the various Diviner, Glimmer, and Seren casually took a seat. Even a Leander sat on a stool that allowed his tail to swish freely behind him. His fur was stuffed inside a tight tuxedo and he wore a ridiculous top hat where space had been cut out for his fluffy ears.

I'd never realized Leander could be so fancy.

Only a few mortals stood by the window, though as Quen went to take a seat, I grabbed his arm and dragged him over. Like his apartment, the glass panes that the elevator was named for stretched from floor to ceiling.

The last few stragglers found their seats and the station staff called time. There weren't enough mortals on board to fill it, and the passengers busied themselves with casual conversations or reading the Chime Courier.

Bright aether lights glared above, and I cringed away from them, staring out of the window. Steam hissed from below.

Then we lifted, and we rose above the station. Higher.

I held onto Quen's arm as the streets of Central Square grew smaller and smaller, and then the buildings and even Quen's tower block shrank to tiny oblongs.

"You know, I don't actually *like* heights," Quen muttered.

"You live on the thirteenth floor of an apartment."

"The thirteenth floor doesn't move up and down."

"It's elevators that bother you?" He'd mentioned being uncomfortable with elevators the first time we'd met, hadn't he? "Why?"

Quen shifted uncomfortably. "I had an accident as a child."

I waited for him to continue, and when he didn't, I asked, "Are you going to elaborate?"

"There's nothing *to* elaborate. I barely remember the event."

"I thought Diviner could explore their past like reading a book?"

His raised eyebrow implied that I'd asked a stupid question. "Would you peruse the worst parts of your past if they brought you fear and pain?"

I supposed not. "But this is amazing. Why is no one else watching?"

"It loses its novelty after a while."

How could it? The buzzing aether grew louder, louder even than the Undercity elevator, and pain throbbed in my head. I kept a tight grip on Quen's arm, this time for stability. "I feel sick. It's the aether."

Quen gently pulled me to a nearby empty chair and forced me to sit. I cradled my head in my hands. The buzzing grew into a deafening screech and I clenched my eyes shut against the blinding light, willing it to go away, but it only grew the higher we rose.

"It takes a great deal of aether to power the elevator," Quen whispered. He rubbed his hand along my back in soothing circular motions. "I'm sorry. I had no idea it would affect you this way."

"Neither did I," I mumbled, and then gagged. "Shit, I think—I think I'm going to decorate the floor."

Aim for a Glimmer's shoes.

Why does aether hurt us, Jinx?

Because we are aether.

Gods, why must you talk in such annoying riddles?

Not riddles, idiot. Everything is made of aether when you break it down.

I was about to break down, all right.

Quen borrowed a spare copy of the Courier and quickly fashioned it into a bag shape. He shoved it between my hands. "Don't miss."

I didn't.

As the elevator came to a shrieking stop, this morning's teacakes made an unwelcome reappearance. Quen apologized to the offended Glimmer nearby, explaining it was my first time, and then he was ushering me off the elevator into bright sunlight.

Actual sunlight. I massaged my temples as I lifted my eyes to the sky.

Gods, I'd never seen the sky like this.

No large plate hung over the city, blocking everything except the horizon in shadow and blinking aether. Instead, an endless beautiful blue dotted with white candy floss stretched over us like a dome.

"How high does it go?"

"No one knows. Are you feeling any better?"

"I think so." I lowered my eyes and blinked against the sun reflecting across the plaza in a glittering mosaic. I could see where the Golden City earned its name.

The rows of tiny cafés and boutiques weren't too different from those in Central, though the town houses here weren't simple brick and plaster, but beautiful brass and gold with vines of lush leaves and sprouting wisteria trailing down the walls.

Everything looked so *clean*.

No soot. No grime. Not a single flier taped to a lamppost, or an abandoned copy of the Courier fluttering into the gutter. In fact, the streets were so clean, it was as though no mortal stepped foot on the surface at all, and they simply hovered across the cobblestones.

It was then I noticed that no aether buzzed in the air, either, and for the first time, I could truly breathe.

Though my attention was pulled elsewhere.

Each of the store windows held an enticing treasure, from extravagant hats covered in feathers to luxury purses, gorgeous heels, and the latest fashions.

Floral tea dresses were *in* this season, it appeared, and by the gods, I wanted one.

I ran up to the nearest window and squashed my nose against the glass.

Only Glimmer and Seren browsed the various blouses, skirts, and dresses; they didn't need to stare forlornly from outside the window. I swallowed a sigh at the ridiculous price tag for a simple pair of shoes. Hundreds of bocs!

A Glimmer shoved past me, her large parasol almost clipping my ear. "Watch where you put your dirty fingers. Honestly, the hired help these days have no manners."

Hired help?

Right, I was still wearing the face of an Umber.

If I'd been a Vesper, no doubt she'd have called the Wardens on me for trespassing.

I wished Malk were here to knock her down a peg. He'd make an obscene joke about the Glimmer and their wealth. These high-class tarts wore enough bocs to feed every mouth in Grayford.

They've got so much gold, they shit out bocs in their golden toilets.

Thank you for filling in, Jinx.

Quen strode to my side. "If you've finished gawking, we're running a little late." He pulled out his fob watch again. though I wasn't sure why— even as a fake Diviner, I'd held a vague sense of the time. "We'll take a carriage to the Academy—"

"Not a tram?"

"We don't want to draw any more attention to ourselves." He looked down at me over the rim of his eyeglasses, which was an impressive feat considering I stood taller. "Unless you need time to rest?"

"I'll rest when the gods do."

"Eloquently put. Now do remember we're entering the heart of academia in Chime. We wouldn't want to offend anyone with your, ah, uncultured opinions."

"I'd have thought the heart of academia would be interested in expanding their horizons."

"We're here for a purpose. Let's not jeopardize it."

Yes, the purpose of allowing some Amnae boffin to root through my memories.

I pulled away from the boutique window.

This wasn't my world and never would be. My world was hidden in darkness and buried deep underground where mortals could think freely.

I could never forget that.

In my quest to find a god, I was certain I wouldn't like the god I'd find.

XV

While most domains have their own unique peculiarities which must be accommodated on Chime, the Amnae are the most difficult.
Most come from Memoria ill-equipped to breathe Chime's air and struggle to adapt. The gills on their neck mean they must have access to a regulated water source should breathing difficulties arise.
Many suffer from asthma as a result.
Businesses must strive to make their premises accessible for Amnae by providing a 'steaming' station where moisture can be pumped into the air.
Alternatively, suitable saltwater beverages can offset these difficulties.
—Q. Corinth, *Warden Dossier on the Amnae*

AH, THE ACADEMY. ONE of my favorite places in Chime.

The carriage made good time as we rode through the cobblestone streets. Kayl's head was practically hanging out of the window the entire journey, playing the part of impressionable tourist remarkably well. I supposed to an Undercity resident, or even a Central citizen, the Golden City had its charm. All brass buildings, marble statues, flowing fountains, and perfectly tailored bushes.

It was a work of art carefully maintained by a council of Diviner, Glimmer, and Seren, though the Amnae and Zephyr made their contributions.

Like the gods, the golden veneer was more show than character.

The only exception being Chime's Academy.

"We couldn't have stopped by the theater?" Kayl pouted as we exited our carriage. "Their shows only last, what, six hours?"

"I'm sure you'd rather not suffer six hours of a Glimmer play." I certainly didn't fancy the thought.

We took a leisurely stroll across the campus green. Kayl skipped and bobbed ahead with the boundless energy of a Fauna pup, and not the more demure and reserved nature of the Umber whose face she now wore. There I was, trying to categorize her again, but she truly baffled me. The more time I spent in her company, the more confused I became.

"Why do they look so different?" She pointed ahead to the two main buildings.

We walked the path which split the Academy into two schools; the School of Art and the School of Mechanics. While the School of Art's more traditional architecture of gothic stone and marble fit in with the aesthetic of the Golden City, the School of Mechanics was more of a brass workhouse full of cogs and contraptions. They were essentially separate, with their own lecture halls, library, and student dormitories, but the departments often mingled.

If not, I might never have met Elijah. "One is for the philosophers and artists, and the other is for the engineers and scientists. It's like that old saying: art is the heart of Chime, but engineering is the backbone holding society together."

"Art brats and nerds? Got it. You were with the nerds, right?"

I straightened my spectacles. "What makes you say so?"

"No reason." She flashed a smile. "You told me you trained to be a tram driver."

Ah, so she *had* listened to my rambling back on Eventide. "That's why I joined the School of Mechanics. But my particular talents were wasted there, and so I transferred to the School of Art."

I could have studied in any of the domains; indeed, it was expected of me to attend the most prestigious university on either Kronos or Memoria. But Chime was my home, and one of the few places offering mechanical scholarships for tram drivers.

Alas, fate swung me into the study of horology, philosophy, and mnemonics. How fortunate that my favorite professor ended up being an Amnae.

"And they didn't teach you how to organize your papers?"

"My papers *are* organized," I said with some indignation, and pushed on ahead, diverting our path to the School of Art.

At this time of day, lectures would be in full swing, and as we climbed the stone steps leading to the main hall, only a few students passed by on their way between classes; Glimmer and Seren mostly, studying either literature or other arts.

"This looks like a museum," Kayl said as we stepped past the outer columns.

The main hall appeared just as impressive inside as it was out, what with its domed glass ceiling and wall frescoes depicting some of the more famous alumni mid-lecture. Portraits hung in the alcoves above carefully carved marble busts; these, too, were some of Chime's more well-known saints and ambassadors, including my dear Elijah.

Though his jutting marble chin didn't quite match the flesh I knew more intimately.

The School of Art had once been a place of sanctuary, and, as Kayl had rightly put it, a home for free-thinkers. But since the Glimmer took over much of the Golden City, their influence poisoned the waters of the Academy, and many of my favorite philosophy professors were silenced, if not outright exiled.

Ironic, that the last bastion of free thought belonged to the Undercity, to those my peers would likely sneer at. To the blasphemers.

Gold didn't buy freedom; it only enshrined it with gilded locks.

I beckoned Kayl along one of the many tiled halls and she bounded from one side to the other, peeking inside the classrooms. "Are they playing music? Is that allowed?"

I glanced around her shoulder. Seren were gathered inside one of the orchestra halls for their harp recitals, though neither of us could hear it. "Soundproof rooms. The Academy is one of the few places in Chime where Seren are legally permitted to sing."

"How depressing that they need a Warden's permission to perform such a natural act."

"When a mortal's 'natural act' can endanger others, then such laws must be set." One of my very first cases as a Warden was to arrest a rogue

Seren who'd used their siren's call to manipulate a jeweler into handing over a small fortune.

"I'm surprised the Covenant doesn't cover who gets to fuck who, you're all such busybodies. But then I could just imagine the horror of Diviner needing to negotiate in marital disputes. They'd blow a gasket."

Well, she was right in that; in marital disputes, the Wardens often sent Umber. They possessed a more sympathetic ear, and if disputes became rowdy, they also possessed the brawn to deal with them. "You'd be surprised how far our jurisdiction goes."

"Would I?" She slid to the next classroom window before I had a chance to form a retort. "Oh, look, a Glimmer sermon disguised as a play. Apparently, you can break the Covenant so long as your preaching is considered art."

"Self-expression *is* allowed—"

"Only for Glimmer? Would you watch a Vesper play? They make far better actors with only shadow puppets for props." She glanced around the hall. "Not that I've seen a single Vesper student. Shouldn't the Wardens be advocating for scholarships for *all* mortals? I'm sure I read *something* about equality in the Covenant—"

"We're not here to debate ethics."

"I thought this would be the ideal place to debate ethics—"

"You're supposed to be my assistant. Please act like it."

She came to my side and bumped into my shoulder. "Yessir. Who is this professor we're meeting?"

"Professor Walter Burns, a lecturer in mnemonics and memory recall. That's what his research is based on—the concept of memory storage, transference, and retrieval between mortals of different domains."

"Sounds complex. Do you trust him?"

"I'd trust him with my deepest, darkest secrets." And memories, too.

"Do you have many deep, dark secrets, Quen?"

"I'm gallivanting with a Godless, so there's that." We approached the back end of the building, which opened out to various glass conservatories and greenhouses. Here, the school taught horticulture, popular with the Umber students who helped tend the Golden City farms that kept Chime fed. And it was in one of these greenhouses we'd find Walter. "You may want to remove your jacket. Walter's laboratory can get quite stuffy."

Sure enough, upon entering the greenhouse I was immediately beset by humidity that steamed my spectacles. I pulled out a cloth and cleaned them as Kayl's blurry shape wandered in front.

"Quentin! Good morning, dear fellow!" called a cheery Walter from somewhere. His voice always sounded a little garbled, as though he spoke from underwater. "And you must be his lovely new assistant."

I shoved my spectacles on to see Kayl offering a polite curtsy. "Yes, I'm one of Quen's deepest, darkest secrets."

Heat rose to my cheeks that had nothing to do with the humidity, and I found my tongue suddenly tied.

Walter laughed her off in good humor. "Aren't we all, my dear? Would you like some tea? I've got a pot brewing. Quentin can never resist my herbal recipes." He sat by a table covered in a mass of alchemical bottles, glass jars, and burners that were bubbling away some bizarre purple liquid next to a kettle of green tea. I wasn't one for herbal teas normally, but his brews perked me up.

"This is incredible," Kayl whispered.

Yes, it was.

Flowering rosemary, thyme, and other herbs cascaded down the glass walls of Walter's office, acting as a natural curtain for privacy. Brass pipes ran across the ceiling and puffed a never-ending supply of steam into the air, which generated the humidity Walter needed to work in comfort. Amnae needed the moisture, though the room also contained an enormous bathtub, deep enough to soak in.

Metal contraptions filled half the room, connecting to the pipes needed for his memory recall experiments—all waterproofed, of course—and leading straight to his alchemical setup. He didn't have any books or scrolls to keep his ideas and formulae in order; he kept all that inside of his head.

All he required was his font of memories, a small basin where he could dip in and retrieve them at will. Though his shelves were stocked with various alchemical ingredients: Vesper mushrooms, Mesmer candies,

Umber rocks, plus coral and kelp from his own domain, which gave off a strong salty scent of seaweed.

"How does he breathe?" Kayl asked as she observed the good professor.

I supposed they didn't get many Amnae in the Undercity. "Carefully."

Walter was fairly typical for his domain; his skin was translucent teal with spots of gold that looked more see-through around his webbed feet and fingers. He never wore shoes, only slipping into sandals around campus, and his office attire consisted of loose slacks and a shirt that was never buttoned to the collar.

The gills at his neck had adapted to Chime's air. His face thankfully resembled a mortal more than a fish, though to those unaccustomed to Amnae, he still cut a surprising figure with sharp ridges atop his head instead of hair, and flapping fins instead of ears.

He approached, balancing a tray of tea. "Please, take a seat." He gestured to the spare recliners, and Kayl and I made ourselves at home. "I'm afraid we're out of snacks. I like to keep stocked up on these exceedingly good cakes from Mr. Kipler's back on Memoria, but alas. They pair so well with my teas."

I helped myself to a cup. "We didn't come for tea and cake, Professor."

"It's just as well." Walter sat and faced Kayl. "Quentin tells me you're having trouble recalling your childhood. Is that right?"

I nodded to Kayl, urging her to answer as I blew across my tea. "Tell him about your friend, Jinx. Spare no detail."

Kayl took a deep breath and recounted our last few days together in haphazardous detail. If Walter had brows, they'd be furrowed right now as he took it all in.

Instead, he leaned back and his slitted eyes blinked. "You don't know your own god, but you have a voice speaking inside of you? A twin soul?"

I cleared my throat. "I know it sounds a little far-fetched—"

"No, no, I've come across something similar through reading accounts of Necro surgeries. The gods create variance among their mortals, that's how we're so different, but sometimes mortals are born with abnormalities. Six fingers instead of five, one eye instead of two, a mortal who feels trapped in the wrong body, and so on."

"You're saying I'm abnormal?" Kayl's voice raised in alarm.

"I don't mean it negatively, my dear. We are all wonderful as we are. Though there have been accounts of two mortals born connected to the same body; twins conjoined by their limbs or vital organs. I've never heard of a conjoined soul, but it follows the same logic."

"What does that mean? Can we be separated?"

"Without a body, it's highly unlikely. Even conjoined twins cannot be separated if their organs are too interwoven. It would kill them both. There's no technology on Chime that could separate a soul, and even if there were, it would likely kill you."

Kayl cringed. "Jinx doesn't approve. If the gods are so perfect, then why create such abnormalities? Why make their mortals suffer so?"

Her words were bordering on blasphemy, but Walter again shrugged that off. "Because the gods like to test us, and to experience variation of mortal bodies for themselves."

"So the gods made me wrong as an experiment? A test?" She scowled in my direction. "Are you sure I'm not Diviner?"

"Whatever you are, you and your twin's souls are the same," Walter said. "Same domain, same god. A body cannot possess the soul of another domain."

It came down to discovering Kayl's true patron god. At least that meant she hadn't been manipulated or possessed by another domain. But this only answered one of my questions. "Can you check her memories for any clues?"

"Of course. If you're ready, my dear?"

Kayl slurped her tea and leaned back in the recliner. I'd experienced Walter's memory-tinkering many times, enough to understand the procedure didn't hurt, but could feel a little odd. She giggled slightly as the suckers which formed his fingertips lodged onto her forehead, beside the petals sprouting from her brows.

Walter closed his eyes. "Now, my dear, try to relax as I ride the rivers of your memories."

"Don't get lost in the stream." Her silvery-blue eyes met mine, and she winked.

I hid a smile behind my cup as I finished the last dregs.

We sat in quiet anticipation as Walter went *hmm* and *ahh*, and then he released her with a frown. "Confound it."

I placed my cup down and leaned forward. "Your powers don't work on her, either?"

"Apparently not."

"What if she touched you? Became an Amnae?"

Kayl sat up. "You want me to become a *fish*? No offense."

"None taken," Walter said. "Will this work?"

I grinned. "Only one way to find out."

Tentatively, Kayl wrapped her hand around Walter's wrist. For a second, nothing happened, and then I stared in wonder as the change took hold. The flowers of her brow receded, replaced with fleshy ridges and fins. Gills materialized on her neck, and her skin changed to semitranslucent silvery-blue scales with spots of pink.

The same colors she'd transformed into as a Diviner, an Umber.

The same colors as her eyes.

The colors of aether.

She examined her webbed fingers and tested the suction of her fingertips on the back of her hand as Walter strode around her in circles, examining her from all angles.

"This is incredible!" he exclaimed. "I've never seen anything like it!"

"You see why we need to keep this quiet," I pointed out.

Kayl opened her mouth to say something and gasped. She sucked in air and rubbed the gills at her neck, which now flapped erratically. "Can't breathe," she croaked.

I was on my feet in an instant.

"The tub," Walter ordered.

Together, Walter and I lifted her up and carried her carefully over discarded wires to the bathtub. She continued to make awful rasping sounds as we gently lowered her into the water. She sank below the surface with a gargled scream, and for a terrible moment I thought we'd drowned her.

But then her head breached the surface and her breathing returned to normal.

She gripped the edges of the bathtub and glared up at me. "You do realize," she panted, "that I'm still wearing my clothes."

Yes, I suppose she was, even the shoes.

Blast it.

"It's no bother," Walter said. "We'll fetch one of the Ember engineering apprentices, they'll dry your clothes."

Kayl's cool aether eyes met mine. "You want me to bare myself to you after all?"

Such a thought warmed my cheeks. "Let's stay on task. Professor, if you will?"

Walter placed his fingers on her forehead. "Ah hah!"

"You can see her memories?"

"Yes, now *shush*."

I rocked back on my heels. My Diviner power still hadn't worked, even when she'd taken on the role of a Diviner. It was a blessing, I suppose; I couldn't violate her memories, nor would I be cursed with visions of her death.

It was impossible to maintain relationships with anyone, even my fellow Diviner, when a single touch would show me their demise. How could I look them in the eye with such knowledge? At first, I'd wiped those memories and chosen ignorance in order to maintain friendships, but every touch brought them back.

So I'd chosen the next available path; I'd distanced myself. I couldn't confess why, and over time those relationships crumpled into nothing. Forgotten.

Only Elijah knew my true nature and demanded such obedience that he forbade me from distancing from him.

But Kayl... she didn't realize how precious that gift was.

Somewhere in the tub, she'd lost her shoes, and her webbed toes were making tiny splashes as she hummed some nonsensical tune. I didn't truly know what was her, and what was the being inside—Jinx, she called it— though I supposed it mattered not.

Whatever Kayl or Jinx were, their protection came under my jurisdiction.

Even if Elijah and the Wardens would ultimately disagree.

Walter hissed and yanked his hand back as though he'd been stung.

"What did you see?" I asked as Kayl craned her head around to listen.

"Your memories only stretch to thirteen years. A wall of light blocked me after that. Such light typically denotes birth or creation."

Kayl looked appalled. "You're saying I'm only thirteen years old?"

"Essentially, yes. I saw no parental figures, nothing that indicated birth."

That wasn't entirely unusual. "What domain?" If we knew that, then we had our answer.

Walter looked stricken. "She appeared in darkness, in soot and muck, under aether lights."

"The Undercity," I whispered. "That's impossible. Births happen on Chime, yes, but no god can send a soul through the Gate to materialize there." The Gate was deliberately warded to prevent immortal energies from making the crossing, which effectively stopped the gods from directly interfering with Chime or other domains. But the Gate recycled such massive amounts of aether to power it—surely a soul couldn't survive?

"Souls travel through the Gate upon death. Perhaps one of the gods learned how to do it in reverse. It might explain why she possesses two souls, if they got jumbled together."

Then we were back to square one. I removed my spectacles and rubbed my forehead.

Which god would be foolish enough—ambitious enough—to attempt such a feat?

And which was capable of creating a mortal with shape-shifting powers like hers?

I was going to find the nearest brick wall and smash my skull against it. *Make it make sense, Quen.*

"My advice," Walter was saying, "is to seek one of the Mesmer's dream parlors. They can regress into another's subconsciousness far better than you or I. And they have experience of sharing minds. Perhaps even twin souls. It's worth looking into."

It came back to the Mesmer.

"Thank you, Professor. Your expertise is appreciated as always, as is your discretion."

Walter bowed his head. "It's my pleasure. Now, my dear, let's sort out your clothing situation. I'll summon a custodian."

He left us as Kayl removed her clothes and slid the soggy mess over the tub. I couldn't see anything from where I sat, but I averted my eyes anyhow. A gentleman never looked.

"Are you sure you trust him?" she asked as her soaked blouse fell with a squelch. "I *am* Godless. He would have seen many incriminating things."

"Don't worry. He'll wipe his own memories of them."

"That easy, is it?"

"That easy."

"So what now? I go for a nap?"

I dabbed the sweat off my forehead with a handkerchief. The humidity was finally getting to me. "There're plenty of Mesmer parlors in the Golden City or down in Central, not counting the domain of Phantasy itself, of course. I'll need to do some research; it's imperative we find one that takes client confidentiality seriously. Which rules out the Golden City, and also Phantasy." The last thing I wanted was to attract the attention of Mesmorpheus. Though if all signs kept pointing to Kayl being a Mesmer, we'd need to have that confrontation sooner than later.

"You probably won't approve, but I have a suggestion—Sinner's Row."

"You're right, I don't approve—"

"It's the only place where we'll be guaranteed absolute confidentiality. When your clients are criminals, it's poor business to spread secrets."

Damn it, I hated that she was right. The businesses of Sinner's Row could get away with all sorts of depraved and illegal activities, which is exactly what my Godless friend here needed. That, and I was on good terms with the Ember ambassador. He would ensure our visit went unnoticed.

"I'll have to touch you before we go," she said. "I won't be going anywhere in this state." She wiggled her webbed fingers.

Right again. Blast it, we'd just have to hope no one noticed a female Diviner leaving the Academy.

The greenhouse door opened and Walter returned with a nervous looking Ember lad dressed in a blacksmith's apron. Hrm. An Ember persona would work better for where we were headed.

I slapped my thighs and stretched to my feet. "Well, then—"

Blinding light flashed in my vision, and I staggered back.

Then the familiar and comforting darkness of eternity found me.

The creature stood in the shape of a mortal, but it radiated silvery-blue light. It reached for me, pointing a damning finger that sparked pink.

All around me, the air hummed, thick with the taste of raw aether.

Gods. No. It had found me.

It knew what I worked on deep underground.

It knew what souls I worked to rend.

And now it had come for mine.

"Father!" I screamed. "Save me! Please, Father—"

"Is Quen all right?" Kayl was asking.

I panted and squeezed the bridge of my nose. Slowly, the black dots of my vision cleared and reality returned with only a mild headache. Though the images remained.

Another aether creature. And in the background, my quarry so clearly stood within an engine room full of hissing pipes. The steamworks.

Walter held my arm steady. "A vision, dear boy?"

I sank against the recliner as both Kayl and the Ember student gawked at me. "Yes, sorry." I offered them both an apologetic smile. "Don't mind me. I sometimes receive urgent visions from my god of a mortal's, ah, unfortunate circumstances."

Kayl sat up in the tub, splashing water over the sides. "What did you see that was so unfortunate?"

Death.

Always death.

So many of my fellow Diviner experienced random bouts of déjà vu, usually innocent and mild visions of no consequence. Occasionally, if Father felt it necessary, He'd bless us with greater visions that put a Mesmer's dreams to shame. Visions that helped correct our paths should our hearts and minds stray into sin.

But it wasn't enough for me to be cursed with seeing a mortal's demise through touch. My indenture with the Wardens meant Father could direct me to danger He'd foreseen Himself—transfer those visions to me—and I'd have no choice but to act on them.

And always, I dreamed of death.

"There's been another Diviner attack down in the steamworks. I need to investigate it immediately." I grimaced. "It looks like we'll be visiting the Undercity after all."

16

The Zephyr are an inquisitive lot that like to tinker with machinery. Many of Chime's innovations are incorrectly credited to the Diviner and were instead created by Zephyr minds. Their domain of Tempest is full of such technological wonders which, unfortunately, are far too advanced for Chime's infrastructure.

Their brilliant minds, however, do not translate into social skills, and they lack an awareness of the other domains. This aloofness can cause friction. The Zephyr require space to spread their wings, both physically and metaphysically.

—Q. Corinth, Warden Dossier on the Zephyr

IT HAD BEEN DAYS since I last stepped foot in the Undercity.

A part of me relaxed in the familiar company of the dim aether lights and beckoning shadows, but a stronger part nurtured guilt.

The Godless believed me to be caught in the clutches of the Vesper-murdering Dark Warden while Malk quite literally was in the clutches of an all-powerful Vesper-enslaving monster. I had to remind myself I was doing this for him—to find answers for *him*. But the more I learned of myself, the less sure I felt we'd find the right answers at all.

What would appease a god like Valeria? What treasure was worth Malk's soul?

At least my new body was entertaining. The Amnae professor had brewed a particularly pungent concoction he'd tricked the poor Ember boy into drinking, which had knocked him out cold. But at least I could leave in his form without arousing suspicion.

My skin had turned a dark pink, rather than the flame-red of Sinder, and the two horns growing from my skull had silvery-blue tips. Though the most remarkable part was the power to summon flame with a snap of my fingers. An ability Quen warned me not to play with.

Now we can burn our way through Eventide.

The thought had apparently crossed both of our minds.

Though the Amnae boffin had confirmed Jinx and I were stuck together. I wasn't sure how I felt about it. My thoughts had always been mine, so I'd once assumed, and having another soul joyriding inside my head was both comforting and violating.

I didn't ask to be stuck with you either, Jinx had said on the way back to the glass elevator. *But I want what you've always wanted, so we'll make the best of it.*

What do we both want?

To end the reign of gods.

An ambitious goal that enticed my sinful heart. But could that even be possible?

Anything's possible if you put your mind to it, and you've got two minds.

Somehow, I didn't believe our combined minds would be enough to end the reign of gods, but at least we were on the same page. Though I supposed we'd never have made it this far together if Jinx possessed the pious constitution of a Glimmer.

Riding the glass elevator down to Central had renewed my nausea, and so Quen and I had stopped by a tea stand and I'd ordered myself a lemon iced tea, though he hadn't approved. "Tea should be hot. Anything less is a travesty," he'd muttered.

He'd sent off a telegram warning our destination of our impending arrival and then, as we'd found a quiet bench to rest my stomach, he'd turned to me with knitted brows. "You should return to my apartment and wait with Miss Smith. Where I'm going may not be safe."

"You know I was quite literally born in the Undercity." A fact that I hadn't wrapped my head around yet.

"I'm chasing a Diviner-killer. Whoever—whatever—is killing them isn't likely to be a friendly fellow."

"I can handle myself." I'd snapped my fingers and produced a flicker of fire. "See?"

"It's not your, ah, abilities that concern me. I'll be heading to the steamworks which contain the largest aether generators in Chime. You won't be able to withstand that much aether. You barely managed the elevator."

"Let me concern myself with what I can and cannot withstand. I thought the whole point of this exercise was to find the connection between myself and these aether attacks? How can I do that if I hide in your apartment?"

Quen had appeared uneasy, the first real time I'd seen him so uncomfortable, but he'd relented in the end. And so we rode the elevator down to the depths of Chime and caught the woefully empty tram.

I'd never set foot inside the steamworks. I'd had no reason to. But many of Grayford's poorest found work there and shared their tales. The Godless's mystery benefactor had blown the whistle on a few cases where mortal safety hadn't been adhered to, resulting in lost fingers or worse.

It was dirty, dangerous labor, but the pay was better than what the Glimmer offered for their factories and workhouses. Vesper could work in the dark and cramped tunnels with ease, Umber didn't feel the extreme heat and steam, and neither did the Ember, whose flame came in handy to relight the engines.

The steamworks were the heart of Chime, and their pipes were the vessels which kept the city alive. Without them, the aether lamps wouldn't burn, the elevator wouldn't rise and descend, and the Gate wouldn't cycle between the domains.

As the tram pulled into the station, it wasn't hard to miss our destination.

A monstrous black building not too dissimilar to Valeria's castle filled the skyline, but instead of harsh angles and sharp points, curved pipes protruded from its back like threatening tendrils.

Some pipes were the size of mansions and connected to the Undercity's ceiling plate, no doubt delivering power. Others pumped out steam and soot. Even from a distance, I could sense the hum of aether in the air, and it groaned and hissed as though a beast truly made its nest underground.

An ache was already forming in my forehead.

Quen observed me over the rim of his eyeglasses. "How are you feeling?"

I scowled at him. "Annoyed by your constant questions and concern. I'm fine, Quen. Honestly."

He looked unconvinced. "Honesty isn't one of your abilities. We should have made you transform into a Seren. At least they're small enough that I'd stand a chance of dragging your carcass out of here should you collapse."

I pulled a face and skipped off the platform.

With each step, the foreboding hum grew louder.

I hate it here, Jinx whined.

Why?

Can't you taste the death in the air?

I could taste soot and oil and sense an odd static discharge. If my Ember body contained any hair, I was sure it'd be standing on edge.

Diviner in jumpsuits guarded the metal gate that blocked our entrance. They let us in with a flash of Quen's badge, though they spared no interest for me. I supposed an Ember entering the steamworks wasn't unusual.

We passed through double doors and the monster swallowed us whole.

The inner steamworks was just as oppressive. Aether lamps buzzed and flickered above a dismal reception desk. Metal chairs cluttered the waiting area, which stocked copies of the Courier as well as a magazine on energy solutions, or something equally dull. Both were stained with coffee.

A bored Vesper woman slouched at reception and was too busy picking her nails to notice our arrival.

"Isn't this charming," I whispered.

Quen simply tutted.

Footsteps echoed from a corridor labeled 'Maintenance–Employees Only' and a man stepped through covered in a mane of white hair.

At first, I thought he was another Diviner; his hair was almost silver in the glare of the aether lamps. He was dressed in a white lab coat over a gray suit and held a clipboard with that arrogant air of disinterest that most Diviner carried.

But as he approached, I realized the mane of hair wasn't hair at all, but tufts of white feathers which turned sky blue at the tips. And the long shadow of his nose was actually a beak that took up half of his face. A bird's beak. The fingers clinging to his clipboard were claws, and his feet were long talons supported by custom-made sandals.

A Zephyr. But where were his wings?

The Zephyr approached and offered Quen a curt nod. "Master Corinth, I presume?" he said with a shrill voice. "By my estimations, you are late." He cocked his head sharply. "I do believe you must be the first Diviner in Chime to suffer from tardiness. I hope there is a cure."

How rude!

Quen gave me an exasperated look, as though he blamed *me*. "We came as quickly as we could, Master...?"

"Doctor Zachery Finch."

"A pleasure to make your acquaintance, Doctor. This is my assistant—"

"Yes, yes. Please follow me and keep up. The subject is waiting." The doctor turned sharply into the corridor, and I couldn't help but stare at his back.

I'd heard terrible stories of both Seren and Zephyr losing their wings as punishment from their god, but there were no bumps or ridges protruding along the doctor's spine like Varen's scars. Nothing to indicate he'd ever owned wings at all.

A Zephyr without wings was like an Amnae without gills. An Ember without flame. A Vesper without shadow. A Diviner out of time.

Utterly unnatural.

Was he another abnormality like me?

Ask him, Jinx prodded.

Gods, no. I may be terrible, but I wasn't going to pry into another mortal's business.

I kept up with the doctor's brisk pace, his clawed feet tapping the concrete floor. Grime clung to the upper corridor walls, and the aether lamps flickered menacingly. I cringed away from their brightness. We passed door after door and the corridor seemed to twist and turn for an eternity. The hum of aether grew louder and rattled under my feet, as though the growl of a belly welcomed such tasty mortals in its lair.

Don't go any further, Jinx warned.

We need to examine the body.

You won't like what you'll find.

At last, the doctor stopped before a metal door with the word 'Coolants' written across it. "We thought we needed to store the subject somewhere cold. It appears that wasn't necessary."

We followed him inside a freezing room and my Ember skin instantly rebelled at the temperature. Large canisters were stacked inside, most covered in a powdery white. Icicles hung from a grate in the ceiling, which blew in cold air.

Below that, a gurney had been left covered in a fire blanket. Though the blanket was thick enough to hide what was underneath, the outline was clear.

A body. A physical shell of a mortal without its soul.

I crossed my arms over my chest and kept my distance.

Bodies weren't supposed to linger, were they? The Vesper woman who'd escaped from the Glimmer workhouse had crumbled into dust almost immediately. Even Vincent had described the grotesque experiments the Necro performed on bodies; they were catatonic when they were dissected and examined, but still alive.

Quen's eyeglasses were perched on his nose, ready for business. "Tell me everything, Doctor. Let's start with the subject, and then we'll cover the circumstances."

"We found the subject beside one of our reactors approximately two hours and fifty-three minutes ago." Doctor Finch flapped a hand at the body, and a stray feather came loose. "A Diviner named Doctor Hector Bezel. Day shift. Worked here for thirteen years, eleven months, six weeks, two days—"

"Yes, thank you. What was Hector working on at the time?"

"Doctor Bezel headed the project designed to trap energy leaking from the clock tower. He'd been running calibrations to the pressure pump for Reactor A, Pipe C. It converts steam to aether."

At the very word, my head throbbed. "How does that work?"

"We're not here to discuss physics," Quen chided. "Tell me more of this project."

These eggheads play with forces they don't understand.

And you understand them, do you, Jinx?

You don't hear the screaming.

What screaming?

"Our calibrations have been off with the recent aether leaks and thus required more extensive fine-tuning," Doctor Finch was saying. "In other words, the aether is malfunctioning and creating more volatile reactions. We assumed Doctor Bezel's death to be an unfortunate electrical accident, but... not even we can explain this." His eagle eyes turned sharply to the body.

"Do you know what's causing these leaks?" I asked.

The doctor glanced at me then for the first time, as though he'd forgotten I was there. "The conclusion is an obvious side effect."

"Assume I never passed my engineering classes at the School of Electric Lamps or whatever. What is so obvious?"

His feathers ruffled, though I didn't think it was possible for a beak to scowl.

"A city as large as Chime requires a tremendous amount of power," Quen explained, apparently *now* happy to talk physics. "And as Chime grows, it consumes more. The steam power we rely on is no longer sufficient, hence the need for aether. You know there're rivers of lava below the Undercity, yes? Those, along with artificial water tunnels, generate steam, and the steamworks convert it to aether, but this process is volatile. Essentially, the more power that's generated and piped throughout Chime, the more of it leaks out at the seams."

I still didn't understand *how* steam became aether, or what aether even was. A staticky-discharge of something. "That's what the clock tower reconstruction is? To patch the seams."

"Precisely."

"And that'll mean no more deaths?"

"One would hope."

"So why are only Diviner being killed by the aether leaks? There must be hundreds from other domains working on these pipes." Ember and Vesper, at least.

"That's what we're here to find out." Quen turned to the doctor. "Would you kindly give us some privacy? I'd like to examine Hector."

The doctor stepped out without hesitation. It seemed he didn't want to be here, and I didn't blame him.

Quen removed his eyeglasses and cleaned them with a cloth. "It's not that simple, of course."

"Is it ever?"

He took a deep breath, steeling himself for the gruesome task of examining a body. "If you'd like to wait outside, this could be disturbing—"

"I'm part of this investigation."

"Right you are. Listen, Kayl, I have an, ah, ability. One I have not disclosed to you." His expression looked grim.

"It's not playing the harp?"

"Sadly not. Diviner power can examine a mortal's recent past, as you know, however, I... I can experience a mortal's death with a single touch. It's the first thing I see, actually."

I gawked at him. "Can all Diviner do that?"

"I've never met another who can. Most can only travel up to an hour in someone's immediate future. But I can see the precise time and nature of their death."

This was why he'd gained a reputation as the Dark Warden. Why the famous Quentin Corinth always turned up when death was nearby. The ability to witness another mortal's death would be invaluable for preventing murders, though perhaps not as useful for solving them, given most bodies faded back to their god.

"This is what you do, Quen? You have visions of a mortal's unfortunate circumstances and investigate them? They say death follows you."

"It's the other way, really. I follow death. I use whatever details my visions grant me and try to prevent them."

That was certainly a different picture of the Dark Warden than most Vesper believed. "How many mortal lives have you saved?"

"None." The word blew out in a hot cloud of breath and hung in the air.

I asked the question I knew I shouldn't. "Have—Have you seen my death?"

"No. My powers don't work on you."

I supposed I should have felt relieved. "Did you see the deaths of the Vesper before you killed them?"

His breath hitched, and I bit my lip.

Why had I asked that? What in god's name had possessed me?

Whoopsie.

Did you make me say that out loud, Jinx?

Maybe.

Shit. If I explained, Quen wouldn't believe me. *You arsehole, Jinx!*

He's a Diviner. Who cares?

Oddly enough, I care.

Quen turned his back to me and pulled the blanket from Hector Bezel. I glanced over his shoulder and swallowed a curse. I wasn't sure what I was expecting—a Diviner sleeping peacefully, maybe? But there was nothing peaceful about this.

Hector Bezel was dressed in a tweed suit and lab coat, not too dissimilar to the Zephyr doctor. His silver skin was ashen, even for a Diviner, and his mouth was gaping open, as though still screaming in fear.

But it was his eyes that made my skin crawl. They were missing, leaving only empty sockets. I knew, in the depths of my soul, that this wasn't right.

Hector Bezel wasn't a mortal anymore, or a Diviner. He was a shell. A nothing. Wherever his soul roamed, it was long gone from here. How could aether cause this?

"Did—Did I do this to my Glimmer boss?" Had I ripped out her eyes? Her soul?

"No—well, yes—but that was an accident. Whoever is targeting Diviner is doing so with malicious intent."

Gods. I'd never touch another mortal again if this was the power lurking within my fingertips. I kept stealing glances of the Diviner's missing eyes. There was something about this particular Diviner that seemed familiar...

You saw him in Lady Mae's.

Shit. I had. "I know him," I blurted out.

Quen shot his gaze to mine. "What?"

"He met with the Diviner ambassador the evening my Glimmer boss died. They sat together—I overheard their conversation."

"Why did you withhold this from me?"

"I didn't withhold it! I said your ambassador was up to no good. It's not my fault you refused to listen—"

"Just tell me what you overheard."

What *had* I overheard? *Jinx, you'll need to help me out with this one.*

Nuh-uh. I'm not helping any Diviner. Figure it out yourself.

Great. Thank you for your assistance. "They were talking about the clock tower repairs, I don't quite remember. But the doctor was nervous. Oh! Yes, they mentioned something about testing the Vesper workhouse staff."

Quen rubbed his jaw, and I could see the cogs in his eyes grinding against each other. "I'll need to speak with Eli—Ambassador Karendar. It's no coincidence this attack targeted the good doctor, here. Let me see if I can find anything from his residual memories." He held his hand over the body. It shook, and his teeth rattled. "It's the cold," he explained. And maybe it was.

I slid my body against his and wrapped my arm around his waist. He flinched, but didn't push me away, which I supposed was a good sign. Carefully, I let the heat of my Ember power flow, warming us both.

"Thank you," he whispered.

And then he placed his palm on the doctor's forehead.

Quen's body spasmed, and I held him steady, afraid he might fall. He'd said he didn't just see the visions of the dead, but also *experienced* it. That couldn't be pleasant.

A heartbeat later, Quen yanked his hand free with a gasp. He staggered from my hold and stumbled back into the wall, resting his head on it as his chest rose in shallow pants.

"Quen?"

His pained gaze fell to mine. "He died the same way as the others. A creature crawled from the aether; no, *born* from it."

Born from aether? "But aether is just energy. How can it take a form?"

"Technically, our souls are a type of energy provided by our gods. Whatever is powering these aether creatures, they can take forms—and have done."

"And this creature attacked? Sucked out the doctor's soul? Why?"

Quen pushed away from the wall. "I need to investigate the reactor. Go to the reception area and wait there until I return."

"And let you walk into this monster's trap alone? Don't be an idiot."

"There's too much aether below; I have no idea how you'll react to it." He was out of the door before I could stop him.

I quickly covered up the doctor's body and reached for the door.

Locked.

Shit, he'd locked me inside! "Quen!" I yelled. "Doctor!"

I didn't think he'd intended to freeze me to death given my new Ember powers, but that arse was going to walk straight to his own death for the principles of chivalry. Why offer himself as bait? Why bring me here just to abandon me?

Melt the door.

Good idea. *I didn't think you cared for him, Jinx?*

I don't. I want to watch his eyes get eaten.

Why must you be so morbid? If Quen dies, we don't get Malk back, and we end up tied to a table in a Warden correctional facility. I don't fancy the idea of a Necro opening my brain to find you inside. Why do you hate Diviner so much?

They hurt our mother and don't care. Why should I care about their pain?

Great, we were back on *that* subject again, but I didn't have time to argue. I placed both my palms on the door and thrust all my fire power out.

A ripple of heat burst across the metal, and the door began to melt. I quickly hopped back as it oozed into a molten heap at my feet, and the cool air whooshed out of the room.

I'd left the poor doctor with little privacy, but I couldn't worry about that. I scanned both sides of the corridor and spotted a stray white feather belonging to the Zephyr doctor. I ran along the trail he'd left behind.

The corridor continued to snake around in a bend and I came to a set of double doors. These led to a metal staircase lit by aether lights on the walls. I kept my eyes downcast as I descended, though the deeper I went, the stronger the hum of aether grew.

And then I came to another set of doors with the sign 'Reactor A.'

I slid quietly through the doors and emerged into a long metal tunnel that was half-filled with a pipe. It was like being inside that Glimmer factory again. I kept a good pace as I strode alongside the pipe, past a door labeled *Pipe A*, then *Pipe B*, and eventually I found *Pipe C*.

Gods, what was I going to find inside?

A headache, most likely.

I stepped through, and the screech of aether assaulted me.

She's screaming.

I covered both ears and tentatively stepped forward, though each step felt like pushing against wind, and the screeching grew louder.

More metal pipes filled the reactor room, deafening me with their hissing and churning. They ran along the walls and led to an engine of sorts. I couldn't get a good look as two figures blocked the way: Quen and the Zephyr.

Quen came to my side and grabbed my shoulders. "I told you to stay put! There's too much aether here!"

"Really? I hadn't noticed!" I yelled over the screeching.

Quen cringed, and the doctor snapped his head around. Couldn't they hear it?

My gaze was pulled to the engine. Colorful sparks danced inside, tumbling and twirling like a machine in one of Central's laundromats. Silver-blue with flashes of pink.

The beautiful ballet of aether.

It is the sun and the moon and the stars, Jinx crooned. *The dusk and the dawn. The beginning and the end.*

What are you talking about?

Aether. It is the cosmos and everything beyond.

The aether glowed brightly, and the pink sparks spat with menace.

"Remarkable!" the doctor declared. "I have *never* seen aether behave this way." He stepped toward the engine.

Quen grabbed his lab coat. "Stay back, Doctor. It's too volatile—"

"Nonsense!" The doctor shrugged him off. "I ran the calibrations myself—"

"Does that *look* safe to you? It's overloading!"

The aether twisted into sharp angles, and they took on a form—a mortal form—that crawled out of the engine and stood tall on its own two feet.

An aether creature. An actual being made of rippling silver and blue and pink.

The pounding in my head filtered into my blood, causing my veins to vibrate and ache.

Shit! I was going to pass out at this rate!

My knees buckled. Quen caught me before I fell, and I sank into his arms, my hands still clasped against my head, but they did nothing to stop the agony pulsating in my blood.

The doctor squawked and dove behind me as Quen slowly stood, using himself as a shield to protect us both.

The creature stepped forward.

Quen raised his spare hand and slowed time to a stop.

The aether engine kept churning, completely ignoring the laws of time. I risked a glance behind me at the doctor, who'd fallen backwards in his haste to escape and now hung comically suspended in the air, his mouth wide open.

But the creature still advanced.

Time doesn't stop for the cosmos!

Shit, we're going to lose our souls, and you're happy about it, Jinx?

"Run, Kayl," Quen whispered. "*Run!*"

And leave him to his death? Not a chance.

The aether creature lunged for Quen, ignoring me altogether. I threw up a spear of fire and it collided with the creature, knocking it aside.

Don't! You'll scare it.

That's the idea.

"If you're looking for a soul to eat, mine tastes a lot better than Diviner."

The creature's attention turned to me. A searing pain tore through my chest. I screamed and fell once more against Quen, my hands slapping over my ears to stop the horrid sounds scraping the inside of my skull.

What was this thing? Why did it *hurt*?

I can stop it, Jinx said. *Let me take over our body.*

What? How?

Trust me, sister. Relax our body. Let me take over.

I had no other options.

I sucked in a breath and let my limbs go loose. Quen grunted as the full force of my weight fell atop him, but then my legs were moving on their own with no input from me. A whirl of dizziness overcame me as I stood, or Jinx stood.

I—*we*—held out our hand. The creature offered its own in turn.

"Kayl, get back," Quen rasped behind me.

I should have been scared. I would have been pissing myself right now if I'd retained any control of my body.

The creature's hand wrapped around mine, sending warm tingles up my arm, but it didn't hurt. It felt like...

Like when I touched someone and transformed.

I had no idea what this creature was—in fact, I had no idea about anything anymore, but at its touch, the throb of my head lessened, the screeching lulled to a hum, like a soft lullaby filling my heart with a sense of peace. Belonging.

What are you? I wanted to ask, but my lips wouldn't move.

Instead, Jinx spoke for me. "You want to be free, but it's not your time yet. Wait for when the clock strikes thirteen."

And then the creature vanished into a thousand tiny particles of aether; wisps of silvery-blue that faded into the air.

Exactly like a mortal death.

Jinx's control of my body lifted, and I staggered. What did that mean? When the clock struck thirteen?

It understands its place in the universe, as do you.

I did. I wasn't sure how we shared a connection, but in that moment, I realized a fundamental truth.

That creature didn't have a god. It didn't belong to any of the twelve domains. It was made from the energy of the universe, as Jinx had described. It came from the aether—*was* the aether—and somehow, the Wardens of Chime had enslaved it, converted it into energy to fuel the city.

And now it wanted to be free.

We were Godless, and I helped lost souls like that one. How though?

The screeching of the aether had faded, and the engine hummed away as I imagined it was supposed to. Time resumed, and the doctor fell into a heap.

"What—What just happened? You! What *are* you?" He pointed a talon right at me.

Quen scrambled to his feet and stared at me with his eyeglasses askew. "Blast it," he muttered, and he subtly nodded at me.

I examined my hands. They weren't the dark pink of an Ember anymore, but the silvery sheen of a Diviner. Shit. I must have accidentally transformed while in Quen's arms, but then... Why hadn't the aether creature attacked me? Stolen my soul?

Quen righted his eyeglasses. I could see the mask of calm sliding into place, the cogs whirring in his silver eyes as he tried to make sense of what had just happened. "It seems we've fixed your engine problem. We're done with our investigation here, Doctor Finch. Thank you for your cooperation."

"But she—she was an Ember!" the doctor exclaimed.

"*Me?* An Ember?" I touched my hand to my chest with mock shock and gave a haughty laugh I'd often heard from the Glimmer. "You've been overworking yourself, Doctor. Perhaps you should pay more attention to the assistants." I looked down my nose at him. Another trick I'd learned from the Glimmer. Or perhaps from Quen?

The doctor spluttered a series of questions, but Quen had already wrapped his arm around mine and was dragging me out through the door.

XVII

*One may be forgiven for assuming that Sinner's Row is a bastion of sin.
And it is. The entire strip is made up of businesses which operate outside the
Wardens' purview of legality. However, I aim to posit that a haven of sin
holds many benefits.*

*For one, mortals are drawn to sin. Despite what Glimmer doctrine may
deduce, simply abstaining from sin does not work. Ember are drawn to
illicit engagements much as a Vesper indulges in drugs to escape drudgery.
If we Wardens cannot fix inequalities in Chime, then we must provide a
healthy outlet for sin, one that can be monitored, because mortals will find
destructive methods to sin, regardless.*

*The businesses of Sinner's Row seek to accommodate the individual needs
and desires of the domains without disrupting the flow of Chime. Sinner's
Row is conveniently tucked away from puritanical eyes, much as Rapture is.
If one finds the existence of Sinner's Row distasteful on the basis of
promoting sin, then do remember: they pay tax.*
—Q. Corinth, *Redacted Warden Dossier on Sinner's Row*

THE PAIR OF US stumbled out of the steamworks like two drunken Leander
desperate to forget the night's mistakes. A colloquialism I wouldn't have
shared if I hadn't felt like retching. I'd taken Kayl's arm and hurried her out
of there before anyone noticed my Ember assistant had suddenly
transformed into a Diviner one, though other than Doctor Zachery Finch,
none of the steamworks guards or maintenance staff noticed as we scurried
away. Hopefully, they wouldn't pay much attention to the good doctor,
either; Zephyr had an annoying habit of latching onto puzzles, much like
Diviner.

The time was early afternoon; too early to retreat to the Silver Suite and let unconsciousness wash away everything I'd seen. I needed a drink, something strong, but I also needed answers.

Kayl, though she cringed at the aether in the air, wanted answers, too.

And so I found myself at Ambassador Erosain's private bar in Sinner's Row for the second time in as many weeks. Truly, it was becoming a bad habit.

The Ember ambassador welcomed me in with a kiss to both cheeks. "Quentin, my good man! You just can't keep away, can you? And who is this young beauty? Gosh, my heart is aflutter!" He took Kayl's hand and planted a lingering kiss.

Kayl feigned embarrassment, though I could tell she delighted in his fawning. "I'm Quen's assistant, though he never informed me he kept such distinguished company."

"An assistant, Quentin? Is it true? You're finally stepping into the world of the socialites?" He winked.

Erosain was ever the flirt. He cut a stunning figure as his fiery skin complemented his impeccable tuxedo and matching heels. Unlike most of the Ember, Erosain sported a thick tuft of sleek black hair and a thin beard which curled into a spiral—a Necro hair transplant, which must have cost a small fortune. Two large onyx gemstones hung from his ears and glittered in the oil lamps.

"I'm afraid this isn't a social call, Your Excellency. We're here on business."

The ambassador dramatically touched his forehead as though about to faint. Ever the actor, too. "Alas, you wound me. Then to what do I owe the pleasure?"

I explained our desire to commune inside a Mesmer parlor, preferably one he recommended as having absolute confidentiality, and he swept us into a private booth in the meantime, likely to earn some Bank o' Chime's out of me, as the Undercity put it.

The ambassador's bar was much like the rest of Sinner's Row; a little slice of Rapture here on Chime.

Lava flowed beneath our feet, separated only by thick glass that somehow remained cool despite the heat, and its molten rivers cast the sandstone room in an orange glow. Painted murals of Ember in various compromising poses decorated the walls, and real diamonds hung in the air in twirling chandeliers.

Such decadence wasn't reserved for just any mortal who wandered in off Sinner's Row, no. Erosain's bar welcomed only those with the notes to show for it.

To the back of the bar, a band was rehearsing an energetic ditty with an Ember lad on piano and a Seren woman on vocals. Seren weren't legally permitted to sing in Chime, but this one kept to low, unassuming notes. A melody designed to relax one's inhibitions for a night of expensive debauchery.

I leaned back in our booth. There were many more like this one, for illicit conversations. Some were already occupied, even at this time of day; two Seren discussing business, a Leander guzzling wine with a Fauna cat-girl straddling his lap, and an Ember woman trying to flirt secrets out of a Necro, with little success.

You never found Glimmer in these places, and rarely Diviner.

Kayl made herself comfortable on the plush satin cushions opposite me as a server came to take our order; another Ember, dressed in a maid's outfit with black eyeshadow and lipstick. A tattoo was inked just under their collarbone which said *sinner*.

"Look at you two gorgeous sweethearts. On a date, are we? Oh, he doesn't deserve you, darling." The Ember bent close to Kayl and whispered something salacious I couldn't hear as they handed her a menu.

Again, she feigned embarrassment and waved them off. "Naughty! I'm afraid I already have company with my friend here. He'd look awfully sad if I abandoned him."

"I'd be more afraid of the trouble you'd get up to." I studied the Ember as I took my menu. There was something painfully familiar about them, but my memories drew a blank—likely for good reason. "How may we address you?" So many Ember blurred the lines between the sexes, and this one was equally ambiguous. Certain domains liked to play with gender more than others—the Seren were especially hard to keep track of as they switched hats on a whim—thus it always paid to ask rather than assume.

The Ember fluttered glittering eyelashes. "Aren't you lovely? I'm a boy with the tail to prove it." He spun around and gave a swish of a thin horned tail protruding from his skirt. Kayl whooped a laugh. "What drinks can I sort you?"

"I'll take a classic hot toddy, please."

"Tea?" Kayl raised an eyebrow. "I thought you wanted something strong."

"That *is* strong." Besides, I didn't want to enter a Mesmer parlor with my head foggy.

She shook her head and scanned the menu. "Oh my, there's so many amazing things on here. You're paying for this, right? No limit?"

My coffers weren't exactly fit to bursting, but I forced a smile. "Indulge yourself."

I should have been wary of that mischievous glint in her eye.

While we waited, Kayl turned her attention to an oil lamp on our table. I could feel time distort as she studied the rhythmic flicker of the fire.

"It's best you don't do that," I said. "Time isn't a toy."

"Diviner play around with time constantly and we mere mortals don't even see it. What stops your domain from using your power to pickpocket or abuse others?"

"Our moral creed, for one. I told you before; Diviner are uniquely attuned to time, and we know when others are abusing it. Time is a tool that deserves reverence. Though while on the subject, I should warn you; Diviner may have some control over the past and present, but it's not wise to tamper with the future. Doing so can have disastrous consequences. It's the first thing a Diviner learns during their horology classes. I forget you've not received the same tutelage."

"Horology?"

"The study of time. Promise you won't mess with it."

She leaned back with a sigh. "I promise I won't fuck with time."

Exactly thirteen minutes later our server wheeled out an entire platter of appetizers and slid them onto our table. Mushroom crostini, sprout canapes with spiced fruit chutney, baked Camembert on toasted bread, tiny cucumber sandwiches, mini cheese pastries with a glazed onion dip, strawberries dipped in yogurt... and a large crème brûlée that our Ember server caramelized with a spark from his own finger.

"I couldn't decide," Kayl simply said, and toasted me with her mimosa.

I nursed my hot tea and took a sip of the burning lemon, honey, and whiskey. "We need to talk about what happened at the steamworks."

She sat up straight, her shoulders going rigid, as though ready to square up to me, though in a fight she certainly held the advantage. "Yes, we do. What were you thinking? You knew that creature would come after you. What made you think chasing it was a smart idea?"

Her silvery-blue eyes burned into me, and I took another hot sip to avoid them. "I'm a Warden. Protecting mortals is what I do, and I couldn't let Doctor Bezel's death go to waste." And I needed to find out more about the creature... to know what it was.

"Don't give me that. This wasn't about one dead doctor. We're supposed to be partners, Quen. Why did you leave me behind when I expressly told you not to?"

Because she was reckless, because none of us knew what effect strong aether would have on her. "To keep you safe, naturally."

"You locked me inside a freezer with a dead body."

"The body wasn't going to hurt you—"

"I don't appreciate your concern. You can shove your chivalrous shit up your arse if you expect us to continue as partners. If you don't trust me, then what's the point of all this?"

Her harsh words lashed me with a fury I'd never reckoned with, not from any mortal or god. Hot shame curdled in my stomach. "You're right. I'm sorry I disappointed you."

The insane part of this was that I *did* trust her. I could almost hear Elijah's judgement criticizing my own. She was a Godless, I mustn't forget.

Perhaps I had forgotten already.

Her shoulders relaxed. "You're forgiven. Just don't do it again." She popped a strawberry into her mouth. The way she licked her fingers clean stabbed another sliver of guilt into my gut, as though I'd been caught soliciting her affections by merely basking in her presence. I took a measured gulp of tea as penance.

"So, what wholesome activities does your god consider sinful?" Her playful smirk returned, for which I was glad, though the hot toddy was making my cheeks burn.

That, or the Seren's dulcet tones were getting to me.

I busied myself with a cucumber sandwich. How did they cut them so perfectly? "Father—Dor—has strict rules that classify sin. We're a stoic domain. We're not supposed to seek pleasure, but seek enlightenment."

"Like the Glimmer? No cake, no dancing, no masturbation under the sheets?"

"None of that. Our god demands logic, order, sense. Anything which cannot be explained is discarded. Anything which doesn't further our betterment is worthless. But we find pleasure in the smaller aspects of life, rather than the finer."

"And what pleasures have you found? What great sins have you committed?" She leaned over the table. "There must be at least one. The Glimmer say mortals can't help themselves."

I couldn't keep a smile from rising to my lips as I covered part of my mouth, a conspirator about to whisper my greatest secrets. "Well, right now I'm drinking tea with whiskey."

"What an absolute scandal! And does your great god of order know how you organize your papers?"

"Sadly." Father liked to pop into our heads during prayer now and then to check we weren't engaging in erroneous habits.

In truth, I'd sinned many times throughout my life, though not all I could remember.

Edana herself had tried to seduce me and discover my greatest desires, to blackmail and control me; a trick I'd seen so many young Wardens fall for. Even a god liked to have a Warden in their pocket. Erosain had attempted the same with considerably better success—I'm a mortal of flesh and bone, after all—but they both failed to realize that forbidden pleasures weren't my interest.

I couldn't lust after another when my heart, body, and soul weren't mine to bargain with. Nor did I desire to. Not when getting intimate with another mortal meant witnessing their death. "I'd ask what sins you've indulged in, but we simply don't have the time to cover them all. And there's still the little matter of discovering your patron god."

She flumped against her cushion dramatically. "It's always business with you."

It was my turn to raise my cup in a toast. "That's why I'm here. I'm not entirely sure how we survived our encounter at the steamworks. It's a shame we couldn't have examined Doctor Bezel's office and learned more of his project."

"Just what are your Wardens working on? It's not simple clock tower repairs. Whatever the Glimmer are doing in their workhouse used a massive amount of aether. I think... I think I saw that same aether creature there before I passed out."

She was right. Something didn't quite add up. I trusted Elijah, of course, but I had a gut feeling he wasn't telling me everything about the clock tower maintenance.

The fact he'd held secret meetings with Hector Bezel didn't bode well. I needed to know why. I needed the full picture.

These aether leaks weren't just bursts of wayward energy. They were organic. Deliberate. Alive. "We know the aether is creating actual mortal creatures. But such a thing is impossible. A being cannot just be born into existence. A god needs to give them a spark of consciousness, whether mortal or immortal."

"Are we talking physics or theology?"

"Quantum mechanics, I suppose."

"You and your fancy words. A question, then—what *is* aether?"

"The textbook definition is that aether is a type of energy generated by steam power, but energy cannot be created in a vacuum. It comes from somewhere; from the gods."

"Aether is cosmic power, so Jinx says." Her eyes took on that wistful, spacey look which I'd come to understand meant she was communing with her soul-twin.

"Quite right. Each of the twelve gods reside over their own domain. Without their power, their worlds and we mortals simply would not exist."

"Then how does Chime exist? Who rules it? What powers it?"

"Chime's power comes from all twelve gods, who generously keep it balanced via the rotations of the Gate. The Gate isn't just a portal to their worlds, but also serves as a conduit for their power. And this power rather conveniently keeps them *out* of Chime so that mortals may live in relative peace."

"They teach you this in your Academy? Never mind, tell me later." She waved me off with a cucumber sandwich. "So, aether is energy which comes from the gods and is converted via the steamworks to light our pretty little lanterns."

"Residual energy, but essentially, yes."

"Well, then it's obvious, isn't it?"

I cocked my head. "Is it?"

"These aether creatures, whatever they may be, are the manifestation of the gods' combined residue. Which makes them either a product of all twelve gods, or godless."

"The act of creating a mortal is deliberate. The gods are precise in this endeavor. They don't throw their power about willy-nilly."

"Perhaps the gods lost control of their cosmic willies and shot out a few mortals through their own unsuspecting wet dreams."

Such a blasphemous image, I almost covered my ears! "Life cannot exist without the gods' knowledge—"

"Yet here we are. Are you so certain you'll find my god? My profile doesn't match any of the domains, you admit it yourself. Perhaps that is what connects me to the aether."

I'd considered it myself; that Kayl and these creatures were one and the same, though I hadn't dared yet voice it aloud. The signs were all there, right down to the aether in her eyes, yet the implications were enormous.

If these creatures could form a consciousness on the same scale as Kayl, then they were mortals; functional beings. They'd need protections, rights... And no wonder they were attacking the Diviner. We made up the bulk of the Wardens, and it was us, our policies, our sponsored technological developments, which bled the stars dry of energy. We needed it to power Chime and the Gate, and maybe our greed had given rise to these creatures. It had certainly enslaved them.

Would Chime accept a new breed of mortal—one born without a god, with powers that leeched from the others? Each of the domains had the means to cause harm with their powers, yet none were quite as appalling as the ability to devour souls.

The Wardens would never allow such beings to walk the streets.

Nor could I discount that these aether creatures could well be the design of another god, a weapon from one of the domains to attack Diviner. Our powers enveloped all others. The Glimmer certainly had ambitions, though I imagined others did as well.

Kayl could just be an unfortunate victim who got caught and infected with an aether being, a twin soul. That was the answer I was sure Elijah expected.

And a far more terrifying thought; had our experimentations orchestrated the birth of a new domain? A new god? A mortal without a god was unfathomable, but perhaps these beings weren't fully mortal at all.

This would throw the whole balance of Chime, of the domains, into disarray.

None of these conclusions pleased me, for I could see where they'd end.

Right down to the visions of my death.

A far better conclusion was to continue reinforcing the clock tower, trapping these aether creatures within the steamworks, and to find Kayl's patron god. Even if it meant choosing a false one. "We can't reach a consensus until we speak with the Mesmer."

"You still believe I may be one of them?"

"They'll find whatever's hidden in your subconscious."

Kayl fell into a sullen silence.

I stirred my tea. "You act like you don't want to find your god."

Her aether eyes met mine with cool detachment. "I don't."

What must it feel like to live in ignorance of one's god? To not share that personal connection? That gratitude? "Your god could be searching for you as we speak. Desperate to meet you, know you."

"I'm one in millions. If a god created me, they likely don't even know who I am, and why would I *want* to know them? If you'd grown up hearing the stories I'd heard, you'd realize how pompous and privileged you sound. *Your* god cares for you. You're lucky. There are many mortals who aren't so lucky, who are trapped with a vindictive god and who live in fear of their whims and mercy. Or have you forgotten our trip to Eventide already?"

I hadn't forgotten.

There were some memories I chose not to erase.

No matter how much they pained me.

"Did you see the deaths of the Vesper before you killed them?"

Only every night in my dreams. "You're afraid your god will punish you."

"I'm Godless. Of course I am. The gods are cruel in their punishments, and don't look me in the eye and willfully deny it. They made mortals in their image, so they say, and if mortals are capable of evil, then so are the gods."

I glanced over my shoulder to check no one lingered nearby to hear such brazen blasphemy.

"Relax, Quen. Do you think the sinners of Sinner's Row care what I say?"

"The sinners of Sinner's Row need their gods more than we do," I muttered. "We cannot fathom a god's intentions—"

"You've met the gods. You've spoken to them like old friends."

"They are still beyond me. Perhaps they are cruel from our perspective, but they are almighty. They are everything. They work the inner machinations of the universe in ways we will never comprehend. And they have given us much—"

"They've given us the Glimmer and look at what fanaticism they've wrought." Kayl snorted. "Truth is, the gods don't care enough to make life comfortable for their mortals. Do you know how many hungry children beg on Grayford's streets because Valeria demands such crippling tithes? The gods have the power to eradicate poverty and hunger, yet they ignore it. No, they take pleasure from it. Mortals are forced to rely on each other. It's we mere mortals who have created true wonders without aid from the gods. Chime is one such wonder, ruled by mortals, and not divine intervention."

"I thought you Godless despised Warden rule?"

"Only because you cannot see your own potential. You bow and scrape to the gods' demands and do their dirty work for them."

The Godless were right to complain about some aspects of Warden rule, and I wished we could offer greater protections and support for Chime's citizens, but Kayl failed to see that we were beholden to the gods. That bond could never be broken. "You exist. By virtue of a god, or gods, you exist because they made you."

"And I should *thank* them? Don't you understand how fragile we are? We're nothing but an idea, a spark as you say, a manifestation of the gods' thoughts and dreams. They made us. They can unmake us. We have no freedom beyond what they give us."

"They gave you free will to think that."

"They punish us for exerting our free will. Who owns your thoughts, Quen?"

I sank back in my seat, aware that my breath had grown shallow. She'd almost caught me in her net, seduced me with her Godless dogma, because she'd uttered the words that kept me awake at night. The words inked into the flyer I carried with me, always.

Who owned my thoughts?

A hand wrapped around our booth and I jumped as Ambassador Erosain leaned in. "Enjoying my fine delights, are you? When you're both ready, I have a room booked for you with a most lovely Mesmer at the Dreamcast parlor."

Kayl finished her mimosa and wiped her mouth with a napkin. "I'm ready."

I scanned over the platter of appetizers. "You've barely touched anything."

"I can wrap these up to go?" the ambassador offered.

Kayl stood and straightened her crinkled blouse. "Send the leftovers to Ambassador Varen's office in Grayford." She gave me a cool stare. "If that's fine with you?"

"Are you sure?" Erosain raised one of his fake eyebrows. "Transport will cost a few hundred notes to ensure they arrive fresh, you understand."

Well played. I pulled out my wallet. "As the lady commands."

She winked at me as she slid from the booth.

Well played indeed.

XVIII

When traversing the strip of Sinner's Row, one must be wary of one's surroundings and valuables at all times. Pickpockets are rampant, though it's the more persuasive beggars and business owners you need to beware. They can spot a Warden coming from a mile away, as well as a mark. Don't fall prey to the various tempting stores which beckon you. While most will simply overcharge you with counterfeit goods, some will attempt to manipulate your mind to steal Warden secrets. Don't ingest any unknown food or drink. Don't stop by a Fauna cat café. And for pity's sake, don't visit a Mesmer dream parlor. They'll pry open your subconscious and sell whatever they find to the highest bidder.
—Q. Corinth, *Redacted Warden Dossier on Sinner's Row*

WE STRODE FROM AMBASSADOR Erosain's bar along the main strip of Sinner's Row. Stores and quaint boutiques lined the cobblestone path, their windows lit with all manner of intriguing and illicit goods, from Vesper pharmaceutical mushrooms to counterfeit jewelry. Amber oil lamps dangled overhead, beckoning us with a warm welcome. It was almost like taking a jaunt past the cozy teahouses, bookshops, and candy stores of Central.

Only the coziness was a facade, and hidden behind the carefully painted exteriors were dens of mischief and mayhem. The teahouses were cat café's where Fauna donned whatever half-mortal half-animal form their clients desired, the bookshops traded in censored works and illegal laundering, and the bright candy stores sold brews and powders that would make a mortal believe oneself a god for a time.

And these were just the windows we passed.

The back alleys hid worse within their shadows. Gambling huts, fighting rings, Necro-owned clinics that offered cheap if not deadly cosmetic surgery.

All completely illegal in the eyes of the Wardens, but we let it go for a few reasons. For one, it fell under Ambassador Erosain's protection. He still paid his taxes on time—and no one wanted to offend Edana's favorite mortal. And for another, it gave the mortals of Chime an outlet for their sins.

Oh, the Glimmer didn't approve, but they didn't see the benefit of keeping the criminals of Chime in one location—they were much easier to track.

I avoided glancing into the windows as we made our way to the Mesmer's dream parlor. To Kayl's credit, she kept by my side and didn't bounce from one window to the other, though her eyes certainly darted. But I forgot she grew up in the Undercity. She'd know all about Sinner's Row, its vices and virtues.

"Do you come here often?" she asked. "You and the Ambassador seemed awfully close."

"I have traipsed here from time to time when working a case." In fact, the last time I'd been investigating the workhouses by sniffing out a lead that went absolutely nowhere. "There are benefits to making friends in high places, and Erosain appreciates having a Warden on his side."

"A crooked Warden? Do you take bribes?"

"I can be swayed by an excellent cup of tea."

"You've visited all twelve domains, yes?" She pointed to my arm. The passport tattoo poked out from under my sleeve. "Have you truly met all the gods?"

"I have."

"So you must have lots of stories?"

"I do." My voice sounded wary, then. When it came to Kayl, I never knew which direction a conversation would steer.

"Then which domain produces the best tea?"

That I wasn't expecting, and I choked back a laugh. "Hrm... That's a tough question. There's so much variety in tea, and the domains each have their own unique flavors. To declare one superior would be subjective on my part, and not an objective summation. The Ember enjoy their iced teas, the Mesmer add far too much sugar, the Seren add spice and fruit, and so forth."

"Your favorite, then."

"There's no tea quite like home. The measured temperature, the correct number of leaves..." I trailed off as we reached the dream parlor, the Dreamcast.

Like most buildings on Sinner's Row, the dream parlor's brickwork had been painted in gaudy colors and patterns. This one was covered in bright purple and decorated with white stars. The paint peeled at the edges and looked run-down, cheap and tacky.

But this was the one.

Kayl bounded in before me, and I followed to the tinny ring of the parlor bell.

The inner Dreamcast fared no better. Cheap plaster covered the walls in a painful mauve. A single Mesmer lay slumped at the reception desk, their glossy eyes staring at nothing as drool dripped from their chin. They could have been daydreaming as Mesmer do, or they could have been high off their buttocks. In Sinner's Row, it was hard to tell.

Other mortals filled the cramped waiting room; another Diviner with his arms bunched around him and his head averted to avoid attention, an Ember staring blissfully at the ceiling as though already high on some Vesper mushroom, and a Seren woman dutifully reading through a copy of the parlor pamphlet.

Lavender incense burned from somewhere alongside hints of bitter coffee, and I felt ill at ease. Coffee always triggered my worst nightmares.

"Master Corinth, we've been expecting you."

Kayl and I both jumped as a Mesmer woman came gliding toward us, seemingly out of nowhere.

Her skin was a dark purple, almost Vesper in shade, only freckles of starlight rippled across her cheeks, and even her long black hair glittered with starlight. It had quite an aether quality to it. She wore a tight black dress as though ready to attend theater, though I supposed dream parlors were their own type of show.

I pushed my spectacles up. "Ah, yes. I believe you have a room for us?"

The Mesmer woman smiled with assured serenity. "Of course. I am your host, Lady Nara, and I'll be your guide to the stars and beyond this day. If you'll follow me."

We entered a corridor just as bland as the reception, and I wondered if that was part of the illusion. We passed room after room, all closed with the word 'Occupied.'

"Popular place," Kayl commented.

"Many mortals come here to seek meaning from their lives, or to find new ones," Lady Nara explained in her soft voice. "Our rooms are booked weeks in advance."

"We must be quite lucky." Kayl offered a raised brow in my direction. Lucky indeed.

The favor I'd owe Erosain wouldn't be paid off lightly.

Lady Nara stopped by an unmarked door and ushered us inside a dark room. At first, I worried we'd walked into a trap, but then tiny lights lit up around us. Kayl gasped, and I shared her wonder.

The ceiling hung over us in a dome shape, like a Diviner observatory, and its surface shimmered with painted stars. No, not painted; they *were* stars. Glowing orbs and colorful constellations which came to life in the swirling dust of the room.

It was like standing outside at night and staring at the glory of the universe, observing the makings of it all.

That was the one thing I loved about the Golden City, save the Academy; the beauty of night undeterred by aether lamps and plates. It was those nights on campus that I'd lay on the grass and quote Diviner philosophy.

The universe is a machine; the gods are the gears, and we are the cogs.

A large circular bed stacked with cushions filled the room, but there was no other furniture, save a shoe rack and coat hanger beside the door. Lady Nara gestured to it. "Please, take off your shoes and make yourselves comfortable."

"We're going to share a bed?" Kayl said with a giggle. "I hope you don't snore."

I raised my hands. "Not me. This is for my good friend, here." I nodded to Kayl as I explained to Lady Nara. "I'll be observing, if you don't mind."

Lady Nara placed the tips of her fingers together as though in prayer. "I'm sorry, Master Corinth, but His Excellency's instructions were quite clear on the payment. We'll be happy to explore her dreams in exchange for one of yours."

Ah. This was how Erosain was able to slot us in so quickly. A Warden's dreams held all manner of secrets, and no doubt both he and the Mesmer would welcome a chance to unlock some of mine.

Who knew what lurked in my deepest subconscious? Blackmail material, certainly, but also information pertaining to my Warden colleagues and Ambassador Karendar. Even memories of the Warden HQ layout would be of use to some rogue.

Which was why we Wardens were warned against attending dream parlors. As far as I could remember, I'd never stepped foot inside one, nor had any intention to until today.

"I'm afraid my dreams would bore you, Lady Nara."

"He's right, you know," Kayl added. "It'll be dreams of tea and stacking papers."

Lady Nara ignored her. "Oh, I'm sure the Dark Warden holds many dreams. Many nightmares." Her dark gaze held mine, and I suppressed a shudder. "Though if I'm mistaken, and you no longer wish to bargain with us, I have clients waiting."

Damn you, Erosain. Who knew a Mesmer could be so menacing? "Very well, Lady Nara, though I'm sure you'll be disappointed by what you find."

I tucked my spectacles safely away inside my jacket pocket and left that and my shoes by the door. Even with my poor vision, I managed to wobble on over to the edge of the bed and sat, trying to create as much space and privacy as possible.

Kayl leaped on the bed and sent a cushion flying.

"Behave, please. We're here for answers, not to frolic under the sheets."

"Well, I know you're a good boy who wouldn't even *dream* of sinning under the sheets." She tackled my arm, pulling me backwards so that my head hit the collection of pillows. "What would your god think now?" she whispered into my ear.

Goodness, her words sent a shiver down my spine, and I suddenly ached for more tea. Dark, bitter tea. "You're wicked."

"So they tell me." She sat up on her elbows, gazing over me with those silvery-blue eyes, brighter than the stars dancing around us.

I could lose myself in those eyes.

Die in them.

"Shall we begin?" Lady Nara coaxed.

Warmth flushed through my gut, and I twisted my head away. "Yes," I croaked. "Please do."

Kayl flumped beside me and wiggled until she found a comfortable spot. "I could do with a nap. So what now?"

Lady Nara stood over us. "First, you must relax. Allow your mind to drift. I will begin a slow chanting hypnosis that will lull you into a deep and refreshing sleep. Only then can I reach inside your subconscious and guide you to whatever answers you seek."

"What answers do mortals seek?" Kayl asked.

"Our clients come to us for many reasons, not just to answer their questions. Some seek peace in their own minds where they may be free to be whoever they wish, to explore a world of fantasy where there are no demands and no repercussions."

Freedom in your own dreams. But even dreams, like thoughts, belonged to one's god—more so for the Mesmer whose god walked freely within those dreams. Were any of us truly free? I closed my eyes and dreaded to think what I'd find.

Too many sins. Too many mistakes.

Lady Nara chanted a soothing rhythm.

Kayl's hand brushed against mine, and my heart fluttered for a moment, reminding me why I was here. *Don't be afraid*, I wanted to say. Of the Mesmer? Of what Kayl might discover about herself? Of me? I wasn't sure.

I took her hand and squeezed it with a soft reassurance.

I hadn't held another mortal's hand in years.

Not without suffering their death over and over.

She squeezed back.

And while I was sure my soul remained intact, I felt myself fade into oblivion.

Sunlight warmed my face as a gentle breeze rustled the grass of Meridian Park. The woman of my dreams rested her head on my lap, my fingers idly stroking her dark hair, which flickered with silver starlight even under the sun's glare. She held a copy of *Saints and Sinners*, a lurid tale by one *H. Arabesque*, that I read over her shoulder. I wasn't paying much attention to the words. Being here offered enough contentment, and my gaze instead drifted to the round swell of her belly.

We were creating something impossible together; combining my Diviner with her Mesmer. A girl, the Necro doctor had proclaimed. A daughter.

We'd already settled on a name.

Jinx.

"Are you keeping up?" she asked, never taking her eyes off the page.

My fingers stroked down to her nape, her skin a brighter indigo shade compared to other Mesmer. "Of course."

"You're not even reading, are you."

"My attention is fully engaged."

"I'm sure it is." She reached up and kissed me.

A soft kiss. One of many we'd shared and would continue to share until the end of our mortal existence. The end of time. We'd been there, seen the end of everything, and had ripped domains apart only to piece them together again, one atom at a time, for this moment. This bliss.

Is this the future you dream of, Quentin Corinth? came a female voice in my head that wasn't my own. *Is this what you seek?*

Why wouldn't it be what I want? Hadn't I suffered enough to warrant a slice of peace? An experience of normality? The chance to build a life on my own terms without a master's whip dictating it?

You crave freedom.

Didn't all mortals?

You don't trust the path your god set for you.

I'd always known my path. All Diviner did. I'd rebelled, once, when I was younger and more prone to imprudence. My path had swerved, and I'd taken destiny into my own hands, to train as a tram driver, of all things. But it was what I'd wanted.

Something normal. Something mundane.

My love faded from my arms and I blinked. The scene changed from Meridian Park to an empty classroom in the School of Art. It appeared just as I remembered, with stuffed bookcases, wooden desks carved with silly Undercity slang, incense burning from the professor's pulpit, and the piano in the corner. A bronze-haired boy sat there playing a mournful note.

This was a memory from my childhood. One I did not wish to see.

I wanted to pull away, to keep myself from reliving it again, but the memory forced me on, and I found myself acting it out like some cursed puppet on a string.

The boy glanced over his shoulder and smiled at me, his brass eyes twinkling. "Now you know my secret."

Saints, he was beautiful.

I slid onto the seat next to him and watched his slim fingers work the keys. "I had no idea you played." And played well.

"It's all in the timing. That's what most art is, you know. Patterns. The Seren say you can't paint by numbers, but I beg to differ."

True, there weren't many Diviner artists in Chime, but there was beauty in the synchronous and symmetrical. Eli was proof of that. His high cheekbones in perfect balance, the curl of his hair a golden spiral. Truly, his mortal body had been painted in sublime strokes. A work of art.

He shuffled close to me, his thigh rubbing against mine.

My heart fluttered. And not for the first time in his company.

It was sin, what I felt. We knew the rules; knew courting was forbidden within the Diviner dormitories on campus, but we weren't *in* the dormitories. The masters said nothing about the classroom.

"I could teach you to play," Eli said, his voice low, husky.

"The piano or my heart?"

"Both."

He turned, delicate hands moving so slow, so painfully slow, as one hot palm slid to my thigh, and the other grazed my cheek. His lips pressed to mine.

Goodness, he tasted like the first rays of dawn.

And then light flashed, and the classroom warped into chaos.

I watched a vision of the future bloom through Elijah's eyes.

Mortals were screaming, running in fear as strange silvery-blue creatures tore the life from them without a hint of blood or bone. The aether lamps flickered erratically, plunging us in spurts of darkness. Dusk should have illuminated us from the Gate, from Eventide, but Eventide was lost.

Saints preserve us. It was *gone*.

"What have you *done*?" I screamed. Not my words. Elijah's.

The clock tower's hands were spinning out of control.

And the bell rang out *dong* after thunderous *dong*.

Not twelve.

I counted thirteen.

My future self stood there panting, my jacket discarded, my shirt torn—disheveled and stained with sweat. Blood dripped from my nose and my spectacles were cracked, dangling askew from my nose.

My trembling fingers reached for the brass pistol holstered at my hip.

"Don't," Elijah warned.

The line of Wardens beside him readied their weapons—pistols, batons, and tasers.

"Think, Quentin, please *think*!" Elijah begged.

My future self didn't say a word. But my silver eyes said everything.

Hate burned where there was once love, once lust, and in Elijah's mind I felt the fear, the despair. *Father was right. He covets Chaos.*

There was no redemption waiting for either of us.

Time had run out.

Elijah raised his hand to slow me.

But my future self moved quicker, lifting both hand and pistol.

Time rippled across the space between us, twisting and distorting; our wills equally matched.

"I remember what you made me do!" My future self yelled, his voice hoarse. "You made me shoot her. I *killed* her!"

"I tried to cure you of sin, Quentin! I tried to save your soul! No one will ever love you as much as I do!"

"You don't know what love is."

The shot rang.

My vision pulled back, returning me to the classroom.

I'd felt it. Saints. I'd felt that bullet pierce Elijah's head as if it were my own brain matter being forcefully ejected from my skull.

And I'd been the one to pull the trigger. An older Quen.

But that—that could never happen! Saints, I could never!

It wasn't me. It could *never* be me.

I scrambled from the piano seat, practically tripping over my feet in my haste to distance myself from Eli's touch.

"Quentin?" Elijah called, his voice full of concern. "Are you all right? Was that a vision? What did you see? *Quen*—"

But I was already running. Out, I ran through the halls and along the campus green. I lost all sense of time as my feet pounded the streets, racing through the Golden City crowds to the station. Tears streamed from my face and I shoved between angry mortals.

The glass elevator doors were closing, but I ran for it.

I needed out, I needed to be *gone*.

"Mind the gap!" the station staff called. "Son, slow down! Or you'll—"

My feet slipped on the platform.

And then I fell.

I didn't even know how, but I fell into darkness with such speed, the wind ripped screams from my lungs. Silvery-blue lights flashed by me, and I thought it must be the end of my short and pathetic mortal existence.

Killed by a kiss. By a vision of death.

No, killed by my own stupidity.

And I hadn't even finished my mnemonics coursework. My professor would be so deeply disappointed in my tardiness. Though not as disappointed as my Father.

But then I landed with earth-shattering force and pain found me. It quaked through my bones with such absolute agony, I knew I couldn't be dead, though my death would surely come soon. My breath came in fighting rasps, my chest so tight I could barely cry out.

I'd die how I was born. Alone and in darkness.

But at least I wouldn't kill in my future.

At least I wouldn't become *that* monster.

I fumbled in my pocket for my fob watch. My only companion, though that too had cracked on the landing and would no longer soothe me with its melodic tick and tock.

A CHILD OF TIME, came a voice deep in the abyss.

It wasn't my Father.

My breath caught in an agonized wheeze. "Who—Who's there?"

Aether lights blared in the dark and I squinted.

WHY DID YOU FALL?

"Please, it hurts—"

WHY ARE YOU HERE, CHILD?

I must have died, and this was a test of faith. "Forgive me, Father. I—I witnessed a vision. Of destruction and chaos and I... I shoot someone. In the future. I saw it." Tears ran down my cheeks. "I'm sorry, Father. It scared me, and I ran, I—"

SPEAK OF YOUR VISION, the voice called. *AND I WILL SAVE YOU.*

The memory paused, and the Mesmer's invading presence filled my mind.

This is what lies buried deep in the subconscious of Quentin Corinth. You've had this dream erased, haven't you? I see the meddling scars of an Amnae. But the dream returns over and over again.

This wasn't a dream. It was a memory. A nightmare. I never wanted to relive it.

I'd spent my entire life running from it.

Is this your desire, Quentin? Your fantasy? Or one of Dor's visions?

No. You don't get to question me on this. You've seen enough. Let me go.

Is this the future, Quentin—

Get out of my mind!

I woke with a gurgled scream.

"It's okay, Quen." Kayl was leaning over me, her brows knitted together. "It's just a dream."

I sat up and rubbed my forehead, wiping away sweat. It wasn't *just* a dream. It was my greatest fear. And that—that Mesmer had forced me to relive it. I snapped a glare in Lady Nara's direction.

The stars of the observatory blinked softly around her, as though confused by my ire. "The payment has been made, Master Corinth."

"And what did my payment earn?" I glanced at Kayl. "What did you see?"

Kayl made an awkward shrug.

"Her mind is full of many noises and colors," Lady Nara said. "There were many dreams cascading one after the other. It was too nonsensical to make sense of."

"You learned nothing?" My hands clenched around the bed sheets.

I'd endured my worst nightmare for nothing?

"Sorry," Kayl whispered.

It wasn't her fault. I'd dragged her here, so desperate for answers, yet the truth continued to elude us.

Or I continued to ignore it.

"Let's get out of here," she urged. "We'll go back to your place, have a cup of tea, and think about what to do next."

Yes, that sounded like an ideal plan. The day's events had left us both rattled. A calming tea was what we needed. And I'd need something strong to face what lay ahead.

My dream had served as an ample reminder of what future lay in store. Time would wait for no man; certainly not me.

Kayl scooted past me, and as she bent to retrieve her shoes, the sight of her curves caught me off guard.

I'd dreamed of her as a Mesmer, the literal woman of my dreams, and the carrier of my progeny, but that *had* to have been a dream, an illusion, because Diviner didn't birth children, not in that way. Nor could mortals breed with those of other domains.

What did such a dream say about me? About my innermost thoughts and desires?

No, Lady Nara had been toying with my head, nothing more.

It was another memory I'd have to wipe clean.

Along with every other sinful thought.

19

On the morning of the incident, I'd been ordered to the Undercity slums known colloquially as Grayford along with twelve other Wardens. While my colleagues searched the empty buildings, I remained on standby in case of accidents or injuries. Specifically, I'd been informed that the runaway mortal we sought was a pregnant Glimmer and my skills might be required in the worst-case scenario.

At approximately thirteen minutes past twelve, I heard three gunshots coming from inside an abandoned warehouse. I rushed to the scene and came across my Diviner colleague, who stood over the faded bodies of two dead male Vesper with his pistol in hand. Both shot. The trajectory of the blood splatter corroborated my colleague's report.

A third male, an Ember, was also shot at the scene, but fled and presumably survived as we found no trace of him.

We recovered the Glimmer female; however, her pregnancy had been forcibly terminated. I examined her and found traces of an illegal substance which induced the miscarriage. The Glimmer refused to concede whether she'd willingly ingested the drug herself.

—V. Holcroft, *Warden Dossier on the 'Grayford Incident'*

THE GATE WAS SET to Witheryn when Quen and I returned to the Silver Suite, and the snowy landscape of the Necro home world clashed with the setting sun.

We found Dru snoring on Quen's couch. Poor dear must have been waiting hours for us to return. I slid onto the cushion next to her. "Miss me?"

Dru woke with a start. "Where have you *been*? And you're a Diviner again? I thought you were one of us—an Umber—this morning?"

"It has been an awfully long day. First, I had flowers, then gills and fins, then fire, and—"

"I don't want to know." Dru scowled as Quen sat in his armchair. "I thought you said you'd be back by lunch?"

"Apologies, Miss Smith. The day ran ahead of us. Thank you for clearing the dining table. I hope you were able to successfully entertain yourself." His eye fell on a pile of neat papers Dru must have tidied away. I swear Quen's eyebrow twitched. "We'll order dinner in, I think, if you'd like to return to your domicile."

Dru's scowl moved to me, and her flowers wilted. "You're not going to tell me what took all day?"

I opened my mouth to explain and caught Quen's expression. He was staring out of the window at the clock tower. Rather forlornly, I might add. Whatever he'd seen at the Mesmer's dream parlor had left him rattled.

Probably dreamed of iced tea, Jinx said. *Or the sight of some woman's bare legs. The horror.*

Oh, hush, you. "It's been a long day, Dru. Come back for breakfast and we'll discuss it in the morning."

Dru grabbed my wrist and yanked me off the couch. "If you'll excuse us for a moment." She dragged me into the hall and blocked it off with her arms crossed over her chest. "I'm not letting you stay here with *him*," she whispered.

"Oh, give over—"

"I'm serious. He's dangerous."

I raised my brow. "Trust me, he's anything but." Gods, the man was so pure he couldn't even wank under his bed sheets.

"Why are you so intent on staying here and playing house with a Warden?"

"I'm not playing *house*." I rolled my eyes. "For god's sake, we found a body."

Dru winced. "Another dead Diviner? Where?"

"Down in the steamworks. Listen, something big is going on with these aether leaks—a story like you'd never believe." And I was at the heart of it. "Quen is the only one who can help me unravel it. I'll tell you everything tomorrow, I promise. Did you find anything in his apartment while we were gone?"

"No. He's got stacks of records, but it's all nonsense—just dates and times. A few files on Godless activities, an entire stack of our fliers, but nothing incriminating. Nothing on the Glimmer workhouses. Though..."

I leaned close. "Though?"

"I found a pistol. A fancy brass pistol hidden under his bed. I told you, he's dangerous. Stop falling for his bumbling gentleman act, or whatever he's peddling you. Corinth is the Dark Warden, and he is not on our side. He'll drag you off to Kronos next and you'll never return."

She's right, you know.

No, she wasn't. I chewed my tongue to keep myself from saying something rash. Dru was my closest friend, and the Godless were family; Harmony, the older sister who chastised me when I needed it, Sinder and Vincent, the uncles who alternated between encouraging my recklessness and helping me recover from it, Reve, the younger brother we all needed to guard. But they guarded me as well. They didn't trust me to make competent decisions or handle dangerous tasks. Gods, I was twenty-six—

Thirteen.

I possessed the body and mind of a twenty-six-year-old. That had to count for something! "I can handle Corinth. And I'll stay for as long as he's useful to us." I glanced toward the hall, checking he wasn't eavesdropping on our conversation. Harmony suspected that the Godless's mystery benefactor might be a Warden, so they could be bought. Maybe not Quen. He was too straitlaced for that, but he sympathized with us at least.

He'd said it himself; it paid to make friends in high places, and I couldn't get much higher than the Silver Suite.

"Is this still for Malk and the workhouses?" Dru whispered.

That hurt. "Of course it is."

She raised her hands in surrender. "Fine. I'll be over at Harm's place. If you need to get out for whatever reason, find me there."

I pulled her into a hug before she could object. "I love you, you know."

Dru sighed into my shoulder and patted my back. "I know you do."

I left Dru to make her own way out and found Quen still staring at the clock tower. He hadn't moved an inch and gave no sign he'd overheard my conversation. "Tea?"

He slapped his thighs. "Yes, right you are."

We ordered in some food and waited for the concierge service to work their magic as Quen brought out a tray of tea with another glittering array of biscuits. Before he could retreat to his armchair, I pulled him onto the couch beside me. "You and I need to talk, mister, and I'm not shouting all the way over there."

He sheepishly sat with as much space between us as politeness could afford and crossed a leg over his knee, a teacup perched precariously in his lap.

Dru thought this idiot was dangerous? I'd met mold with a more threatening aura. "So the Mesmer were a bust and we've got aether creatures lurking in the steamworks. What now?"

Quen took a slow sip of his tea, as though trying to steel himself. "I'm fresh out of ideas."

"You? The great Quentin Corinth?" I fidgeted with a lock of my silver hair. "You said my god was waiting for me out there. We just need to keep looking."

"We've already drawn too much attention in search of inconclusive results. You are, quite simply, an enigma."

No. I knew what I was. Some bastardized aether creation. Quen just couldn't admit it to me, or himself, because...

Because of the threat you pose.

I hated that Jinx was right. Sure, I hadn't stolen any Diviner souls yet, and honestly, it wasn't like I was *trying* to. But my existence still proved problematic. I could see how it appeared from his Warden eyes—a true Godless. A mortal without a god. I wouldn't pretend the thought didn't thrill me; I might be the first mortal in all of Chime to be born free. I was a living, breathing blasphemy. Apostasy in mortal form.

And wow, did that feel good.

No god owned me. They never would.

We could take a tour around all twelve domains, and I was certain I wouldn't find my god. None of the domains pulled me. I was an amalgamation of their best and worst parts. A chaotic mixture that didn't belong anywhere except in Chime.

The question now was... would the Wardens accept my existence?

And the second, more pressing question... how could I leverage this to free Malk?

Valeria wanted answers, but neither Quen nor the Wardens would allow her the truth of my existence. Not unless I went to Eventide alone.

The bell to Quen's apartment rang and our food order of afternoon tea turned up with a bottle of chilled wine. He fumbled with the stopper as I stared in disbelief.

"Alcohol, Quen? Whatever will your god think?"

Fizz bubbled from the open bottle and Quen hastily filled two glasses with a sparkling pink. "It *has* been a long day. What's a little sin between friends?"

I took my glass and clinked it against his. "I'll drink to that."

The wine had a mild fruity taste to it, like the strawberries or raspberries that Dru grew in our depot.

We leaned against the couch in comfortable silence and watched the sun set over Central Station, forcing Quen to light a few oil lamps that only added to the cozy ambience.

Truly, there were no nights like this underground.

The food went ignored. The concierge's afternoon tea was a glorious selection of tiny sandwiches, fruit scones, and cakes, including meringues, macarons, cherry bakewells, and a healthy slice of Battenberg, but it seemed both of our appetites had waned. Perhaps I could smuggle these away too.

I'd guessed Sinder would be waiting for me at Sinner's Row. He used his natural charm to spy on Erosain's customers on behalf of the Godless and had likely been tasked by Harmony to eavesdrop on my conversations. I'd had to subtly turn down his rescue attempt when he whispered in my ear to go hide in the powder room.

Seeing him made me ache for the Godless, for my home back in the depot. I'd been gone less than a week, but that was a week too long.

Gods, I missed Malk. Missed his easy smile no matter what foolishness I'd wrought, his strong arms wrapped around mine whenever I needed them, his hot breath panting against my ear... My gut warmed from the wine.

From the wine?

Yes, the wine. How does alcohol affect you, Jinx?

I feel everything you do. Though I can remain clearheaded when you can't.

Interesting implications. Gods, I was starting to sound like Quen.

"What *did* you dream?" Quen suddenly asked, interrupting my thoughts.

Dream? Oh yes, the Mesmer. I swirled my wine glass. "Honestly, I can't remember half of it. Just pictures of things, places, mortals I'd never seen before." Like I'd taken a tour around the domains and spoken to each of the gods in turn. Ludicrous dreams. "And what of your dreams?"

Quen gazed toward the clock tower again, though I could almost hear his thoughts whirring, the gears grinding to a halt as he couldn't—or wouldn't—say whatever it was he needed to confess.

"Quen," I coaxed. "What did you dream? Was it a nightmare?" He'd woken up screaming, which had snapped me from my own reveries.

He turned, flustered, and shoved his eyeglasses up his nose. "It was just a dream."

"*Quen*. You were glaring at that Mesmer. I've never seen you glare. What did she show you? You'll feel better if you air it out."

"Will I?"

"It's customary to share problems over a bottle of wine, and gods know you've seen enough of mine. I promise I won't tell a soul. I'm no god; I won't judge you."

His expression was caught between cringing at my blasphemy and relief. But his shoulders relaxed, releasing whatever pent-up tension he'd been carrying since we left Sinner's Row. "I've killed mortals." His voice was little more than a whisper.

My heart skipped a beat. "You dreamed of the Vesper?"

"I dream of them often. I know what you must think of me. I'm aware of my reputation, and I don't blame the Vesper of Grayford for acting as they do, but I... I didn't kill those Vesper in cold blood. I'd understand if you didn't believe me." The words tumbled out of him as the wine loosened him up. Or perhaps because he'd never said them, and this was his first chance.

It was difficult to reconcile the bumbling Quen I knew with the Dark Warden, but Dru was right. I mustn't forget who I sat beside. "I was there when it happened."

The infamous 'Grayford Incident' as the Courier headlines referred to it.

Quen took a deep gulp from the wine and suppressed a cough. "Then you have no doubt heard the Wardens' version of events."

"They marched on Grayford looking for illegals. Some nonsense about certain domains putting on pressure to return them; Eventide, Rapture. I think even Solaris's name came up, which *was* nonsense, because Glimmer don't congregate in Grayford."

"You'd be surprised. I'd been serving the Wardens only a few years when I and an entire legion of us were ordered to Grayford to hunt a runaway Glimmer. Oh, the Glimmer like to keep their business quiet, but they deal with many runaways. It's the natural consequence when one forces their own mortals into workhouses. They suspected this particular Glimmer had run to Grayford."

"So the Wardens went rioting through Grayford on the mere suspicion of one hidden Glimmer?"

"The Glimmer support and fund the Wardens, so yes, we marched to their beat."

"I thought Diviner ruled over the Wardens?"

"Technically, the Wardens are run by a council of all twelve domain ambassadors, though it's Diviner policies they choose to implement. But Glimmer influence has grown considerably. Besides Dor, Gildola is the only god who cares about the internal politics of Chime, and who wants a piece of it. They take an active part in Chime's council. Diviner and

Glimmer have been butting heads and wrestling each other for control for years. Why do you think the Wardens come down so hard on apostates?"

I suppressed a shudder. I cared little for Diviner rule, but if Glimmer ruled the Wardens, they'd have total control of Chime, and the city would never become a godless state. And I would never have my freedom.

They'd already used their influence to force the Vesper and Ember underground.

"Did you find a Glimmer in Grayford?"

"I did. A young girl. Pregnant. The Glimmer had told us that she'd been blessed by Gildola to carry a daughter, but the girl... She wasn't happy to be blessed."

"I know."

"You... know?"

"I told you; I was there."

His silver eyes widened. "You were one of the Vesper who helped her?"

My insides churned, perhaps from the wine. "She'd escaped the workhouse with an Ember." With Sinder, and Malk's mother, though I didn't want to mention either Sinder or Elvira's name. "And they'd come to Grayford to seek shelter, and because they knew the Vesper had poisons which could end her pregnancy. We tried to help her."

I waited for Quen's reaction: shock, disgust? To the Glimmer, nothing was more sacred than life and birth. No wonder they'd thrown together everything possible to find the girl and stop her. To kill an unborn child was worse than apostasy in their eyes, though she wasn't the first to have a pregnancy forced on her by her god. Nor would she be the last.

Instead, Quen looked sad. "I arrived too late to stop her. The girl had already... ingested. She was squirming on the floor when I found her. I still remember the blood."

"I'm sorry."

Are you? Jinx asked.

No, but it feels like the right thing to say.

"I tried to help her, and two Vesper males turned up," Quen continued. "They only wanted to protect the girl, and they thought I'd come to take her away, to send her back to the Glimmer so Gildola would smite her. And they were right. That was exactly my purpose. They lunged for me, and in the scramble, I grabbed one of them. I saw their death. I witnessed myself killing them through their own eyes." Quen rested his head against the couch. "The shock of it made me hesitate. I... I didn't want it to end that way. But they pulled a knife on me and I reacted on instinct in the end."

Silence hung heavy in the air, punctured only by the tick and tock of the mantelpiece clock.

I placed my hand on his knee. "You acted in self-defense."

His silver eyes met mine. "I acted like a Warden. They covered it up. The Glimmer wouldn't allow news of a runaway girl to get out, especially not one who'd aborted her own child. News spread that I'd tried to bust some drug-dealing Vesper and had overreacted, leading to their deaths, and so the legend went."

"What happened to the girl?" She'd been taken, along with a bunch of Grayford's illegals, including Elvira. The Wardens had caused a riot that day. Malk had been stabbed trying to get to his mother, and he still bore the scar. One of Quen's stray bullets had hit Sinder, and I'd been the one holding his blood in. He'd have died if not for Vincent.

Quen gave me a level stare. "What do you think happened to her?"

The Glimmer took her back to Solaris. To Gildola. Never to be seen again.

Just as they took Elvira.

He'll do the same to you. He won't even hesitate.

I batted Jinx's thought aside. "You didn't question it? You didn't try to save her?"

"I had no power, no authority—"

"That's a crock of shit and you know it—"

"I spent time in a correctional facility."

My heart almost stopped entirely. "What?"

"For three months on Kronos and then another three in the Warden HQ."

"But... why?"

"Part punishment for failing to save the Glimmer's bounty, part public appearances; someone needed to pay for the Wardens' failure. And partly because... I *had* questioned it. I'd questioned sending that girl to her doom. The Wardens needed to ensure my mind was still pure enough to serve them, still free of taint and sin, and that I hadn't suddenly started sympathizing with heathens and apostates. So I sat on my hands and did what was expected of me like a good boy. And when they saw fit to release me, I tried to use my unique ability to save lives. But perhaps the Vesper are right; death follows me."

Shit, I didn't know *anything* about Quentin Corinth.

He eyed me over the rim of his wineglass, and there was a wariness in those silver flecks. He'd told me too much, he realized. I'd uncovered a side to him no one ever had, or likely ever would.

"Is that why you became a Warden?" I asked. "Because of your ability?"

"Not entirely. You know I wanted to be a tram driver." A subtle smile tugged at his lips. "But Father—Dor—he wanted me to serve with the Wardens. That was the path he set out for me."

"So you did what your god told you to do?"

"He's my god. I had to trust he wouldn't lead me astray."

Only lock him inside correctional facilities for six pissing months when he *did* go astray. Didn't Quen see what I saw? The abuse his god put him through? "Does Dor order you about often?"

"I receive visions of future events occasionally. Cases that need my attention. Mortals who... Well, you know." He fumbled for the wine bottle and topped up his glass.

I'd forgotten that Diviner could see the future as clearly as the past, though I supposed the clue lay in their name. Visions weren't just the realm of Mesmer; their visions, and Reve's, were more like dreams. Full of possibilities of how events *could* play out, but often not how they did. "I saw a vision. That first time I took the Diviner form in the Glimmer mansion." The first time I touched Quen.

His head spun around and he almost dropped the bottle. "You did? Why didn't you tell me this before?" He hastily slapped the bottle down and wine spilled onto the table. "Describe it, please."

I tried to recall the details as much as I could; the chaos, the screaming, bodies falling from the sky, blood splattering the streets of Central, aether burning in the air like wafts of static cloud. Each new detail made his eyes widen further until I was sure they'd fall out.

"I've had a similar vision," he said all too quietly.

"What does it mean? Is it the future?"

His throat bobbed. "Yes. Undoubtedly so."

Shit. "Can it be changed?"

"The future is a set course. It cannot be altered by mortal means. Trust me, I've been searching for a way to change my fate for years, but all my visions come true. Even knowing what's coming cannot change it. I've seen..." He placed his wineglass down and ran a hand through his hair. Gods, his hands were shaking.

"What have you seen? Quen, tell me."

"Deaths I know are coming. Deaths I know I can't stop. I'm going to kill again soon. I saw myself do it from the eyes of my victim. I saw... such scorn on my face, twisted beyond recognition. What kind of man do I become to transform into that? Into a being that kills with no mercy? No remorse? What horrors will make me that way?"

Dor had done this to Quen; plagued him with visions.

But I wouldn't accept these visions as true.

Despair contorted across his face, and it sent a dull ache through my chest. What must it feel like to touch another mortal and see their death? To experience it?

"I can't—I can't touch anyone," he said, as though reading my thoughts. "Because I know as soon as I do, I'll see their end, condemn them to it as sure as the sun rises."

In that, we shared a joint pain. Would it be safe for me to touch others in the future, knowing my power could steal their souls if I wasn't careful?

His powers didn't work on me. Maybe we were safe.

"You can touch me." My fingers wrapped between his and I pressed my palm down. The tingle was there, but no tug—perhaps because I'd already taken on a Diviner form? Was that why I'd never hurt Malk? "See? No visions."

His expression was unfathomable as he cupped my cheek. "No visions."

I leaned into his warmth. "And I haven't stolen your soul."

"I wouldn't mind if you did."

Then his lips pressed against mine. My mouth parted in surprise as I tasted him, all sweetness and sorrow. I felt the touch of his tongue like a budding promise.

And that promise was snatched away.

Quen pulled back. "I'm sorry." He stood, scarpering like a wounded Fauna. "I am *so* sorry. That was entirely inappropriate of me. I never meant to—"

"It's all right." I sagged against the couch. "We were just... testing our limits—"

"Testing our limits," he repeated in disbelief. "Right."

The bell to his apartment rang, and Quen bolted for it like he was chasing a tram. A few minutes earlier and it would have saved us some awkwardness.

Time was never on my side.

I warned you he wanted to fuck you.

It was just a kiss, Jinx. A drunken kiss between two lonely souls. I pulled my knees up to my chest and tried to stop the buzzing that wasn't wine or aether, but my own stupidity.

Quen returned, his face looking even more haggard than before, a strip of paper clutched tight in his hand. "A telegram. I've been summoned to Timefall Estates to speak with Ambassador Karendar."

"At this hour?" I glanced at the clock tower. It was almost nine. Rapture would open soon.

"Eli—Karendar often summons me late. I owe him my report." He took a deep breath, steadying himself. "Tomorrow, I think it would be prudent to visit Kronos."

See?

I sat up. "Whatever for?"

His eyes didn't meet mine. "I don't know what you are, and we've run out of time. My god may be able to examine your timeline and discover exactly what made you."

Why hadn't this been an option before? What had changed? "And then what? The Wardens subject me to tests? Lock me away?"

"Don't be so dramatic," he snapped, and I recoiled. He'd never lost his patience like this before, either. What was wrong with him? "You know how the Wardens work. They only remove those who pose a threat to Chime."

Had he forgotten who I was? Godless? I *was* the threat. The Diviner god would see who I was, all right. "If I go with you, will your god put pressure on Valeria to release Malk?" Perhaps this was the only card I held. I had no intention of meeting Dor, but if I could leverage Malk's release, I gods-damn would.

Quen rolled his eyes. "Is that all you care about?"

Why was he being so cruel? "Of course it is."

"We'll visit Kronos at the midday crossing. Can you handle being alone for a few hours?" He glanced at the clock tower. "I'll be back by midnight."

I offered a mute nod as he strode from his apartment without another word.

He's locked you in. He doesn't trust you anymore.

I waited until I was sure he was gone and then ran for the door and gave the handle a good yank. Jinx was right. He'd locked me inside.

What had gone wrong? Quen and I were partners, we'd been getting along great until the kiss—until he'd spilled his darkest secrets.

Shit.

He no longer saw me as his partner, but as a liability. I now knew things about him and his past that no mortal should. But I hadn't judged him; shit, I'd *sympathized*, and I thought he'd shared that sympathy. There'd been signs of his sinful nature here and there that had leaked through our time together, and I'd thought... I'd honestly thought I could coax that side out of him. Set him free.

He's a Warden. A Diviner. What did you expect?

He'd spent time in a correctional facility, for god's sake. It was no wonder his world view was warped.

You can't save him. Don't even waste your time.

Shit, Jinx was right. I'd been such a fool to trust him, to assume he was different. Dru had seen it coming, but I'd wanted to save Malk—to find *something* on those pissing Glimmer workhouses, and now I was back to square one.

So what now? I asked Jinx.

Get the fuck out of here.

Yes, that sounded like the best plan. I stumbled to my room, half-dizzy with wine, though mostly reeling from the absolute turn of this evening. My uncoordinated feet accidentally kicked over a stack of papers in the hall. Fuck it, I wasn't coming back here. I kneeled and rifled through them.

Some were copies of the Courier with events circled and times and dates written in the margins. Others were scraps of paper that were a completely nonsensical jumble of words, dates, times. Lists of items and places and description of mortals. None of it seemed relevant, as Dru had suggested, but they were written in a familiar way...

Gods. These were lists of things Quen needed to remember. I recognized the format; I'd used a similar form of note-taking when working at Lady Mae's. My brain was so unfocused and scattered at times, I'd needed the mental prods to steer me. But Quen? He didn't appear overly scattered to me.

Why would he need to remember so many things?

That Amnae professor. He could wipe memories. Had Quen asked him to wipe his? All of these? What in god's name was Quen doing to his own mind?

If he regularly wipes his own memories, then he could erase his memories of you, Jinx said. *That'll make it a lot easier for him to hand you over to his god and destroy you.*

He wouldn't do that. Would he?

What else have the Wardens done to him in that correctional facility?

Shit, shit, *shit*! I needed to get out of here. I returned to the guest room and quickly dressed in something casual and unassuming, shirt and slacks. I dug out the fresh lockpicks Dru had hidden under the bed thanks to her paranoia.

Waltzing out of the Silver Suite wouldn't be easy, not with the body of a Diviner. No doubt the Glimmer in reception would be spying. But if I knew how Glimmer and Diviner ran estates like these, their concierge service would employ Vesper.

The lock clicked open easily in my hands and I slid out into the Silver Suite's hallway. I walked casually, but instead of taking the elevator, I found the stairwell and took a brisk pace down to the basement. As I expected, the basement door opened out to the kitchen and laundry rooms full of busy Umber and Vesper. I could take my pick of either persona, but Vesper suited me better, and I may need their shadows.

Now, how would I grab one of them without them noticing?

The laundry room. Vesper are lazy arses.

Rude, but Jinx was right; I slipped in and heard the telltale snoring of a Vesper slacking off. Sure enough, I found a young Vesper girl dozing behind a trolley of cushions in her own makeshift fort. Carefully, I touched her wrist.

One light touch was enough to transform my pale Diviner skin back to indigo.

To my luck, the Silver Suite had a back door going out of the basement for supplies, and I used a faint stretch of shadow cover to slip out undetected and merge with the early evening air. While gated, the guards paid little attention to Vesper workers leaving for the day.

I joined the path through the gardens that separated the various tall apartment blocks of the Tower View district. Harmony's apartment was a comfortably small place in the City Rise block, a step up from the shabbier Stackhouses. With any luck, Quen wouldn't know to follow me there, but I'd grab Dru and catch the next elevator down to the Undercity before anyone noticed I'd gone.

The night air was cool and dark, though the aether lamplight hummed with its usual oppressive glare. I didn't expect anyone to follow me, but I played it safe and diverted to the dirt path between the trees and away from the lights. Darkness never bothered me; indeed, darkness was a companion welcoming me home.

I pushed my way through the bushes, but a light shone further ahead in the shadows. Not the silvery-blue of an aether light or the orange of an oil lamp, but... bright sunlight.

Glimmer.

Shit. I hastily beat a retreat and walked straight into a tall pale-faced woman.

A Necro. I hadn't heard her sneak up on me because they didn't need to pissing breathe!

The Necro leered at me. "In a hurry somewhere?"

Wait, she wasn't just any Necro, but the one who'd examined me in the Glimmer estate. Which meant I was in some deep shit.

The light grew brighter as two more Glimmer emerged from the bushes. Their light expanded, surrounding me in a circle. My Vesper powers were useless against them; I should have stayed as a Diviner.

But I could grab one of them and turn their own light against them.

One of the Glimmer approached cautiously, as though afraid that was exactly what I'd do. "Take her."

I leaped for the nearest bush. Or attempted to.

The Necro pounced on me before I could even take a step.

I jostled in her grip, desperately trying to pull away without touching her—I didn't want to accidentally brush up against a Necro and become one of them!

But the Necro left me with no choice, as her icy hands went straight for my windpipe.

Panic choked the breath from me. I tried to pry her tight fingers away, to take her power, *anything*, but a painful spasm shot down my neck and along my spine. My limbs dropped, and I would have fallen in a heap if the Necro hadn't caught me.

Shit! I tried to move, to scream, but my body wouldn't work.

Jinx? Please take control of me, do something!

She's paralyzed us. Sorry, we're fucked.

Great. Just great. I couldn't even muster a scowl as the Glimmer peered over my inanimate body and smirked.

XX

Every Diviner is required to check in with our educational facilities on Kronos at least once a month. This will be recorded by Wardens and any late appointments will be noted. Chime offers many avenues for self-expression and indeed sin, but we must remember that our Father places limits on self-expression for a reason; to avoid sin.
Duty comes first for any Diviner, for we are the cogs of the universe. It is by our laws that the Gate operates, and by our logic that Chime functions. We are the example that Chime must follow.
—E. Karendar, *Commandments for the Diviner*

IT WAS A RISK heading for the Academy at this time of night, but I knew Walter would still be in residence, perched over a book or fiddling with some machine or concoction. There was no rest for the wicked.

The familiar campus halls were empty as students left for either a night in Rapture or the welcoming safety of their dormitories. As I predicted, the lights to Walter's greenhouse were lit, and I burst inside.

"Code red," I declared after quickly scanning the room to check we were alone.

Walter sat at his alchemy bench and blinked beneath thick goggles, two vials of green liquid in his hands. He hastily placed them down and yanked off his goggles. "Good gods, man, what have you done now?"

I'd already made my way to a recliner and settled in, leaning my head against the headrest. "What haven't I done?"

"Is this about that woman—Kayl? Did you discover what she is?"

"Yes. Elijah is expecting me within the hour, so make this quick."

Walter muttered a curse I didn't quite catch, and then he was over by my side. We'd performed this dance so many times—I'd forgotten exactly how many—and he understood the necessity and urgency. The suckers of his fingertips pressed into my forehead and formed a tight seal.

"Have you been drinking, Quentin?"

"A little wine." I hiccupped. There was no point lying, he'd see for himself soon. My fingers drummed against my thighs, my feet tapping an impatient beat. Every last nerve was shredded to pieces.

"Sit still."

I obeyed, taking in a steady breath and closing my eyes.

The images of my recent past—my memories—flashed before me as Walter zipped through them at breathtaking speed. I couldn't keep myself from cringing at the guilt of memories I couldn't quite grasp, and the shame of ones I could.

I'd kissed her.

In one blind act of selfish stupidity, I'd kissed her.

I hadn't meant to, but I'd let myself fall, let myself get close, because I couldn't go one single blasted week without needing to push others away and wipe the evidence clean from my mind. With Kayl, I'd been doomed from the start.

A Godless woman. A brilliant Godless woman, who, in another time where gods didn't rule the mechanics of the universe, could have been a Warden—a better Warden than I—and made a difference. She cared for the mortals of Chime in a way I couldn't.

I knew she'd be gone by the time I returned. I wanted her to run. I'd planted that seed of doubt and fear by mentioning Kronos, but my words hadn't been a lie; that was exactly where Elijah would demand I take her next. Because she—

"Oh my," Walter gasped. "She truly is godless."

He saw the conclusions and possibilities racing through my mind. "I can't save her. But I can give her a head start." I knew she'd hate me for my *chivalrous shit*, but I saw no other way.

The Wardens would kill her. No, strap her to a table and have a Necro root through her organs first, dissect her while she was still alive, and try to find whatever connected her to the aether. Death would be kinder.

They'd never let her walk free.

She threatened the existence of the entire cosmos.

"You want me to wipe it all clean?" Walter asked.

"Wipe my visit to Sinner's Row. Keep the body in the steamworks, but distort the memories with Kayl. Elijah will only grow suspicious if I wipe the lot. Plant some lie, that my proximity to her, to the aether, muddles my memories."

"And the past few hours in your apartment? Wipe those too?"

His voice held no judgement, only kindness, and for that I would be forever in his debt. "Distort my conclusions, but the part where I—wipe that."

"You found happiness with another mortal for the first time in however many years, and you want me to wipe it? You'll run out of good memories at this rate."

That brief spark of happiness was a mistake best left forgotten. Elijah would punish me for getting close to another. "She has a lover. I brought her nothing but misery. Wipe it. I'll need to believe she's waiting for me in my apartment." Though *I* knew she wouldn't be, the man who left this greenhouse wouldn't have that assumption.

Walter released my head and crouched in front of me, his expression pitying, or whatever passed for pitying in an Amnae. "You can't keep doing this to yourself. It's going to cause permanent damage one day."

What did it matter?

I'd seen my future; I knew where it led.

When we'd entered the steamworks and I'd touched Hector Bezel and saw the creature that had stolen his soul, I'd assumed then that my time had come. That was why I'd gone to the reactor alone. Kayl would have been fine; she'd have made her way to Grayford or wherever the Godless made their base.

But she'd saved me.

And while the creature that had crawled from the reactor had glowed with the same radiant aether, it wasn't the same shape, the same death, and I'd earned a reprieve.

Then that blasted Mesmer had gone rooting through my mind and pulled out the one memory I'd wiped over and over and still it returned.

Every time I touched *him*, it came back with more clarity, more painful than ever.

That vision always pushed me over the edge.

It brought back memories I couldn't wipe, because to do so would cast me adrift and then I'd be useless to everyone. Memories of the Vesper. The Glimmer girl. My stint in a correctional facility. Wiping them would have been easy, wouldn't it? I could have moved on. But Elijah never wanted me to forget, because to forget was an absolution I didn't deserve.

Moving on didn't happen for mortals like me. We suffered, and we served.

Though now the Mesmer knew. They could have sold my darkest secrets to Erosain. If Elijah found out, he'd be furious. Another correctional facility would be the best I could hope for. Not that it mattered in the end.

Time was running out for me.

Not just the death of my mortal body; the death of my soul.

Tears ran down my cheeks and I removed my spectacles to rub them away. "Look at me, Walter. I'm a bloody mess."

He put his hand on my shoulder. "Find the Godless. Join them."

I glanced up through bleary eyes. "You know I'd only bring trouble to their door."

He smiled with a shared fondness. "You bring trouble to my door. Chime needs godless heathens, and they need you."

No. The last mortal they needed on their side was the Dark Warden.

From outside the greenhouse, the Academy's clock tower rang out ten o'clock. I patted his hand in thanks. "You best get to work."

His fingers returned to my forehead. "You're a good man, Quentin."

"I wouldn't know." I squeezed my eyes shut.

This part of the process always felt odd, as though a Necro surgeon wiggled his fingers into my brain and cut out the rotting parts. Worst was the vague feeling of bewilderment that came afterwards, like wandering through mist, knowing that something lay beyond, but not what.

263

To his credit, Walter was a master of his art. He could leave subtle hints and traces in my subconscious telling me what to do and where to go next, to protect me from myself.

I'd forgotten so many regrets.

But for these precious few seconds, I could be free. I could blaspheme as much as I liked, because soon those thoughts would be wiped clean and the pious Quen would emerge.

For these precious few seconds, no one owned my thoughts.

No man.

No god.

Only one woman.

I'd enter oblivion thinking of her curves, of the swell of her belly in my dreams. I'd think of my tongue tasting hers, tasting the sweet bud of her sex, of throwing her atop that table in Erosain's bar and fucking her for all I was worth with Erosain watching over my shoulder, complimenting my form.

"What would your god think now?"

Dor would be delightfully disappointed in His son for oh-so-many things.

Good men didn't indulge such lustful thoughts.

They didn't crave sin.

I'd hurt her. I'd forget that. And now... Now those lustful thoughts drifted away, lost to more guilt and shame. Not even in the sanctity of my mind did I want to come between her and the Vesper who remained in Valeria's clutches.

I couldn't forget him; Malkavaan Byvich needed me. As did many more like him.

No, for these last few seconds, I wanted to imagine a world where women like Kayl ruled it; godless beings that could shape Chime into a haven for all mortals, not just for the pious, not just for those sodding Glimmer. A world where indulging one's natural pleasures didn't make you a sinner. A world where the gods couldn't control us. Maybe with Kayl, it was possible, but I'd never see it.

Chaos was coming.

Could a god feel fear? Feel pain? I'd pray... one day... they... would...

My carriage pulled into Timefall Estates at exactly thirteen minutes past ten. So much of its architecture was square, precise, clean, and modern. It didn't blend with the rest of Chime's brick and brass, or even the Golden City's extravagance, as though someone had bought a life-size snow globe of Kronos from some tacky Central souvenir shop and dropped it right here. Timefall was, quite simply, an estate plucked out of a future that had yet to come to pass.

Darkness shrouded the estate, and the silvery-blue glare of the aether lamps cast everything in an odd chrome. It felt asynchronous.

It didn't feel like Chime at all. Like home.

Or that was the wine talking. I'd come straight from my apartment after indulging in a few glasses, a sin I was destined to pay for later, and it left me feeling a little shaky and lost. Though both Kayl and I had returned from the steamworks shaken from what we'd discovered down there. Another dead Diviner. How many more would we find before we learned the truth of Kayl's god?

The carriage stopped outside the familiar lavender bushes of House Karendar.

The ambassador's home was a grand one, tucked in the far corner of Timefall where it didn't attract the noise of Chime, though at night, the silence and darkness wrapped around me like a suffocating cloak. Only the hoot of owls followed me—their hooting a precise alarm from Fauna Wardens on watch over the estate to announce my arrival.

I bid goodnight to my driver and strode up the pristine pathway to Elijah's home. Aether lamps lit the gated entrance where two Diviner Wardens stood guard. They nodded as they allowed me through. I was expected.

I'd never been fond of the clean architecture of House Karendar. The angles were too sharp and there was too much empty space; wide open grass with nothing to decorate it, rooms with the barest of furniture and no one to occupy them. It felt lonely. Oppressive.

A mournful melody welcomed me as I stepped inside and left my shoes and jacket by the door. Bitter coffee battled with the lavender bushes outside for dominance, and the conflicting scents made me queasy.

Elijah's living room resembled the open studios of Kronos with plain walls and mirrors, the complete opposite of my oak and brass furnishings. Even the bookshelves were neatly organized, where dust wouldn't dare tread. In the corner by the patio, Eli sat playing on his grand piano, the notes rising to a crescendo. Funny, I'd forgotten that he played.

His fingers slid over the keys with such beautiful precision, it made my heart flutter.

Then they slammed down, and the music stopped with the jarring clang of a bell toll. "You're late."

"Apologies, Your Excellency, I came as quickly as I—"

"You disobeyed my orders. Can you provide an adequate reason why?" He rose and snatched the mug of coffee that rested on top of the piano. He leaned against the piano, still dressed in his usual pinstripe suit; his brass eyes narrowed as they awaited my answer.

That golden stare always made it hard to speak, and I swallowed a lump in my throat. "I explained in my telegram—I didn't believe this woman to be in league with the aether creatures, but with her cooperation, I intended to learn more—"

"And did you? Where is this woman now?"

"She is, ah, locked inside my apartment. There was another death in the steamworks. A Diviner named Doctor Hector Bezel." I paused and watched for any flicker of recognition across Elijah's face, but he gave no indication. Perhaps Kayl had been wrong on who she'd witnessed at Lady Mae's. "I saw the aether creature with my own eyes, though I cannot fathom how the aether is able to take shape or form a consciousness. My findings have been inconclusive thus far. I need more time to—"

"I've given you enough time. You should have brought her to me as I explicitly commanded you to. A mere telegram is not sufficient." Elijah took a swig from his coffee and then strode for me, so quick that I had to force myself to remain in place and not run for the door. "Show me what you've found."

I sucked in hot air as Elijah's hands grasped onto me. His palm against my hip, pulling me close as though about to embrace, and his fingers went straight to my throat. They traced a soft line down to my pulse.

Then my memories flashed by in reverse as Elijah filtered through them, slowing in places to enjoy his perusal.

He saw everything; my visit to Eventide, the questioning I placed Kayl under, her own remarkable transformation into a Diviner, an Umber, an Amnae, an Ember, and back again, the aether creature we confronted in the steamworks—

"These memories are muddled." Elijah pulled back suddenly and his brass eyes glared with hateful accusation.

"They—They are? I mean—it must be the proximity to the aether."

His grip tightened on my neck, his sharp fingernails digging into my skin, and I fought to rein in my composure. Elijah owned me in more ways than one; my indenture with the Wardens, the specialized cases he and Father arranged for me.

My thoughts. My memories.

My body.

"What are you hiding from me, Quentin?"

My pulse raced as his fingers remained pressed painfully into my neck. "You've seen my memories—you know I couldn't hide anything from you—"

"You visited Professor Burns."

"To examine Kayl's past, to find out what she is—"

"And you didn't come to me straight away with this information? You waited until I summoned you and then acted tardy with it?" He leaned in close and breathed me in. "I can smell the wine on you."

"Eli, please—"

"Do you like her?"

The audacity of his question made me blink. "Pardon?"

"This woman. Do you want to fuck her? Is that it?"

"No, why would I—"

"A woman who can turn into a female Diviner. That must have been quite a shock for you, Quentin."

I'll admit it had surprised me when I first saw her change, and every time after that. I could be forgiven for acting a little goggle-eyed, couldn't I? Female Diviner were so rare. "She means nothing to me. Nothing but a case to solve."

"Is that so? I assigned you a case to solve three years ago; to investigate these so-called Godless and eliminate them by whatever means necessary. And instead, you gallivant with them across the Golden City and then invite them into your apartment to drink wine. What does that tell me?"

"I employed her assistance to stop the aether creatures, nothing more—"

"I went through great effort to convince the Wardens to reinstate your badge. How do you think I feel when you disrespect me like this? Where is your loyalty?"

"With you," I blurted out. "With Father. I'm sorry. I never meant to bring you shame." Tears came to my eyes, and I blinked furiously to stop them from spilling.

The pressure around my neck relaxed. "Good. You're so impressionable. You know it's important I watch over you, don't you? We've been down this path before. It would hurt me deeply to see you fall into sin again."

Because I toed the line when it came to sin. I'd always justified my actions as being part of my intent to understand the various domains that we Wardens served. But such radical thinking had once earned me six months in a place I'd rather not think about.

I knew I should have been grateful for Elijah.

Without his advocacy, I may well have never escaped.

But what freedom had I earned if he kept me on such a short leash? If his love squeezed me like chains?

The shame of Elijah's stare burned in my stomach and I swallowed the words that had bubbled forth in my throat, desperate to spill out.

You don't own me.

"We need to keep this under control," he said. "These Diviner deaths are connected to the aether, but without aether we cannot expand Chime and grow. The reinforcement of the clock tower is one such measure to contain it. Thankfully, the Glimmer workhouses are almost finished with their plating. We're fortuitous that this contract between our domains has proved fruitful."

"You knew the Glimmer bribed Valeria for Vesper. Are you aware of how they treat mortals inside their workhouses?"

"I don't appreciate you questioning me, but yes, I am aware—"

"This goes against the Covenant!"

His brass eyes narrowed, and I flinched as he reached for his coffee. "The Vesper are Valeria's mortals to do with as she wishes. If she consents to Glimmer methods, then no breach has been made. I know you feel some modicum of responsibility for these mortals, but such actions are necessary to protect the greater good of Chime. These aether creatures won't stop at Diviner souls. The quicker we finish these clock tower repairs, the safer we'll all be, even the Vesper."

Blast it. I'd wasted weeks investigating those workhouses, and he'd known about their depraved practices all along. No, he'd *encouraged* it.

I didn't like it; allowing the Glimmer to take Vesper slaves to build our reinforcements in exchange for Glimmer indoctrination was obscene. The Wardens—Elijah—were turning a blind eye to their atrocities.

Hadn't I promised to end them?

"I need you to believe in the work we're doing," Elijah continued. "In our vision."

"I—I do."

"I worry this won't be enough. The more aether that pumps through the steamworks reactors, the more of these creatures could manifest. We need methods of destroying them, which is why it is imperative we discover the connection between aether and your Godless woman. It's time we brought her to Kronos."

My heart skipped a beat. "Give me a few more days, and I'll find—"

"I want her making the crossing tomorrow."

Now I truly struggled to maintain my composure. Dragging her to Kronos meant the end of this case. It meant Elijah no longer trusted me with the answers.

And it likely meant the end of Kayl.

I knew what they'd do; rip her in half to find where her consciousness began and the aether—the twin soul—connected. They'd come to the same conclusions I had, that she was an innocent possessed by an aether creature, and by pulling her apart they'd sever that connection, destroy the aether. But that would destroy her, too. They wouldn't even care.

"We could bring her to Warden HQ and run a few examinations—"

"She's too dangerous to leave running around Chime. Remember, she killed the owner of a prominent Glimmer business—"

"That was an accident—"

"An accident? Nothing about Lady Mae's death was an accident. This woman is an illegal and an apostate. I thought she meant nothing to you?" Elijah's brow quirked. "I thought you cared about this case?"

I felt caught in a trap. "I do, but she's mortal. If one of the gods discover our tests—"

"None of the gods have claimed her." Elijah waved me off. "But Father will examine her and discover her domain one way or another. Leave me to handle the outcome. Whichever domain owns her soul has already breached multiple protocols and the Covenant. This is no longer a matter of diplomacy, but urgency. I trusted *you* with diplomacy, and you've given me nothing."

I could formulate no counterargument. Fogginess blanked my mind— curse me for drinking wine before I came here! There were no words that could convince Elijah otherwise.

It would always come down to this.

Perhaps I could keep her safe in Kronos. Watch over her as an advocate of the Godless. Someone needed to give them a voice.

"I want you off this case," Elijah commanded as though he'd read the conspiracy on my face.

"What—why?" I spluttered. "Haven't I served you?"

"You're too close to this woman. She's a bad influence. Your decisions of late have been tardy and irrational. You'll deliver her to Kronos, and then you'll wait for my next orders. Given your disrespect of my *previous* orders, a week or two inside the HQ's correctional facility may be required to remind you of your duties."

This was a punishment, but what did the punishment matter when a mortal life was at stake? Not just Kayl's; these aether creatures had souls. I knew it in the depths of my own.

What power did I have to help them?

And there was the question of Malkavaan Byvich, the poor man left to suffer Valeria's whims on Eventide. With no answers, I held no bargaining power to set him free. Elijah could put pressure on Valeria, but he'd also question why. And I, to my great shame, couldn't stomach to ask him.

If I could only save one, it needed to be Kayl. She wasn't bound by a god, at least not yet. Malkavaan was already lost to us.

"Well?" Elijah demanded.

I bowed my head. "It will be done, Your Excellency."

Elijah placed his mug aside and beckoned me close. "I don't do this to hurt you. I do this to save your soul and Chime's. Don't pout. It's unseemly." An easy smile came to his lips, more the casual boy I knew from our Academy days. He rested both hands on my shoulders and squeezed with gentle reassurance. "Tell me you'll do this for me."

"I'll do this for you. Of course I will."

"Good." His lips brushed my forehead with the softest of touches, sending a flush of guilt into my stomach. Then, as he withdrew, his brass eyes hardened. "Take off your shirt."

The guilt in my stomach curdled into panic. "Please don't—"

"You've sinned tonight. You know how Father feels about sin."

"It was only a little wine—"

"And cavorting with a Godless woman? Disobeying my commands? I hate to do this, but it's for your own good. Take off your shirt."

This was my penance. Father didn't demand my flesh and blood, not like some gods did, yet it pleased Eli. Thus Father allowed it.

I undid the buttons of my waistcoat and shirt with trembling fingers. With penance came pain.

With pain came forgiveness. Or should. Did it ever?

I kneeled and held my hands together in prayer. Elijah tugged off his tie and wrapped it around my wrists, pulling it tight so I wouldn't squirm. He didn't offer a gag. He knew I wouldn't scream. Screaming was a confession of guilt.

He moved behind me out of view, making my heart leap once more as the heat of his palm rested on my back. His touch burned me. Possessed me.

The touch withdrew, leaving me both bereft and relieved.

And then he unbuckled his belt.

Elijah was my heart. My salvation. Everything I did was for him, to please him. So why did this leave me feeling so empty? Why now did my thoughts betray me?

Why did they turn to a Godless woman?

The crack of his belt seared across my back, marking me for the sinner I was.

To scream was to confess.

To bleed was to repent.

To cry was an absolution I did not deserve.

"Who owns your thoughts?"

I didn't know anymore.

It was past midnight when I returned to the Silver Suite. The Gate was set to Kronos, and in twelve hours' time, I'd be making the crossing there—dragging Kayl to her doom, though she didn't know it yet.

It left me sick to my stomach.

The walk to my apartment hurt, and I carried my jacket over my arm. I couldn't bear the touch of cloth on my back, though it was nothing a warm shower and lotion wouldn't fix. Elijah had been rough with me. He was always rough when I'd displeased him, as though punishing me was the only way he could get through to my sin-addled mind.

I craved it. I despised it. I could never categorize my emotions when it came to Elijah. The hardest part was the visions that followed whenever he made me touch him.

Another memory to wipe. Had I already?

Though I couldn't shake off the feeling I was missing something. I'd have to scan my papers for whatever clues past Quen had left me.

I hadn't wanted to leave Kayl alone this long, or to lock her inside my apartment, but it was for her own safety—no, it was for my peace of mind. I didn't trust her, did I?

It was dark inside and eerily quiet. Had Kayl gone to sleep? I slipped off my shoes and carefully crept along the hall. Her bedroom door was open, her bed empty. My heart raced as I ran into the living room and yanked on a lamp.

Belatedly, I realized her shoes weren't by the door.

Blast it! She'd gone.

I could have scoured my entire apartment and not found her. Had she known this was the end? Had I given her some indication? Some hint?

I stared out at the clock tower, at Kronos through the Gate below.

Elijah would be furious.

I wasn't sure whether to laugh or cry or scream. Kayl had gone, and now my work on this case resumed. She'd saved my life once more; granted me one final reprieve.

I ran into my room and scrambled under the bed, dragging out my old case. It flipped open with ease and I stared at the single brass pistol still resting there.

This pistol had killed before. It would kill again.

Nothing could stop the march of time.

My fingers curled around the cool handle. It had been years since I'd wielded it, but the mechanics were like controlling a tram. Familiar. Monotonous. Its condition was absolutely pristine. Not a single dot of dust. I'd need it now if I was to hunt my Godless quarry. Who knew if bullets would be enough to stop a creature made of aether? But perhaps my old faithful could earn me a few more reprieves.

Wardens were permitted to carry weapons. I was the only one who didn't.

Just as Wardens were supposed to work alongside a partner, and I'd elected not to, given my unique abilities.

Until Kayl had named herself my partner.

I'd allowed it. Accepted it. A mistake on my part, perhaps, for I knew Elijah would question my judgement, and my sore back paid the price. Kayl was no Warden and never would be, but Chime needed heathens like her.

And I needed her for this case.

As I glanced around my empty apartment, at the discarded wine bottle, the cold sandwiches and cakes still sitting on my dining table, an empty pang gripped my chest.

For the first time in days, I was alone.

Truly alone.

With not even the heathens for company.

Part Three

21

You were made in the image of your god, but they aren't you.
You possess your own heart, your own mind, your own soul.
You do not own their cruelty or greed.
Nor are you responsible for their deeds.
You are mortal. You will live, you will age, and you will die.
None of these things make you lesser.
In the words of the Covenant, you are equal.
—Anonymous, Godless affirmation

APPARENTLY, ALL IT TOOK to kidnap someone in Chime was to throw them in a sack and travel down the service elevator to the Undercity. None of the station staff checked to see if the suspicious body-shaped package actually contained a living mortal and not legal Vesper mushrooms. I couldn't kick or scream to get their attention—the Necro had completely paralyzed me—and I heard the station staff's dismissal as the Glimmer whisked me off to my doom. I knew where they'd be taking me; back to their workhouse.

But why? Did they remember who I was and what I had done? Did they mean to question me? Torture me? Discover what I was? Was it even about my odd powers, or my Godless connections? Had they seen me escape from Quen's apartment and assumed they could pry intel of the Wardens from me? Or had they just seen a Vesper out for an evening stroll and decided I'd make an excellent addition to their workhouse?

My captors gave no indication they recognized me at all, save the Necro, who kept obsessively patting my head through the sack's rough cloth. Perhaps they liked to play with their food.

They wouldn't go through all that trouble to eat you. Besides, you'll taste terrible.

Thank you, Jinx. That fills me with confidence.

They lifted me onto a carriage, not a tram, from what I could tell, though I had no idea how long we bumped along the Undercity roads. I'd almost nodded off when I felt them lift and carry me, jostling me like I truly was a sack of mushrooms.

Whoever carried me eventually emptied me from the sack, unceremoniously dumping me onto a lush carpet. Bright oil lamps burned my eyes. I cringed against the light and felt myself being dragged onto a chair, my arms and legs tied tight like the Wardens had. Thankfully, my hands remained glove-free.

I squinted as my Vesper vision adjusted to the brightness.

This was the Glimmer ambassador's room. Shit.

"You can undo your magic now," a familiar woman drawled.

The Necro touched my neck, and an icy shock washed over me, as though I'd been dunked in water. I gasped and shuddered against the restraints. Drool had run down my chin and my slacks were hitched up over my ankles. I must have looked a right state.

You've more pressing concerns?

The kidnapping. Right.

The Glimmer ambassador leaned on the edge of her desk, wearing a silk minidress too tight to be modest. Her golden skin and flowing hair glittered in the lamps and her long crimson nails idly tapped the wooden surface. She was a gorgeous woman, the absolute pinnacle of her domain, though for the life of me I couldn't remember her name. Glenys or Glory or—

Gloria, Jinx said.

There was a chance she'd not remember me from before—I had an entirely different nose, after all. I put on my demure Vesper act and let tears come to my eyes. "Who—Who are you? Why have you brought me here? Please, my lady—"

"Spare me your pretense. I know who you are, Anne Arkey, if that's your real name. Only a Godless would infiltrate my estate and pass my test with such *passionate* hatred for their patron. Really, I expected your kind to shove your nose into our affairs long before now."

Well, shit. "If you've brought me here for sermons and hymns, I'm afraid I'm not interested. More to the point; what are you doing to the Vesper?"

"And there it is. The real you. So defiant." Gloria's red eyes smoldered. "You've seen for yourself what we're *doing* to them; we're freeing them from the chains of Valeria. I thought the Godless would approve."

"You're stealing them from one god and chaining them to another!"

"We didn't steal them from Valeria. She volunteered them in exchange for gold. A simple transaction. We take the labor of her mortals, do as we wish with them, and when their time's up their souls simply return to her. No one is hurt, though blessed Gildola's influence on Valeria grows through her own greed."

"No one is *hurt*?" I snarled. "What of the Vesper you work to death?"

"The Vesper are happy to be here. We give them food, shelter, medicine, and a purpose free of sin—"

"Do you mortals not smell the shit spewing from your mouth?"

Go on, keep insulting her, Jinx urged. *I'm sure that'll help our situation.*

But the ambassador only flashed her smug Golden City smirk. "You're rather invested in Valeria's mortals, considering you don't even share her domain. But then we're not quite sure what you are. A Diviner? An Umber? An Ember?"

Shit, they *had* been spying on me, likely following Quen and I through the Undercity. "What can I say? I like to play dress up."

"You can save the theatrics, my dear. Who and what you are does not concern me."

"So you kidnapped me for sport? I already said I wasn't interested in your sermons."

"You'll be interested in what information I have to offer you."

What information could a Glimmer possibly offer me? "Free every single Vesper in your workhouse and we'll talk."

"That could be arranged."

Now she was shitting me. "What do you want?"

"You don't trust Quentin Corinth, do you? Why else would you be escaping his apartment in the dead of night? Though I'll admit the pair of you made an odd partnership."

The thought of Quen returning to an empty apartment made my chest tighten, though I couldn't explain why. "If you think I can play spy for the Wardens, you're wrong. Corinth held me on a leash, that's all. His apartment has nothing of value—we already scoured it."

"I'd expect nothing less of a Godless. You're aware of the work we're doing here, correct? To create the plating and parts needed to reinforce Chime's clock tower?"

"The Wardens contracted you, and you used the opportunity to snatch Vesper away from Eventide and enslave them."

"Would you believe me if I said the Vesper willingly came to us seeking sanctuary? That they chose to accept Glimmer rule because we've found a key to true freedom? A method of separating a mortal from their god? What would you say to that?"

"I'd say you're out of your mind."

Gloria chuckled. "Does this sound more far-fetched than a Vesper who can change her physical appearance between domains? We know the Wardens have been hiding the real reason behind their urgent clock tower repairs. Ambassador Karendar couldn't keep something this large from us. Aether has been leaking throughout various generator hotspots, and these leaks have given rise to creatures that lay beyond mortal comprehension—beyond the domains. Am I correct?"

Painfully correct. "What does this have to do with separating a mortal from their god?"

There was a gleam in Gloria's eye. "Everything. Perhaps it's easier if I show you." She gestured for the Glimmer standing by the door.

They came over to my chair and undid the straps, allowing me to stand. I rubbed my sore wrists and my eyes darted to the window.

Run. Get out now while you still can.

I'd tried that before and wasn't successful. In Vesper form, their sunlight would blind me. Not to mention there were too many of them.

And, gods-damn it, I wanted to know what the Glimmer—and Wardens—were truly up to. I wanted the truth. Quen hadn't given me anything to help shut these damn workhouses down, but perhaps there was something here which would.

Gloria led me through the halls of the Glimmer estate with a small entourage surrounding and watching my every movement; three more Glimmer and the Necro woman from before, who kept leering at me and licking her lips. I ignored her and followed dutifully as we stepped outside and strode for the factory building where they'd previously taken Malk.

My heart ached as I remembered this was the last time we'd been together before Eventide. Before everything went wrong.

They could be leading you to your doom.

Why bother with the preamble if they meant to torture or kill me? Though who knew with Glimmer; they liked to play the martyr.

The Vesper remained inside the factory, toiling on the Wardens' pet maintenance project—even more than I'd remembered. Regardless of what conspiracy I was about to become privy to, I couldn't forget that these were enslaved here because of the Glimmer. They may treat me with courtesy, but they weren't my allies.

Rather belatedly, I realized where the Glimmer were taking me.

Underground to where the aether screamed.

I followed them into the tunnel, which was now lit by the Glimmer's glowing skin. We walked in single file, but each step felt heavier than the last, as though I pushed against wind and needed to force myself forward.

Stop it, Jinx whined. *Turn around and run.*

Are you fighting against me?

You don't understand what's beyond that door.

Which was exactly why I needed to see it.

Down we went and the static of the air *popped* and *cracked* around me, though none of the Glimmer noticed, or cared.

And then we approached that odious metal door.

There was no flash of aether this time, no colorful sparks dancing through the tiny square window. Despite that, I held my breath as the door clanked open and I crossed the threshold.

Inside, the room appeared circular in design, not unlike the reactor from the steamworks. But instead of a generator, the room encircled a metal chair bolted in the center. Large pipes and wires spread from its back in a sprawling heap of steel tentacles. Beside it stood a control panel where various buttons lit up with an ominous red glow.

My heart caught in my throat. "What is this?"

Gloria stopped beside the chair and ran a fingernail along the leather straps. "Your salvation. The Wardens have been creating these machines in secret. This one is a failed prototype we salvaged and pieced together. The rest were taken to Kronos for further testing. It is designed to attract and capture the creatures created by the aether leaks."

If I were truly one of these aether creatures, then I wasn't attracted by this thing at all—I was repulsed by it. "To trap them?"

"To destroy them."

My heart fluttered anew. "How does one destroy aether?"

"This machine works much in the same way as these creatures who have been killing Diviner; it separates a mortal from their soul."

That's exactly what power those aether creatures possessed; the ability to steal the soul of a mortal and leave their body behind. How had the Wardens been able to recreate the same process?

And what did that mean?

What do you think it means, idiot?

It meant nothing good. Such a machine could rend the soul from a mortal, destroy the sacred covenant between mortal and god. It went far beyond the apostasy of the Godless.

Shit, I was going to be sick.

Why aren't you running already? Get out of here!

From the corner of my eye, my Glimmer guards hadn't moved to grab me, but they blocked my only exit. "This was the Wardens' plan all along? Not to simply repair the clock tower, but to destroy the aether creatures?" I had to believe that splitting a mortal from their god was so profane that even the Glimmer wouldn't dare touch it. And yet here we stood.

"That was Karendar's intended purpose, I'm sure. However, my god and I have recognized an alternative use for this machine. A machine which can separate a soul from a mortal also separates that soul from their god. Her sacred holiness Gildola believes we can reconfigure this device to induce the process without tearing the soul from the body. In other words, we can separate a mortal from their god permanently."

Was such a thing even possible? I couldn't believe my ears.

The implications were enormous.

"Why are you showing me this?"

Gloria blinked, as though confused why I'd ask. "I thought your organization would leap at the chance to use it. To become truly godless."

"Why would a Glimmer want to help us? You hate us and everything we stand for."

"This is true. We abhor your apostasy—"

"And now you wish to advocate it?" But as the words passed my lips, I understood why the Glimmer would be interested in such technology.

They'd long believed themselves to be the one true domain, powered by the one true god, the god of life and light and all that. Their correctional facilities had preached their sermons and enticed mortals from other domains to reject their gods in favor of Gildola. The Wardens tried to tamp down their behavior, though not hard enough.

Apostasy included the worship of a god not your own. But of course the Glimmer didn't care for other gods, nor the sanctity of the Covenant, it seemed.

With this machine, they could split mortals from those so-called lesser gods. And then they'd be free to become Gildola's acolytes.

Such a thought sickened me, but then I too could see the possibilities, the shiny bauble that the Glimmer ambassador dangled before my eyes. The Godless could also be free. Harmony would never need to answer to Serenity. Sinder would no longer live in fear of Edana. Vincent could finally free himself of The Nameless One. Reve could cut the tether from Mesmorpheus and end his plaguing nightmares. Dru... Well, I wasn't sure if Dru would ever want to leave her god, but the choice would be there.

And Malk. Gods, I could free Malk. He'd no longer be trapped in Valeria's clutches.

This changed everything.

It changes nothing, Jinx said.

Don't you see, Jinx? With this, we would end the reign of gods. Because if mortals were no longer reliant on their patron god, those gods ceased to matter.

The Glimmer want Vesper slaves. They can't be trusted.

Yes, *they* couldn't be trusted, and gods knew this was likely a trap, but I could save Malk. And perhaps bring down the Glimmer and Wardens along the way.

"Why do you need me, Ambassador?" I glanced at the machine with its array of pipes and wires. "It's not yet functional, is it?"

Gloria grinned with the arrogance of someone who knew she'd won. "As I stated before; we believe it can be reconfigured, but we are missing the necessary parts. A Diviner scientist named Doctor Hector Bezel possesses the schematics needed, though these were lost after his death. I believe his apprentice, Doctor Zachery Finch, may have hidden them. We also require a series of crystals—prisms—to capture and deflect the aether."

An odd coincidence that the Diviner doctor now lay dead and soulless. "You can't retrieve these yourself?"

"Karendar may grow suspicious if I send my mortals into the steamworks. I believe you are already acquainted with Doctor Finch? The specific crystals we require are also in the possession of Ambassador Erosain. We sent one of our mortals there to retrieve them, but she has yet to return—blessed Gildola believes she may have fallen victim to Erosain's wiles. While we cannot step foot in Erosain's bar, *you* can."

"Say I retrieve these for you; what then? You allow the Godless free rein, and then hoard this device for yourself?"

"That is the deal we're willing to offer."

A deal that sounded too good to be true. Even if their intent was to steal Vesper from Valeria, if the Vesper became split from her, the Godless could save them from the Glimmer, too. I detested the idea of helping a Glimmer, but the Godless needed this.

I needed this.

This is a mistake.

No, it was our salvation.

I didn't know if a god was out there waiting for me like Quen believed. I didn't know if these aether creatures were truly godless beings, a weapon made by one of the other gods, or a bastardized mixture of all twelve.

But all mortals deserved their freedom.

And we, the Godless, could actually deliver it.

I offered my hand. "Then we have a deal."

To my great surprise, Gloria took it. "Don't disappoint me, Godless."

It was well past midnight when I left the Glimmer estate and made my way through the tunnels to Grayford. Though I ached to return to the depot and explain everything, I needed to make one stop first.

The lantern in Varen's window glowed. He was in residence, and up rather late, possibly working on reports. Vesper enjoyed their nights. That was no surprise, though a part of me balked at Varen's presence here. Shouldn't he have been watching over Malk? Had he been making enough crossings to Eventide to ensure Valeria wasn't torturing him to death?

I picked up a small pebble and threw it at Varen's window. A few seconds later, his face appeared. I couldn't tell his expression from here, but he'd seen me. A few more minutes and he came striding out the front door.

His lips were pursed into a frown. "Kayl? What in god's name are you doing here?" he whispered.

"I could ask you the same."

Varen placed a hand on my shoulder and glanced around to check no one saw, but the main square was quiet—any loiterers were hanging around the night market. "Come." He steered me inside his home.

I'd spent my youth exploring this building when I'd run Varen's errands and he'd taught me Chime's secrets in return. The weathered furniture and threadbare curtains of those earlier years were gone, replaced now with sturdy oak and gaudy wallpaper. When had he come into fortune? And why hadn't he shared it with Grayford?

We strode past the empty reception to his study on the second floor. This, too, had been renovated. Even the carpet had been replaced with something plush under my shoes.

No wonder we'd stopped holding meetings here, and he came to me in the depot instead. How much wealth had he been hiding?

And where had it come from? "You've redecorated."

"I'm an ambassador," he snapped, hearing the accusation in my voice. "If I am to command respect among my mortals and the Warden Council, then my status must reflect my position. I thought you were with Corinth?"

I tucked my hands into my pockets. "I escaped."

"Are you insane?" Whatever calm Varen had cultivated now fled, and his words came out with a snarl. "He'll be tearing his way through Grayford come dawn in search of you! You remember the last time he and his Wardens tore Grayford apart on their hunts?"

"I was there." Though it reminded me that the Glimmer couldn't be trusted and I was foolish for ever bargaining with them to begin with. "He's ordered me to Kronos."

The anger wilted from Varen's expression and he sagged against his desk. "I can't help you. Not anymore."

"I know."

"The Wardens suspect I've been assisting the Godless. They've brought me to heel and there's nothing I can—"

"I *know*. What of Malk? Is he... safe?"

"Valeria has kept him imprisoned, but unharmed. Though she grows impatient. Do you or Corinth have *anything* that could appease her? Do you know what you are?"

"I haven't the foggiest."

"So all this time you've been doing *what* with Corinth?"

His tone riled me. "I've been trying to discover the truth! Will you listen to me for one moment? The Glimmer have a machine, a Warden-sanctioned machine, which can separate a mortal from their god."

Varen stared at me, dumbfounded. "This is a poor time for a joke—"

"It's no joke." I tried to explain what it was, what it did, and what task the Glimmer had set me on. Each word I uttered pained Varen, and he cringed until he'd sunk into his office chair.

"The Wardens couldn't have built such a device," he said, more to convince himself. "It's inconceivable. In Glimmer hands, they could enslave so many Vesper."

"We won't let that happen. But think; this device could free Malk."

"Free Malk? Without Valeria's blessing, Malk isn't going anywhere."

Those words were a blunt truth. "You're supposed to be her voice. Speak with her at the next crossing. Tell her I've uncovered a plot by the Glimmer—some lie, it doesn't matter. She suspects the Glimmer of foul play, regardless; she'll believe they're backstabbers who have taken her Vesper for nefarious reasons. Tell her the Glimmer have a weapon and Corinth and I will destroy it, but I won't act unless she releases Malk—"

"Valeria is no fool. She'll want proof—"

"Then give her proof. Give her anything. *Please*," I pleaded. "Bring him back to me."

Varen ran a hand down the full length of his face. Deep lines were etched across his forehead, and his black hair had more streaks of silver. When had he become so old? "What are you, Kayl? Truly, what are you? Are you beholden to Valeria? I saw you turn into a Diviner. That's... This whole situation is insanity." He shook his head.

"Truly, I don't know what I am; I haven't yet found a god who owns me. But you know me, I'm Godless. I'm me. None of that has changed."

"Do you believe this god-splitting machine can save the Vesper?"

"It's worth a try, isn't it?" I took a tentative step forward. "You don't love Valeria. I know you don't."

Why trust him? Jinx asked. *You saw the way he slobbered over Valeria's feet.*

Faced with one's god, one has no choice but to prostrate oneself. How could Varen possibly love his god? When Valeria had once given him wings with one hand and then ripped them from his flesh with another?

Then where did he get that fancy desk? Where are your Godless donations going?

I *wanted* to ask, but I needed his help, and pissing him off wouldn't bring Malk back.

Varen leaned into his chair and sighed. "You're killing me, Kayl. You've always been that way. Pushy. I liked that about you." He fidgeted with a silver band studded with a large sapphire around his finger. "I've witnessed many things in my lifetime. Horrific things. Do you ever wonder why I bend myself backwards to serve Valeria? Why I'm complicit in her foul deeds?"

I swallowed a lump in my throat. "Because you have no choice."

"There's always a choice." He pulled off the ring and allowed it to roll underneath his desk. "I could have chosen death. I could have chosen oblivion. Valeria owns my soul, but she'll never own my will. Not completely. It's through sheer stubbornness that I'm still here, and through sheer stubbornness that I've assisted you and your Godless, if only to prove I retain some aspect of my will. That, you and I have in common." His dark eyes met mine; shrewd, as I knew them, though I could still recognize the affection. "Valeria wants to break my will, and so she forces me to act in her name. It's a game to her. One I fear she may win."

"If there's freedom for you, I'll find it. I promise."

He dipped his chin in a modest bow. "Vesper, or whatever you are, this is the last favor I can grant. Do you understand? After this, you're on your own."

I offered a curt nod. Varen had once played the part of mentor and father as I played doting student and the daughter Valeria had denied him, but we'd both outgrown those roles.

"Can I stay here tonight? For old times' sake?" Exhaustion weighed down my bones, and I wasn't yet ready to face the Godless and their onslaught of questions.

Or, more specifically, Harmony and her onslaught of questions.

It had been a terribly long day. Only this morning I'd been making my way to the Golden City with Quen. Funny how things could change so fast.

Varen relaxed into a smile. "One night. I'll make the crossing tomorrow morning. Be out before my staff show up."

"Thank you. For everything." And I meant it.

22

"There are thousands of mortals.
The gods can't be expected to watch them all!"
The Wardens say this to justify their existence. That without Warden rule,
Chime would descend into chaos. How could twelve domains otherwise
coexist without Wardens? How could society function without the Covenant?
They say we need the Covenant to make us equal.
When a Vesper hates a Glimmer or a Leander outmatches a Seren, it's the
Wardens who keep the balance.
But it's the Wardens who perpetuate the animosity between our domains.
When we agree with their estimations, we are divided.
Divided, we fail to see their shortcomings.
And then we are better controlled.
—Anonymous, *Godless flier on the Wardens*

PLEASURE WARMED MY BODY, and I woke to the sensation of touch on my breast and rubbing my sweet spot. Many times, I'd woken in Malk's arms and he'd gently nudged me in such a way to coax me out of slumber, and I'd encouraged it; his fingers and tongue exploring where they wanted, my moans muffled so as not to wake anyone else.

But Malk couldn't have returned so soon.

My eyes snapped open, and it was my own hands exploring where they liked, only it wasn't *me* touching myself. I wasn't moving my fingers.

I leaped from Varen's couch and hastily pulled up my pants, half tripping over myself. "Jinx, what the *shit*?"

You were sleeping. I was having a little fun.

A little fun? With my body? What gave you the right?

Our body.

Just because we share a body doesn't mean you can take over without my consent and do whatever you want!

The key word being share.

An icy shiver crept down my spine. If Jinx could take over my body whenever they—she?—wanted, then what control did I have over myself? What other times had Jinx possessed me in such a manner? I'd often felt an odd out-of-body experience during the deepest throes of pleasure when making love to Malk; what if they'd been Jinx taking over? What if Jinx had been fucking Malk instead of me?

I may have a few times.

Holy pissing gods.

Why should you get all the fun? Don't you think it's unfair that you get the body and I'm forced to play voyeur?

I paced Varen's study. I'd tolerated Jinx's presence inside my mind as much as Jinx tolerated me, I supposed, but where did my thoughts end and Jinx's begin? What separated us? Was my love of blueberry pancakes mine, for instance, or Jinx's?

We're twins. I like what you like.

I like not being violated, thank you. If Jinx could take control of my body whenever she liked, then was my body truly mine?

The clock inside Varen's study rang eleven o'clock. Eventide would have closed by now, and I could only hope Varen had made the crossing. Within the next hour I'd know if he was successful or not, which meant I had work to do.

I'd argue with myself later.

I straightened my blouse and dress pants. My clothes were a right mess, but I'd be able to change once I returned home. I quietly slipped from Varen's office and made my way through the trash heaps to a sight I longed to see. The depot.

The familiar painted brick archway welcomed me in, and I sighed with relief. I'd expected to bump into Harmony or Sinder first, but the figure waiting for me on the platform was the last I'd thought would be up and walking around.

"You have returned as I have foreseen," Reve said with his booming voice. He stood there, small and frail, his fists clutching his nightgown like a lost boy. Yet the intensity of his speech and those dark eyes flecked with starlight spoke of a life beyond mortal ages.

"Good morning, Reve. What, uh, else have you seen?"

"Many things. They get clearer with time." He cocked his head. "You'll rip the domains apart. Tick. Tock."

"What are you talk—"

"Kayl!" Sinder yelled from across the platform. He bounded over and pulled me into a warm hug before I could react. "Darling, where have you *been*?"

The door to the small printing office opposite my room slammed open. Harmony poked her head out. "Kayl's back?"

Vincent appeared from underground, and then Dru came running into the depot behind me. "Kayl's gone, I can't find—*you?*" She stared at me.

My family converged on me like clockwork. "Yes, I'm back, I—"

"She brings news of some consequence," Reve announced, and all eyes turned to him, including mine. Had he already envisioned the Glimmer's god-separating machine? I could see why Quen had assumed me a Mesmer. They were beyond understanding.

Don't flatter yourself, Jinx said. *You're not that mysterious.*

I beg to differ.

Harmony climbed down the stairs, taking one at a time due to her small stature, while balancing a stack of freshly printed fliers in her arms. "News of consequence? I'd say. Should we be expecting a horde of Wardens at our doors?"

"Hopefully not. But Varen is coming with Malk." If all went to plan.

"With Malk?" One of her fliers fell with a flutter, but she didn't notice. "What in god's name have you done now?"

I raised my hands. "I'll explain everything, but can I *please* get changed and grab something to eat first?"

"You've got ten minutes, now scat." She waddled off to the tram.

"Charming."

Sinder scooped up the discarded flier depicting a terrifying image of Valeria, ironically. "Don't mind her. She's been going out of her mind worrying for you. Get changed, I'll bring something for the meet." He embraced me in another quick hug, and then I jogged up the stairs to my dangling room.

Gods, I'd missed this tram.

I took a moment to catch my breath and appreciate the sanctuary of my room. It remained just as cluttered as I'd left it. Staying with Quen hadn't been a traumatic experience, truth be told. His sheets were soft, and I'd terribly miss his bathtub with working hot water, not to mention his concierge.

But this was where I belonged.

It felt good to change into fresh clothes that were mine; I paired a black pleated skirt with a lighter blouse and flats. It would have been nice to dig out my nail polish and add a splash of color, but Harmony waited.

I found her and the rest of the Godless huddled inside our tram meeting room. Harmony sat at the head of the table with a notepad and pen poised for action. Dru fussed over Reve as he stared at an oil lamp dangling from the railing above. And Sinder and Vincent sat close enough for their shoulders to rub together.

The only one missing was Malk.

Harmony scowled and tapped her pen. "That was twenty minutes."

"What are you, a Diviner now?" Sinder scoffed as he shuffled aside and made space for me. He'd laid out a small platter of cheese and crackers across the table, complete with a pitcher of dandelion and burdock—an Undercity favorite, since the weeds managed to grow everywhere.

I slid between Sinder and Vincent, giving both a grateful smile.

Vincent returned the smile with restrained subtlety. He and Quen would get along. "Are you well, Kayl?"

I picked up a cracker and hesitated before shoving it into my mouth. They were all staring at me expectantly. "I'm pissing starving," I said with my mouth full.

Harmony snorted. "You're still you. It's good to have you back with us." She winked. "Dru tells me you now possess the ability to transform into mortals from other domains, along with their powers. If I'd known you'd be this useful, I'd have rescued you sooner."

I pulled a face. "I rescued myself, thank you."

"It's like no one noticed I *tried*," Dru muttered.

Sinder's hands went to my shoulders. "Are you really all right, darling? You've had a traumatic time. But... you were a Diviner in Erosain's bar. How did you do that? Can you turn into me?"

I grabbed another cracker, this time loaded with a thick wedge of cheddar. "Not you exactly, but other domains, yes. Give me your hand and I'll show you."

Sinder eagerly offered his palm, and I squeezed it, savoring its warmth. The heat of his skin tingled up my arm, and I pulled back before the tug. My hands turned their dark pink shade from before. I snapped my fingers and summoned a small burst of flame.

Harmony almost fell off her seat. "Holy *shit*."

"Language, Harm." Though she wasn't the only one staring at me, except for Reve, who acted like he'd seen this all before, which he probably had.

Sinder held his arm up to mine, comparing the color. "You're not as red as me. Can you control the shade?"

"*That's* your question?" Harmony spluttered as she righted herself in her seat. "How are you doing this? There's not a god in all twelve domains that can do that. Have you ever seen anything like it?" she asked Vincent.

Vincent's brow furrowed. "I've only ever seen Fauna transform this way. The gods can manipulate their form and their own mortals however they wish, but... none have the ability to mimic power from another domain. None."

"Trust me, I've been there," I said.

And so I laid out *everything*.

What happened at the Glimmer estate with Quen, the questioning afterwards, our visit to Eventide and my meeting with Valeria, our ill-fated partnership, our visit to the Academy to examine my memories, then Sinner's Row and the Mesmer dream parlor.

I left out the kiss and Quen's odd behavior. There was no point going over that, and Dru had judged me enough for daring to befriend the Dark Warden.

The rest listened with rapt silence as I described it all. Harmony started scribbling down notes as I described the aether creature I'd met in the steamworks and my suspicion that they were a new breed of godless mortal. It confirmed what she knew about the dead Diviner and their connection to the aether leaks.

Then Harmony burst out laughing.

"What?" I asked.

She waved me off. "Don't you see how ridiculous this is? You, the most disorganized and indecisive mortal I've ever met, can swap domains on a whim?"

"Not quite on a whim—"

"Don't you see what gift you possess, girl?"

Honestly, I hadn't really thought of it as a gift, but I could see the potential from the gleam in Harmony's diamond-shaped pupils.

I'd always fancied myself an actress, and here I was with the ability to take on any role as the key star of my own play. Not only could I steal the powers of any domain I wished—and who wouldn't want the Ember's fire magic or the Diviner's ability to control time—but I could take on their face as well. For a Godless, the skill of blending in and spying was a useful one, and I'd made it much easier.

I still didn't know where my power came from, but Harmony was right. I owned this gift. Why not use it to the Godless's advantage?

"Sadly, the Wardens don't care for my gift, otherwise they wouldn't be trying to drag my sorry arse to Kronos. But I have a real scoop for you, Harm. One that could destroy them and the Glimmer."

"Destroy the Glimmer?" Sinder repeated with nonchalance, though I could detect the slight quiver in his voice. "Don't tease me, darling."

Harmony leaned over the table. "Go on."

I patted Sinder's knee, aware that the words about to spill from my mouth would startle him the most. "The Glimmer have a machine which can split a mortal from their god."

Sinder downed the dandelion and burdock as I explained why I couldn't meet Dru at the safe house last night, and what I'd offered Varen in exchange for Malk's freedom.

Harmony sank back on her cushion. "Well. This is news of some consequence, I'll give you that." She glanced to Reve. "I'd never thought the Wardens capable of building such a machine. Certainly not the Glimmer. *Shit*. What a scoop."

"You're welcome." I blew her a kiss.

"If this got out, there'd be mass outcry. Can you imagine? The domains would be tearing themselves apart to steal it or destroy it. Public trust in the Wardens would evaporate, their precious Covenant would mean nothing. It would throw the entirety of Chime into chaos."

"You've heard no mention of this from our benefactor?" Vincent asked.

"Not a peep. In fact, I'm starting to get concerned. I haven't heard from them in weeks, but how does one check in with an anonymous contact?"

"You believe the Wardens may have finally gotten to them?"

"Could have, which may be bad news for us. They've certainly dropped nothing of *this* magnitude in my box, which means it must be hush-hush of the highest level."

I squirmed in my seat. The Godless had been founded thanks to the generosity of our mystery benefactor, who regularly donated bocs and intel into Harmony's drop box at the Chime Courier. We'd never met them— we had no idea who they even were—but we'd have never gotten this far without their support.

Not even Reve could use his visions to determine our benefactor's identity. When questioned, Reve would only answer that we'd discover their identity in time. And then he'd go back to staring at the wall.

With the level of information our mystery benefactor provided us, we suspected they must be a crooked Warden. Thus, if they'd been quiet this long, then the Wardens could have caught them committing treason without us ever knowing.

I'd always hoped to meet them one day, if only to thank them.

"We need to destroy the machine," Sinder said, his voice low and lacking his usual warmth. "Before they use it. We go and destroy it now, burn it to molten metal—"

"Wait a moment," I said. "Don't you see the potential? If we took this machine, we could free you." I scanned around the carriage. "All of you. We'd be truly Godless."

Sinder grimaced. "While I appreciate the sentiment, dearest, don't *you* see how the Glimmer would use this? Because I do."

"To rip Vesper from Valeria in order to serve the Glimmer. I got that. But we can save the Vesper before then—"

"No. If the Glimmer have the means to reconfigure this machine, then what else could they do? Think! If they can remove a mortal's connection to their god, couldn't they then force a connection? Force their golden whore of a god on others?"

Oh. I'd assumed they'd want Vesper free to worship Gildola—I hadn't thought they could literally enslave Vesper souls to the Glimmer. Gods. They wouldn't need bribes to entice and trap mortals into their workhouses then. "We'll just have to make sure they don't."

Sinder slumped against the cushions with an exasperated hiss that blew smoke from his nose. "It's obviously a trap. They use us to build the machine, and then they rid themselves of our kind once and for all. Harm?"

Harmony's expression was hard to decipher. "It's most definitely a trap. But it's worth the risk. Who among us wouldn't free ourselves if we had the chance?"

"Um, I'm not sure I would," Dru said.

"I'd gladly risk my soul." Vincent reached over the table and took Sinder's hand. "And give it up to protect yours."

Sinder blinked. "I would never ask that of you."

"You wouldn't have to."

The two of them stared at each other as though telepathically sharing a conversation. They both knew each other's mind without needing to utter a word, and it made my heart ache for Malk. The only man who understood *me*.

"We shouldn't be tampering with the gods," Dru whined as she wrung her hands in her lap. "We'd be playing with cosmic forces beyond even the Diviner's understanding. It won't end well."

"Malk has been trapped in Eventide for days," I said. "I—I have no idea what state he'll be in when he returns, but his situation embodies our greatest fears. I'll do what it takes to free his soul for good." Even if it meant fucking with cosmic forces. "Reve? How do you see this playing out?"

We all turned to Reve as his gaze slowly lowered from the wall to me. "I see myself sitting on this machine. I see... my salvation."

Such talk made Dru look uneasy. Her god was arguably the kindest of the twelve, but the Umber were still beholden and enslaved to its every whim. I could see the dilemma churning over her expression; while she didn't hate or fear her god as we did, she cared for Reve, and ending his suffering would be enough.

"Then our path seems clear," Harmony stated. "We play the Glimmer's game. At worst, we gather evidence of what the Glimmer and Wardens have been doing. At best, we have the means to save mortals from the tyranny of the gods. I like our chances."

Sinder scowled. "I don't."

"But we have our secret weapon." Harmony gestured to me. "How could we fail?"

Sinder snorted and then grimaced at me. "Sorry, darling."

I nudged him in the side.

"He's here," Reve suddenly declared.

Malk!

I scrambled past Sinder and practically leaped out of the carriage.

Two figures stood on the platform under the gold of the oil lamps. I completely ignored Varen as my gaze roamed over Malk.

Gods, he was here, all limbs intact, his long hair the same length, dressed in the black Warden attire he'd worn the day of the crossing.

The last time he'd kissed me.

"I love you with everything I am."

How I wanted to echo those words!

It was him—*my* Malk—and thank the gods he bore no visible scars or injuries, though as I raced toward him, his eyes widened, and he shrank away from me.

I slowed to a stop. "Malk?"

Varen, too, was staring at me with slight horror.

You're an Ember, you idiot.

Oh shit. I'd forgotten I'd touched Sinder! "Malk, it's me." I extended my hand. "Please. It's me."

He tentatively reached out. I grabbed his palm and my Ember skin rippled back to the indigo of my Vesper form.

He yanked his hand free as though I'd burned him. "What the—the fuck *are* you?"

"I'm still me. Kayl." I reached for his arm.

He recoiled. "Don't touch me!"

Gods, he was scared of me. Actually scared. "What did that bitch do to you?"

"Valeria kept her word," Varen said, as the others came rushing behind me. "He has been returned to you unharmed, as promised. However, his release is conditional."

That wasn't part of the deal. "On what conditions?"

"You'll deliver this Glimmer machine to her by next morning's crossing or his body will be obliterated."

Malk's gaze fell to the floor, confirming Varen's words.

My heart caught in my throat. "You *told* her about the machine?"

"She's a god. She ripped the information straight from my mind. It's lucky for us both that Valeria wants this device, otherwise neither I nor Malkavaan would be standing here. She offers his return as a gesture of good will."

Good will? Fuck that starry-arsed bitch, but it didn't matter; we'd get the Glimmer's machine working and save Malk before Valeria laid her cursed fingers on him.

But could we get it working in only twenty-four hours? It was a dangerously tight schedule.

"Do you have any better news for us, Varen?" Harmony asked as she came beside me.

"I have nothing more for you. I told Kayl; no more favors. The Wardens are getting too close and I can't risk Grayford."

Harmony nodded. "I understand. We thank you for all you've done for us, Ambassador. We'll continue to support Grayford as we always have."

Varen wore a wry smile. "I can't say it has been a pleasure."

He'll happily keep taking your bocs, Jinx said.

To help Grayford's mortals. That's what it's all been for.

Keep telling yourself that.

The sound of a loud *click* made me jump, and Varen spun around to a stranger who'd entered the depot.

No, not a stranger.

"Corinth," Varen gasped.

Quen stood by the depot's main archway, a brass pistol cocked in his hand and pointed directly at Varen. "Ah, so this is where the Godless make their home. Thank you for leading me here, Your Excellency."

301

XXIII

Not much is known about the shadowy organization which calls itself the
Godless. Their activities began after the 'Grayford Incident' and are likely
a direct consequence of Warden interference within the slums.
The 'Godless,' as they refer to themselves, operate by defying the Covenant to
spread blasphemous propaganda of the gods and Wardens. They bask in
their apostasy, and no domain is spared from their abhorrent disrespect.
There are no known members of the Godless, and we have no estimation of
their number, however they are believed to operate from Sinner's Row. They
spread their propaganda through professionally printed fliers. Such fliers
continue to propagate, despite our increased patrols, which leads me to
suspect the Godless have support beyond the Undercity.
—Q. Corinth, *Warden Dossier on the 'Godless'*

I'D LONG SUSPECTED THAT the Godless had made their home in Grayford.
But an abandoned tram depot? Very clever.

I'd also suspected that this was where I'd find Kayl. In a stroke of
genius, I'd sat outside one of the cafés by Central Station, waiting for a
certain Vesper ambassador to make the crossing to Eventide. Truly, the
wait had been worth the abysmal, overpriced tea I'd been forced to
consume, though even *I* hadn't expected the good ambassador to return
with a healthy-and-whole Malkavaan Byvich. That only piqued my
curiosity further.

Following Varen had been all too easy. It was almost as if he wanted to
lure me into their lair.

My records didn't give me an accurate number of how many served the
Godless, but judging by the many faces staring at me—Ember, Mesmer,
Necro, Seren, and the lovely Miss Smith, of course—I knew I'd rounded
up most of them.

I kept my pistol trained on Varen, though my eyes moved to Kayl.

She didn't look pleased to see me.

Did *anyone* ever look pleased to see me?

Varen raised his hands. "Put the pistol away, Corinth."

"I don't think so. I'm here on official Warden business, though it looks as though my morning is now fully booked. Ambassador Karendar would be most perturbed to learn that the rumors are true, Your Excellency."

"Karendar needn't know, and you needn't make this difficult. Do you think you can outmatch all eight of us?"

"Let's see, now... I'm the only one in this situation who can stop time, so yes."

"You're not the only one," Kayl said, and her defiant aether glare burned right through me. My goodness, did she realize how terrifying those eyes looked? "Why are you here?" she demanded.

"I thought that was obvious. Though now I'm here, perhaps you can explain what this Glimmer machine is that Valeria is so intent on getting her hands on?"

A flicker of fear passed over Kayl's face.

What trouble had she wrought?

Shadows ripped from Malkavaan, plunging the depot's hangar into darkness as he lunged for me. At the same time, flame burst from the Ember.

I raised my spare hand and slowed time to a stop. The rolling flames hung in midair, cutting light through the clouds of Malkavaan's shadow. The effect was rather pretty, like a storm trapped in time.

Or it would have been if Kayl wasn't charging right at me.

She barged into my side, knocking my balance askew, and then grabbed the wrist holding my pistol and tried to wrench it free.

"Kayl, stop—"

Her fingernails pinched a pressure point in my bicep and I yelped, dropping my pistol. She caught it with one deft movement and swung the pistol round, pointing it at me. "Get on your knees, Quen. I won't ask twice."

I shook off the spasm in my arm. "It's not loaded."

Her anger somehow intensified. She jabbed the barrel into my chest and squeezed the trigger once. Twice. Multiple clicks that would have left a gaping hole in my chest. She growled in annoyance and threw my prized pistol, letting it clatter along the platform.

"Was that quite necessary?" If she'd scratched it, I wouldn't be best pleased.

She stomped to a locker beside the depot door and returned carrying a crowbar. "Get on your knees."

"This isn't very gracious of you, I must say—"

"We have a Necro who specializes in healing broken bones, but do you really want me to smash your kneecaps and test his abilities?"

Such dramatics. I sighed and kneeled. "You ran from me."

She stood over me and tapped the crowbar menacingly in her hands. "You were going to drag me to Kronos. Don't deny it."

"What now, then? Are you and your Godless going to murder me? Beat me bloody? Torture me for Warden secrets?"

"Don't be ridiculous. I'm going to tie you up and make you wear gloves so you can't fuck with time and fast-forward your way out of here. And then we'll talk."

"You know fast-forwarding time is a bad idea."

"Then I'll trust you not to. Speaking of, do you mind?" She waved a hand at the stop-motion around us.

"Right you are." A headache was already building in my temples; I wouldn't have been able to hold time for much longer, regardless. With a flick of my fingers, time resumed its infinite march.

Malkavaan stumbled to a halt, clearly confused, and the Ember's flames flared and then suddenly shrank. They blinked at the sight of Kayl holding me hostage with a crowbar. Getting so easily captured by a ragtag group of Undercity residents would have been embarrassing if I hadn't counted on it.

Now I'd find my answers.

"Find the Godless. Join them."

Those words lingered in the back of my subconsciousness, but I couldn't fathom why.

"Tie him up," Kayl ordered.

It was the Necro, a pale-faced chap in a sharp suit, who tied my hands with Warden-like efficiency and offered an apologetic grimace while doing so. I didn't particularly enjoy being bound on my knees this way, and my back still ached from my visit to Timefall Estates last night, but the Godless didn't seem the flagellating type.

Kayl passed the crowbar to the Ember, who slung it over their shoulder. She ran up some metal stairs and returned with a rather lovely pair of pink fluffy gloves.

"Don't let him touch you," the Ember warned.

"Don't worry. His powers don't affect me." She at least placed them on my hands with some care. Truly, I'd worried she'd snap my fingers.

"They're not my color," I said, but no one listened as the Godless surrounded me.

The very mortals I'd spent years studying and attempting to track.

Elijah would be delighted by my success.

The Seren, a small woman with lilac skin, whooped a laugh. "You crazy bitch, you caught a Warden. A Diviner Warden."

"Kill him," Malkavaan seethed. "Sinder can burn his clothes. We'll scatter their ashes with the trash."

"And lose out on valuable intel?" the Seren countered.

"We're *not* killing or torturing him," Kayl said, and I was relieved to see her lips pull into a frown.

"He dragged me to Eventide!" Malkavaan yelled, spitting. He thrust a damning finger an inch from my nose. "He's the reason I suffered *her*!"

Kayl came to his side and placed a hand on his arm. "Malk—"

"Don't *touch* me." He yanked his arm free. "None of you know what it was like." His frantic eyes darted between the Godless. "None of you."

"You're tired, Malk," Varen said. "You need rest—"

"Piss off!" Malkavaan stomped away from the group to a stairwell that led underneath the hangar.

Kayl stepped after him and then hesitated. "Vincent? Could you check on him?"

The Necro bowed his head. "Of course." And then he followed the Vesper.

Kayl rounded on Varen. "I thought you said he was unharmed!"

"Unharmed, but caged. We left him there for days. Of course he's going to be irritable. But you have bigger concerns." Varen's eyes landed on me. "You can't kill Corinth."

Relief flooded through my bones. "Thank you—"

"If you kill him, everything he's seen today will go straight back to his god." He shared a knowing glance with the other Godless, though what that meant, I couldn't deduce. "Gag him and shove him somewhere quiet for now."

"And I thought we were friends, Varen."

The ambassador looked upon me with disdain. "You're nothing but Karendar's puppet. You'll soon see how much he cares for you when he cuts the strings." Varen took Kayl's arm and guided her out of earshot for a private conversation. Obviously about me, since Varen kept glaring in my direction.

At least Kayl didn't want to see me bloodied to a pulp.

"So you're the famous Dark Warden?" the Ember named Sinder said. "You're not much to look at. How did a Diviner become the unluckiest mortal in Chime?"

"I've never gambled, so I couldn't possibly say. Have we met before?"

Sinder gave me an odd look. "You don't remember me from Erosain's bar? Served you a hot toddy?"

"You work for Erosain?"

"Typical." They rolled their eyes and turned to the Seren. "Diviner think we look the same."

I hadn't stepped foot in Erosain's bar in over a week, nor could I remember the last time I shared a whiskey and tea with anyone. Either this Ember was trying to trick me, or my past self had erased the memory for good reason.

If I'd shared a moment with an Ember, there could have been any number of sins I'd committed working a case. There was something about this one that struck some subconscious bell. Had they served Erosain in some capacity? Had we dallied? Likely not, as even my past self would avoid getting handsy—and Elijah would flay me for a start. Male bodies were undoubtedly my preference, though this Ember blurred the lines between the sexes. Lately I'd found my dreams exploring the female form. Their soft skin. The taste of their sex. The swell of their breasts.

Saints. Captured for less than half an hour and my mind was already sinning.

Perhaps I *should* let them kill me.

I glanced toward where Varen was now striding out of the hangar and abandoning me to my fate.

"Well?" the Seren demanded as Kayl returned to our cozy little group.

Kayl brushed a strand of dark hair behind her ear, an oddly vulnerable gesture I'd never seen her make. "Varen is right. We need to keep Quen—Corinth—hostage. I'll lock him in my room. There's nothing incriminating there."

"Can we even trust Varen?" Sinder said. "He allowed Corinth to follow him here in the first place. He's never been that sloppy." The Ember's burning eyes turned to me. "Who's to say there aren't more Wardens on their way here now? They don't work alone."

"You're right," I said. "We don't work alone. In fact, my partner is standing right here." I turned to Kayl.

If Vesper could blush, I was sure she would have. Instead, her features morphed somewhere between embarrassment and a scowl. "He's an idiot, but he's harmless. Right, Dru?"

Miss Smith sighed. "You both are."

"I'll take that vote of confidence." I flashed a smile.

The Seren was rubbing her forehead. "Take him to your room and lock him *securely*. If he tries to get out, we'll have Vincent induce a permanent coma." Her harsh gaze leveled on me.

"I assure you I make an unassuming guest."

The Seren snorted and strode away as Miss Smith took the Mesmer's arm and guided him down the same stairway as Malkavaan and the Necro.

Kayl dragged me up.

The Ember tapped their crowbar. "Are you sure about this, darling? We shouldn't be leaving a Diviner alone and conscious."

"His powers don't affect me, remember? Trust me." She pulled me awkwardly, and we climbed shaky metal stairs up to a secondary platform overlooking the hangar.

"So kind of you to introduce me to your friends," I said.

"Don't be an arse."

"But no, thank you for not murdering me."

"Don't thank me yet."

An office awaited us at the top of the stairs, and that was where I'd expected Kayl to imprison me. Instead, she steered me to what appeared to be a tram carriage dangling from a thick hook attached precariously to the ceiling.

"Oh my," I gasped.

"Watch your footing," Kayl said, though she gave me absolutely no time *to* watch my footing as she shoved me forward and I awkwardly hopped from the secure metal platform to something decidedly less secure. She jumped in behind me, and my heart caught in my throat as the entire carriage swayed.

I was about to remind her of my absolute *love* of heights when I stepped into what could only be described as utter chaos.

Beautiful chaos.

The tram carriage had been repurposed into a bedroom of sorts. A mishmash of clothes hung from the passenger railing, acting as curtains, though piles of dirty clothes were scattered across the carriage floor. Glittering fairy lights twirled around the center pole and hung from the ceiling like streamers. And the back, which was once a driver's caddy, now acted as shelves for all manner of trinkets, from tacky hourglass Chime souvenirs to bottles of colorful nail varnish, a stained and tattered copy of *The Traveler's Handbook to Chime and Beyond,* and a clock that was ticking one minute behind.

"And you complained my apartment is messy? Though I suppose my apartment isn't stuffed inside a loco-13 model carriage. Chime stopped using *these* years ago. Did you know they were the first carriage to combine aether with steam..." I trailed off as Kayl gave me a look which suggested now was *not* the time to discuss the history of Chime's trams. "That's, ah, not keeping time, by the way." I gestured to the clock. "I could fix it for you."

"It doesn't need fixing." Kayl pushed me backwards onto a pile of cushions. She sat opposite with her arms crossed. "Why did you come here, Quen?"

"Because we're supposed to be partners."

"We stopped being partners the moment you discovered what I am."

Had I discovered it? I had my suspicions, certainly, but had we found out which god she belonged to? I'd left no clue in my apartment, and now I wasn't sure I wanted to know. Past Quen certainly didn't. "I was going to take you to Kronos."

"That's what you said. The Wardens only remove those who pose a threat to Chime, and that's what I am, aren't I? A threat to you?"

"That's not how I see you."

Anger flared in those aether eyes. "How do you see me, Quen? Not as a partner."

"What have I done to hurt you?"

"You kissed me."

Oh. Well then. My past self was a blithering idiot. "Was I that bad?"

Kayl glared, and for a moment I thought she'd barge over to my seat and slap me silly. *Wrong question, Quen. Wrong question.*

But then the anger slipped from her expression into sudden realization. "You don't remember, do you?"

"Well, I—"

"Shit. You don't remember last night?" Her arms uncurled as she stared at me. "You don't remember going to Sinner's Row? The Mesmer dream parlor? *Any* of it?"

This conversation was breaking all of my protocols, and I found my tongue suddenly heavy and thick in my mouth.

She stood now and towered over me. "All those papers in your apartment... You went to your Amnae boffin, didn't you?"

I held up my tied and gloved hands in surrender. "Please, let's not—"

"How many times have you wiped your own memories? How many memories of you and I have you wiped? What do you even remember?"

"I remember offering you more courtesy than you've shown me."

She grabbed my shoulder, her grip painfully tight. "What in god's name are you doing to yourself?"

I met her glare with my own. "You know what I am. You know who I report to. Does it not occur to you that I take these precautionary measures to protect you? So your secrets cannot be plucked from my mind and turned against you and your Godless friends? By having this conversation now, I'll only have to wipe my memories *again*."

She snorted a joyless laugh. "Oh, cut your chivalrous shit! You warned me not to fuck with time, and you're fucking with your own memories? I didn't realize you were this much of an idiot!"

"Consider me thoroughly chastised. I'm sorry if I hurt your feelings—"

"My feelings?" Her brows raised. "This isn't about me. You're a disaster."

I glanced over the rim of my spectacles. "It takes one to know one."

She threw her hands up and returned to the edge of her bed, slumping onto the cushions. "Why are you here if you can't even remember?"

"You're right about Kronos. I have my orders to escort you there, where you'll be thoroughly interrogated and not with pleasant questions over a cup of tea."

"And you're telling me this because you *want* me to murder you?"

I raised my bound hands. "Well, I shan't be performing any arrests in my current state. But answer my question—what is this machine Valeria is after?" It had to be of some importance if it convinced her to release Malkavaan.

Finding the truth of Kayl's existence and the aether creatures was one problem, but whatever the Glimmer and Godless had stumbled upon worried me far more.

Kayl responded to my smile with her own saccharine grin. "If I told you that, then I'd have to kill you."

"Or find a nice Amnae to wipe my brain clean."

"Sadly, we don't find many Amnae in the Undercity. The air's too dry and the water dirty. Our Necro could probably melt your brain inside your skull for you, though."

"Please don't toy with my brain. What are the Glimmer doing?"

"We're Godless. Do you honestly believe I'm going to share my organization's secrets with a Warden?"

"I've shared mine—"

"You've told me nothing I don't already know."

I leaned forward. "What if I agreed to impart some Warden secrets in exchange? Would your organization make use of that?"

"Is this a bribe, Quen?"

"I like to think of it as a mutual exchange of information that could benefit us both. And I'd rather like to know what dirty shenanigans the Glimmer are involved in."

Her lip quirked. "I don't know why I trust you."

Neither did I, but I hoped she'd take that chance.

"The Glimmer have a machine. They say your Wardens built it to deal with the aether leaks, but they have a prototype that they've asked us to help fix up. You've not heard of any such developments?"

Now my interest was truly piqued. "I'm aware of the Glimmer's involvement with the clock tower, but not the specifics."

"You wouldn't have wiped this memory?"

"Possibly. Possibly not. I work cases, I don't deal with maintenance or public traffic laws. How did you gain this intel? What does this machine *do*?"

"It's designed to capture the aether creatures leaking from the clock tower. But the Glimmer discovered an alternative use."

"What use?"

She clasped her hands in her lap. "It can separate a mortal's soul from their god."

My heart fluttered. I could well believe Elijah would commission a device to capture these aether creatures, perhaps even turn their own power against them to split their souls apart and return them to the primordial aether they spawned from, but to split a mortal from their god? That...

It was utterly depraved.

No, Elijah must not know of its unintended side effects. Damn the Glimmer, of course they'd find such use for it—and the Godless too. "You said the Glimmer asked you for their help? Please don't tell me you intend to assist them with this."

Her lips formed a tight line.

Father, save us. "Do you understand what threat this poses to Chime? To all mortals of the twelve domains?"

"We're not stupid. We understand the risks—"

"*Do you?* You've seen what happens to a mortal when an aether creature takes their soul—they die, their soul split forever, and their body is left behind!"

"You didn't wipe that memory then?"

"This is serious, this is... This is insane. The Wardens need to know, they need to destroy—"

"Your Wardens built this machine in the first place!"

"But not for this!" Surely not for this. "We protect the vested interests of the domains, of the gods. I can fathom what use the Glimmer would have for such a device."

"So can we, which is why we'll take it from their hands—"

"And hand it to Valeria?"

"Of course not. This machine shouldn't be in the gods' hands—not Glimmer, not Vesper, and certainly not Diviner."

"Do you truly believe your organization can be trusted with this?"

Her hard stare burned a hole into my soul. "Yes. I've told you how the Godless came to be, how we've been tortured under our own gods—if you haven't wiped those memories anyhow. We want to be free. That's all. This machine gives us a chance. It's our salvation."

Salvation?

It was Chime's doom.

A sick thought came to me. "Do you intend to force mortals on this machine? To force *me*?" That's what Varen had implied. If the Godless split me from Dor, I wouldn't be able to transmit my thoughts and memories back to Him. Then the Godless could do with me as they wished. I sank against the cushions.

They could rip me from my Father.

Death, even having my entire memories wiped from existence, was more bearable than losing that connection.

"You know I wouldn't do that."

Did I? Did I truly know this woman? She'd been quite clear about what the Godless meant to her, and quite content to shy from her own god. I had no idea what Kayl was capable of.

I had no idea who she was and how she came to be.

Why *had* I come here? Why had I sought her out?

To arrest her? Save her? Save myself?

Elijah knew what threat the Godless possessed. Did he truly know?

In these past few years, I'd brushed against the Godless, but never gotten close. I couldn't help but wonder if my past self had held my investigation back more than the Godless's own competence.

Because I'd not considered them a threat. Because I believed Chime needed heathens like these. They were the one voice in Chime who actively stood against the Glimmer and their workhouses. And I'd switched to investigating the workhouses too, convinced that fixing the Undercity's inequalities would somehow solve the Godless problem and appease the Wardens.

Past Quen believed the Godless could be saved. *I* believed they were worth saving.

But now...

Elijah had been right. Empathy was a curse.

I could beg and plead all I liked, but what good would it do? I knew my death was coming—the loss of my very soul at the hands of an aether creature. But perhaps the colors I'd witnessed in my visions weren't a mortal after all, but myself strapped to this machine.

This was the path I'd been set on from the day of my conception.

For I'd seen worse in my visions.

The destruction of Chime itself.

I sat here in the heart of enemy territory. If the Godless believed me a threat and not some bumbling idiot, then it wasn't just my life at stake, nor my soul—but everyone in Chime. The entire balance of the domains. The gods themselves.

Aether creatures be damned! Regardless of the danger they posed to my domain, this device was the *real* threat. I needed to stop both the Godless and Glimmer from unleashing it, somehow. This was why Dor had anointed me His Warden, why Elijah trusted me to do what was right in the end. He knew of the darkness in my heart and had given me this final chance to prove myself pure.

I'd always flirted with sin, but this device... It went beyond simple sin and apostasy.

"I need to do this," Kayl whispered. "I need to do this for Malk."

Desperation tinged her voice. She'd risk her life for this, I knew.

And so would I. To stop her.

"Find the Godless. Join them."

Destroy them.

If I had any hope of success, I needed to play this smart and convince the Godless I could be trusted. I needed Kayl to trust me. "For Malkavaan, then. How do you intend to help the Glimmer?"

"They have a few errands for us to run. Parts and schematics to fix it up and get it running. Then we'll take it for ourselves and ensure the Glimmer never use it."

"Then keep me here. Use me as a hostage, leverage, whatever. Just promise me you'll prevent them from using it, and when the time comes, let me go. Your Godless, the Glimmer—neither of you are a match for Diviner power. You need my help."

She cocked her head. "I could take your power from you. I don't need you."

"You barely know how to command time. If you want every success, you'll need someone who can effectively wield it."

"And why would the Dark Warden help us?"

"Because I'd sooner this device disappear into the shadows of the Undercity than find itself into the hands of any domain. Besides—" I forced a smile. "We're partners."

She smiled back. "A partnership with *some* caveats."

Caveats indeed.

I'd make myself her prisoner and play the part.

And then I, Quentin Corinth, would betray my own heart to save this damnable city.

24

Every mortal is born with a gift from their domain, and none are more deadly than the Seren. Despite their diminutive form, which requires some adjustments throughout Chime, and their ability to fly as Zephyr do, it is their power for song which one should not underestimate.

A Seren can manipulate their voice to induce a hypnosis-like state in other mortals. This state cannot be easily shaken off or defended against. Through song, a Seren can convince a mortal to hand over their possessions or even harm themselves and others.

It is unfortunate that we must regulate singing when other domains are able to freely embrace their abilities, but outside of the Diviner, no other mortal has such mass influence.

—Q. Corinth, *Warden Dossier on the Seren*

TIME WAS GETTING ON, and I didn't want to waste any more of it when I only had twenty-four short hours to fix the Glimmer's god-splitting machine and save Malk. But I couldn't walk out of the depot without checking in on him first.

I waited outside Vincent's office and picked at my nails. My skin remained the indigo of my Vesper form, but soon I'd have to take Quen's visage for my impromptu meeting with the Zephyr doctor. If I went as a Vesper, I'd give the poor soul a heart attack, and we needed those schematics.

That was the plan; head to the steamworks first, then Ambassador Erosain's bar later for the Glimmer's crystals, and we could have this wrapped up with time to spare.

The door opened quietly, and Vincent slid out, his hand resting on his cane. Whatever power he'd just performed must have taken its toll. "I've sedated him," Vincent said as he limped over to a couch outside his office and slowly eased himself down.

I remained standing and hugged my arms. It wasn't a question I wanted to ask, but I forced the words out. "What did you find?"

Vincent stretched his stiff left leg out and rested the cane across his thighs. "I found no injuries on his body. No cuts, broken bones, or bruising. However..."

"However?" My breath hitched.

"His mind holds scarring. It's a telltale sign of manipulation, either by Necro or by... more divine methods."

"Meaning what?"

"Meaning his body has been reset to factory settings, as we Necro call it. Any injuries or changes he may have endured have been wiped clean. Reset."

"Like how an Amnae might wipe parts of their memory?"

"Precisely."

I suddenly felt sick. Both Valeria and Varen had promised to return Malk unharmed, and in their twisted definition, they had. They could have tortured him in so many ways and wiped the evidence clean. I wanted to barge into that room and speak to him, hold him. Run my hands through his thick black hair and whisper how much he meant to me.

But more than that, I wanted to get this gods-damn machine working. Then Malk would never suffer that vile bitch again.

I thanked Vincent and headed upstairs to where Quen sat tied to a wooden chair on the main platform, guarded by Sinder and Harmony.

Quen strained against his bindings as I approached. They'd taken off his jacket and rebound his wrists. He looked wonderfully helpless with his limbs restrained, my fluffy gloves stopping him from experiencing the memories and deaths of my friends, his eyeglasses somewhat askew and his silver hair flopping over his brow like some ridiculous Academy student who'd been caught vandalizing a desk with naughty words.

Barf, Jinx said.

No one asked for your opinion.

"Is it quite necessary for this fine gentlebeast to threaten me with a crowbar?" Quen whined as he eyed Sinder. "Especially since they can quite literally burn my entire body?"

Sinder's eyelashes fluttered as he affectionally stroked the crowbar in his hands. "Perhaps I enjoy holding something big and firm, darling. Besides, I am under strict orders *not* to scatter your ashes, as much as I'd enjoy it."

Harmony lifted her brows at my approach. "I've considered gagging him, but I'm still waiting for this intel he has to share."

"I do loosen up over a nice cup of tea," Quen said.

"You're out of luck. We have coffee or dirt, your choice."

"Is there a difference? Coffee will be fine," he amended at Harmony's glower. "Any chance of a biscuit? Bourbon if you please?"

"Don't push your luck. Are we ready to go?" Harmony asked me.

I leaned over Quen and cupped his cheek. "Try to behave, and my Ember friend will take good care of you. While you're in the company of my friends, you should get to know them. Hear their stories. Discover what makes us Godless. We sacrifice Glimmer children at noon and make cocktails with their blood for our evening chanting, if you'd like to join our festivities."

Quen's silver eyes widened as they met mine. "Do you actually?"

"No, you dolt. We drink wine and play card games." My palm transformed from Vesper indigo to the silvery-blue of a Diviner.

"What trouble are you going after, dressed as a Diviner?" His voice dropped to a whisper. "You shouldn't be playing with time alone."

I patted his cheek and stepped away. "I won't be gone long."

"Kayl—"

"You'll just have to trust me. Painful, I know." I winked.

"Shit, I'm still not used to you doing that," Harmony said as she took in my Diviner form. She carried a briefcase under her arm and together the two of us headed for the depot doors.

We shouldn't be leaving him alone, Jinx said. *He can't be trusted.*

He'll have Sinder watching over him. Besides, I didn't think Quen would try to escape. He needed to know we'd get this machine from the

Glimmer. I didn't trust him not to sabotage our mission, though, which was why he remained tied to a chair.

Once a Warden, always a Warden.

Quite. Though what mad games was Quen playing?

He hadn't joked about wiping his memories—I could see it from his face, though I didn't know the extent of his memory wipe. He remembered me and my purpose at least, as well as our excursion to the steamworks, but he'd wiped our blasphemous discussions and intimate wine drinking. I could well understand why.

If the Wardens explored his memories, they'd have good reason to throw him back into one of their correctional facilities. Quen had told me of his past, the truth of the Vesper killings, and then absolved himself of the memory.

Why? Because he trusted me?

Or he used you to confess and absolve himself of his guilt, knowing you'd be pathetic enough to forgive him.

He didn't use me—

He kissed you, knowing full well you were mourning Malk and struggling with your own identity. He's nothing more than a selfish prick. Or have you forgotten what he said to you already? How he doesn't care?

I hadn't forgotten the harshness of his words, but they hadn't been uttered by the Quen I knew. The real Quen.

You don't know the real Quen.

No, perhaps not. But the Quen I knew had turned up here to warn me, which was more than our mystery benefactor ever did. Regardless of Quen's intentions, he wouldn't let this god-splitting device remain in Glimmer hands.

But I couldn't afford to let it pass into Warden hands, either.

"You okay there?" Harmony asked as we entered Grayford.

"Yes. Sorry. There's a lot on my mind."

"Try to keep focused. This is our biggest operation yet. We can't afford to fuck it up."

Gods, I knew that more than anyone. There was too much at stake for me to fail now. Such as Malk's soul.

All right. I could focus.

Sure you can.

The Undercity tram arrived outside the steamworks just after one o'clock, and the gloomy building appeared as uninviting as the last time I'd come here with Quen. He'd been able to steer us inside by flashing his Warden credentials and his charming Diviner face. Little did he know that I'd swiped his badge from his jacket pocket, and by spinning some Diviner charm of my own, I hoped we'd get past the guards.

My backup plan was Harmony. For such a short woman, she had a big mouth and knew how to wield it. Harmony hadn't become leader of the Godless by chance—she'd practically barged into the depot one day and declared herself in charge. She strode now with a confident swagger that said she'd take down anyone who got in her way. Dressed in her black suit and armed with her briefcase, she looked the part.

Gods, I didn't think she'd need me at all.

We stopped outside the main gate to the steamworks as a huge Leander guard prowled out to greet us. This one was broad-shouldered and all muscle, his navy-blue suit straining across his chest, and his unruly mane spilled over his collar. Of course Leander made the best security guards. They had tackling and pummeling down to a fine art.

They're just big kitties in suits, Jinx said.

I'd never dare say that to their face!

"Can I help you ladies?" he huffed, and my imagination lingered on how cute he must have been as a lion cub. Maybe he wore a little bowtie.

I flashed Quen's badge, carefully placing my fingers over his name so the Leander couldn't tell I wasn't a Master Corinth. "We're here to speak with Doctor Zachery Finch regarding an investigation." I'd practiced saying Doctor Finch's name on the tram ride here to ensure I'd remember it.

"Let me see that badge one more time."

"I came here yesterday, if you recall—"

"I weren't on shift then, Miss." The Leander huffed again with a slight growl, and his tail swished behind him.

I'd hoped my Diviner skin would be enough to deter most fools, but this giant kitty had a brain, it seemed.

Scratch behind his ears. They love that.

Harmony dramatically sighed and slapped her briefcase. "Just yesterday you had a body in there. A *body*. Where was security then, huh? Where were *you*? We're here to clean up your organization's mess. If you want me to start the paperwork now, I'm happy to oblige." She flipped open the locks with a violent *snap*. "Can I take *your* name and badge?"

The briefcase sprung open, obscuring Harmony's face. At that signal, I slapped my hands over my ears.

And Harmony began to sing.

"Hush little kitty, don't say a word," Harmony warbled in a high-pitched tone. *"Forget you ever saw us, and we'll walk by unheard."*

The hairs on the back of my neck bristled as Harmony's otherworldly melody lulled me into a false sense of security, her voice almost convincing me to take a nap right here in the dirt.

I'd never heard Harmony sing before. Now that I'd been blessed with her delightful voice, I never wanted to hear it *ever* again.

The Leander stiffened, then his arms went slack. "I never saw you," he said, as though half-asleep like a Mesmer, and his feline pupils stared into the distance at nothing.

Wow. No wonder the Wardens banned public singing.

Harmony closed her briefcase and strode off for the main doors before the Leander could recover his senses.

I shuffled next to Harmony and bit back a giggle. "That guy was twice the size of you and you practically had him by the balls."

"Hardly. I'd have to stand on tiptoes to reach his balls."

Why can't you be more like her?

Because none of the Godless could ever compare to Harmony. We entered the dreary main reception of the steamworks. It was just as empty as it had been yesterday, with the same Vesper girl working the desk, and already the buzz of the aether lamps was giving me a headache. Now we needed an excuse to get Doctor Finch's attention so I could ransack his office, find these schematics, and snatch them without being caught.

Harmony strolled up to the reception desk, which towered above her height. She sighed dramatically once more. "Are there no Seren who work here? I can see why. This is discrimination and goes against the equality clause of the Covenant. Where are the Wardens of this jurisdiction?"

The Vesper girl stopped chewing her pen and leaned over the counter. "Uh, can I help you, ma'am?"

"Is this how your organization treats visitors? Typical." Harmony threw her briefcase on the counter, making the Vesper girl jump. "My associate and I are here on behalf of Master Quentin Corinth. We came here yesterday regarding a most unfortunate incident? We're here to clear up the paperwork, if you don't mind."

The Vesper girl blinked, and her confused stare moved to me. I waved, and I could see her thoughts clanking like a Diviner's. She recognized me, but hadn't been paying enough attention to separate my face from that of an Ember to a Diviner. "How can we help with that?"

Harmony rolled her eyes, becoming increasingly more agitated, though it was all for show. "We spoke with Doctor Zachery Finch and need him to sign these papers. If you would be a dear and escort us to his office?"

Now protocols set in as the Vesper girl straightened in her chair. "If you'll both please wait here and make yourselves comfortable, I'll bring Doctor Finch out for you." She scurried off into the same corridor I'd entered only yesterday.

Harmony grabbed her briefcase and climbed up to a seat. "They really don't get Seren visitors." She tutted. "Sure you can do this?"

I cricked my neck from side to side. "Have a little faith."

Harmony gave me a look that said she had no faith at all, which I suppose for the leader of the Godless, could be considered a compliment.

It's not.

Well, it could be.

Footsteps echoed along the corridor, and I recognized the frantic pace of Doctor Finch.

"You're up," Harmony said. "The gods leave you to your fate."

Now to do the one thing Quen warned me not to—fuck with time.

I clasped an imaginary lever to slow time to a stop. Dust motes hung in the air, and even the static buzz of the lamps quieted. I wasn't sure how long I'd be able to hold this effect since this was my first real attempt, therefore I had no time to dally.

Doctor Finch waited for me inside the corridor, his leg sticking out comically in a frozen mid-walk. I carefully slid my hands into his pockets and pulled out his ID and office key. A quick flip and I had the number of his office. All I needed to do now was find it.

I ran down the corridor, not bothering to muffle my steps. Anyone I raced past would see a flickering shadow when time returned to normal, with any luck.

Between using a Vesper's shadow to sneak around this place and the power to quite literally stop time, this seemed the smarter way of searching a building I had no business being inside. Speaking with Doctor Finch was out of the question, I'd realized. He'd have too many questions of his own, and I doubted he'd just hand over his former master's schematics.

The corridor twisted around to the icebox where the poor Diviner's body had last been laid. The door hadn't been replaced, so I couldn't resist popping my head inside to see if Hector was still there, but no. Someone had moved him.

Good. I didn't want to go rummaging through a dead man's pockets.

Doctor Finch's office is further on, Jinx said. *We passed it yesterday.*

You remember where?

One of us has to pay attention to these things.

I jogged out of the cooler and scanned the numbers as I strode past. Eventually I came to Doctor Finch's office. Getting inside wasn't a problem.

His office was almost as badly organized as Quen's, with papers scattered over his desk. A bookshelf filled the far wall, but instead of books, there were odd-looking mechanical contraptions and piles of nuts, bolts, gears, and wiring. Truly, the man was a Diviner in disguise. But how would I find the schematics in this mess?

Check the desk.

Good plan. I closed the door and used my hand to drag time back to normal. A wave of dizziness came over me, and I staggered against the desk, knocking over an inkpot and quill. Ink splashed over a collection of papers and dripped over the side. Shit!

You fucked with time too long, idiot.

Had I? I hadn't realized stopping time would have an effect on—

Forget about that now. Search the desk.

Gods, right. My legs wobbled, so I slid onto a stool without a back—a good choice for a Zephyr with wings, even if Doctor Finch was missing his. I quickly searched the desk for anything resembling schematics. Even the drawers were filled with gadgets, but no folders or papers.

Where in god's name would a doctor hide their most precious documents?

Something caught my eye; an hourglass model of Chime. Among the papers and gadgets here, this gaudy figurine stood out. I stumbled over to it and lifted the heavy base. Underneath lay an ID badge and key.

Hector Bezel's ID. The dead Diviner doctor.

Why would Doctor Finch hide them?

Though what were the chances these schematics were still locked away in Hector's office?

I again slowed time, but my balance didn't seem to right itself. There wasn't any point cleaning the ink I'd spilled since Doctor Finch's office was such a mess regardless, but I locked the door behind me. I ran as quickly as I could, but a raging headache was building in my forehead that had nothing to do with aether.

The ID clasped in my trembling hand stated office thirteen, which I found further along the hall as I passed some Umber who stood as still as a statue. The key fit inside the lock and I practically fell as I pushed open the door. Something wet dripped from my nose.

Blood.

Oh shit, was my brain bleeding?

Stop playing with time! Jinx yelled at me.

I let time catch up as I slid against the wall of Hector's office. My heart pounded, and I wiped away a smear of blood with the back of my hand.

Quen hadn't explained time powers would melt my pissing brain! I suppose it made sense; fucking with time took a lot more effort than playing with shadows.

After gulping a few steadying breaths, my gaze turned to Hector Bezel's office. This was more what I expected a Diviner office to look like. Neat, orderly, and minimalistic in design. The desk had been cleared of everything except an inkpot, though the bookshelves were full of thick books, all organized alphabetically.

At least I wouldn't have to search too far. I crawled on over to Hector's desk and rifled through the drawers.

There, in the very bottom drawer, I found a folder with diagrams of what looked like the god-splitting machine along with various numbers and equations written in the margins, though one word stood out among the jumble: aether.

Had that Diviner doctor died for this?

"You're the one I sensed stopping time."

I scrambled off the floor.

A Diviner leaned against the doorframe, but not just any Diviner. I recognized his bronze hair and brass eyes from Lady Mae's café.

Ambassador Karendar.

What was he doing here in the steamworks? He wasn't dressed in his official tabard, but in the pinstripe suit from the café.

His brass gaze scanned over me, from my face to my clothes, to the smear of blood on my hand, and then to the folder clutched by my side. "I believe that's mine."

I straightened up and tucked the folder under my arm. "I'd rather like to borrow it, if you don't mind."

He didn't move from the door. "I rather do. But there's no rush. My Wardens are currently securing all exits to the steamworks to ensure you don't slip by me again. I'm afraid I have a great many questions for you. Although—" He glanced at his watch. "It appears we've missed the crossing for Kronos."

Shit. I'd walked myself and Harmony into a trap, though she'd have fled at the first sign of trouble. We Godless didn't like to leave anyone behind, but we also understood the pointlessness of chivalry; we couldn't rescue one another if we all got caught in the same net.

"Where are you holding Corinth?" he asked, and that question caught me off guard. He knew I held Quen captive, then, just not where. Luckily for me, he wouldn't be able to grab me and scan my memories for the Godless's location.

"Quen is spending quality time with my blaspheming friends. We're quite a bad influence, and you know Quen; he's such an impressionable boy."

Karendar's eyebrow twitched with restrained anger. Oh, pissing him off probably wasn't the brightest idea, but I did so enjoy it.

"Kayl, is it? No known family name, no known domain. Your existence provides many opportunities for study. It is quite clear, for example, that you suffer from an explicitly chronic case of apostasy. You simply drip with sin, my dear." His eyes unflatteringly roved across my body to prove some twisted point. "What is it about you that attracts sin? I could have easily blamed it on your Vesper blood, and yet that wouldn't be accurate. Which domain created *you*?"

Pious types like Karendar were obsessed with sin, though I didn't see what was so sinful about enjoying mortal existence.

I slid around the edge of the desk and angled my feet to run. "The answer is obvious, isn't it? All domains suffer with sin. Even yours. As I am an amalgamation of each, I incorporate their best bits. Their finest sins."

"That is what would make you an excellent subject for study, yes. Would it be possible to rectify your sins? I'd like to invite you to our HQ and find out."

"I'd *love* to accept, but I'm afraid I must turn down your kind offer as I'm rather attached to my sins. And, well, I surely don't have the time for torture. Your Glimmer friends would happily take my place, though."

His brass eyes burned into mine. "Please. I insist."

Grab him, Jinx urged. *Take his soul.*

Shit. Leaving Karendar's empty body wouldn't help the Godless cause, but it would certainly help my predicament. I didn't believe that the Wardens held no knowledge of this god-splitting machine, as Quen assumed. Even if they didn't know, these schematics could point to the Glimmer's use, and who was to say Karendar wouldn't use it on me?

I was an aether creature to him. An anomaly. I could read it in his eyes.

It was either my soul or his.

I charged at the ambassador which, due to my unsteady gait, made me quite literally fall onto him. I grabbed his wrist and felt the tug pulse in my palm.

His eyes opened wide, clearly aware of what I meant to do. "Get off me!" he snarled, and shoved me away.

We both stumbled out into the hall. I'd not taken his soul, but now I was free of Hector's office and ran for it.

"There's nowhere for you to go!" Karendar called after me, but I didn't care. I'd find a way out. There would be pipes leading out of the steamworks somewhere underground. Gods, if there were an Amnae or two nearby, I'd be able to swim out.

I ran around a corner and bumped straight into Doctor Finch.

He threw up his arms in alarm, scattering an entire folder of papers. "It's you! Guards!" he yelled. "She's here! Guards!"

"Oh, shut up," I snapped, and turned to run.

"No! You're not taking that!" He snatched Hector Bezel's folder from my hands.

I tried to pry his claws from the document, but they dug into the paper with an iron-gripped tightness.

Wings burst from my back, ripping through my blouse.

Holy shit!

Doctor Finch squawked and released the folder, falling onto his arse. "How—How did you do that? How did you transform? I *need* to know!"

I quickly glanced at my hands, which had become the same clawlike fingers as Doctor Finch's, while talons also cut through the leather of my shoes. Plumage sprouted across my face, sending a flutter of silver feathers in the air.

Great. I didn't have time to admire my change, however, or the wings protruding awkwardly out of my spine.

Fly out of here.

Good thinking. Becoming a Zephyr hadn't been my plan A, B, or C, but it would have to do. I shoved past the doctor and ran for the stairs which lead to the reactor, my feet flopping awkwardly with each step.

This time I went up instead of down. The Wardens might have every door blocked, but would they count on me flying off the roof? As I reached the top, I was vindicated to discover they hadn't.

Oh, I *loved* making fools out of Wardens.

I clutched the folder tightly as I ducked through the maintenance door. My new wings caught the sides, scattering more feathers, but I didn't have time to hide the evidence. I emerged out onto some sort of ledge, where more pipes ran up to the large plate above. Wires and panels with various switches surrounded me, but no maintenance staff. I ran to the edge and glanced over.

Shit, it was a damnable fall from here, and I'd never flown before. Gods, I didn't even know how to fly!

Just open your wings and glide down, Jinx said. *It can't be that hard.*

Glide down? I was going to fall to my death!

Shouting came from behind me—my pretty trail of feathers had led the Wardens to my position. I had no choice but to jump. Karendar seemed like the sort to take great pleasure in plucking a Zephyr.

I shuffled along, making space for the wingspan I'd surely need, and then climbed over the ledge with shaking legs. Spreading my wings came easily, as though my body's instincts knew how to move them like a third limb, though not even that filled me with confidence. I was up pants-shittingly high.

A flash of light caught my attention, and I spotted someone waving a mirror by the far steamworks gate—Harmony. Thank the gods. She'd gotten out and was now signaling my attention. The gate looked so far away, but all I needed to do was glide down.

Shit, I couldn't do this.

It wasn't like the safety of my room swaying in the air, or riding on top of an elevator.

Wardens burst out of the maintenance stairway. "She's here!"

Shit! I just needed to jump, I needed to—

For fuck's sake, you're going to get us both caught! Jinx wrenched control of my body and flung us both forward.

I swallowed a scream as I plummeted through the air. Then my wings flared sideways, tugging me back for a heartbeat before my body corrected itself, and I casually rode whatever air currents flowed underground.

"You're a bloody bitch!" I squawked at Jinx, but then the adrenaline caught up with me and a laugh tore through my lungs.

You love it.

I did. I actually did. I soared down, aiming for the far corner of the steamworks gate where Harmony waved her arms. But as the ground grew closer, the elation of flight was replaced with panic.

Falling and flying had been easy. But landing?

That'll be easy too, when you go splat.

Jinx, help me with this!

Oh, so now you want *me to take over our body?*

It won't be anyone's body if we crash!

I could feel Jinx roll our eyes as she once again took control. We approached the ground at breathtaking speed, and I worried that she'd let us paint the ground with our mangled body out of spite.

But then our wings flared once more and our legs bent, ready to take the impact. I stumbled forward, my body suddenly returning to my control as Jinx let me fall flat on my face.

Thanks, Jinx.

You're welcome, bitch.

"Shit, are you all right?" Harmony grabbed my arm and attempted to pull me up. "It didn't take long for the Wardens to show their faces. I had to serenade my way out. What did you do? Run into that irritating Zephyr doctor, I presume?"

I dragged myself to my battered feet and checked the folder of Hector's schematics was still intact. I'd gripped it so tightly my talons had dug grooves into the paper. "It was Karendar." My voice came out in an odd trill, and I rubbed the smoothness of my beak.

Harmony let my arm drop. "Ambassador Karendar?"

"How many Karendars do you know?" I glanced toward the steamworks. Wardens were running out of the main building and straight for us, and I'd landed on the wrong side of the pissing gate. The walls were so tall, I wasn't sure if I could manage to fly over it.

"This way." Harmony stepped aside, revealing a small hole in the wall. Large enough for a Seren to squeeze through, but certainly not me with my massive wings. She held out her hand. "I can stand you copying my style for one day, girl."

Shame, I hadn't even gotten the chance to admire my new wings, and I was going to need to shrink them. Better that than attempting to fly and failing spectacularly.

I took Harmony's hand, and the world shifted slightly as my eyes became level with hers. I glanced at my hand; the skin had turned a lovely pastel blue. Aether blue.

My blouse slipped from my shoulders, flashing Harmony a lacy white bra. I'd ripped it with my Zephyr wings. "Damn it, this was my favorite."

My pleated skirt also slipped, becoming more of a ballooning dress. I struggled to keep my oversized clothes in place and preserve some modesty, and my shoes flapped loose. The holes my clawed feet had poked through had ruined these, too.

"I'll get you a new one." Harmony took Hector's schematics and shoved them into her briefcase. "Smart thinking, flying out of there, by the way. Now let's go."

The tips of my Seren wings fluttered at the compliment. Coming from Harm, they were a rare treasure indeed.

I followed her through the gap, tucking in my new and much smaller wings as I ducked under. It was a tight squeeze, which meant the Wardens wouldn't be able to follow easily. We'd have a head start and take the tunnels back on foot. They'd hopefully not find two Seren hiding in the dark.

But now Ambassador Karendar knew the extent of my powers and knew I held Quen captive. He seemed to know a great deal more, possibly thanks to Quen, or perhaps the Wardens had caught our mystery benefactor after all.

And Karendar also knew what I'd stolen and likely what I planned to do with Hector Bezel's information.

Which meant the Godless were in more danger now than we'd ever been.

XXV

The Wardens have received ongoing reports of discrimination against the Necro. We depend on their ability to manipulate mortal bodies, both inside and out. Their skills for physical modification aren't just required for healing and other medical surgeries, but also for designing passport ID's, without which Chime cannot exist.

The truly gifted Necro are also in high demand within the Golden City for their cosmetic abilities; face tailoring, hair growth, wrinkle and blemish removal, coloring, and so on.

You'll likely know that the Necro's gifts come with a price; a hunger for mortal flesh and blood. But even these can be catered to without the need for discriminatory action.

Do remember the Covenant. The Necro are mortal, too.

—Q. Corinth, *Warden Dossier on the Necro*

THE COFFEE TASTED DIRE, but at least it kept me on my toes, so to speak. I wasn't going anywhere with my hands bound like this, not that I wanted to leave any time soon. The Ember had shoved me into an abandoned tram on the platform which had since been reconditioned into some sort of lounge. The cushions were more comfortable than that blasted wooden chair at least, though I couldn't say much for the company.

"Too bitter for your tastes, darling?" the Ember asked, the crowbar resting lovingly by his knee—a male Ember, as I'd deduced by a flash of his tail. I still couldn't remember if we'd dallied, though it seemed this Ember liked to play flirt with everyone.

I cradled the hot mug in my gloved hands, which required both to drink it. "I've suffered worse. You wouldn't want to drink any beverage made by a Necro."

As I said the words, the Necro—Vincent—stepped into the tram and sat beside the Ember, placing an affectionate hand on his shoulder. "Get some rest before tonight. I can entertain our guest."

The Ember looked me over as one might judge a dirty cup unfit for drinking, but then he shrugged. "Don't get too acquainted, dearest." He kissed the Necro on the cheek and swaggered out of the tram.

"A Necro and an Ember?" I commented aloud. "How unusual."

Vincent settled in the Ember's seat and placed my pistol on the table, angled and pointed at me. I could see it was loaded—they must have ransacked my jacket for bullets. Whether this Necro knew how to use it, I couldn't guess. "We're an odd pairing, I'll grant you. This is a beautiful design." He tapped the intricate brass barrel.

"Thank you. I customized it myself. I didn't think your kind dated? Certainly not outside of your domain. How do you maintain your urges?"

"We make it work. You're not bothered by the thought?"

"Why would I be?" Though I noticed the subtle way Vincent carried himself and sat. There were so many misconceptions regarding the Necro, so many fears based on half-truths. I didn't fear them, though the younger Warden recruits kept their distance.

Some sought the Necro *for* their danger, for the pleasure found in pain. Sinner's Row ran boutiques covering the fetishes of those who enjoyed a 'feed and fornicate,' as they called it, to the darkest and most macabre desires, where the thrill came in becoming a meal, quite literally. And there went my pure, innocent mind, languishing on such thoughts.

Death and lust were often intertwined, so the Ember said. Personally, I liked to keep the two apart.

"My god does not care if we are feared," Vincent said, a polite smile coming to his gray lips. "Nor does my god care if we hunger, so long as that hunger is sated. Sinder offers me his blood, and I give him my devotion in return. I haven't eaten flesh in some time."

The old-fashioned feed and fornicate, then. Not my style, but fair play to them. "The other Godless accept you?"

"More so than the Wardens or my own kind would. I'd marry him in the eyes of Warden law, but neither of our gods would allow it."

No. Both Wardens and the gods held strict rules for cohabitation between the domains, often for good reason.

We dealt with so many cases of one domain abusing another, even in consensual relationships; Necro biting their partners, Seren using the power of song to make others fall in love with them, pushy Leander who failed to inform lovers of their prickly penises before the night's event, and they certainly *were* a shock.

It wasn't easy serving a melting pot of twelve unique domains, but that was why I loved Chime—and all its saints and sinners.

Mortal lives were messy things.

I took a sip of my bitter sludge. Kayl had suggested I speak with the Godless and try to understand them, and I did so enjoy conversing. Elijah wouldn't approve, but Elijah rarely approved of anything I did for myself these days, and why make my captivity dull? Damn it, I *wanted* to understand them—to understand Kayl.

I wanted to know what would drive these mortals to such desperation that they'd look upon an infernal device and see salvation. It couldn't be as simple as marriage rights.

Though perhaps it was.

When I'd entered this den of apostasy, I'd expected blood lettings and chanting and mass orgies. So far, the Godless had disappointed me with their normalcy.

"Tell me, Vincent, if I may address you by your name; why are you here?"

"If you mean to question me to build some sort of dossier on our past and histories, then I have no interest in speaking further."

I glanced over the top of my spectacles. "If I wanted your history, you know I could very well take it."

"With your hands bound?"

"Well, this pleasant coffee is running straight through me, so unless you want to handle my manhood or allow me to ruin your cushions, I daresay you'll be untying me at some point soon."

His smile turned predatory, and I caught the glint of a fang. "Sinder would be delighted."

I was sure he would be. "Don't tell me the wheres or the whens. What I want to know is the whys and the hows. Tell me as much or as little detail as you will."

"Do you seek to understand us so you may destroy us?"

Partly. "Is seeking understanding not enough? We live our own pathetic mortal lives through the lens of our god, our own domain. I don't know what it means to live as a Necro or an Ember, only what it means to be a Diviner and to share that connection with my god. However, the Wardens exist to serve all domains and all mortals of Chime. How can we achieve this when our vantage point is so limited? So please. Enlighten me."

Vincent clasped his hands together over the table. "What do you know of The Nameless One?"

"They have no name, for a start."

My comment brought no smile. "The Nameless One takes on many personas. Many faces. An entire collection of masks cut from the mortals of other domains. They are fascinated by the inner workings of a mortal body. They like to play with the mortals under their command, because that's all we are. Toys wrapped in shells that bleed and scream such delightful sounds should you pull them in certain ways."

There was a reason why The Nameless One appeared in so many Mesmer nightmares. "You don't like your own god?" Despite their god's depravity, most Necro didn't seem perturbed by it.

"My history, Quentin Corinth, is that I was made in Witheryn and studied on Memoria to learn biology. To please The Nameless One. There, I caught a taste of life from a world that was not cold and dark. I wanted to use my talents to heal. My god had other designs for me.

"Upon my return to Witheryn, The Nameless One ordered me to perform operations and dissections on living subjects, and to speak of whatever findings intrigued them. I ripped the wings off a young Seren. And then we threw them off a cliff to see if they'd still try to fly." Vincent's bloodshot eyes stared through me. "The mortals of my domain did not see what I saw. A life, full of color, that became dulled in death. My god has committed many such atrocities, and yet you—your Wardens—never once stepped forth to put an end to it."

"I'm sorry. You're right. We should have."

"You didn't then and you won't now. You say you serve the mortals of all domains, but the domains are unbalanced. They kill each other. But so long as the gods and their ambassadors are happy, the Wardens won't interfere. And that is why we Godless exist."

"The rest of the Godless have a similar tale?"

"Yes. Most of us have been abused and tossed aside by our god in one way or another. We see the gods as cruel."

"Not all are."

"Enough are. A mortal has no choice which domain they are born under. Who would choose to live like this? To be forced to drink the blood of their loved ones, or suffer the urge to hurt innocents in order to sate an insatiable hunger? If mortals are lucky, they'll be born as a Diviner or Glimmer. If not, they'll be enslaved. Even the others, like the Amnae, Seren, and Zephyr, are no stranger to their god's cruelties. But to even entertain the idea of choosing another god or none at all is blasphemous in your eyes."

That I couldn't deny. "The Wardens are not perfect by any means, but we seek to work with the less, ah, *reputable* gods and protect mortals from the worst of their whims. No mortal can stand against a god, but we place pressure where we can—"

"With all due respect, your pressure means little. The gods still torture their mortals, only their screams are hidden behind doors that no Warden dares tread past."

Therein lay the fundamental truth of the Wardens; we only held so much influence. The gods listened and allowed us to assert our authority on Chime, but we were only mortal, after all. We did what we could. We thought it enough.

I thought it enough.

Didn't I?

"I cannot walk for long," Vincent continued. "For my god made me arthritic, though Sinder's heat helps ease the pain. Each of us suffers from a similar deficiency that our gods inflicted. The Wardens' Covenant means nothing when our gods punish our very mortal existence. Do you yet understand why we wish to be free?"

Elijah believed that the Godless embodied the flaws of mortal sin while the rest of us strived to obtain purity. Which meant the Godless were built wrong, somehow. But were their flaws, their imperfections, any different from my eyesight or Kayl's double-soul problem? Why would a perfect god build an imperfect mortal?

To test us? Challenge us? Give us meaning?

The gods made us imperfect for a reason, and that included notions of apostasy. That included the Godless. A blasphemous thought that would get me thrown out of the Wardens.

But even the Godless were owned by their god.

Unless they could truly become free.

What meaning would such a life hold then?

Saints. I couldn't let my sympathy for these mortals cloud my judgement. Not when they held knowledge of the Glimmer's device. I squirmed in my seat. "I appreciate your testimony, but I truly must visit your restroom."

Vincent stood and shoved my pistol into the band of his belt. "I'll accompany you."

Hopefully, he'd untie my hands, otherwise we were about to become well acquainted.

I followed him out of the tram and across the platform to another set of metal stairs that descended to an underground factory floor. This, too, had been converted into a hospitable living space.

Where there were once storage bays, now resided private rooms, personalized with signs denoting each of the Godless, I presumed, as well as a medical bay and restroom. These surrounded the circular central conveyor belt, which served as a breakfast bar and makeshift kitchen.

Miss Smith sat on a stool by the conveyor belt, eating from a bowl of colorful pebbles while browsing the latest edition of the Chime Courier. She gave me a startled look as I shuffled past. I offered a polite nod, but alas, she did not return the courtesy.

Oil lamps gave the room a cozy golden glow. It was far more spacious than my apartment, stuffed with couches, bookshelves, and a table that had been reserved for a board game in session. The furniture appeared threadbare, and even the game pieces were a random assortment of items, likely scavenged within the neighboring slums. But the room looked lived in. Homely.

"Who's the artist?" I asked, while pointing to a series of crudely painted images of the gods on the walls. The same imagery that often appeared on their fliers.

"That would be me," Vincent said. "I like to keep my fingers active, even if they ache some days. Do you approve?"

One painting depicted Dor pulling the strings of a Diviner like a puppet. So horrifically offensive, I couldn't help but gawk. "I can't say that I do. If you're the artist behind your organization's fliers, who's the author?"

"That would be Harmony, though we all pitch in with our ideas. I assume you're not a fan of our work?"

"On the contrary, I rather like collecting them. How do you manage to print so many so quickly?"

Vincent gave me a wry smile. "Where there is a will, there is a way. Here you are," he announced as we stopped outside the restroom. "I'd rather not wake Sinder to watch over you, thus I ask, can I trust you, Master Corinth?"

"I swear on my gentleman's honor that I shan't do more than see to my mortal needs." I held up my gloved and tied hands. "I'll keep my hands to myself. I promise."

The edge in Vincent's eye betrayed his doubt in my sincerity, though I could see it from his perspective. With my hands free, I could stop time and fast-forward my way out of here, as Kayl put it. None of the Godless could stop me. Within the hour, I could have a legion of Wardens marching through Grayford to round up every last Godless and Godless sympathizer in the area.

But I wasn't going to do any of that, and I had no interest in viewing the Godless's memories or deaths. "Until Kayl returns, I'm not going anywhere."

That seemed to convince him. He untied my hands, and I breathed a sigh as those pink gloves came free. "One moment, then."

The scent of pear perfume welcomed me into the Godless restroom. I wasn't sure what I'd expected—a hole in the ground? Rot creeping up the walls? Urine splashed across the tiles? But this restroom looked just as cozy as the rest of their base.

Verdant potted plants and candlelight in jars sat happily under a clean mirror. The lavvy wasn't as modern as mine, and the seat wore a fluffy cover to match my gloves. How much of this restroom had been designed by Kayl? It certainly had a woman's touch.

I went about my business and was glad that the plumbing actually worked, despite the loud gurgling sounds it made on the way down.

On my exit, neither Vincent nor Miss Smith were waiting for me, though she'd hastily abandoned her bowl of pebbles, judging by the few which had spilled out.

Angry voices came from the next room over, but my Warden instincts recognized a different noise elsewhere; pained whimpering.

I followed its source to a room marked 'Reve' and slowly opened the door, peeking my head around.

A young Mesmer boy stood on the other side and stared right at me.

Gods! I jumped back, my heart leaping to my throat. "Sorry to bother you. I heard noises. I thought you needed help—"

"She calls you Quen," the Mesmer said with the deep voice of a much older man that did not match his boyish face. With the Mesmer, it was so difficult to tell what age they were. This one stood as still as a statue, though those dark eyes moved with the twinkling constellations of stars.

"She does. And you must be Reve?"

"You don't remember me."

Not a question, but a statement.

I glanced over my shoulder. My Necro guard wasn't in sight, and the shouting a few doors down grew louder. Whatever they were arguing about sounded heated. "Have we met before?"

The Mesmer held out his hand. "You are the reason I'm here."

I was? What trouble had my past self wrought? "I promised not to touch any of you. I'm a man of my word."

Reve lowered his hand. "You've already seen what I would show you. You've seen the chaos to come."

This was why no one liked Mesmer. The way he stared at me and spoke felt profoundly uncomfortable, but if he'd witnessed the same visions I had... "Do you know what she is?" I asked, keeping my voice lowered.

"I have seen her true form."

Holy saints. "Then who is her god? Do you know?"

"I will tell you my story."

"Your story?"

"You wanted to know Vincent's story. I want you to know mine."

I sucked in a breath, caught between impatient agitation and apprehension. Reve did not move to sit somewhere more comfortable, keeping me trapped here outside his door, but I feared losing his concentration if I so much as twitched. Mesmer seldom retained their lucidity for long. "Please do."

"One moment I swam in a river of nothing. A blissful darkness. I existed as an idea that should never have been thought. As a synapse that should have never fired. And then I appeared in light and noise. I was born into *chaos*." Reve's eyes flashed at the word. "It pained me. Existence. I tried to end it. I came to Chime and threw myself in front of a tram and splattered its window. I embraced that blissful darkness once more. But then the light and the noise and the chaos returned. My god brought me back. Mesmorpheus did not wish for me to die. I have tried many times."

"How—How many times have you tried?"

"Twelve. The thirteenth will be my last."

I'd come across suicidal mortals during my tenure as a Warden. Often, they weren't mortals who wished to escape their god, but lonely souls who wished to be closer. Umber were especially prone to such melancholy.

However, both mortals and gods were meant to obey the Covenant, which meant *one* mortal life bound to the laws of time—to live, to age, and then die. If Mesmorpheus had brought this mortal back twelve times, then they'd only gone and broken the Covenant *twelve* damn times. Again, not unheard of, but it set my Warden sensibilities twitching.

Though no wonder such a mortal would hide among the Godless. Who was I to judge? "There must be something you enjoy about life?"

Reve pondered my question. "No."

"Then why are you here?"

"I await my salvation."

The Godless's cursed device. "You know what that device will do? It will rend your soul apart." Though perhaps that was exactly what a suicidal Mesmer wanted.

"I died in your arms twelve times." He cocked his head. "You cried after each one, though I told you not to, yet you don't remember."

My mouth went dry. It was entirely possible I was there for each of his deaths, or that he'd witnessed it through a vision. And entirely possible I'd have wiped such memories.

But none of those memories mattered now. The stars in his eyes held more knowledge than I dared ask, yet I needed to know. "What is she, Reve? Which god?"

"You know what she is."

"An aether creature, born from the combined energies of the twelve domains?"

"We're all aether, Quentin Corinth."

I raised my spectacles and rubbed my eyes. "But more specifically?"

"What time is it when the clock strikes thirteen?"

Riddles, now? "Time to get a new clock."

"Reve!" Miss Smith exclaimed as she came running over to us. She pushed me aside and grabbed the Mesmer's arm, pulling him away as if *I* were the dangerous one!

Then something slammed into me, knocking the breath from my lungs, and I was shoved painfully against the wall.

Malkavaan.

The Vesper snarled, splattering my cheek with spit. His fist curled around my waistcoat, pinning me so tight I could barely move. I tried to raise my hands, and a sharp object pressed against my throat.

"Move, and I'll saw your pissing head off."

I swallowed a heavy lump. "I wouldn't advise it."

"Don't condescend to me, you time-keeping twat." His hot breath blew over my face. "Do you want to know what Valeria did to me? What you left me to suffer?"

"Malk," Vincent called. He limped over with his fist wrapped around a cane and came to stand beside Miss Smith. Both looked visibly uncomfortable, though not as uncomfortable as I, I was sure. "Let him go, Malk."

"The fuck should I? He condemned me to Eventide! He left me there to *die*!"

"You look alive to me," I said.

Malkavaan's nostrils flared. "Do you want me to slice your throat and send you back to the darkness that spawned you?"

I met his sapphire eyes with my own cold stare. "You won't kill me, Malkavaan Byvich."

The knife pressed into my skin, biting ever so slightly. "Won't I?"

"No. For three reasons." I kept my breathing steady. "For one, if you send me back to my god, Dor will see all you've done today, and the Wardens will hunt you and your fellows down. And for two, I've seen my own death, and it is not by your hand."

Malkavaan scoffed. "You said three reasons."

"The third is because it would be poor form to kill Kayl's ally. We are, after all, partners." I forced a smile, despite my best judgement. One could afford a little spite with a knife pressed to one's throat.

Rage boiled in his eyes. He released his hold on my chest only to shove me again with such force, the back of my head smacked against the wall. I blinked away starlight.

"What is she, you miserable fuck? What did you do to her?"

"I didn't do anything to her—"

"Then what is she?"

"Malk, stop this," Vincent urged.

Malkavaan tossed his knife aside, letting it clatter to the ground, and then raised his fist only inches from my nose. "*What is she?*"

I'd never suffered a broken nose before, but there was a first time for everything. "Believe me, I wish I knew."

I winced as Malkavaan pulled back his arm, readying his strike.

"Malk," a female voice called from the stairs. Kayl. She'd returned.

All eyes snapped to Kayl standing with her hands on her hips. Her skin had changed from the silvery-blue of a Diviner to a more pastel blue, and her hair was now a vivid pink with silver highlights.

At first, I thought the angle of her pose made her seem smaller, but no; she'd shrunk in height. Her skirt's length now covered her shoes, and her blouse had been tucked and tied at her waist. She'd damaged it, somehow, and I dreaded to know the reason. A pair of silver wings peeked out above her shoulder.

My goodness. She'd changed into a Seren.

She did look rather adorable as a Seren. Albeit a furious Seren.

Malkavaan released me from his grip. I sank against the wall and rubbed the imprint of his knife against my neck. Malkavaan, however, stared at Kayl with his jaw slack. Well, they all were. I couldn't blame them.

"Malk," Kayl called again. "If you're done acting like an arse, we'll talk."

The poor Vesper nodded mutely and then stalked up the stairs after her, leaving Vincent and Miss Smith to continue staring.

"Are you heathens always this dramatic?" I asked.

Vincent and Miss Smith turned their bewildered stares to me.

And then the Mesmer laughed, and we all jumped.

I didn't think Mesmer could display emotion, but Reve's laugh was hearty and bold. Miss Smith took his arm and guided the still-chuckling Mesmer to his room. "You need sleep, Reve, this isn't good for you."

"What's so funny?" I called.

The Mesmer's laughter died as quickly as it appeared and he glanced over his shoulder. "You don't remember the punchline, Quentin Corinth? You soon will."

26

No mortal embraces sin quite like the Ember. In fact, they relish it.
While most domains have strict rules when it comes to pleasure, especially
the Glimmer, the Ember take these rules and turn them upside down. To
not sin is considered a sin.
Anything and everything can and must be indulged in, so Edana demands.
This of course makes her one of the more popular gods, and Rapture a prime
destination for revelry.
Most forget that pleasure often comes with a price, and Edana so enjoys
burning mortals who fail to pay up.
All things in moderation, as Father says.
—Q. Corinth, *Warden Dossier on the Ember*

WHEN I'D RETURNED TO the depot and found it empty, I'd feared the worst.
I hadn't expected to find Malk threatening Quen downstairs. Malk
followed me now into my private room, his expression a painful mixture of
annoyance and anxiety.

"He threatened Reve," Malk blurted out by way of an explanation as
soon as he entered.

"That's not what I saw." Quen may be many things, but he wasn't the
sort to threaten mortals—least of all Reve. I wanted to get changed out of
my ridiculous oversized clothes. Though more than that, I wanted to
switch from this ridiculous Seren body. Climbing up those steps had taken
more effort than I was used to.

You could have flown up, Jinx said.

Oh, I suppose I could have. How did Harmony manage in a city much
larger than her? She rarely complained about her lot because, like the rest
of us, we channeled our complaints into action. Though now I appreciated
what her efforts were worth.

"Why is he even here?" Malk paced the length of my tram, causing it to sway. "He said you were partners? What does that mean? That you and him have been, what, frolicking across Chime while I was rotting in Eventide?"

His height now towered over me, and I strained my neck just looking at him. "Can you sit, please?"

"Why?"

"So I can actually look you in the eye when you accuse me of abandoning you."

He flumped onto a cushion, though his glare didn't soften. "Corinth dragged me to Eventide and left me there—and you let him."

He's making valid points, Jinx said.

No, he's being an ungrateful arse. I leaned against my bed and tucked my hands behind me to stop their shaking. I'd expected Malk to be hurt, yes, but... I hadn't expected this level of hate. Not from Malk. I steadied myself for the words to come. "Quen and I—"

"Quen!" he exclaimed. "He's *Quen* to you? As soon as you were rid of me, you shack up with a Diviner? The Dark Warden of all pissing mortals? Have you forgotten who he is? What he *did*? If not for him, my mother would still be here!"

My cheeks burned. "I haven't forgotten." Nor was I about to launch into the truth of the Grayford Incident without Quen's permission. "Quen and I worked together to discover who I was—to find a reason for Valeria to release you. You're welcome, by the way. And I won't take judgement from a Godless on what company I choose to keep."

The anger slipped from his expression a little as his eyes roamed across my face, to my Seren wings, as though fully seeing me for the first time. "Who are you, Kayl?"

Not what, but *who*. "I'm still the same as I ever was. Who I am hasn't changed. What I am is a different matter. Corinth tried to help me find my god."

"You're not a Vesper."

"I don't think I ever was."

He let out a breath and his shoulders sagged. "Valeria... she doesn't know what you are, either. Who is your god?"

"I don't know."

"You... don't know?" He stared at me incredulously.

I tried to explain everything that had happened between Eventide and now, but he became even more confused. Though he stopped looking so angry, so frightened.

He came to sit next to me. "If you touch me, you'll turn back?"

I held out my hand. "Try it."

He placed his palm against mine and I felt at home in the rough texture of his skin, the warmth of it. It enveloped my smaller Seren hand until I felt the tug, and my hand grew in size along with the rest of me. I accidentally bumped his head, and my blouse popped open, my breasts swelling to fill my bra. Truly, swapping from a Seren to Vesper had not been as easy as swapping from any other domain.

Malk rubbed his forehead. "That's... incredible. How come you never did this before?"

"Honestly, I have no idea." I tried to pull my blouse together and preserve some modesty.

"Don't." He took my hand, stopping me. "I like what I see." The glint in his eye was more the Malk I knew.

"I missed you," I whispered. "Every night I cried for you. Everything I've done is to get you back—"

And then he was kissing me.

Desperate and deep kisses.

Time apart always intensified our lovemaking, and he'd often returned from Eventide eager to replace those memories, but *this* burned with an all-consuming energy. Malk ripped my blouse open and his hands were pawing at my breasts before I could even open my mouth to breathe.

"Slow down," I gasped, but he didn't.

His hands slid to my thighs, hoisting my skirt as his palm traced my indigo flesh. I wanted this, wanted him, but he was moving too fast and had me pinned against the cushions, his body sliding atop mine, his belt undone, as I struggled to adjust.

"We shouldn't, the motion—*shit!*" I winced as he entered me in one rough thrust. I hadn't warmed up enough to accommodate his size, and the speed and force of it *hurt*. "Please Malk, slow down." We'd never fucked inside my tram before, but now he hammered into me with no regard for the tram's sway, or my comfort. "Malk, stop."

He wasn't even looking at me, but looking through me, as if I weren't even here.

"You're hurting me!" I pushed against the solid muscle of his chest. He hadn't even bothered to take off his shirt or undress in his haste.

Shadows burst from my skin, but it wasn't me—Jinx had yanked control of my body.

"She said *stop*!" Jinx yelled with my voice.

The vacant look in his blue eyes turned to panic. He rolled off me, tugging up his slacks, and collapsed against the couch in a fit of sobs.

Gods. I pulled up my skirt and tried to adjust the blouse. Malk sat with his head in his hands, tears streaming between his fingers as he rocked back and forth. His shirt had ridden up slightly, exposing the skin above his hip where I knew a scar should have been—a scar from when Wardens had marched on Grayford five years ago. But the scar was no more.

Valeria had erased it.

I lifted his shirt to check, and Malk jerked away from me. "Don't touch me!"

"What did she do to you?"

Fear returned to his eyes, and he wiped them and his nose dry with his sleeve. "I hear her. She's in my head, she... She wants me to hurt you. *I* want to hurt you. I'm not safe around you, I'm not—" He scrunched fists against his head at some imaginary pain, or it could have been real for all I knew.

Valeria could be torturing him now from afar.

I reached out to comfort him, but he recoiled as though he couldn't bear it. My hand dropped. "Go to Vincent. Let him help you sleep."

"And then what?" he asked, his voice cracking into another repressed sob. "You have no idea what it's like. I'm hers. I'll always be hers."

"No, you're mine, and I don't care to share." I couldn't stand to see him this way. "Sleep, and then I'll fix the Glimmer's god-splitting machine and free you. You'll never be owned by a god again. I promise you. I'll free you."

And I would. I'd rip Chime apart if I had to. I'd destroy Valeria and her domain if it meant freeing Malk. I'd do whatever it took.

For the second time this week, I stepped into Sinner's Row, only today my arm was wrapped around Sinder's, not Quen's.

Harmony and I had debated the best way to retrieve these prisms the Glimmer so badly needed for their god-splitting machine; Ambassador Erosain would recognize me as a Diviner and friend of Quen's, which might open up the doors of conversation and negotiation, but ultimately, we didn't want a man such as him to learn about our plans. Quen had stressed the importance of keeping this knowledge out of the other domains' hands, and so far, only the Glimmer and Diviner were aware of it, and potentially Valeria. If we approached Erosain directly for his prisms, he'd want to know why. And if he learned of the machine, so would Edana, and then things would surely get messy.

No, the best way to approach this would be to avoid Erosain entirely.

Fortunately for me, Sinder had already earned a place in Erosain's kitchen thanks to a tip-off from our mystery benefactor, and I, in my Ember form, was about to join their staff. So long as Erosain himself didn't notice me and examine too closely, he'd never suspect.

"Nothing whets the appetite like a little espionage for dinner, darling," Sinder said cheerfully, as he guided me through alleys to the back door of Erosain's bar. We'd had to wait until evening to make our move. Erosain liked to play host, and the best time to sneak into his private quarters would be when it was busy enough for us to blend in.

An Ember guard standing by the back door blocked our entrance. "You new here?"

I fluttered my eyelashes and bobbed a little curtsy in the pinafore I'd worn at Lady Mae's. "I know, I am *so* lucky to get this chance to glimpse the glamor. I'm Fira." I gave a little giggle.

"Ignore my lady friend here, she's an awful flirt." Sinder swatted me on the arm playfully.

Truly awful, Jinx said.

Quiet, you.

"Boss was looking for more waitstaff with pretty faces," Sinder said. "Fira here knows cocktails and offered to help cover. And she is lovely, isn't she?"

I gave another little twirl of my pinafore.

The guard looked me over with a scowl. "She'll do. Make the boss happy, and I'm happy, got it? Any trouble and you're both out." He waved me inside.

Sinder led me to the kitchens, which were twice the size of Lady Mae's. It wasn't just Ember who worked the stoves, but Seren chefs as well, which didn't surprise me. Of all the domains, the Seren were unique in their talent for turning anything into art, even a plate of cucumber sandwiches. The exquisite platter of edibles I'd ordered thanks to Quen had come from these wonderful minds.

Ember servers rushed about in impossibly tall heels, carrying trays of canapés and bubbling wine. From what I could see of the main bar, the tables and booths were packed. It wasn't quite Rapture, but it was the closest that most Undercity folk would get.

"Here." Sinder handed me a black apron as he donned his own. "The color suits you. Now, I'll coordinate your plates and try to get you as close to Erosain as I dare. Remember, dearest, you're here to watch him, not jump into bed with him."

I rolled my eyes. "You're as bad as Harmony. You know I've done all this before at Lady Mae's."

"Your short tenure at Lady Mae's resulted in a legion of Wardens hunting you." If Sinder had eyebrows, he'd be raising them. "I've been working this gig for months. I should be the one doing this."

"And ruin my debut as hostess?" Besides, Sinder's knowledge of Erosain's businesses would pay off tonight as we hunted for these prisms. I needed him to work his charm in the background as I worked my charm out front.

"That's what worries me, darling."

I patted his arm. "Let's put on a good show."

The bustle of the kitchen swallowed us both, and we fell into a pattern of orders and customers. The sheer number of tables didn't compare to Lady Mae's tiny café, and it left me reeling. I had no little notepad to help me this time. But I did have a friend.

Jinx, you need to help me keep track of these tables.

Why should I? Helping you just means I'm helping the Glimmer.

You helped me escape the steamworks.

Because I didn't want our body to get ripped apart by Wardens.

Please, Jinx, I pleaded. *I'm doing this for Malk.*

Why should I help him? He hurt you.

He didn't mean to. He's scared. We have no idea what Valeria did to him. But with this machine, we'll make her pay.

My mind went silent for so long I'd thought Jinx had somehow blocked my thoughts. *Fine*, she said at last. *I'll be the brain for us both.*

With Jinx's help, we cleared table after table. We truly made excellent partners as she freed my mind to focus on my actual task—spying on Erosain.

The Ember ambassador played the gracious host well and lavished attention on his eager patrons while lapping up the adoration they offered him. As planned, my tables brought me close to the ambassador's own movements, allowing me to eavesdrop on choice conversations here and there, though nothing of importance. Erosain drew customers in, and not just because of his status.

Dressed in his sharp black tuxedo and high heels to match his curling black beard and the black eyeshadow and lipstick, he stood out as a classy figure among the other Ember. Gods, he was undeniably beautiful too, and that smooth voice of his could melt butter.

You're supposed to be spying on him, not admiring his arse, Jinx said.

I can appreciate art when I see it. I admit I found myself drawn to Ember. How could I not, when they were so quick to sin? Though speaking of art, I'd scanned the bar thoroughly while waiting tables and not come across anything resembling the prisms.

I carried yet another tray of sparkling gold wine to a booth where a lively group of Seren women were hanging on Erosain's every word. Their pastel-colored skin and wings were a fluttering rainbow against the bar's beige sandstone.

"Oh, Ambassador, you are really spoiling us. Can we see it? You promised us last time, and it's quite rude to turn a lady down," whined a Seren with pale pink skin.

"Ladies, please," Erosain purred, a delighted smile on his lips. "One cannot just whip out one's goods in public."

That earned a smattering of giggles.

Another Seren playfully slapped him on the wrist. "What use is a private art gallery if you never share it? Come now, you know we'd inspect your goods with *great* care."

I gathered up the empty glasses, lingering on the table and their conversation.

"Apologies, ladies, but my collection contains many valuable and delicate items I dare not trust with the inebriated, and since I plan to get all of you *very* sloshed, we'll need to schedule a tour some other time, I promise you."

The Seren laughed and clinked their glasses together as I hurried away the empties. I ducked into the kitchens and beckoned Sinder over into a quiet corner. "How do we gain access to his private art collection?"

"You think he's hiding the goods there?"

"Where else would he put a random assortment of prisms?"

Sinder rubbed his chin. "Only he carries the key to his private collection, and I doubt even you'd be able to pick his pocket in this crowd, darling."

"I could if I stopped time." Though there were no Diviner among Erosain's clientele for me to accidentally brush against. The ambassador wasn't the type to let just anyone into his private collection, least of all another Ember.

No, men liked him craved power and possession. If I were to get his attention, I needed to offer something he wanted.

My eyes scanned over the patrons. Plenty of Ember, Leander, and Seren, with some Fauna and Vesper working alongside various clients. The

Diviner and Glimmer held power in Chime, but none of them frequented Erosain's bar.

I needed to become someone unique. Intriguing. And perhaps a little dangerous. My eyes landed on the pale flesh of a man lurking alone in a booth. "The Necro."

Sinder followed my eye. "Darling, you cannot be serious."

"We'll spike his drink. Then I'll take his form while no one's watching, and you'll direct Erosain's attention to me."

"We're supposed to be *avoiding* Erosain. Besides, Necro aren't known for their sex appeal, dearest."

"Vincent would be devastated to hear it."

If Ember could blush, Sinder's face would burst into flames. "And what if the urges get to be too much? Even Vin..." He cleared his throat. "Even Vincent struggles occasionally."

"Then I'll eat Erosain and get his key that way. Problem solved."

Erosain might not be the suck and fuck type, Jinx said.

No, but I needed to take a chance. "We can't keep standing around playing spy. We need to do this now. Malk needs me to." Otherwise we'd never make Valeria's deadline.

Sinder sighed. "Harmony is going to slaughter me, if you don't first. We'll need to swap you out of those clothes."

I followed Sinder to his private locker and quickly swapped out of my pinafore into a tight shirt and slacks. I was taller and broader-shouldered than Sinder, which pushed my chest out more.

He fixed up a sparkling white wine and added something hidden in the pop and fizz. "Necro often aren't ones for alcohol, but he'll appreciate this." Sinder pricked his finger with a cocktail stick and allowed a few drops of blood to swirl in the wine.

I took the glass in hand. "So this is how you and Vincent spend your evenings."

"Oh, you know Vincent. He likes to take his drink straight from the source." Sinder adjusted the scarf around his neck. "The key is not to drain too much. A man still requires some blood to raise his cock." He winked.

I stifled a giggle and headed back into the throng of bawdy bar-goers. As the night wore on, more and more entered to seek drink and companionship, though the Necro sat alone. No doubt he worked in one of the back-alley clinics of Sinner's Row.

I slid into his booth and placed the sparkling wine before him. "Dying for company?"

The Necro appeared much older than Vincent with drier, tighter skin pulled over the blue veins visible in his pale complexion. His bloodshot eyes narrowed. "We're all dying," he said, his voice raspy. "Some quicker than others."

"Then misery likes company." I pushed the glass forward.

He eyed the glass, his gaze examining the droplet of blood. "I don't come here to indulge the sick fantasies of harlots that should know better."

"Then why do you come here?"

"To see life."

"Not taste it?"

"In Sinner's Row? Everything tastes rotten. But where else do freaks like me go?"

You may have found the one Necro with a heart, Jinx said.

Vincent has a heart. Though Vincent was a lot easier to flirt with. "Well, between us freaks, it's far more fun to partake in life than merely observe it. That's why *I* come here—for a new story every day. I'd like to hear yours."

"Nosy, aren't you?"

"So I've been told."

He smiled, baring a fang, and took the glass. For a painful few seconds, he sniffed the contents. Finally, he dared a sip.

I held my breath, hoping that whatever Sinder had tipped into the wine would be potent enough, but I needn't have worried. The Necro's tongue lingered on the glass, enjoying the taste of Sinder's blood. Then he downed the drink in one. He slurred something I didn't quite hear, and his head slumped against the booth. I felt a little guilty for drugging his drink, but I wasn't here to steal his wallet—only his persona.

The thought of becoming a Necro didn't appeal to me, truth be told, but needs must.

I checked no one was walking past and shuffled next to him, laughing slightly as though we were sharing some joke. My hand touched his cold one. A shiver traveled up my arm, and I turned my face away, hiding it in the booth's curve as hair sprouted from my head and my skin turned from bright pink to a pale white.

A shadow appeared over my booth, startling me, but it was only Sinder. He slid next to me and placed a sparkling gold glass on the table.

"You look ravishing, darling. How do you feel?"

I ran my tongue over my teeth and felt the tips of fangs. Though apart from that, I didn't feel any different. "You look like a snack." I gnashed my teeth.

"That's always been true." He fluttered his eyelashes. "Think of food later; we need to deal with this fellow." He nudged the Necro with his foot.

Rather awkwardly, we rolled the unconscious Necro under the table where anyone walking past wouldn't see. He'd likely wake up confused later, but we'd be long gone by then.

"Now, this is the bar's most expensive champagne," Sinder explained as he tapped the sparkling glass with his black fingernail. "And most potent. Don't drink it. Sip, if you must, but *remember,* it is strong."

The drink didn't look that fancy. "How many bocs is it worth?"

"An entire mansion in the Golden City, I shit you not. Now, *don't* drink it. It'll go straight to your head. Erosain will be over as soon as he learns you 'purchased' it. Trust me." Sinder left me alone in my booth.

I took my incredibly fancy champagne and gave it a swirl. How could a mere drink be worth so much?

Drink it, Jinx urged. *I dare you.*

And piss out glitter like a Glimmer? No thank you.

Footsteps approached my booth in a joyful staccato to match the upbeat piano, and I bit back a smirk as Ambassador Erosain appeared with a swooping bow.

"Are you enjoying this evening's entertainment? Oh, have I made your acquaintance before, miss...?" His unnatural brows drew together, caught between familiarity and confusion.

Ideally, I didn't want to risk identification, but who would ever believe a Diviner could become a Necro? Though I hoped a player like Erosain would be too caught up trying to make a few bocs to care where my face came from.

"Please, call me Nadine, Your Excellency." My voice came out huskier than normal, which would only help to disguise me. "I don't believe we've met."

"Apologies, I'm sure I'd remember a stunning face like yours. Though you needn't trouble yourself with formalities, Nadine. All sinners are made equal in my bar." He flashed a charming smile. "Though what's your sin? A taste for the finer things?" His eyes followed my finger as I traced the rim of my champagne glass.

"Sadly, the finer things no longer tempt me. I dabble in art. An odd choice for my kind, I know. My Seren associates from Windsong no longer cater to my particular tastes." I casually name-dropped one of the richer estates of the Golden City. "I don't mind bloodying my wallet for the truly sublime."

The gleam in Erosain's eyes brightened. "You've come to the right place. We accommodate a wide variety of tastes here, even tastes such as yours. It so happens that I have a rather unique collection of antiques. Would you be interested in taking a perusal?"

I didn't mask the glee from my face. A player indeed. "I'd love to."

Erosain offered his arm. I took my champagne and allowed him to lead me away from the main bar. Sinder caught my eye from the kitchen, and I winked as I passed.

We entered a darkened hall lit by dim fire braziers. Multiple rooms like those in the Mesmer's dream parlor lined the hall, only these walls were made from glass. Other patrons loitered beside them, watching whatever was going on inside. I peeked over their shoulders and wished I hadn't.

These rooms were full of Ember engaging in various acts that would make Quen faint. Most were Ember women with mortals from the other domains, though some Ember men were also on their knees for the pleasure of whoever paid.

"As you can see," Erosain said as we strolled past two Fauna in dog-form quite literally going at it. "We cater to all tastes here." We stopped outside a window where a soft orange glow flickered like a candle, only it emanated from a woman.

Not the red skin of an Ember, but golden.

Shit. This was where Ambassador Gloria's missing Glimmer had turned up.

She'd been chained to the wall, though her head lolled to one side, delirious not with drugs, but... blood loss. A thick vein pulsed at her throat. Funny, I'd never noticed such details before, and now I couldn't help *but* notice it.

Dark blood dripped from two sore punctures on her neck and ran down to her naked breasts. I should have been disgusted. I should have recoiled at the sight. But some inner hunger yearned to get closer. To taste her for myself.

"Can I tempt you?" Erosain asked, his voice curling as much as his beard.

It should have come as no surprise that the man who ran Sinner's Row would force such tortures on other mortals. To him, they were commodities that could be bought and sold. "She is most exquisite," I said, trying to disguise the bite in my voice. "But I find my appetite strongest after discussions of business."

Erosain turned to me with his lip quirked. He'd lost the handsomeness of his features, as though I now saw the beast for what he was, and I instead wanted to sink my fangs into *his* throat and tear it out.

He's a pretty prick, what a surprise, Jinx said. *I bet he tastes like ash.*

Maybe we'll get a chance to find out.

We moved on from the corridor of sin and pushed through a double door guarded by Ember males in matching tuxedos. The room we entered resembled the rest of Erosain's bar, with glowing lava underneath the glass at our feet, and brazier flames spreading across the walls. Though this seemed more of a private lounge with its own well-stocked liquor cabinet.

Erosain led me to a locked door. He released my arm and produced a key from his inner jacket pocket.

"Welcome to my wonders," he announced as he opened his gallery with dramatic flair.

I stepped into a marble chamber filled with all manner of treasures that truly made my room at the depot resemble a flea market.

There were so many delights: intricate pottery vases with a mosaic of gemstones, golden statues in the shapes of the gods, detailed paintings, and rows of jeweled pendants.

The ambassador strode around the room and explained which domain each piece came from. Some were as tall as me, and each were precariously balanced on stone plinths. I could see why he wouldn't want a rowdy group of drunk Seren bumbling around in here.

"Does anything catch your eye?" Erosain asked with a sly smile.

My gaze roamed the carefully curated museum of artifacts. And there—hidden in the corner were three triangular prisms the size of my fist. My bounty. Now, how to extract them without anyone noticing?

I moved my gaze from them and turned to a giant golden statue of the Leander god, a sculpted man with three lion heads atop his shoulders. I didn't want Erosain to guess where my heart lay. "Is this solid gold?"

"Indeed it is, though not the most expensive item of my collection, as I'm sure Lionheart himself would be devastated to learn."

Are you thinking what I'm thinking, Jinx? I asked my devious inner self. *Destroy it all.*

I didn't know if Jinx could smile, so I grinned for us both. "What of that vase?" I placed my drink onto a table and gestured behind him.

Erosain turned his back to me. "Which?"

I ran behind the golden statue and shoved it with all my might.

He whirled around with a look of horror as the golden figure of Lionheart came crashing down. He dove out of the way, but not quickly enough.

The statue landed across his legs. Erosain howled with pain, though his pain twisted into shocked gasps as the statue knocked over a vase, which then knocked over a collection of glass figures and sent a wave of destruction cascading through the room with the deafening roar of a Leander.

Hopefully Erosain's guards hadn't heard, but I'd rather not linger.

The poor ambassador tried to pry himself free from the statue, but what do you know, the gold actually *was* solid, and it pinned him to the ground. "You bitch!" he yelled. "Who sent you? The Nameless One? Serenity? When Edana hears of this—"

"I'm sorry, Your Excellency, but I don't care for your taste in art."

Smoke rose from Erosain's fake eyebrows as his face twisted with rage. It would have been amusing, if not for the flames which then burst from his hands. He took aim at me.

I snatched the nearest painting—a portrait of Edana, ironically—and wielded it like a shield. "Careful now, Ambassador! You wouldn't want to damage such priceless art!" And certainly not art of his patron god.

Poor Erosain visibly deflated, and his flames faded. I strode around the room and sent a few more prized pieces clattering to the ground. Each crash made Erosain wince, and sparks flickered erratically from his fingertips as though he debated whether it was worth burning his precious art just to stop me. I wasn't sure if I'd broken his legs, but it was nothing a Sinner's Row Necro couldn't fix, or so my new instincts told me.

I stopped by the prisms and hastily tucked them into my inner jacket, cradling them in a way Erosain couldn't see. I helped myself to a few smaller items as well—a pendant made of pearl from Memoria, a golden diadem from Solaris, a ruby ring from Rapture. Small things I could carry with me to make this jaunt worthwhile.

Erosain shook his head with a bitter laugh. "Are you stupid? Are you fucking delirious? Do you think you can rob me, *me*, and walk out of Sinner's Row with your mortal body intact? Nadine, or whatever your fucking name is, you're a fucking idiot. It won't take the Wardens long to find a whore with your rotting face."

Saliva dribbled down his chin. Why had I ever considered him handsome?

Because your taste in men is atrocious, Jinx said.

I considered using my Necro abilities to knock him out, but I didn't want to get within reach of his flaming hands, nor did I trust myself not to induce an aneurysm.

Instead, I poured the contents of my golden champagne onto a *very* expensive-looking rug and tossed my glass aside, not bothering to dignify him with a reply. His raging shouts followed me out of the door. It clicked shut behind me, and I wedged the door handle with Edana's portrait.

Nothing but muffled whines passed through the walls. Perfect.

In his lounge, I found a leather bag for my stolen goods and carefully slung it over my shoulder. I nodded at the guards on the way out, and they nodded back, none the wiser for their master's plight. But I needed to get out of here quick.

On my way out, I stopped by the room with the bleeding Glimmer. No one watched over her, so it was easy enough to slip inside. The scent of blood made my stomach rumble—actually clench with hunger—and I swallowed the sensation. My fingers moved to her pulse, and she moaned at my icy touch.

"What's your name?" I whispered.

"Joe—Josephine," said the Glimmer's whimpering voice.

"Don't be afraid, Josephine. I'm a friend, and I'm getting you out of here." Through her pulse, I could almost sense where her veins traveled to her heart. Necro had the ability to manipulate physical bodies, to modify them and heal them. But even with a natural understanding of physiology, Necro healers still needed to learn how to heal wounds—a skill that I lacked. All I wanted was to send a little jolt to her heart and get her moving.

A static shock passed through my fingers, and her eyes opened wide and alert with a gasp. I let go at the tug.

Shit. In the moment between blinks, I'd swapped my Necro body for a Glimmer one, which I'd *not* planned to do. I suppose it helped; as soon as Erosain freed himself, he and his guards would be searching for Nadine the art thief, not some Glimmer.

Though two Glimmer inside his bar? I'd only draw attention to us.

"Wha—What's going on?" the Glimmer asked, panic in her voice as her consciousness caught up with her predicament.

With a quick burst of sunlight, I melted through her chains. I no longer desired the taste of mortal blood. Instead, heat danced at my fingertips, and

I longed to destroy this room with righteous, blinding anger. "We're getting out of here. Can you walk?"

She nodded. I led her out of the box and through a side door that led to the staff locker room. Sinder was already there waiting for me and his eyes bulged at my Glimmer form. I'd had no chance to warn him.

"Sorry," I said. "She needs clothes, and we need to leave."

He scowled at me. "We're helping the enemy now?"

"You know how these things go. She's bleeding and needs our help—"

"Then she can pray to her golden whore."

The poor girl shrank from Sinder's glare.

I didn't have time to deal with his grievances. "The Glimmer may be our enemy, but this woman isn't, and neither was the one *you* helped escape during the Grayford Incident. Now, are you going to help me, or are we going to argue about this until Erosain catches us?"

Smoke flared from his nostrils. I could read the hurt in his blazing eyes—I'd crossed a line. But he helped me sit her on a bench, even if his shoulders tensed in our presence.

I understood his discomfort around Glimmer. And perhaps it wasn't wise to help someone who would likely betray us later. But I wasn't going to leave a mortal naked and chained at Erosain's mercy, regardless of which domain they came from.

I pulled off Sinder's tight shirt and slacks and swapped them for my pinafore, handing Sinder's clothes to the Glimmer, who sat dazed. "Listen, you have a choice. You can return to your masters in the workhouse, or you can take the ruby ring inside this pocket and find your freedom."

The Glimmer dug out the ring. "I can—I can go? Anywhere?"

"Go anywhere and be whoever you wish to be. That's worth a whole pile of gold. Just don't get caught with it, and don't pawn it off in Sinner's Row, you understand?"

She clenched the ring tight to her chest.

Shouting came from inside the bar.

Time to go, Jinx urged.

"Shift's over," I declared to Sinder as I slung the leather satchel over my shoulder. I tentatively reached for his hand. "May I?"

"Please." He cringed. "Gold is not your color."

One touch of his hand and I'd become Fira the barmaid.

"Earn any nice tips?" Sinder asked, returning to his old charming self as we hurried through the kitchens.

I patted my satchel full of illicit treasures. "You could say."

XXVII

Diviner aren't the only mortals to receive visions. While our visions unravel the threads of time and thus focus on the immediate future, the Mesmer are able to 'dream' visions. These aren't constrained by the concepts of time, but instead explore the realms of possibility; to see thousands of possible outcomes in any given situation.

They may be dreamers, but the Mesmer's imagination far surpasses any Seren artist. Don't discount their ramblings as words of lunacy.

And while we Diviner explore the future, and Amnae explore the past, the Mesmer can delve deep into a mortal's subconscious and explore what it truly means to be mortal.

—Q. Corinth, *Warden Dossier on the Mesmer*

THE GODLESS HAD LOCKED me into a spare room downstairs for the night, but I'd hardly slept a wink. The creaky spring mattress was serviceable enough, but my room bordered the Mesmer's—deliberately, I assumed, for all the screaming he did in his sleep.

"You don't remember the punchline, Quentin Corinth? You soon will."

Reve had seen the same visions I had, and that too kept me awake as I stared at the low orange burn of an oil lamp and mentally wrestled with my conscience. I'd wiped so many of my memories that trying to piece together everything I knew left me with a migraine. Memories regarding the Godless and how I felt about them versus how I was *meant* to feel about them, at least according to Elijah and the rest of the Wardens.

My past self had wiped those memories for good reason, but if there was anyone left in Chime I could trust, then surely it would be myself?

There was little else to do to pass the time except ponder life's greatest mysteries: The Glimmer and their cursed device. Kayl, her missing god, and her bizarre relationship with the aether. The aether creatures themselves, and their penchant for stealing Diviner souls. These strands were connected, somehow.

And why, blast it, were the Godless so enamored of coffee? That alone was their greatest sin.

The door to my little cell creaked open and Kayl popped her head inside, back to her Vesper form. "Awake? I've made you breakfast and tea."

"Tea? Thank the almighty gods." I slid off the bed and stretched.

Kayl opened the door wider and tutted. "Careful. We don't use such colorful language in this place."

I tried to straighten my crumpled shirt and smooth my hair, but I knew I must look a mess. My chin sported more stubble than civility dictated. At least the Godless had untied my hands and allowed me to discard my frilly gloves.

"What's that?" Kayl stepped into my room and tugged my shirt collar to one side, exposing my collarbone.

Heat rushed to my cheeks. "What are—"

"How did you get these welts?"

For a second, I wasn't sure what she was blathering on about, but I caught my reflection in a mirror. Bright red lines ran over my shoulders, and I vaguely remembered their biting sting further along my back.

I snatched my collar and did up the top button.

"Quen, who did this to you?"

"That's none of your business—"

"*Quen.*"

I should have shrugged her off, made light of it with some foolish quip. But the concern in her voice gave me pause.

"If you want to talk about it, we can talk," she said all too quietly. "These aren't the marks of a caring lover."

No. They weren't. I rubbed my hands together. "Where's this tea, then?"

She gave me a worried look as I followed her out to the underground common room of the Godless's hideout. None of Kayl's companions sat at the conveyor-belt-cum-breakfast-bar, though footsteps thudded above, so we weren't completely alone.

Kayl made herself comfortable on a stool and gestured for me to join her. "It's a little something."

I sat before a plate of crumpets and melted butter, and a steaming mug of tea next to not one, but *two* bourbon biscuits. "Milk and sugar? You spoil me." I dug into a crumpet with polite restraint and took a measured sip of tea. They couldn't mask the hardness of the water down in the Undercity, but it still hit the spot. "I thought you heathens drank coffee."

"I did a little shopping on my way home."

"Your way home from where?" She'd returned well past midnight and convened with the other Godless as I languished in my room. A part of me had wanted to sneak out and eavesdrop, to discover what chaos she'd engaged in, but Kayl would have spotted me, and I didn't want to break her trust so soon. That, and breaking my door to escape would have looked rather suspicious.

She fiddled with a pearl necklace dangling around her neck. Odd, I thought I recognized it. Such expensive taste reminded me of Erosain. "We've gathered the parts the Glimmer asked for. We'll be leaving soon to test it."

"All of you?"

"Me, Malk, Sinder. And Dru is bringing Reve. Harmony and Vincent will remain behind to keep you company."

I placed my tea down slowly. "We're partners."

"If the Glimmer ambassador sees you with us, she'll never let us inside."

"You don't trust me."

"Apparently the feeling is mutual." Her gaze flicked to my collarbone.

I ignored the flush of heat in my gut. "You know I could have escaped from this delightful pit anytime I liked. It wouldn't have taken much for me to gather your entire organization and march them to Warden HQ, as I probably should have. But I've been a good boy and kept my hands to myself."

"Perhaps you should touch my friends so I'll know what's coming and correct my course if need be."

"You can't stop the future. Once you know what's coming, you have no way of preventing it. At least if you don't know, you stand a chance of succeeding."

She looked sad then, as though remembering the chaos we'd both seen in our visions of the future. That was one reason why I didn't want to get intimately involved with Kayl's friends; witnessing their deaths would not bring me joy or peace. These mortals held no love for me, but I had no desire to see them suffer.

The Wardens wouldn't see it that way. They'd want this mess cleared up, wiped as clean as my memories. They wouldn't see the Godless how I saw them; mortals who deserved protection the same as any Chime citizen.

And that was the decision I'd come to. While I didn't trust the Godless with this device, I understood their reasons for attempting to use it. They were apostates. Sinners. But still citizens of Chime. Weren't we all sinners in our own way?

Justice would be done, I was sure, but someone needed to ensure that justice didn't destroy the mortals it served, otherwise there was no point to the Wardens.

I had to give Kayl one last chance to do the right thing. "Let me come with you as backup. I need to be there. I need to know what this device is capable of. I'm not speaking as a Warden or a Diviner, I'm speaking as me. The Glimmer cannot be trusted."

Kayl let out an exasperated breath. "I know that. If the Glimmer turn on us, Sinder will burn their machine and we'll fight our way out of there. No harm, no foul."

I glanced at her over the rim of my spectacles. "And now I speak as your partner; it's not worth the risk."

"I wish you hadn't wiped your memories. I wish you remembered all I'd told you of the Godless and why we need to do this—"

"I understand your intentions."

"Do you? You love your god. We don't love ours."

"You don't even know who your god *is*. How can you want to wipe that connection when you've never felt it? Embraced it?"

She cocked her head and smiled at me. Such a wondrous thing. Even in the guise of a Vesper, I could still see the Diviner within her, enough for me to keep on wondering who Kayl was deep down. I'd been enamored of her Diviner body, I'll admit, but she carried that smile, that mischievous glint in her aether eyes, whatever form she took. It was the first thing I'd noticed.

If I wiped my memories a hundred times over, I'd still dream of those eyes.

Saints, I was cursed.

"The difference between you and I," Kayl said in her silken voice, "is that I wish to be free of all chains. No matter who my god is. No one owns my soul. No one ever will."

"What of Malkavaan?" I asked, my own voice suddenly hoarse. "Doesn't he own your heart?" *Your body?* As Elijah owned mine.

Again, that smile. "He doesn't own me. I allow him to enjoy me. There's a difference." She slid off her stool. Standing at my full height, she still stood taller than I. "I'm sorry. I need to do this. But when we are free mortals, I'll come for you and release you. Then you can go on and live your life as we'll live ours."

"The Wardens won't give you peace so long as this device exists. You know that."

"Then I'll trust you to wipe these memories and bury our secrets with them." She kissed me on the cheek, a lingering warmth that pressed into my skin and sent fire through my veins. "You deserve better, you know," she whispered.

When she withdrew, her Vesper form had changed to Diviner.

"Please," my voice cracked. "A Diviner persona is no insurance against an entire mansion full of Glimmer. If you're not careful, you could do yourself and others harm."

"I promise not to fuck with time." She winked and left me staring as she strode up the stairs to the rest of her waiting Godless.

I touched the imprint of her lips, and my stomach clenched. This wasn't how I wanted our partnership to end. But so be it.

Less than an hour later, Miss Smith came for Reve, and then Vincent came for me. The tea and crumpets were untouched and cold. My brass pistol was still stuck inside his belt.

"Would you join us for a coffee and a chat, Master Corinth?" He pulled out the frilly gloves and rope from his inside jacket.

I stood and held out my hands. "I'd be delighted."

Vincent tugged my hands together tightly, and I dutifully followed him upstairs to the lounge of the abandoned tram. I caught no sign of Kayl or Miss Smith, though the Seren—Harmony—waited inside the tram with a flier in her hand, my jacket discarded on the seat beside her. They'd quite clearly rummaged through my pockets.

"Where did you get this?" Harmony asked as I sat opposite her. She waved one of the Godless fliers I carried with me, the one scrawled with *'Who owns your thoughts?'*

"You designed it. You tell me."

"Don't play cute with me, Corinth." The Seren's diamond pupils held a sharp edge. She turned the flier over to where a message had been scrawled at the bottom. "This is a drop-box address for the Chime Courier. Specifically, *my* drop-box address. Where did you get it?"

I blinked. "You work for the Courier?"

"Answer the question."

No wonder the Godless were able to gather so much information, if they'd infiltrated the Courier. Very clever. "No coffee before my interrogation? My throat is a little dry."

Vincent placed my pistol on the table, the barrel aimed at me once more. "You promised us intel in exchange for your fair treatment. Please answer her questions."

I swallowed a sigh. "It's my handwriting. My past self must have written it."

"Your past self?" Harmony's brows shot up. "What are you talking about?"

"I may have already dropped intel into your drop box. It's something my past self would do. Though my question for you is, have I? And what?"

Both Harmony and Vincent shared a glance.

"You can't—You can't be our fucking benefactor, no way," Harmony stammered. "How do you not remember?"

"He doesn't remember me," Vincent said slowly, his wary eyes scanning me. "We served together in the Wardens, and he doesn't remember a single detail I've told him."

I struggled to contain my shock. "You're a Warden?"

"Ex-Warden. I was the Necro on call during the Grayford Incident. I was there when you shot those Vesper and Sinder. I thought the Wardens helped mortals, but I witnessed the truth for myself that day. I quit and joined the Godless."

"I'm—I'm sorry, I don't remember shooting your friend—"

"But you remember the Vesper, don't you?" Vincent turned to Harmony. "The Wardens employ Amnae. While the Amnae on Memoria sell their services to remove regrets and lost loves, I've heard of them being employed for more... sinister means. To wipe information which could be dangerous in the wrong hands."

"So the Wardens know of us? Of you?" Harmony asked.

"No," I said. "I mean, yes, you're right, the Wardens do indeed employ Amnae for such work as you rightly guess, but they've never touched my memories. I have a friend who wipes mine. Though obviously I cannot remember why." I smiled at my own joke.

Harmony stared at me. "You—You don't even remember who you are? What you've done?" She gestured to a framed placard hanging above the lounge. Vincent took it down, placing it in front of me.

It contained a tattered, worn note, likely some years old, with just two lines:

"Chime needs godless heathens.
May the gods leave you to your fate."

"That's my handwriting." My insides churned. "What is this?"

Harmony's single wing was quivering. "This note was left for us roughly six months after the Vesper Incident, along with a small fortune. And every month since then, such notes and donations have appeared in my drop box; all money that we've used to build a better life in Grayford and help mortals escape their gods. We chalked it up to a mystery benefactor. Gods, for so long I assumed it was a crooked Warden, not the Dark Warden himself!" She let out a delirious laugh.

I stared at the note, at the traitorous curl of my penmanship. "How— How much have I donated?" My coffers often ran low, but my past self had never checked *why*. I'd assumed I'd spent it all on sodding biscuits!

"Hundreds. Thousands. Not just bocs, but intel on the Wardens' operations, on the Glimmer workhouses, and other things you've warned us of over the years."

My heart pounded in my ears. "This... This couldn't possibly be me, the handwriting—I'm sorry, I must be mistaken—"

"There's no mistake, is there, Master Corinth?" Vincent said. "Why else would you be here? Why help Kayl at all?"

Harmony was still staring at me as though I weren't quite real. "You're our benefactor. You. The Dark Warden."

Holy saints.

This *had* to be a mistake, because if her words were true, then I'd been betraying the Wardens for years. And I didn't even remember doing so!

Walter must have manipulated my subconscious. Perhaps he was a Godless sympathizer who'd altered my memories to support these mortals and then wiped the evidence.

Or past Quen had been a complete and utter idiot. I always thought my past self knew what he was doing, but now I feared I'd been playing the traitor all this time and had likely wiped my memories from guilt. Shame had always been my closest companion. I felt it deep in my bones whenever Elijah looked at me.

If Elijah knew what I'd done—what my past self had wrought—this wouldn't just end my tenure with the Wardens.

I doubt I'd ever see the outside of a Kronos correctional facility again.

"Why did you wipe your own gods-damn mind?" Harmony asked. "You stopped sending us intel weeks ago. What changed?"

"I—I don't know. I must have wiped these memories for a reason. For my protection or yours." Had Elijah known when he'd ordered me to round up the Godless?

"What now?" Harmony demanded. "Where does the present-day Quentin Corinth's conscience lie?"

With stopping this damnable device. "With doing the right thing. And then I'll wipe whatever I've seen clear from my conscience."

Harmony crossed her arms. "How can we trust you? You may be our benefactor, but that man's dead, and you're still a Warden. I care for these godless heathens, and I'm not letting some well-dressed idiot in specs endanger them."

Well-dressed? Now I was truly charmed. "Apparently, I care for your godless heathens, too. I'd rather not see you locked inside Warden HQ. And I'd rather not see your souls torn apart by this device you're hunting. Surely you must understand the danger it presents? If not the device itself, then the Glimmer's intentions?"

"The Glimmer are your bedmates, not ours. And it was your organization who created this device—"

"To stop the aether leaks. Listen to me; this device, whatever it is, cannot hope to separate a mortal from their god and it is absolute foolishness to attempt to do so. I have seen what happens when a soul is split from a god—the body remains, hollow and lifeless, and the soul becomes lost to the aether. What guarantees do you have that this device won't do the same? Are you willing to gamble with your life? Your soul?"

Vincent's bloodshot eyes burned into mine. "Yes. You've heard Reve's nightmares. If freedom means death, then we'll take death."

"This isn't just death—it's darkness, it's nothing, it's existence without connection. It is breathtaking arrogance to live a life without one's god. To spit at the life granted you. Is this ghastly existence who you wish to be?"

"You've clearly forgotten who we are, Corinth," Harmony said, her cool stare meeting mine. "We're Godless. You speak as though we should thank our overlords for our very existence—"

"You *should*—"

"But the truth is, the gods may own us, but we also own *them*. They experience existence through *us*. Without our mortal lives, our mortal thoughts, they are nothing. They have nothing. And if they cannot afford us basic dignity, then we deny them."

If my hands were free, I'd be pulling out my hair! "This isn't just about your gods and your soul—this could affect every mortal in Chime! *Please* listen to me. There's still time to stop this madness—"

"Why did you ever help us if this is what you think of us?"

Honestly, I wished I could ask past Quen the same. "I know what you think of the Wardens, and yes, there are aspects of our organization which need work. But the fundamental heart of my kind is to protect the mortals of Chime. Even the Godless. I'm trying to understand you—"

"We're not some curiosity for you to ponder," Vincent said. "We're made of flesh and blood and hopes and dreams. If the gods cared for us, for their children, they wouldn't allow us to suffer."

I didn't have time to keep debating theology. "How else would mortals learn from their mistakes? Like the ones you're making now?"

Vincent bared his fangs in a terrifying smile. "Our mistakes are products of the gods. They create rules for how we should think and feel. What if our thoughts don't align? Are we abnormal? Wrong? If mortals are capable of mistakes, of evil, then so are the gods."

Such blasphemy. But what did I expect from a group of apostates? "May I have my dirt-laden coffee now, please? I daresay I've earned it."

Harmony rubbed her forehead. "You'll get your damn coffee when I know I can trust you, and right now, I'm not favoring your chances."

Fine. If that was how the Godless wanted to play it.

I wasn't going to allow this madness to progress any further.

Time slowed to a stop. I hadn't moved an inch, as far as the Godless could see, and that had been my first trick; allowing Kayl and her friends to believe I needed my hands free in order to manipulate time. Working invisible gears was a technique taught to children, to those new to the concept of horology, which was why I'd passed it onto Kayl. But I hadn't taught her everything for good reason.

Ah, trust. Such a rare commodity these days.

I leaned across the table and clasped my bound hands together in prayer. Truly, I didn't want to do this, and I didn't want to see the Godless punished, which was why I scrunched my eyes closed and tried to focus less on Grayford and more on the Glimmer estate and their device. There wasn't any time to wipe my memories, so I needed to guide my thoughts and hope—pray, really—that Dor didn't see everything.

That He didn't see my betrayal.

"Forgive me, Father. I am in urgent need of your wisdom."

Warmth flooded my veins, as though I were drunk on whiskey, and I felt His presence with me.

MY SON, the otherworldly voice of an elder god echoed in my mind. *WHAT MACHINATIONS HAVE YOU WROUGHT?*

"The Glimmer have a device, Father. One capable of rending a mortal from their god. I have come to learn this recently, and I have not had time before now to warn you or Elijah."

I SEE ITS INFERNAL WORKINGS. GILDOLA MUST BE HELD TO ACCOUNT. ELIJAH WILL MOVE AT ONCE.

"This device... It was created by us, Father. The Wardens. Why would we devise such a thing? I understand these aether creatures are dangerous, but—"

THEN YOU UNDERSTAND WHAT MUST BE DONE.

I wasn't sure I did, but I couldn't question my Father.

YOU HAVE SEEN CHAOS. YOU HAVE COVETED IT.

I chewed my lip as shame rose in my gut. One could not commune with one's god and not feel helplessly naked in their presence. All that I am, that I was and ever would be, was laid bare for Dor to examine. Even the Godless. Even Kayl.

THIS WOMAN. SHE IS NOT YOUR SALVATION.

"I know, Father, I know—"

SHE IS NOT ONE OF US. SHE IS AN ABNORMALITY.

"What would you have me do?"

WHAT MUST BE DONE. I GUIDE YOU, MY SON, TO WHERE YOU MUST BE. WHERE YOU ARE NOW CONCERNS ME. DO YOU NOT REPENT?

Hot tears slid down my cheeks. "I'm sorry, Father. I didn't mean to disappoint you. I didn't mean—"

CORRECT YOUR PATH, QUENTIN.

The warmth in my blood flooded my face and then dissipated into the aether. Father had left me alone with my tears and my shame, the harshness of His command a punch to my gut. Blood dripped from my nose and I became vaguely aware of time slipping away.

I opened my eyes as time caught up. I must have looked a state, for Harmony instantly recoiled and Vincent grabbed my pistol, pointing it at me.

"What did you do?" Harmony shrieked. "The fuck have you *done*?"

I wiped the blood from my nose, staining the pink gloves with a red smear. "What I had to do."

Vincent limped around the table and pressed the barrel to my head. "Explain."

I glanced up, the barrel pressing hard into my forehead as I stared through blurry vision. "The Wardens will be heading for the Glimmer estate to stop this device. And perhaps here; I cannot be certain what my god saw. You'd best prepare for the worst."

"Fuck!" Harmony slammed her palms onto the table.

My pistol shook in Vincent's grip. "You've left us with little reason to keep you alive, Master Corinth."

"Don't worry yourself. My end is coming. Just not by your hand." To illustrate the point, I allowed time to pause once more. With a quick twist of my wrists, I wiggled free from Vincent's bindings. When time resumed again, I was standing behind both Vincent and Harmony, my pistol lovingly returned to my palm and pointed at them.

Vincent deflated against the tram's couch as Harmony stared daggers at me.

"You've damned her," she snapped. "Do you realize that?"

That was what my Father wanted. To correct my path. Though I rather thought I'd damned us both. "Kayl's a resourceful woman. She'll make it out. Though neither of you are in any position to mount a rescue attempt."

"What now, Corinth? You arrest us? Drag us to your HQ?"

"I'll give you the only gift a Diviner can offer." I lowered my pistol. "Time. As for me, my interest lies with the Glimmer and this device. I'll be leaving now, if you don't mind. I'd thank you for the hospitality, but your coffee was truly appalling." I headed for the tram's door.

"Wait!" Harmony called. She jumped from her seat and waddled toward me. "Some part of you cares—why else would you have dropped so much intel in my box? You could be one of us, Corinth. With your powers—"

"I belong to my god. I'm sorry." I yanked open the tram door and stepped out before more of the Godless's cursed words polluted my ears.

Dor owned my soul. That was how it was meant to be.

Without my Father, I was nothing.

I wiped my eyes clear as I strode from the abandoned depot, turning my back on whatever sympathy I'd held for these mortals. I'd been such a fool to flirt with apostasy, with *her*. I'd almost forgotten who I was.

Quentin Corinth.

Dark Warden.

I hated that title. Hated the reputation that went with it.

I'd not saved a single life yet for all the visions I'd suffered, so perhaps it was fitting. I'd tried, hadn't I? I'd tried to make a difference. Even if I couldn't save a mortal life, I'd been there to offer a small comfort in their final moments. Not that I could remember them.

Would death comfort me in the end? Or would time simply forget me?

They'd certainly never name the Dark Warden a saint.

The past didn't matter. What mattered was the chaos to come, and what role I'd play.

And knowing the future would break me.

Correct my path? Could I even? My path had derailed long ago.

"The difference between you and I is that I wish to be free of all chains. No matter who my god is. No one owns my soul. No one ever will."

Though Dor owned my soul, there was a shard of it that belonged elsewhere. That thought should terrify me, for I no longer dreamed of Elijah's beautiful brass eyes.

But aether eyes.

I steeled my resolve, for I had work to do. Though deep down, I knew Kayl was going to be the death of me.

28

Grant me not your mercy, your miracles, nor gift.
Let every suffering I bear be mine to sift.
I welcome not your judgement nor honor your deeds.
For I am a mortal, with mortal desires and needs.
Demand not my tongue or words you dictate.
I pray aloud; may the gods leave me to my fate.
—Anonymous, *a Godless prayer*

AT LEAST I HADN'T needed to run for this tram. My Diviner form came with some perks, including a remarkable awareness of time. Our tram from Grayford to the workhouses rumbled through the dark tunnel on schedule. Vesper mostly filled the seats on their way to work at the factories this morning, though they gave a wide berth to our little group. I supposed we made an odd bunch.

My silvery face could have marked me as a Warden. Malk's Vesper face fit in, but even sitting, he towered over everyone with a scowl. Sinder's bright red Ember skin stood out among the sea of midnight blue and gray. And Dru's green Umber skin looked dull next to Sinder, her golden flowers drooping over her eyes.

Though the most startling sight was likely Reve. We'd dressed him in day clothes, but they didn't suit him. He'd thankfully remained quiet during this journey and was staring out of the window at nothing.

It wasn't unusual for Ember, Umber or Vesper to find work within the Undercity. Even Diviner weren't an odd sight in the factories or steamworks. But a Mesmer?

I leaned against the center pole as Dru came to stand with me. "We shouldn't have brought him," she said over the rattle of the tram, her worried frown pinned on Reve.

"He wanted to come."

"If things get dangerous, I might not be able to protect him."

"He's seen a vision of our success."

"You know his visions don't always play out."

Dru's flowers had wilted further. She'd always been the worrying type, but when it came to Reve, she mothered that boy. It was comical, really, that an all-seeing being such as the Mesmer required so much coddling. If it wasn't for Dru, he'd be sitting in his nightgown.

I wrapped my arm around Dru's shoulder. "None of us will let Reve get harmed, I promise."

"He's suffered so many nightmares recently. I think they've gotten worse."

My heart skipped a beat. "Do you know what they're about?"

"The usual. Death. Destruction." Dru shuddered and rested her head on my shoulder. We could have been two hungover ladies propping each other up after a night on Sinner's Row, though we were more two conspirators whispering dark secrets. "What about you and Malk?" she asked. "You're normally all over each other, and now you can barely stand to look at one another. What happened?"

I couldn't keep my gaze from turning to Malk. He sat apart from the others, as close to the aisle as he could get in case he needed to make a getaway. We hadn't spoken much this morning, but I needed him with me if I was to save his soul before Eventide opened in a few hours. "He's still shaken. He needs time, that's all."

It wasn't just Malk I worried about. Those marks on Quen's shoulders weren't there when I'd left his apartment the other night. Had he been punished for losing me? Had he punished himself?

He probably whipped his mind free of dirty thoughts after kissing you, Jinx said. *Then again, Diviner and Glimmer are the type to get off on flogging themselves.*

I scrunched my nose. *You're disgusting.*

You have too much sympathy for mortals who hurt you, which is equally disgusting.

"Do you really think this Glimmer machine works?" Dru asked, dragging my thoughts back to the present.

"I hope so." I patted the leather satchel clutched close to my hip containing Erosain's prisms and the doctor's schematics.

Hope was all I had. Hope that this machine wouldn't just free Malk, but fix whatever nightmares plagued him too. Hope that I'd get *my* Malk back. Valeria had turned him into a shadow of himself, and I couldn't stand it.

Half an hour later, our tram pulled into the workhouse station. Dru helped Reve off as I took point, the two grumpy men forming a shield behind us.

Neither Malk nor Sinder looked pleased to be here, and I couldn't blame them. Not only was the workhouse district of the Undercity even bleaker and more oppressive than Grayford, but these buildings held negative memories for them both. This was where Malk had been captured and handed over to the Wardens, and where Sinder had been enslaved by the Glimmer. I hated to bring him here, but we needed his fire power.

Sinder, for all his apprehension, wanted to be here too, if only to burn the entire Glimmer estate down if everything went wrong.

We slogged our way past the various factories until we came to the familiar brass gates.

"Why do I do this to myself," Sinder sighed as he rubbed the black flaming tattoos on his arms where anxiety no doubt crawled under his skin. Vincent had inked those designs for him long ago in order to replace the scars he'd earned from this place. Sinder had changed out of his outrageously feminine style into a more modest waistcoat and pair of trousers—to give him the flexibility to fight, he'd said. Though I wondered if returning here dampened his personality.

I put my hand on his shoulder. "If you want to wait out here—"

"No, darling." He patted my hand. "I should have been with you the first time. If I wasn't such a damn coward, we wouldn't be in this mess." He glanced at Malk.

"That wasn't your fault, you know."

He winced and turned to the gate. "Maybe. But you were right to snap at me last night. I need to face this. I can't keep running from shiny-arsed shadows for the rest of my life, not when I know they could be using their machine to trap more mortals like me. Not when we now have a means to stop the Glimmer for good. I'm doing this for them and us."

"We're Godless. We'll face our fate together."

And so we approached the gate as one mismatched group of mortals. I was glad Sinder was holding it together; between Malk's skittish twitching, Dru's frowning, and Reve being Reve, I was worried I'd be the most competent among us.

What a terrifying thought, Jinx said.

I know. But we couldn't risk bringing either Vincent or Harmony. Neither had the mobility to fight or run. They had the Memoria University education for this sort of diplomacy, but they lacked the street-smarts of an Undercity upbringing that Malk, Sinder, and I possessed. We'd brawl our way out if it came to it.

You could have brought Corinth.

Quen was too much a Warden for my liking. He wasn't one of us. He wasn't Godless. What did he understand of our mission? Our purpose? No, Quen would only mess this up.

We didn't need a Warden sticking his nose into our business. Nor did we need a Diviner to deliver us from our gods. We could manage that ourselves.

Two Glimmer waited by the main double doors to the mansion. As we crunched our way up the gravel, the doors opened, and Ambassador Gloria stepped out to greet us.

"I see you've brought your ensemble," Gloria said, a slight sneer to her lips as her red eyes passed over us. "And you've changed your face. How intriguing. Do you have what we requested?"

I patted my satchel. "If you're willing to honor our bargain."

"But of course. The daughters of Gildola honor their commitments." She swept aside, beckoning us into the mansion.

I nodded to the others, and we followed.

As soon as I entered the mansion, the bright lamps made me cringe. The Glimmer loved their light, and the entire building stood out like an overpowered lamp in the heart of the Undercity. Sinder cringed too, his expression turning sour as though wrestling to remain neutral when surrounded by so many Glimmer.

Entering this place was torture for him, I knew. It would evoke so many memories of the suffering he'd endured under a Glimmer's whip. But we needed him.

And he needed this. If not to overcome his fears, then to confront them and burn them to ash. I'd be by his side every step of the way.

The only one among us who didn't seem perturbed to be here was Reve. His head rolled from side to side, fascinated by the gaudy decorations hanging on the walls.

They didn't check us for weapons at least, which meant they either trusted us or they didn't consider us a threat. My role was to use my Diviner powers if needed, which not even the Glimmer could defend against. Malk always carried a knife or two. Sinder didn't need a weapon, not when he could command flame. Dru's Umber powers would be useless underground, but she'd pummel anyone that got too close.

And Reve was Reve. I didn't know what powers a Mesmer held, besides giving every mortal they conversed with an existential crisis.

The ambassador led us through the mansion and to the same factory where they'd been building metal plating for the tower. As we entered, Sinder stiffened at the sight of other Ember and Vesper hammering away. I wanted to take his hand and offer my reassurances, but Glimmer eyes watched where we walked, and I couldn't afford to reveal any weakness in the home of my enemy.

Then we were striding through the double doors leading underground. The screech of aether proved that we were headed the right way, and I chewed my tongue. No one else could hear what I did.

Why does aether scream, Jinx?

Because it's in pain.

Aether feels pain?

Of course it does. It wants to be alive. It wants to be free like you do, but it's trapped in pipes and machines and that clock tower you mortals love so much.

What'll happen when the Wardens finish reinforcing the clock tower? Will the screaming stop?

No. It'll get worse.

Gods. I wasn't sure I could handle a city full of screaming aether. *How do you know so much about this? And don't give me your 'we're all made of aether' nonsense. Give me a real answer.*

I could almost feel Jinx sigh inside me. *We* are *made of aether, idiot. You just don't understand it yet.*

I didn't have time to argue with myself; the metal door opened and the screaming aether hit me like a gust of wind. The machine sat at the heart of the round room, all pipes and wires coming out the back like dark veins. The console beside it glowed a healthy bloodred, and the hum of energy pulsed around me.

"It's just a chair?" Dru whispered beside me.

"Lots of metal," Sinder said. "May take me a little longer to melt it into scrap, dearest."

"We're not melting anything yet," I whispered back.

Though seeing the machine bolted to the ground here, I wasn't sure how we'd be able to take it from an estate full of Glimmer. Right now, all I wanted to do was check the damn thing worked and free Malk—and then we'd return with a real plan of attack.

Then, I supposed, I'd need Quen's help.

Four Glimmer guards dressed in unusually modest robes blocked off the entrance as the ambassador greeted another wearing maintenance overalls beside the machine's console.

This Glimmer didn't have the sheen of the others—indeed, I didn't think I'd ever seen a dirty Glimmer before. Smears of black oil stained her cheek, forehead, and hands, though her smock had received most of it.

Gloria beckoned me. "We're ready to begin our final adjustments."

I dug out the prisms and handed them over one by one to the eager Glimmer engineer. "Everything you asked for." Though as I tried to pull the schematics out of my satchel, my hand froze. It wasn't stuck on anything—my entire arm went dead.

Jinx, what are you doing? She was controlling my arm. Stopping me from handing over the doctor's schematics.

Don't do this. Corinth may be a prat, but he's right about this machine. Listen to the aether. They're scared of it.

This machine had apparently been devised to destroy aether creatures, but what did they expect when they were stealing Diviner souls? *Jinx, stop. We need to do this to free Malk, don't you see? Reve saw himself sitting on it. This is the future he wants.*

You can't trust a Mesmer to understand reality.

According to you, I shouldn't trust anyone. Why even help me if you're trying to stop me? What happened to ending the reign of gods?

We'll end the reign of gods, but not like this. You can trust me, and I'm telling you—this machine is death.

No. It's our salvation.

"Is there a problem?" Gloria asked.

I yanked my arm free from Jinx's control and handed over the schematics with a forced smile. "None at all."

The Glimmer engineer took the prisms carefully and flapped open the schematics. Her golden eyes scanned from side to side fast. "Ah, yes... This will take no time at all. May I?"

Gloria waved a dismissive hand. "Proceed."

We watched in uneasy silence as the engineer tinkered with the back of the machine, placing the prisms in careful positions, and then returned to the panel to input numbers I couldn't quite follow.

The engineer stepped aside and clapped dust from her hands with a triumphant grin. "These tweaks have now brought the machine in line with its intended purpose. You see these pipes?" She pointed to the large tubes connecting the chair to the ceiling. "These feed aether directly into the machine, providing the power we need. The prisms guide and shape the aether—"

"Yes, yes." Gloria waved her off. "We don't need to understand how it works, so long as it does. Is it ready?"

"Indeed, Your Excellency." The engineer curtsied. "We may proceed with our first test subject."

Gloria turned to me with a wry smile. "Then who would like to go first?"

The Godless huddled together, our backs turned from the prying eyes and ears of the Glimmer.

"I don't like this," Malk said, his fingers flexing in and out of fists. "It doesn't feel right."

"On that we agree," Dru muttered. "How can we trust this is safe? We should ask one of the Glimmer to test it first—"

"No," Reve declared, making me jump.

"Reve?" I asked, turning to the Mesmer.

The usual spaciness of his expression was gone, replaced instead by a hardened resolve in those deep black eyes dotted with stars. "I see myself sitting on this machine. I see my salvation. Let me go. Please. Let me go."

Dru took his hand. "I don't want you to do this."

Reve smiled, the first time I'd ever seen him smile. "Thank you, Druzy. But I have seen it."

My jaw dropped, and I wasn't the only one staring at Reve with such shock. He could barely string together a coherent conversation, and here he was offering his thanks.

Dru sucked in a breath. "You'll be okay, won't you? Won't he?" She scanned our faces. "He'll come back to us whole, right?"

"We're waiting," Gloria called.

"I will be happy, Druzy," Reve said, and he turned to the machine.

Dru grabbed his arm. "Then—return this to me, okay?" She plucked a yellow flower from her brow and pressed it into his palm. "I want it back when you're done."

Gods. She'd never given one of her flowers before.

Reve sniffed it and then placed the flower into his upper shirt pocket. "If reality is but a dream of the gods, then I wish my dream to be of this. Kayl, will you assist me?" He held out his arm.

"Of—Of course." I wrapped my arm around his and guided him to the machine as the rest of the Godless stared after us in silence.

"For mortals eager to rid yourself of your gods, you like to dawdle," Gloria commented as I helped Reve into the seat.

"We're still mortal, so learn some patience."

The Glimmer engineer ignored our exchange as she strapped in Reve's wrists and legs with leather cuffs. She then placed a strange-looking hat onto his head, a metal contraption which covered most of his forehead and had many more wires coming out the top.

"Will this hurt him?" I asked.

The engineer gave me a startled glance, as though asking questions wasn't part of the protocol. "It may tingle, ma'am. You'll want to stand well back when we begin." She moved around to the console and stood awaiting commands.

Gloria strode away from the machine as two of the Glimmer guards in robes came to flank her side. "Then on your time."

I squeezed Reve's shoulder. "Are you sure about this?" I whispered. "We can stop. We can burn our way out of here and forget this ever happened." I don't know where the sudden uneasiness came from. I wanted this for Malk—that was what this had been for—but seeing Reve strapped in made me doubt the Glimmer's sincerity.

You should doubt, Jinx said.

Reve gazed up with a giddy grin. "There'll come a time in the future when you'll fix what's broken. You'll remember me. You'll want to bring me back with the others. Please don't. Let me go. Promise me you'll let me go."

"I—I don't know if I can make that promise."

"No. You and I are alike."

What did that mean? Was I a Mesmer after all?

"We're ready to begin," the engineer said.

I patted Reve's shoulder. "The gods leave you to your fate."

His manic grin followed me back to the Godless.

Dru grabbed my arm, squeezing it in a crushing grip. "He'll be safe, won't he?"

I didn't have an answer.

We watched with bated breath as the Glimmer engineer flipped switches and turned nozzles. The screech of the aether grew louder and their screams pierced my head, sending spasms of pain along my neck that almost made me collapse onto Dru.

A bolt of pure aether shot through the machine. It bloomed into a cocoon of static energy that surrounded Reve with a silvery-blue glow.

More energy crackled from its surface, making everyone recoil. The Glimmer engineer's hair stood on end as she frantically pressed more buttons.

"Is—Is this normal?" I called out.

"One second!" the engineer yelled, but there was panic in her voice.

Reve's limbs spasmed as a current of aether rippled through his body.

And then he screamed.

Dru shoved me aside and ran for Reve, but the cocoon of aether energy sent her flying. Malk had his knives out in both hands as balls of flame burned around Sinder's fists. He glanced frantically from me to Reve—he couldn't damage the machine with Reve still trapped inside it, and attacking the console could cause further damage.

The Glimmer guards drew weapons hidden inside their robes—pistols and batons—though their ambassador raised her hand. "Calm yourselves. This is part of the process—"

"She said it wouldn't hurt!" I yelled and pointed to the engineer. "That's more than some pissing gods-damn tingle!"

Reve roared with hoarse screaming, his head wrenching back and forth as Dru watched on in bloodcurdling horror. Aether static didn't affect her stone skin, but she couldn't press past the waves of energy pulsating from the machine. She glanced over her shoulder at me, her eyes pleading. "Do something!"

Shit! I ran to Reve, intending to stop time and drag him out of there, but the aether cut right through me. I sank to my knees, my hands clasped over my ears.

There was nothing I could do—I couldn't even bring myself to stop time!

"Chaos has awakened!" Reve screamed. "Her children bring the end of the gods! The end of Chime! The end of time itself! Hark for when the clock strikes thirteen! Hark!"

What was he screaming? What—

Waves of aether exploded from the machine, and I clenched my eyes shut. Raw energy washed over me, awakening every nerve and hair on my skin as though it vibrated inside my own damn blood.

A few heartbeats later, the ringing in my ears faded. I opened my eyes. Smoke rose from the god-splitting machine and from Reve's body.

His body.

Because the body remained, stiff and silent, but his eyes were gone, and so was he. It was just like the Diviner deaths at the hands of the aether creatures. This machine had taken Reve's soul, churned it and spat it out.

That's what he wanted, wasn't it? Jinx said with a bitterness I felt.

Shit. Gods-fucking *shit*.

Dru sobbed to my left. On my right, my eye caught a glistening pool of blood coming from the Glimmer engineer. Malk stood over her body, blood dripping from his knife. He'd slit her throat and was now snarling at the Glimmer guards stalking toward us.

The hatred on his face made my heart stop.

He'd killed a woman. Sliced her up without remorse.

He'd *never* killed before. Threatened, yes, but to take a life?

That wasn't Malk!

Gloria sneered at the dead engineer. "What a waste. Still, I think we can operate this machine without her. Who'd like to go next? We have four more Godless to get through." Her burning eyes settled on mine.

I stood on shaking legs. "You meant to do this all along, you *bitch*."

"An insult I'd expect from an illiterate bunch of heathens. I gave you what you wanted. Karendar wouldn't step up and rid Chime of your filth, so I took the opportunity. After what you did to Lady Mae..." Her face contorted with disgust.

"That's what this was for? Revenge?"

"Gildola takes care of her daughters. With this machine, her blessings will spread. Of course, we'll need to fine-tune it for *our* purposes, but it appears to be a success." She snapped her fingers. "Take them."

Fire burst from Sinder's fists. He aimed for the machine and Reve's body, but a crack shot through the air. One of the Glimmer shot him.

The bullet pierced his side, and Sinder fell back with a gasp, both hands holding in the blood now gushing out of his abdomen.

Gods, no! "Help him!" I yelled at Dru, who stood nearest Sinder.

Malk threw one of his knives at Gloria, but her guards were quick to shield her.

They aimed their pistols at his chest.

"*No!*" I yanked time to a stop. The chaos before me paused.

Four Glimmer and the ambassador herself stood suspended before me. I carefully stepped over the dead engineer and pulled their weapons from their hands.

Kill them, Jinx urged. *While they can't fight back.*

Shit, I wasn't sure I could stomach murder.

You killed Lady Mae. Don't balk now. Kill them or they'll kill us.

I'm not a killer!

You're pathetic. Jinx took over my body. She tossed the spare pistols aside and took aim at a Glimmer guard.

Stop! I yelled into my mind, but it was my finger that squeezed the trigger.

The pistol aimed for the next, and the next, each bullet piercing flesh. I tried to wrestle my hand free as Jinx readied to blast her final target, the ambassador.

Time suddenly popped back to normal. The Glimmer guards collapsed to the ground with a spurt of blood, and then their mortal bodies faded altogether, leaving behind their robes. Gloria hissed, clutching her arm. The bullet had missed her heart and caught her bicep.

"You'll regret this!" she snarled.

Blinding golden light burst from her skin and filled the room.

Shit, I couldn't see anything!

A bubble of flame rippled around us, shielding us from the ambassador's harsh sunlight as fire met fire. Sinder stood at the heart of it, his shaking arms raised to hold Gloria back. Blood had run down his legs, dripping to his boots, but the wound on his side now appeared blackened and charred—gods, he'd cauterized it to stop the bleeding.

I caught Sinder's pained expression: his red face had paled into a pink shade. The edges of his flaming shield fizzled against Gloria's own power, and it shrank with each heartbeat. He wouldn't be able to maintain it for long.

Someone bumped into me. Malk. He grabbed my wrist and was dragging me to the entrance. "Run!"

"Not without Sinder!" I yelled.

Sinder threw his blazing shield from us to the ambassador. She shrieked as it wrapped around her, trapping her inside his flames.

"I'm with you, darling," Sinder gasped. "But that won't hold her." He staggered on his feet and would have fallen if Dru hadn't stepped up and caught him.

"Dru, carry him," Malk ordered. "We need to run *now*!"

Dru scooped Sinder into her arms without hesitation, and his head rested against her shoulder, his breath coming in harsh wheezes.

Behind us, sunlight flared once more, warming my back. We scrambled for the door.

I shielded my eyes and risked one last glance at Reve—his body abandoned, his soul shattered, and Dru's golden flower still smoking from inside his pocket.

Was this really what he wanted? To feel utter oblivion? Was this the future he'd seen for himself?

Had all of this been for bloody nothing?

We half ran, half stumbled up the stairs as Dru carried Sinder and I kept my pistol aimed behind us. Malk took point, a knife in his hand, as we burst onto the main factory floor.

And walked into an entire line of Wardens.

At least ten Wardens aimed pistols right at us. Had Quen betrayed us? But no, I didn't see him there, or any Wardens that I recognized.

A Leander pointed a sharp claw in my direction. "By the divine law of Chime and the Covenant, you're all under arrest. Drop your weapons *now*."

29

Your god's love is not unconditional.
If your thoughts wander, if you disobey, then you are judged.
If you sin, if you blaspheme, then their love is revoked.
Why would the gods grant us free will if they then punish us for exerting it?
Why punish our sins when they allow us to sin?
Why create an existence that follows laws and logic if mortal hearts do not?
The Covenant allows us life and liberty, but on their terms.
Where is the fairness in that?
—Anonymous, *Godless flier on free will*

THE LEANDER WARDEN SNARLED with sharp fangs. "I won't ask again. Lower your weapons and raise your hands where I can see them."

We were outnumbered two-to-one. I quickly scanned their faces. These were all Undercity Wardens, a mix of Ember, Leander, and Umber—the heavy hitters, which meant someone had sent this show of force to stop us quickly, but not effectively. There were no Diviner within these ranks, but I had a gut feeling they'd be turning up soon.

And if Diviner Wardens were in play, we didn't stand a chance.

We needed to get out of here, *fast*.

I dropped my pistol and raised my hands. "Listen, the Glimmer have a machine through these doors behind me—"

"Lower your weapons!"

The Wardens turned their pistols on Malk, who still gripped a knife in his fist.

"Listen to me! This machine killed a Mesmer—his body is still down there!"

Dru tensed beside me. There weren't enough weeds here in the Undercity to summon her powers. She carefully lowered Sinder to his feet, though he needed to lean on her shoulder for support. I didn't know if he had the strength to summon more flame when he could barely stand, but even he couldn't match these numbers, and neither could I.

More Glimmer gathered behind the Wardens, which meant Malk's shadow powers wouldn't help get us out of here, either.

The door behind us burst open as Ambassador Gloria stumbled out. "She shot me!"

I turned to confront the Leander, but the Warden's movements slowed, his jaw opening like an exaggerated yawn.

Someone was slowing time.

Shit, had the Diviner turned up already?

Time came to a complete halt, but an awful squeaking noise sounded from outside the factory doors. They opened, and someone pushed a large storage trolley inside.

"My goodness, this is rather dramatic."

"*Quen?*"

"A little help would be appreciated," he grunted.

I carefully brushed past the frozen Wardens and came to his side. "What in god's name are you doing?"

"Saving you and your Godless. I thought that was obvious." He'd lost his jacket somewhere and his pistol was holstered in his belt. "I can't hold time for long, and I don't have the muscle mass to move your friends, so you best step up."

I stared at him. "And do what?"

He lowered his eyeglasses and wiped sweat from his brow. "We're going to wheel them out of here. Unless you'd rather leave them and run? Honestly, I thought this was rather clever of me."

Of all the crazy plans I'd heard, this had to be the stupidest, but I couldn't fault his logic. With time literally at a standstill, it would be easier for us to carry Malk, Dru, and Sinder out of here rather than face an entire factory full of Wardens and Glimmer.

I helped Quen drag the trolley inside, and together we laid Sinder down first, careful to avoid his wound.

"What happened here?" Quen asked as his eyes bulged at the sight of Sinder's bloodstained clothes. "Where's the Mesmer?"

"You were right. The Glimmer's machine, it... Reve's dead."

There was no judgement in Quen's expression. No 'I told you so.' Only painful sympathy. "I'm sorry. Did you destroy it?"

"Couldn't." I sucked in a breath as we lifted Dru's considerable bulk. Women made of stone weren't exactly light. "They shot Sinder. We had to run for our lives."

Quen's gaze moved to where Gloria stood with blood staining her dress. "And you shot her, too?"

"I didn't. Jinx did." Gods, thinking about my finger squeezing the trigger made me want to vomit. I'd killed women—Glimmer women, yes, but I'd still taken their mortal lives.

I saved your arse, Jinx said. *Show a little gratitude.*

This entire operation had been a disaster, but I'd worry about the consequences when I had the luxury to do so. "Can we go back? Reverse time and stop this from happening? Stop Reve from..." I couldn't stomach the words.

"Time doesn't work that way. Once another mortal's life is entwined with yours, the timeline becomes solid. It cannot be altered. I'm sorry."

"Then what use are Diviner?" I snapped.

"We're still mortal. If I could change the deaths I've seen, I would."

Pain caught in his voice. Gods. I wished I could use my time powers to take back my foolish words. "Quen, you're bleeding."

Blood dripped from his nose, and he wiped it away on his sleeve. "We need to move quicker. Ambassador Karendar is on his way."

"Shit. How does he know we're here?"

"I told him."

"You... *what*? Why are you bloody helping me if your intent is to betray me?"

"Because this device should not fall into Glimmer hands. But if I can help you and your Godless, I will. Consider this a final favor. If Eli—Karendar discovers I'm assisting you, it'll be my end as well as yours."

"Why risk this? Why not leave us to our fate?"

A slight smile graced his lips. "We're partners."

He's an idiot with a death wish, Jinx said.

You're not wrong. We angled Dru onto the trolley and went for Malk. His height made carrying him the most awkward, and we could only fit him on the trolley by laying him on top of Dru—which would undoubtedly lead to awkwardness later, but we didn't have a choice.

Together, Quen and I pushed the trolley forward. We made slow progress, but at least we were moving. The effort burned in my biceps and calves, and beside me Quen clenched his teeth. More blood poured from his nose, and he tried his best to shake it away.

It wasn't just me who struggled to hold time, then.

I didn't want to admit that I was glad to see his stupid face.

We pushed the trolley off of the factory floor. "Leave it here," Quen ordered. He sagged against it and caught his breath. "The trolley will block the door, buy us more time. Be ready to run."

I nodded, and he used his hand to pull time to the present.

Malk immediately fell on top of Dru. She squealed, and he scrambled off her, his eyes wide and confused as they darted between Dru, me and Quen. "What in—"

"There's no time to explain!" I snapped at them. "We have to run!"

Both Sinder and Dru looked dazed, but Malk caught on quicker. "Aim for the wall!"

Dru wrapped her arm around Sinder's good side and helped guide him under cover.

Shouting came from inside the factory. They'd be on us soon.

Quen drew his pistol and aimed it at the door. "I'll hold them back."

"And get caught? Don't be a chivalrous arse." I grabbed his wrist and dragged him with me.

Following Malk's lead, I pulled Quen against the estate's wall and we hugged the shadows. They expanded to hide us, and we carefully picked our way past the estate and to the main gates. This trick wouldn't work for long. Soon we'd have Glimmer blasting their light in our direction.

Sure enough, footsteps came running behind us. "Summon light!"

"Move faster," Malk whispered.

Lights burned behind us, eradicating the cover we'd left, but we kept one step ahead of them, even though Dru and Sinder struggled to keep up the pace.

"Shit," Malk groaned. I followed his eye.

They'd closed the metal gates. We were trapped.

"Allow me," Sinder said, pushing to the front. He grabbed the metal bars with both hands, though they trembled, and his body swayed unsteadily.

"You don't have the strength for this," Dru hissed.

"I'll have to rely on your strong arms to carry me again when I pass out." Sinder glanced over his shoulder and fluttered his eyelashes. "You don't mind, do you, darling?"

"Let me," I said. "We've got Time Boy with us now—"

"*Time Boy?*" Quen spluttered.

"You keep time, I'll burn things." I took Sinder's hand and transformed into an Ember without a second thought, then I grabbed the bars. "Tell me what to do."

"Let the heat flow slowly," Sinder instructed. "Don't rush it or you'll explode and take us all out."

"Right." With his guidance, the metal bars began to melt in my grip.

The Glimmer's harsh light grew closer.

"Take your time, but *hurry up*," Dru urged. She helped the process along by bending the bars until she'd created a hole big enough for us to squeeze through. "There. Let's go."

One at a time, we ducked through the gap, careful to avoid pressing against the white-hot metal. Dru once again hauled Sinder over her shoulder.

Then we ran.

Our frantic footsteps echoed as we pelted down the main cobblestone street leading to the tram station. As we approached, a tram was pulling in, but there was something odd about it. It kept stopping and starting, as though the engine sputtered.

Though it wasn't just the tram. Malk, Dru, and Sinder were making odd spasms.

"Time fluctuations," Quen said. "Look."

More Wardens poured out of the tram. Diviner. Shit, they were looking for us.

Quen leaned against the wall, his breath coming in shallow rasps. But the fluctuations eased. "I can stop their power from affecting us, but... they'll know I'm here."

"What's going on?" Dru asked. "What do we do?"

"Wardens on the trams," I gasped while sucking in a lungful of grimy air. "We keep running."

"The tunnels," Malk ordered.

I wrapped my arm around Quen's waist and dragged him along. He practically fell onto me, and it took effort to keep him upright. Time manipulation certainly took its toll.

We followed Malk's command and slid into the darkest corners of the tunnel leading to Grayford. Malk's shadows covered us, and we slid into single file. Any shadows farther than that, and we'd draw suspicion. Quen remained on his feet, though I kept him close by.

"Any chance these Wardens know which direction we're headed, *Time Boy*?" Malk called over his shoulder.

"Warden intel on the Godless states you're hiding somewhere in Sinner's Row," Quen said.

"Sinner's Row?" I asked. "Really?"

"You're blasphemers and apostates. Where else would such wanton criminals hide?"

I supposed in this case, our sinister reputation worked in our favor. We trudged through the tunnels at a brisk pace, occasionally pausing as a tram rattled past. No one spoke, though I could hear Sinder's pained gasps and Quen's uneven breaths. The sooner we got back to Grayford, the better.

Though I now had a moment's respite to reflect.

Reve was no longer with us, and I didn't know how to feel about it. On the one hand, it hurt to lose one of our own. But on the other, he'd wanted this. And then I felt angry, betrayed even, that his vision had brought us to this conclusion.

"Her children bring the end of the gods! The end of Chime! The end of time itself!"

The fuck had he meant? Was he speaking of me? I'd never know if that was one of his nightmares or one of his visions. That was the frustrating reality of Mesmer. Not that any of it mattered now.

We'd lost the god-splitting machine, but would it have ever worked to begin with? I'd been so desperate to save Malk, I hadn't thought the consequences through, and now I'd lost my only chance of freeing him. Quen had been right—how could we stand against the gods? How could I protect Malk from Valeria?

Whatever hope I'd carried had died with Reve.

And Quen. He'd summoned the Wardens on us in the first place, but without his help, we may never have escaped. I didn't know where he stood—where *I* stood.

All I felt was an empty, aching loss.

That's just your stomach, Jinx said.

I'm not in the mood for you. You know more about aether than you've ever explained, but you're nothing but a miserable arse. Why are you trapped with me? Why am I cursed with you? I want you out of my head!

Jinx didn't answer. Had I hurt her feelings? I hoped so.

I was sick of her. Sick of her taking control of my body whenever she felt like, sick of her constant criticisms and nagging, sick of the secrets she kept despite sharing my gods-damn mind. I'd never asked to share my soul with another, and it gave me no peace, no privacy, yet Jinx floated in my consciousness like my own personal, taunting god.

I was Godless. I didn't need—didn't *want* her anymore.

Light eventually shone ahead of us, and not Glimmer light, but the aether lamps of Grayford. We sped up our pace and strode through the streets, where Vesper merely blinked at our presence. No Wardens had arrived yet. Thank the gods for that.

We burst into the depot where Harmony and Vincent waited with Varen.

"Oh, thank fuck," Harmony exclaimed as Vincent immediately rushed to Sinder's side and began examining his wound.

Varen pulled out an odd pistol-shaped object from his belt. "Corinth."

We all turned to Quen as he raised his hands. "Your Excellency, we do keep running into each oth—"

Something shot from the pistol with an electrical zap. Quen's body spasmed, and he collapsed to the ground as though suffering a seizure.

"Stop!" I tried to run for Quen, but Malk held me back.

Quen's body stopped twitching, and he lay on the ground, conscious and panting.

"What the shit!" I yelled.

Varen kept the odd-looking pistol pointed at Quen. "He prayed to his god. He called Dor. And soon we're going to have Wardens stomping through Grayford—"

"He called them on the Glimmer, not us!"

"And you think his god wouldn't have sifted through his mind and found every secret of the Godless? Of Grayford and my involvement? Don't be so naïve."

"Then don't be such a prick! If it wasn't for Quen, we wouldn't have gotten out of there with our souls intact—"

"Where's Reve?" Harmony asked. She took in the dejected sight of me, Sinder, and Dru. "What happened?"

"He's dead." Dru's proclamation cut through the air. "Worse than dead. He's gone."

"The Glimmer tricked us," Malk said, and there was a hint of spite in his voice. "They were never interested in helping us. They wanted to use that machine to end the Godless. Nothing more. Only now we're public enemies."

I yanked my arm free from his grip. "We've always been public enemies. That hasn't changed."

"What's changed is *you*, Kayl." The snarl that ripped from Malk's throat wasn't from my Malk. "It was *your* plan that took us to the Glimmer mansion. Your plan that got Reve killed. And now the rest of us are fucked! We lived in peace before all this started—before you became whatever the fuck it is you are."

"That isn't fair. I never asked for this—"

"Neither did we!"

The rest of the Godless were staring at me. None spoke in my defense. None sought to correct Malk.

Quen dragged himself to his knees, his entire body shaking. "This isn't her fault."

Malk rolled his eyes. "Oh, shoot him again, will you?"

Another zap shot from Varen's pistol, hitting Quen in the chest. He fell onto his side in another fit of spasms that left drool running down his chin.

"Stop it!" I dove for Varen's arm and tried to wrestle the pistol free.

He shoved me away and pointed it at me.

"Varen, stop this," Harmony said. "Put the weapon down."

Varen turned the odd pistol over in his hand as though examining it. "It's not lethal. The Wardens designed it. They call it a taser. It has a short aether current that runs through the barrel and can incapacitate any mortal without killing them. A wonderful design, really, since it also prevents a mortal from summoning their power. Yes, even Diviner."

Run, Jinx urged.

I don't understand what's going on.

Malk isn't Malk anymore. Valeria changed him. You can't trust him or Varen. Run!

Shit. I raised my hands. "Varen, please."

"Malk's right about you. You're a liability. A godless freak. Everything that's happened today is on *you.*"

I flinched at his harsh tone.

I'd fucked up operations in the past, I knew, but this... Was this my fault?

I caught Quen's eye. He was still conscious, barely, and he mouthed one word.

Go.

I stepped back and bumped into Malk. His muscular arms wrapped around mine, holding me in place with a painful grip. I glanced up into his blank eyes.

This wasn't Malk. This wasn't the man I'd built the Godless with.

"I'm sorry." Varen actually sounded remorseful. "I warned you what would happen if you dragged me and Grayford into your mess. I've always liked you. You're smart, funny, and a cut above the usual Vesper vagabonds that scurry to the slums. Truth is, I've always been in the Wardens' pocket. How else could I keep them off my back? And Ambassador Karendar knows *all* about you. About the Godless. Everything you've ever done, every secret you've ever passed on, I've passed onto him. The only reason you're all still here is because Karendar didn't deem you a threat worth cleaning up. Congratulations on finally catching his attention."

What?

No.

I couldn't believe what I was hearing. "You—You were my mentor—"

"As I said, I liked you. It's a shame I had to hand over Malk's mother to the Glimmer workhouse all those years ago, but well... Elvira didn't care for me. Why should I have spared a thought for her?"

I pushed from Malk's arms. "Did you know? Did you fucking *know*?"

A single tear slid down his cheek. "No. But what does it matter?"

I thumped his chest. "It matters to me! Shit, Malk, she was your *mother*!"

Harmony had edged closer to Sinder and Vincent, the three of them staring in shock. "You've been handing Vesper over to the workhouses?" she said, her voice breaking. "After all the donations we raised for Grayford? After everything we did for you?"

"You did nothing for me, and the residents of Grayford don't deserve the pitying handouts you bestow on them. I, however, did everything for you and yours, and what gratitude do I get?"

"Gratitude?" I scoffed. "You'd been funneling our donations and spending it on your own bloody greed! Did you care for our cause at *all*?"

Varen's cool eyes turned to me. "Come on, Kayl. You must have known your little group of heathens couldn't last. But thanks to you, I made myself useful to Karendar. He likes knowing where the apostates congregate. You got too ambitious. You should have stayed quiet. But now it's time to clean out the nest." He whistled a signal.

The windows of the depot exploded, shredding through the curtains and showering the platform with a sprinkling of glass. Vincent knocked both Harmony and Sinder to the ground and crouched over them, shielding them as sharp debris fell.

Wardens came running through the archway and stomped over the crackling shards, pistols drawn and aimed at my friends—my family.

Vines burst from our plant pots—from Dru's power—and whipped at the Wardens. They knitted together in a wall of thorns, attempting to hold them at bay.

An Ember Warden casually burned through them. Dru screamed and shrank back.

"Take cover!" Harmony yelled, and she readied herself to sing.

Varen whirled his pistol round and shot her.

She fell with the same spasms Quen had suffered. Her single wing twitched erratically.

Burn him, Jinx commanded.

I summoned a wave of fire and lashed it at Varen.

Malk shoved me aside, and my fire missed. It scorched through the air and across my dangling tram to the metal cables holding it in place. The carriage swayed violently and made a pained creaking sound.

Gods! My room!

The cables snapped, and the Wardens barely had enough time to scramble to safety as the entire carriage came crashing down. Its windows smashed instantly, tossing glass and the trinkets of the driver's dashboard across the platform.

I took advantage of the chaos and ran.

But Malk leaped in front of me. He grabbed my wrist with a painful pinch and refused to let go. I dug my fingernails into his skin to pry him away, but touching him forced my persona to swap from Ember to Vesper.

He released me with a hiss.

And then agony buzzed through my skin.

I fell to the ground in a crumpled heap. My muscles wouldn't move, but they writhed in unnatural spasms. Gods, I couldn't even open my mouth to scream!

Jinx, help!

Varen's shot us. I can't block it.

Boots marched past as the Wardens barked commands and rounded up Harmony, Vincent, Sinder, and Dru. None of them could fight against such vast numbers. I glanced to Quen who squirmed on the ground as hopelessly as I.

And Malk...

Malk stood at Varen's side like a loyal pet. The sight of it made me want to vomit.

"Fetch his pistol," Varen ordered, and Malk obeyed, taking Quen's pistol from its holster and passing it to Varen.

"*Why?*" I managed to spit out.

Malk tensed. "She killed me. For every tithe I'd missed over the years, she punished me. First, by flaying the skin from my bones." His voice cracked. "And then her Winged Twilights... they locked me inside the same cage that my father had died in, and they stabbed me through the bars, letting my blood drip. I died over and over in that wretched place and she brought me back to feel it again and again and *again*."

Fucking gods. "Malk—"

"You wanted to know what Valeria did to me. That's what she did. And all that time I thought you—you'd left me there to rot. That I'd never see Chime again. You... You'll never know what that's like." Sobs wracked through his chest and he rocked on his heels.

"Easy now, Malkavaan," Varen said. "Get on your knees."

Malk did so, as Varen placed the barrel of Quen's pistol to Malk's forehead.

"Don't," Quen moaned.

"No need to worry, Corinth. I'm merely sending the boy back to where he belongs. As for you, Karendar will be calling to collect your worthless hide shortly. I'm sure the two of you will have *much* to discuss."

"You called me his puppet," Quen gasped. "What are *you*?"

"A mere mortal who knows his place."

Varen pulled the trigger. The blast echoed through the depot.

Through my heart.

Malk's brains splattered across the platform.

I screamed as his body tipped over, his blue, lifeless eyes meeting mine.

Then he faded. His body turned to aether, and his empty clothes crumpled like a hollowed-out shell.

Malk was gone.

Returned to his god.

And my heart shattered.

XXX

Mortals are made in the image of their god, so we have always believed.
And so a mortal takes on the traits of said gods. Except the gods are made
perfect, and mortals are not.
The philosophers ask: how could a god make such an imperfect design?
This is the question of mortality.
Immortals are beings which share the same minds as the gods, and yet they
do not stray or sin as a mortal mind does. One can assume that existence is
therefore flawed by such concepts of aging and death.
However, a mortal is not born with sin. Rather, they are born perfect and
acquire flaws. Often when a mortal enters Chime.
What then leads to sin?
Is it assimilation into mortal society? Is it influence from mortals of other
domains? Is it the temptation of freedom that Chime offers? Or the many
distractions that create distance between a mortal and one's god?
—E. Karendar, *A Question of Sin and Mortality*

I SAT BEHIND THE mirror of an observation room in Warden HQ as though I were still one of them, a Warden. As though I'd been part of this operation from the start and was privy to the meeting going on before me. Elijah sat at the table with Varen, discussing the events which had recently transpired, occasionally taking a sip of coffee or examining a file. Occasionally glancing at the prisoner on the other side of this mirror and her Vesper form. Occasionally glancing at me, waiting for my reaction.

They'd even brought me a cup of tea and a digestive biscuit, but I remained still, sitting with my hands in my lap, just as my Vesper mirror did. Making no movements. Saying no words. What could I say?

"Go over their backgrounds with me again," Elijah said, a cup in his hand, as though engaging in some interesting news from the broadsheets.

Varen flipped open another file. "Their leader, the Seren; one Miss Harmony Arabesque. Works as a copywriter for the Chime Courier. Memoria University stock. She's the brains of their organization, which is saying something." He chuckled to himself. "It's her fliers you'll find littered across Central."

"She's the Seren with only one wing?"

"That's right. Her ex-lover was taken by Serenity some thirteen years ago. A minor scandal at the time, if you recall."

Taken. A polite way of saying murdered.

"Then there's the Necro," Varen continued. "Mr. Vincent Holcroft. Also Memoria University alumni. And ex-Warden, though I believe his files were destroyed. He's fairly tame, for a Necro, and suffers from arthritis, which makes him a lesser threat. He's tight-lipped, but if you torture the Ember, he'll loosen up. The pair of them are lovers."

"A Necro and an Ember? You don't say."

"Odd, I know. The Ember, Sinder, has no known family name. He once served as a prostitute for Edana before she carted him to the Glimmer workhouses. He has an obsessive hatred for the Glimmer as a result. He'd been spying on Erosain for the Godless in some misguided attempt to help the illegals who congregate there."

"Is Erosain aware?"

"I doubt it. Erosain pays little attention to his own mortals, and would likely deem them incapable of subtlety. That leaves us with Miss Druzy Smith, the Umber—"

"What business does an Umber have with a group of heathens?"

"I never understood her angle. She came to Grayford on missionary work and served in the soup kitchen. Then she took in the Mesmer, acting as a sort of caregiver."

"And the Mesmer is now dead?"

"Yes, alongside the Vesper male, Malkavaan Byvich."

I bristled as Malkavaan's name spilled past Varen's lips. At the casualness of it all. Had he ever cared for these mortals? Had he been plotting their demise this entire time?

Elijah gathered the papers into a folder. "Excellent work. Normally, we'd follow protocol in these situations, but an exception must be made in this case. Is this all the intel you have on them?" He tapped the folder.

"Everything, Your Excellency. An entire collection of the Godless's known dealings, contacts, and safe houses. Erosain is a leak that must be plugged, but the vast majority of their intel came through me—though I believe a Warden had been in contact with Miss Arabesque via her drop box at the Courier." Varen's eyes glanced toward me. "Someone had been leaving her anonymous notes and *generous* donations."

I held Varen's stare, but said nothing.

He'd betrayed me. Betrayed the Godless.

Killed Malkavaan too, which was not an outcome I desired, even if he'd lost his own mind by the end.

Following protocol meant that the Godless would be returned to their gods and the Wardens would wipe their hands clean of them, leaving their fate to their god's whims. I dreaded to think of what fate Elijah planned for them now.

How could I possibly protect them? My fate was likely tied with theirs.

For I had betrayed the Wardens, and both men in this room knew it.

Elijah thanked Varen for his information and the Vesper ambassador ducked from the room, though not before throwing me one last sneer. He'd never liked me, had he? I couldn't fathom why. Perhaps past Quen had insulted his mother.

"You've not drunk your tea," Elijah commented.

"I'm waiting for it to cool."

"And your digestive? They're your favorite."

Digestive biscuits were standard Diviner fare; an inoffensive snack that lacked the joy and personality of others. The kind of biscuit one ate when trying to purge oneself of sinful thoughts, such as adding sugar to tea or contemplating treason. My hands shook in my lap, and not just from the aftereffects of the taser. "I've lost my appetite."

Elijah sighed and strode around the table, sitting on the corner. "Look at me."

I pulled out my fob watch and ran my thumb over the cracked glass. This damnable thing didn't keep time, and that was why I carried it. Diviner were drawn to broken things, but while my domain sought to fix that which was broken, I did not. I saw beauty in the flaws. A chaos of its own.

"There's no reason to be angry with me," Elijah said. "We have done what must be done. The Godless's actions would have damned Chime, you know that. They infiltrated the Glimmer's workhouse, shot their guards, shot Gloria—"

"The Glimmer have a device, a cursed device which they say the Wardens commissioned." I dared to meet Elijah's brass gaze. "What in god's name have you built?"

"Language, Quentin—"

"No, you don't get to chide—"

He slapped my cheek with such force, my head snapped to one side. The fob watch fell from my grip and clattered to the floor.

The imprint of his palm stung, though it was the shame of it which brought hot tears to my eyes. My breaths came in rasping gasps.

"Look at me," Elijah commanded.

I refused.

He grabbed my chin, his fingernails digging into my skin, and he forced me to stare into his burning brass eyes. "You don't remember, do you Quentin?"

My heart skipped a beat, and I swallowed thick saliva.

"You don't remember all those times you met with Varen and passed on Warden intel," he continued. "Luckily, Varen is loyal to me, and that's when I first learned you were keeping secrets from me and playing with your own memories."

"Eli, I—"

"You've always held a soft spot for the Godless. You're too impressionable. Too vulnerable to sin. You thought you could help them and keep this from me? You think I've not been watching you fall? That it hasn't broken my heart? Each time you wiped your memories I'd hope it would be the last, that you'd come to me and let me help you correct your path. But you strayed further." His grip released my chin, and his finger trailed to my lips, caressing the bottom one. "Do you remember the first time we kissed?"

A flush of guilt burned my cheeks. I'd never forget it. Even though I'd tried.

Elijah's touch fell from my lips, and I longed to feel their caress once more. "You were meant to destroy her."

All warmth drained from my veins and I couldn't keep myself from glancing at the mirror. To the woman sitting beyond, awaiting her sentence as I was. "What will you do with her—with them?"

Elijah stood and paced to the mirror. "Thanks to Gloria and your ineptitude, we've been left with quite a mess to clean up. You are correct; we commissioned this device."

"For what purpose?"

"To destroy the aether creatures, of course. Once I learned what they were and what they were capable of, we needed to dispose of them for good. The usual methods couldn't destroy them, so we devised a method to trap them and turn their own soul-splitting powers against them."

"Eli, they're conscious beings capable of thought—they have the potential to become mortals—"

"Don't be ridiculous. Are you suggesting these creatures be granted the same rights as the rest of Chime's mortals? To live and breathe among us? They are monstrous."

"Kayl is one of them." As I said those words, I knew it to be true. Whatever these aether creatures were, they and Kayl were one and the same. "And she is an articulated, resourceful woman capable of—"

"She is a Godless heathen who would rather see Chime ripped apart than bow to Warden rule. Don't convince yourself otherwise. Whatever she is, she is an abnormality. These creatures are born from aether—from chaos. And chaos cannot function in a civilized society. Your sympathy is clouding your judgement."

"You won't give them a chance to speak!"

His brass eyes flashed. "When they murder Diviner, I've heard all they have to say."

"And your solution is to use this device on them? To split their souls? Do you understand that the Glimmer intended to use it for themselves? To split mortals from their gods? Do you even realize what danger that possesses?"

"I'm aware of the device's potential."

Potential? I leaned back in my chair. "Then why? Why build it? Why take that risk?"

"It was Doctor Hector Bezel who discovered the device's... alternative use. Trust me, we didn't intend to build a device that could split a mortal from their god. Of course we didn't. But the potential was too great to ignore. We tested it on one of Hector's Diviner apprentices to verify it."

"You... tested it? You destroyed the soul of a Diviner? Father would *never* have allowed such depravity—"

"The test was Father's idea."

No. That I could not believe, *refused* to believe.

"Father confirmed that our test subject's soul hadn't returned to Him. It had floated off to the aether, like the souls attacked by the aether creature. We took every precaution to develop and test this device in secret, though the Glimmer sought to build their own version behind my back, a mistake I must now rectify."

Was this why Hector Bezel had died? My skin itched, as though it were literally crawling. I leaped from my chair, letting it fall back with a crash. "This device is unconscionable! It goes against everything the Wardens stand for!"

Elijah's cool stare looked me over. "*You* would lecture me on ethics? Know your place—"

"My place?" I laughed hysterically. Gods, could I name myself a Warden if we were committing such atrocious acts? "When the other gods discover what infernal device you've made, they'll rip Chime apart!"

"Weren't you listening? That's the beauty of this device. It splits a mortal from their soul, and that soul does not return to its god. It dissipates into aether and powers a lamp somewhere. We can destroy mortals without their soul returning to their domain to tattle, and their god is none the wiser."

I sagged against the table. "And that's—that's your intention? To kill mortals?" Potential, he'd said. "Do the other ambassadors know of your plan? They couldn't possibly agree with this. The Wardens are governed by all twelve—not just you, Eli!"

"Chime has always been under Diviner rule. We alone have the knowledge and temperament to govern with fairness and logic. The other domains are too emotional, too volatile, and you've seen what Glimmer influence has brought us. But even they know the fundamental truth of mortal existence; we may be the gods' consciousness made flesh, but it's mortal sin which returns to them in death to pollute their minds. This device can cull the unworthy and keep such taint from influencing the gods."

Who decided which sins would cost one's soul? Where would the Wardens draw the line? Each domain held their own definition of sin. To a Glimmer, enjoying a bourbon biscuit could be sinful, and the mortals of Chime indulged minor sins on the regular. There were the unforgivable sins—apostasy, blasphemy—worth a stint in a correctional facility, if not exile. Would that now mean the erasure of one's existence?

It wouldn't just be the sinners. Any enemies of the Wardens, anyone who carried illicit knowledge with them, could have their soul ripped apart instead of allowing that knowledge to return to their domain. Chime's secrets—Kronos's secrets—would forever be safe.

And no one would miss a handful of undesirable mortals here and there.

Undesirables such as the Godless. Such as Kayl.

"You're going to submit the Godless to this device." That was what he'd said—they'd abandon protocol. They wouldn't be condemned to the wrath of their gods or a correctional facility, but a fate far worse. They'd be reduced to nothing but memory.

Saints. Malkavaan Byvich had gotten off lightly.

Elijah picked up a Godless flier that had fallen from Varen's file. "We are doing this for the future of Chime. You were meant to destroy them. This is on you."

"I'm not a killer—"

"Aren't you?" He raised an eyebrow. "You're a Warden, and if you expect to continue serving as one, then you will do what is necessary to protect this city."

I lifted my chin. "And if I refuse? Will you submit me to your device, too?"

"Quentin." He lifted his hand to my cheek. I flinched, but he only cupped the spot still sore from his touch. "It pains me to see you this way, to see how the Godless have infected you with their poison. I've believed in you since our Academy days. I advocated for you after those Vesper deaths. Why don't you believe in me?"

"I do, but I can't—we cannot be the arbiters of souls—"

"I'm going to make this easy for you. When you forget about the Godless, then it will be of no significance for you to do what must be done."

I recoiled from his touch. "What?"

"You betrayed me. You betrayed my trust, my love. You betrayed the very values you swore to uphold when you joined the Wardens. And you've betrayed our Father. Neither of us wishes to see you suffer, but there must be consequences. This is not something a correctional facility can fix."

"Eli, please—"

"You'll prove your loyalty. You *will* correct your path. I have already summoned Professor Burns to wipe your memories clean. A factory reset, if you will. You'll forget about Varen, about the Godless, as though you were fresh to the Wardens. You'll forget this whole sorry business and then you'll do what must be done."

My entire life for the last eight years would be wiped in an instant.

Maybe once I would have relished the thought.

But who would I become without the knowledge of the Godless? Without hearing their stories? Without meeting Kayl? Without experiencing my pistol blasting innocent Vesper who'd only tried to protect an abused Glimmer girl?

I would be Quentin Corinth.

But I wouldn't be Quen.

"This is a gift," Elijah said. "You know well I could condemn you to an eternity inside a correctional facility on Kronos, or worse. What I'm offering is no different from what you've attempted yourself numerous times—a fresh start. A chance to redeem yourself in the eyes of our Father."

I knew it was a gift. For all I'd done, the betrayals and sins I couldn't even remember, I knew this was a blessing. An absolution.

So why, dear saints, did it feel like a death sentence?

Who owned my thoughts?

My memories?

My existence?

I wanted to throw myself to the floor and beg Father for mercy. Perhaps the Godless *had* cursed me, for I felt such ingratitude for the life granted me.

A *gift*. I'd forget this wretchedness, forget my sins. Start again and hope I'd not mess it up this time. It was a coward's way out.

Hadn't I always been a coward?

"It's what's best for you." Elijah squeezed my shoulder. "Father loves you. I love you. Say it, Quentin."

I sniffed back tears and choked the words out. "I love you."

"Do what must be done. For me. For Father."

"I... I will."

"Good man." Elijah left me standing in the middle of the room as he strode for the door and summoned a pair of Diviner Wardens. I stole one last look at Kayl.

While I'd acted the petulant child, she'd remained staring at the wall without so much as a twitch or scream. She carried herself with the strength of a woman who knew her worth.

"You deserve better, you know."

No. I didn't.

I scooped up my fob watch, stuffing it into my pocket, and glimpsed the man I currently was reflected in the mirror. Present Quen looked a mess. His hair was tousled, his disheveled shirt smeared with soot and blood.

This was the man I'd become. Dirty and depraved.

The two Diviner Wardens escorted me from the room and led me past the interrogation cells which held the Godless. Miss Smith. Vincent. Sinder. Harmony. Soon I would forget them. Soon I would be their doom.

We entered one such room. Professor Walter Burns waited inside, setting up a pot of murky green tea on a counter beside a memory recliner.

"It's good to see you, dear fellow," Walter rasped.

I glanced around the room. There were no steam pipes or ventilation. No moisture in the air at all. "This cannot be comfortable for you."

"Don't you worry, I have my tea. You may leave us," he said to the two guards.

They didn't move. "Ambassador Karendar insists we help Master Corinth into the chair and make him comfortable—"

"I assure you that isn't necessary—"

"It's quite all right," I said. "I'm here because I wish to be. To correct my *path*." The words came out more sarcastically than I'd intended.

I forced a smile as the two Wardens helped me into the recliner—which loosely translated into them strapping my arms and legs down so tightly I couldn't move a muscle. As they secured each strap, panic rose in my chest, and I had just enough wiggle room to reach inside my pocket and run a calming thumb over my fob watch.

A broken thing. Like me.

"You may leave now," Walter instructed the guards.

The two Wardens lingered. "Karendar ordered—"

"This process takes time and concentration, and your presence interferes with my work." He waved a webbed hand around the room. "We won't be leaving until we're done, will we?"

The Wardens exchanged a glance and shrugged. With me strapped down, and an asthmatic old Amnae, we didn't exactly pose a threat. They finally left the room, locking the door behind them.

Walter huffed a sigh and reached for his tea. "I'm sorry it came to this."

"So am I."

"I don't know what Elijah told you—"

"You reported my visits to him, didn't you?"

Walter deflated in his chair like a sad fish out of water. "I had no choice. I'm sorry. He threatened my daughter."

"You have a daughter?"

"You don't remember me telling you about her?" He huffed a little laugh. "Of course you don't. We have time now if you'll listen."

"I'm not going anywhere."

Walter took a deep gulp of his tea that I could smell from here—salt water and seaweed. "She's a bright girl. My Ilona. It's her final year in the University back on Memoria. She wasn't sure what to study and was torn between philosophy and science. Ultimately, she followed in my footsteps to dabble in mnemonics."

"If she has your brains, she'll go far."

"I hope so. And I hope she'll remember me. I don't remember her mother. I once served with the Wardens, you know. We had a case in Memoria of students being abducted and abused, their memories wiped after. It was a horrid affair, and during the investigation my daughter was born. Or so Ilona tells me. I can't remember her at all, nor my wife. Ilona tells me so many things about her mother and I can't place a single one of them."

"You wiped those memories?"

"No. Anima took them."

A queasy sense of dread washed over me. Some gods demanded tithes from their mortals, like Valeria, who demanded worship and attention and gold.

The Amnae god demanded memories.

It sounded romantic on paper. An Amnae so loved to study that they could read the same book over and over and pass on those first impressions to their god. But the reality was more sinister. Anima enjoyed meaningful memories. Memories that mattered. Cherished memories of first kisses, first loves, firstborn children. Who knew what they did with them?

They'd certainly find my antics quite entertaining. "I'm so sorry, Professor."

"It's the price we pay for our mortal existence, and why I rather enjoy my retirement here on Chime. I'd have never known I sired a daughter until she found me. She is precious to me. I want you to remember her name. Ilona. I want you to protect her."

"I can't make promises. I won't even remember this conversation."

Walter finished his tea and rolled his chair to my side. "You know I don't want to do this." His eyelids were heavy.

"If it's any consolation, I don't want this either." But neither of us had a choice. Walter was bound by his god, and I was bound by mine.

I couldn't disappoint my Father.

"I dreaded your visits, you know. I dreaded to see what craziness you'd gotten up to next, and what information I'd have to pass to Elijah. I didn't tell him everything. I tried to protect you as best I could."

"You were always my favorite professor. I don't blame you for this." I found it hard to look at him anymore and stared at the ceiling. "Please don't wipe her from my mind."

"Elijah ordered me to."

"If you do, I'll kill her. I'll rip her soul apart and not care while I do it." I turned my head back to him. "You told me to find the Godless. You planted that seed in my subconscious."

"My dear boy." Walter patted my knee. "You have always sought the Godless of your own volition. If anything, I tried to weed that seed, but it only buried further within you, as stubborn as you are. You don't remember who you are, Quentin, but you soon will."

"I'm a fool drunk on my own hubris, or my past selves were. Past me thought I could balance the Wardens with the Godless—"

"You wanted to protect them. And you have. I've witnessed everything you've ever done, every sin you've ever committed."

"I suppose you're the only man I have ever bared my soul to. How ugly does it look?"

Walter smiled. A sad smile, and I immediately regretted making light of this situation, but how could I not?

I was about to die.

Not the death of my visions, but a different kind of death, because that was what memory loss entailed. The death of present time. The death of potential.

It was too late to run.

Perhaps a stronger version of myself would have. Perhaps a different Quen would have sided with the Godless and fought against everything I ever held dear to save them.

A stronger Quen would have kissed her.

He would have told Kayl how much he appreciated her company these past few days, even if they held blanks here or there.

No, a stronger Quen would have saved the Vesper she loved. A stronger Quen wouldn't have condemned Malkavaan Byvich to his god.

But that Quen had died. Or he hadn't existed at all.

And now all of those lives would come to an end. I was out of time.

Walter carefully took away my spectacles, placing them on the table, and then his cold fingers moved to my forehead. It tingled when the suckers clasped against my skin. "I'm sorry, old friend. What I'm about to do will hurt you deeply."

I forced a chuckle. "Memory loss never hurt before. Did it?"

"I'm not removing your memories this time."

My heart sped up, and I tried to view his face, his reaction, but he held my head securely in his hands and my terrible eyesight blurred his features. "What?"

"The truth is that I never wiped your memories. Not once. I merely locked them away inside the depths of your subconscious. They're all in here." He tapped my forehead. "Every sin. Every pleasure. Every pain."

"Your jokes need more work."

"No joke, I'm afraid. Elijah ordered me to wipe some memories, manipulate others. He wanted me to make you love him, adore him, worship him. I'm sure you did love him, once. But he doesn't deserve you. He never did. He abused you. And I... I played my part in covering up that abuse. I'm sorry. I hope you'll forgive me one day."

"*Walter—*"

"He wants to own you. Control you. But no one owns your thoughts, Quentin. Not Elijah, and not I."

Agony bored into my brain, like sharp knives lancing through my skull. The pain didn't cut away my memories; it shredded through the bindings holding them together, like ripping stitches from a wound.

Images flashed in my mind, one after another, with the searing clarity of burning sunlight. The fires bathed me in depraved deeds and lingering horrors that should have belonged to any other man.

But they belonged to me.

They *were* me.

The pistol shook in my grip.

"Shoot her, Quentin. She's nothing but an illegal Vesper. Send her back to her god."

"I can't do this, I can't—"

"This is Warden law. Do you want to be a Warden? Or do you want to spend the rest of your mortal existence behind stone walls? Do this for me. For our Father. Shoot her!"

My finger pulled the trigger.

I could do nothing but scream as my entire existence unraveled one thread at a time.

PART FOUR

31

Have you ever asked yourself why you suffer?
If the gods are almighty, why make us suffer at all?
"Without suffering, we won't know happiness! Without suffering, we would
never know gratitude, would never learn from our mistakes!"
If that is true, then why do some mortals suffer more than others?
Why do the mortals of the Golden City live in comfort while those of the
Undercity starve?
—Anonymous, *Godless flier on suffering*

WE WERE TWO VESPER making a name for ourselves in the dark.

And now Malk was nothing more than a memory of his god.

Malk hadn't liked me at first. He'd been smaller than me, a scrappy young thing. Angry at the world, at his god. Elvira had smuggled him out of Eventide after watching his father die in a cage for missing the tithe. They'd sought shelter in Grayford thanks to Varen. And that was when they'd found me.

I couldn't even remember those days with clarity. I remembered being lost in the darkness of the Undercity, hearing the whispers in my mind, the screaming of aether. Elvira must have seen a frightened young girl. Malk saw competition for food.

When Elvira had disappeared, stolen into the Glimmer workhouses, Malk and I had formed a partnership; the two of us sharing whatever we could get our grubby hands on. That was before we'd convinced Varen to tutor us in exchange for running his errands. And he'd taken a liking to us because we proved ourselves useful. We'd hung on Varen's every word and command because he knew so much more of Chime and the twelve domains than we did.

We trusted him. He never gave us a reason to doubt that trust.

Had it all been a lie?

Malk hurt you, Jinx said. *I'm not sad he's gone.*

I'm not talking to you.

You might as well. I'm all you've got left.

Yes, I still had the crazy voice in my head for comfort, though amazingly, it didn't help. All that time I'd spent with Quen drinking tea and eating scones, I'd convinced myself that Malk was safe. That Valeria would keep her word. That Varen would ensure his safety.

While I'd been gallivanting around the Golden City, that vile bitch had been ripping him apart. Torturing him day after day, breaking the man I'd loved these past thirteen years.

She'd destroyed him.

We'll destroy her back, Jinx promised.

How? We're mere mortals. What chance do we have against a god? It's over.

I thought you weren't talking to me?

I chewed my tongue and returned my attention to the mirror.

The Wardens had shoved me into one of their interrogation rooms, strapped once more to a chair, and forced me to don their ridiculous gloves. I couldn't see beyond the glass mirror, but I knew someone lurked behind it; the hairs on my neck bristled with the uncanny feeling of being observed. I didn't know where the other Godless were, but they were likely being held in their own little cells.

Quen, too. They'd taken him with the same regard they'd offered me. I still didn't understand why he'd helped us, but I worried about him.

For a Diviner, a Warden... he was one of the good ones.

There'd be no point in screaming or crying, and I wouldn't give these bastards the satisfaction. So I sat and waited for the judgement to fall.

They'd likely send the Godless off to their own gods.

Harmony wouldn't survive Serenity. The Seren god held a vengeful streak and had already ripped off one of Harmony's wings. No, she'd suffer a fate as bad as Malk, but she was stubborn enough not to break at the end.

Sinder would survive, I thought. Edana too held a vengeful streak, but she liked to play with her mortals rather than outright murder them. If she wanted to be truly cruel, she'd send Sinder off to the Glimmer workhouses again. But he'd grown so strong among the Godless, I knew he'd fight back.

Vincent, I wasn't sure of. The Nameless One didn't care for vengeance as other gods did, but the Necro god would likely imprison Vincent and force him into servitude once more.

Unghard was the most forgiving of the twelve, so I hoped Dru would be okay. We first met while working in Grayford's soup kitchen. Together we'd fed so many mouths, and they could be a rowdy lot. Dru and I had watched each other's backs then, and every day since. She volunteered her time for us, even if she didn't understand or agree with the Godless. Then she'd found a purpose in caring for Reve.

Gods. Reve. He'd always struggled and suffered, and now he was gone. Completely gone. His soul wouldn't even return to Mesmorpheus.

As for myself...

I didn't have a god.

What would the Wardens do with me?

They'll probably kill us, Jinx said.

Yes, thank you. It was a rhetorical question.

They'll rip out your fingernails first.

For god's sake! I cringed at the thought. *Do you want me to shit our shared body?*

Now you admit we share a body?

If I die, you die with me, so there's no point arguing over it, is there?

With no god, where would my soul even go? Would it power some lamp in Central? At least the Godless stood a chance of escaping their domains, should their god not immediately obliterate their mortal bodies and cast their souls into the aether.

The Covenant stated that mortals were only allowed one life. Those who died returned to their god, but they could be reborn again, trapped inside their domain as immortal slaves or ordained saints, depending. While they weren't permitted to reenter Chime, it hadn't stopped some mortals from returning.

Malk's soul was owned completely by Valeria, but there was still a chance I could break the Covenant and get him back, no matter how impossibly slim.

And the Godless too. My family. I'd break the Covenant a thousand times over to save their souls.

But not if I lost my own soul first.

The door cracked open, and a Diviner strode inside that I didn't want to entertain.

Ambassador Karendar.

The Diviner was as impeccably dressed as that day in Lady Mae's, in his pinstripe suit and silver cufflinks. With his bronze hair and brass eyes and sharp cheekbones, he was undeniably handsome. The regal gentleman to Quen's dorkiness.

Karendar casually slid into the chair opposite. "We may finally speak face to face without interruption."

I met his cool brass eyes and hated them already.

He clasped his hands over the table. "Kayl. Why no family name? My intel states you and Malkavaan Byvich were close, yet you never took his name for yourself?"

I bristled at Malk's name, but forced a polite smile. I wouldn't let his ilk get under my skin, but I'd sure try to get under his. "What can I say, I like to live as a free woman. Though Kayl Corinth sounds lovely, doesn't it?"

His brass eyes flashed. Oh yes, that hit a nerve. "Are you aware of who I am?"

He's a sanctimonious time-keeping wanker, that's who, Jinx said.

"Unfortunately. And I assume you're here to question me, threaten me, possibly drag me to some sort of depraved torture chamber and then my eventual death, which honestly sounds very dull. I'll take a cuppa, if you're making. Three sugars and a splash of milk, please."

Karendar smiled as cordially as one's captor could. "In truth, there's very little for us to discuss. I already know who you are and what organization you represent. Your fate and that of your allies is a foregone conclusion."

"Then to what do I owe the pleasure of your company?"

"Curiosity. I do not know everything, as much as it saddens me. And when it comes to *you*, my dear, you simply are a mystery. A puzzle that not even Corinth could decipher. A woman who is immune to time. Who can take the faces and powers of the twelve domains, yet not call any of them home. You have a twin soul trapped inside you, do you not? What do you call it? Jinx?"

That caught me off guard. "Did Corinth tell you that?"

"Corinth didn't need to tell me. I ripped the information from his mind."

Shit, what else had they done to Quen? "Where is he?"

"Corinth? Oh, he's got an appointment with Professor Walter Burns. It seems these past few days have taken quite a toll on the poor boy. He'll be wiping his memories clean of whatever poison you and your Godless have infected him with."

My hands clenched into fists. If they wiped his memories that deeply, he'd forget everything—the Glimmer and their machine, the Wardens' involvement, helping the Godless and listening to their stories... and me. He'd forget me.

How could I stop him?

He chose to wipe his memories, Jinx said.

That was true, but in this case? "Quen helped the Godless. We didn't poison him."

"We both know how impressionable he is." The slight smile on his lips reminded me too much of Quen. "Your blasphemy corrupted him and distracted him from his path."

"Yes, because we Godless don't have better things to do than hang around street corners and hand out candy while whispering blasphemy to anyone who walks past."

"Thankfully, you'll no longer be littering our streets with your filth."

I snorted a laugh. "You Diviner are no different from Glimmer. Do you honestly believe that the mortals of Chime will suddenly clean up their act once the Godless are gone? That Sinner's Row will stop operating? The Godless represent an idea. You may kill me, kill my organization, but you cannot kill an idea. It will always be there, festering in the depths of Chime's subconscious, corrupting poor innocent minds."

Karendar leaned back in his chair. "Actually, I do believe we can correct the thoughts of others. We have many welcoming facilities. The Glimmer quite enjoy operating them."

Of course that would be the Warden's solution to apostasy and blasphemy. Don't like a thought? Consider it dangerous? Then correct it. Or, in Quen's case, wipe it away altogether. "You can't stand the Godless, can you, Ambassador?"

"I pity you. I used to believe you apostates and blasphemers were contrary for the thrill of it. Why else does Sinner's Row bring in such vast amounts of money? Because our citizens seek the thrill of sin. We allow it to exist not just for the taxes that Ambassador Erosain sends our way, but because we can keep a watchful eye on the mortals who frequent such establishments. Their behavior I can understand—much like Corinth, who rebels from some childish yearning to disobey our Father. But yours?

"Now, I believe that some mortals are so tainted with sin, they've forgotten their place. Forgotten who they are. They fail to love and appreciate their patron god and the Covenant. Our correctional facilities try to fix this behavior, but in truth, some mortals cannot be saved. They are unworthy of their god and the existence granted to them. Such a wretched life I pity. But I pity you most of all."

"I don't care for your pity—"

"There is a chance, no matter how slim, that you are truly godless. That you are some anomaly born from the aether of Chime. You have never known the love of your god. You have never felt that connection. It is a pity that there is no god waiting for you."

"Odd, because I pity *you*, Ambassador. Do you know what you are? A coward who is a slave to his god's whims. Your entire existence is owned by a divine figure who cares nothing for you. You're not free. You never will be."

"Neither are you." He gestured to my bindings. "I carry the blessings and conviction of my Father. You'll die alone in a world where no one will call for you."

Not quite alone, Jinx said.

No, not quite.

"Speaking of. Time is slipping away, and I have more pressing engagements." Karendar rose from his chair and sauntered around the table to my side. "I would have valued bringing you to Kronos and having one of our Necro perform a live dissection to truly understand what you are, what makes you *tick*. But I can't risk you escaping on the way to the Gate now, can I? Though, thanks to my Father's insight, I believe I know what you are."

I stared up at his brass eyes and searched them for answers. I certainly wasn't going to beg him for his insight.

He placed his fingers on my wrist, searching for the pulse, and I flinched at his touch. "Remarkable. You truly do resist Diviner powers." He then pressed into the vein on my neck and I resisted gnashing at his fingers. "I had to be certain, you understand."

"What now, Ambassador?"

"Now I meet with the Glimmer and clean up this whole sorry affair. You've already seen their device, haven't you? A rusted prototype, but it works as well as the ones we devised on Kronos. How fortunate for us. I had them bring it here and reconfigure it."

My heart sped up.

Gods.

He was going to force me into their machine. Condemn me to the same fate as Reve. We should have destroyed it when we had the chance. "What of the Godless?" I spluttered.

"Don't worry, my dear, they'll be following you."

"That's not—That's not in the Covenant! They belong to their gods! Leave me, but take them back to their domains!"

"Why would I do that? You Godless wanted to be free, did you not? I'm merely giving you what you want."

Shit, *no*! At least if they returned to their domains, they'd have a chance to escape, to beg for their lives and *survive*—this machine would eviscerate them!

"Please, Ambassador—"

"Please?" His lip curled into an amused smirk. "You've found your manners, have you? Go on. I'd like to hear you beg."

Don't you dare! Jinx snapped.

He's going to rip their souls apart, Jinx! They're my family. I can't let him do this. "Please, Your Excellency. Take my soul. I have no god, it doesn't matter, does it? But let them go. Let them find some—some redemption. *Please.*"

A predatory glint shone in his brass eyes. "If only I could spare the time to hear such delicious whining. You Godless are no different from any mortal when it comes to preserving your pathetic existence, though alas, I have no interest in preserving it." He cupped my cheek. "You are rather lovely. I can see how you corrupted Quentin."

I spat in his face.

He pulled a handkerchief from his jacket pocket and wiped away the saliva. "I daresay no one will miss you or your Godless. I'll ensure your names are scratched from our records and forgotten to time."

And then he slapped me, the blow a burning pain that knocked my head against the chair. I licked my lip and tasted blood.

Wanker, Jinx snarled.

He adjusted his cufflinks. "I'd beat you bloody if I thought that would fix you, but I tried that with Quentin, and you see where it led us."

Gods. The marks on Quen's shoulders.

"You meant to do this all along, didn't you, you arrogant prick?" I seethed. "Those Vesper in the Glimmer workhouses—did you intend to submit them to your machine? To use them, make them build the instrument of their destruction, and then wipe them before Valeria could learn what a sick bastard you are?"

Karendar tutted. "What an imagination you have. You should understand your place in the universe by now, *Miss Arkey*. There are saints and there are sinners. Those mortals who dally with sin carry those sins with them in death, and such sin corrupts. Look at Valeria as proof. A spiteful god that seeks to sell her own mortals for gold. What could twist a god so except her own mortals? By purging those with sin, we'll keep the gods pure. The Undercity is riddled with such mortals."

"You... You think mortal souls corrupt the gods?" I couldn't believe what he was saying. "Mortals were made in the gods' image, not the other way around!"

"There you go, spouting such wicked blasphemy." He strode for the door.

Gods. Karendar was insane. Or he was so far up Dor's arse, he couldn't see the imperfections and cruelties of the gods for himself.

They think you're the crazy one, Jinx said.

"Are we ready?" he asked someone waiting in the hallway outside. "Excellent work." He glanced at me. "Let's not waste any more time, shall we?"

Another Warden stepped into the room and my breath hitched.

Quen.

Only... it wasn't Quen. His silver eyes glossed over me as though he didn't recognize me, as though we were strangers. They'd already wiped his mind clean. *Shit.*

"Escort her to Ambassador Gloria, if you would," Karendar commanded.

Quen bowed his head. "Certainly, Your Excellency."

Gods, he looked a mess; blood stained his shirt, and his eyes were bloodshot, as though he'd been dragged through death and back. And not a flicker of recognition crossed over his face. He roughly grabbed my arm and yanked me up.

I jostled in his grip. "Quen, please, it's me—it's Kayl—"

"Come quietly, now."

"You *know* me, Quen!"

He dragged me forward with surprising strength, and I could do nothing but stagger by his side, my limbs useless.

I told you not to trust him, Jinx said.

But he's not him!

He wasn't my Quen, and he was leading me to my doom.

We strode along a bleak gray corridor. All these Warden HQ hallways appeared the same. Even if I could somehow escape, how would I find my way out of this maze? How would I find the Godless?

"You take two sugars in your tea," I said, to prompt some memory or distract Quen. "And you read the Courier as Rapture opens every morning."

He ignored me.

"Bourbons are your favorite biscuit!"

"I said come *quietly*." He shoved me into one of the many nondescript rooms.

Aether screeched as I entered, and I tensed as my gaze fell upon the chair. The Glimmer's unholy machine.

Ambassador Gloria stood beside it, her injured arm wrapped in a sling, and a smug smirk plastered across her face like a disgusting wound. Another Glimmer and a Diviner were busy fiddling with the wires coming out of its back and the console beside it.

This room wasn't as large or foreboding as the underground chamber at the Glimmer mansion, but the sterile white walls and empty space were oddly more terrifying.

Karendar and an Umber Warden made of obsidian with white lilies for eyebrows entered behind us.

"Are we ready to proceed?" Karendar asked.

The Diviner stepped away from the wires and bowed. "Whenever you are, Your Excellency."

"Then let's give our Godless friend what she wants. Corinth, strap her in. Make sure she's *comfortable*."

Quen dragged me forward. I dug in my heels, but the tiles were slippery and offered no grip. The closer he pulled me to the chair, the louder the aether screamed, as though warning me of immediate danger. I couldn't blot it out.

"Quen, please. Don't do this." Tears welled in my eyes. He really was going to destroy me. "We're partners, remember? *Quen*—"

"Partners with *some* caveats," he whispered.

My heart leaped to my throat.

In one quick movement, Quen shoved me behind him and drew his pistol from its holster. He took aim at the Diviner—no, at the machine itself—and fired a round of bullets. Sparks flew from the console with a *pop*, and the pipes coming from the back of the machine recoiled with a menacing hiss.

Smoke rose from the machine in a dancing wisp, and the screams of the aether faded.

"Stop him!" yelled Gloria, as she dove behind the safety of her Glimmer guard.

But Karendar clapped, as though this were some mild entertainment.

Quen turned his pistol on Karendar. "You'll let her and the rest of the Godless go. You'll do it now."

"Oh, Quentin. You've greatly disappointed me and our Father. What will he feel when he learns his son has strayed so far from his path?"

A warning shot blasted the wall only an inch from Karendar's head. "I'm not playing games with you, Elijah. I'll take you and Gloria hostage if I must."

Karendar hadn't flinched. "Do you think this is the only device we have?"

"You're not taking us to Kronos—"

"Kronos is where we developed them, but we brought them here for testing and general use. It occurred to me and Father that it would be safer for us to conduct our business here in HQ rather than allow random aether to pollute our home. This device is merely a prototype. Or, in this case, a test. And you've failed it spectacularly."

"What?"

"You were meant to destroy the Godless. You were meant to correct your path and redeem yourself. Yet you cannot even achieve the bare minimum of what is required of you."

"The Wardens are meant to protect Chime! Not rip souls from mortals! None of this is what the Wardens stand for—what *I* stand for! What you are doing is obscene, it is depravity—"

"You have an affection for depravity, don't you, Quentin? If you want to throw your lot in with the Godless, then we'll treat you as such." Karendar pulled a pistol from his pocket—the same odd static device Varen had—and fired at Quen.

There wasn't enough time for Quen to evade it. He fired his own shot at Karendar as he collapsed against me in a fit of spasms, dropping his pistol.

The obsidian Umber dove in front of the ambassador, and Quen's bullet ricocheted off his stone chest into the ground.

"Take them," Karendar ordered.

The Diviner pulled me away from Quen as the Umber yanked Quen to his feet. Quen tried to fight him off, but another jolt from Karendar's pistol made his limbs slacken, and the Umber practically slung Quen over his shoulder like a rag doll.

I tried to fight off my own Warden. "Get your hands off me, you prick!"

"Such filthy language." Karendar tutted as he picked up Quen's pistol and shoved it into his belt.

Gloria scowled. "You couldn't have warned me of your plan, Elijah?"

"And spoil the surprise? You were never in any danger."

"I'll be the judge of that," she snapped.

"This was only the first act, my dear, but the rest of the play promises to be far more exciting. Shall we?"

Gloria huffed and wrapped her arm around Karendar's as though they were on a date to some fancy theater production. My Diviner Warden yanked me forward, and Quen and I involuntarily followed. I tried to catch Quen's eye, but he drifted in and out of consciousness.

He was one of us now.

A Godless.

And we'd share the same fate.

We entered a double door and what lay before me made my heart stop. "Quen."

He stirred, and his eyes snapped open at what I saw. "*No.*"

This chamber must have been built weeks in advance. The walls were as sterile as the last, but the machine awaiting me was no prototype—its sleek metal chair was chrome, not rusted bronze, and the pipes and wires coming out of the back connected to the ceiling like black wings.

It looked so horribly dead.

Sitting strapped into the machine was the Amnae professor from the Academy. His eyes were open—lucid, but heavy—though a bruise swelled on his right cheek.

The Diviner Warden shoved me inside as Ambassador Karendar took center stage. "Behold our completed version of the device. Professor Burns has kindly agreed to test it."

"Eli, please," Quen begged, his voice slurring. "Let him go—"

"Actions have consequences, Quentin. You have both betrayed my trust." Karendar snapped his fingers.

A Diviner standing by the machine's console flipped a switch.

The machine hummed to life, and the aether awoke with a mournful cry.

Quen tried to lurch forward, but the Umber held him firm. "Stop this, Elijah! For god's sake, *stop this*! Father, please!" He cringed, his hands going to his head, as though some cosmic voice battered his mind.

The professor's limbs were strapped tight in the chair. His webbed fingers clenched the armrests, his translucent skin even paler.

And then he screamed.

A terrible warbling scream that drowned out the screeching aether.

Make it stop, Jinx said, her voice breaking inside my head. *You have to make it stop.*

I'm sorry, I don't know how.

In my Vesper form, what could I do? I was surrounded by Wardens and Glimmer who'd put me down in a heartbeat.

I could do nothing but stare.

Quen kicked at his Umber captor and raged, but his yells were lost to the horrific screaming of both Amnae and aether. I cringed away from the noise, unable to cover my ears.

The professor's body spasmed as the aether tore through his veins, burning his soul from the inside out. There was nothing holy about this, nothing joyous, yet both ambassadors watched with eager grins.

Minutes passed, and the screaming stopped.

The Diviner wafted away smoke coming from the Amnae's now still body. It showed no visible burns, yet his eyes were gone. The sockets empty.

And so his soul had faded into the aether.

Quen collapsed to his knees, tears streaming down his face. "Why?"

There was no kindness in Karendar's expression. "Because I love you. Is this what it'll take to correct your path? Are you willing to do what must be done?"

Quen's bloodshot eyes smoldered with absolute conviction. "Take my soul next."

Karendar sighed. "Miss Arkey, if you will?"

The Diviner yanked me forward.

"*No!*" Quen screamed and dove for me.

"Quiet him!" Karendar snapped.

The Umber slammed his fist into Quen's stomach, doubling him over. Quen retched, splattering vomit and bile onto the pristine tiles.

The aether in the air grew restless once more, though I could do nothing as the Warden dragged me to the chair. Another Diviner had already unstrapped the Amnae's lifeless body and unceremoniously dumped it onto the floor.

Save us! Jinx urged, her panic mingling with my own.

"Get off me!" I kicked for all I was worth, and even tried biting my Warden captor, but the shrieking aether throbbed inside my head and left me uncoordinated and weak.

Another Diviner grabbed my legs, and they lifted me off the ground, wrestling me into the chair as I writhed and screamed.

Straps tightened around my limbs, locking me into place.

Shit, I couldn't move. I couldn't pissing move!

My frantic gaze shot to Quen, who was dry heaving on all fours, his silver eyes wide and pinned on me.

Karendar sauntered in front of me, his lips forming a tight curl. "Any final words, Miss Arkey? Some blasphemy to take with you to the aether?"

Please, Kayl, Jinx begged. *I'm scared. He's going to rip us apart.*

432

Tears burned in my eyes. It was bad enough facing my death, but my literal other half, my twin-soul, would be facing their end as well. *I'm sorry for what I said before in the tunnels—I didn't mean to hurt you, Jinx. I know you were only looking out for us.*

You're my sister. I've always loved you. Ever since we were young, when you didn't know who I was. I loved you. You're me. My heart. Kayl, please. You've always saved us. Save us again.

I'm sorry. I can't this time.

This was the end of us.

At least we'd face it together.

Mother! Jinx called, and her fear sent me trembling. *I want to return to our mother!*

Who is our mother, Jinx? Who are we?

We are the sun and the moon and the stars, Jinx hummed in time with the aether. *We are night and day. The beginning and the end. The cosmos and everything beyond.*

"No words? No quip? No insult?" Karendar taunted. "How surprising. Very well, let's begin." He stepped back and nodded to the Diviner by the console.

"I'll do anything you ask," Quen was pleading. "Anything, Eli, just please don't."

Karendar drew Quen's pistol and placed the barrel to Quen's head.

The Diviner Warden flipped his switch, and the machine came to life with an angry hum.

It was funny how I'd thought of this machine as my salvation.

Quen had been right all along.

I didn't want him to die for me, or for my family to follow, but time had finally caught up with me. Time, in the end, cared little for my existence, whatever I was.

I supposed my last thoughts should have gone to Malk, to my family.

"I love you with everything I am."

But my gaze held the Dark Warden's.

I wasn't sorry I met him.

I wasn't sorry for the brief time we shared.

Heat burned through my veins. First, as a maddening itch, and then as sharp as needles, a thousand tiny jabs and stabs all over my skin. I tried to writhe, to shake it off, and my struggles became spasms.

The tiny jabs turned to slicing agony.

"We are the sun and the moon and the stars!" I screamed. No, not me. Jinx had taken over my body. "Do you know what we are, Elijah Karendar? Does your Dor know what we are? Chaos comes for you! We will rend you from your god!"

For the first time, Karendar's sneer slipped.

Jinx thrashed and screamed. "We are the beginning and the end!"

I felt myself being pulled away.

Jinx, I called. *Jinx!*

The screech of the aether grew clearer as it reached its crescendo. They'd always sounded like screams to me, but now I could hear them—the voices of mortals left in the dark, wailing with fear. They called out to me. And I was about to join them.

Blinding light burst from my flesh and filled the chamber.

And my heart, my twin-soul, was yanked from somewhere deep within me.

The hum of aether stopped.

YOU FINALLY REVEAL YOURSELF TO ME.

I was dead. I must be dead. Because the feminine voice that echoed inside my head wasn't mine, nor did it sound like Jinx.

Jinx?

SHE IS FREE. AS I WILL BE SOON.

What are you?

The voice laughed. *YOU DON'T RECOGNIZE ME, DAUGHTER?*

I was definitely dead. My eyes blinked open, and I expected to see nothing; darkness, death, or aether souls welcoming me to eternity with a bright banner and some balloons.

Instead, I stared at myself.

At Jinx.

She stood naked in the chamber, glowing with the silvery-blue light of the aether creatures. Only it was my face she wore, my body in aether form.

Not my body. I was still strapped to the machine. Gods, I was still here!

"Jinx," I called, my throat so sore from screaming it came out like a whimper.

She turned to me, her burning eyes moving from her hands to my face. "You hear her, don't you, sister? You hear our mother."

Then she laughed. A manic laugh which rang across the chamber.

And those deadly eyes turned to Karendar.

XXXII

The subject came to me after midday. Fifteen-year-old Diviner male. Name [REDACTED]. A student from my mnemonics class. He'd fallen from the Golden City elevator of all things and somehow survived with only a concussion and broken ribs.

A Necro healed his ribs, however the concussion left him with damaged eyesight that they couldn't fix—nor did the boy's god see fit to correct it. [REDACTED] complained of hearing voices and seeing terrifying visions. I wanted to question him further, but the Wardens insisted I wipe his memory of the event and ease his trauma. A cover-up. What had he witnessed inside the clock tower?

—W. Burns, from the journal of Professor Burns

KAYL STOOD BEFORE ME in the form of an aether creature, only it wasn't Kayl—she was still strapped to the device—and this version, this being, grinned with the disposition of a drugged-up lunatic. Her eyes didn't hold the charm of Kayl's that I was so used to—that I so adored. No, these belonged to another. To the soul once trapped inside her.

My heart fluttered. This was like the vision of my death.

"Jinx?" I ventured.

Her manic eyes turned to me. "The one and only." Kayl's voice, but not.

Almighty gods.

Elijah aimed my pistol and fired a whole volley.

Aether pulsed around Jinx like a shield, and the bullets clanged against it, falling uselessly to the floor.

"Kill her!" Elijah ordered.

Time slowed around us. A fatal mistake. With time screeching to a halt, neither the Umber nor Gloria could move, but Jinx wasn't affected. Her grin only widened as she grabbed the Diviner Warden by the device's console and her palm went to his neck.

It took only a moment for Jinx to rip out his soul. Far quicker than the device. His body fell in a heap of flailing limbs, his eye sockets empty.

Time jumped forward as Jinx's body changed from its aether form to that of a Diviner woman. I trusted Kayl not to mess with time, but Jinx? We were truly doomed.

Jinx ran her hands down her new body, lingering on parts that sent a rush of heat to my blood. "Oh, now *this* is nice. Like what you see, Corinth?" She winked at me.

"Jinx, what are you doing?" Kayl yelled.

"One moment, sister." She pointed her finger at me, then Elijah, Gloria, and the few Wardens within the room, as though marking us one by one. "If I'm going to destroy society, I'll need something classy to wear. You, golden girl." She snapped her fingers at Gloria. "Take off your clothes."

Gloria snarled. Blinding light burst from her skin.

I shielded my eyes as Jinx's figure blurred past me like a shadow. Elijah fired another shot, and I tackled his legs, knocking him into the Umber. My pistol clattered to the ground, and I fumbled for it.

The light snapped out, and I leaped to my feet, swinging my pistol at Elijah, but he was staring openmouthed at Gloria.

He'd only gone and shot her in the head, the idiot.

Blood trickled from the perfect hole between Gloria's brows, her own shocked expression mirroring Elijah. Her body tilted over and then crumpled into a heap of clothes as her soul faded into aether. Elijah had likely done the ambassador a favor in the end.

"Nice work, Karendar," Jinx quipped as she gathered up Gloria's crimson dress. "You better not have gotten any blood on this." She glanced at me. "Be a dear and kill him."

I'd trained my pistol on Elijah, who now slowly raised his hands. "You're in a building swarming with Wardens. Killing me would not be in your best interest."

Jinx pulled on the dress. "Either he kills you or I take your soul. Which is it?"

"He's right," I said, though I loathed to admit it. "Elijah makes a better hostage."

"And why should I listen to either of you Diviner pricks?"

"Jinx!" Kayl called. "Get me out of this pissing thing!"

Jinx rolled her eyes. "If anyone escapes, I'll kill you." She wagged a finger at me. "I may well kill you, anyway." She slipped on Gloria's shoes and finally went to Kayl, yanking at the straps.

"Shoot her," Elijah whispered with urgency. "You don't know what she is, she'll—"

"I think not."

"You believe this is what Father wants?" he hissed.

"Quite honestly? I don't give a damn." I cocked my pistol. Only two rounds remained, but I only needed one to send Elijah back to Dor.

Walter's body still lay stiff on the floor, and I'd almost lost Kayl—the thought of it sent tremors through my limbs, and I held my pistol steady with both hands.

Only an hour ago, I'd embraced Walter for the last time. Him, trying to silence and comfort me as I'd been wracked with screams and sobs, reminding me of the danger we faced. Me, trying my best to hold it together. A remarkable effort on my part, considering.

He'd shredded my mind quite thoroughly, pulling back years' worth of memories as though I'd experienced them only yesterday.

The carefree days at Chime's Academy.

My first kiss. My first vision of death.

The day I joined the Wardens and made an oath to serve and protect Chime.

My first mission and the fateful operation that led to the deaths of Vesper.

The months I'd suffered in a correctional facility because I'd dared question it.

And every single mistake since then.

Kayl came free and instantly bounded to my side, flinging her Warden-issued gloves to the wall. "Release the Godless," she snarled, her rage pinned on Elijah. "Or I'll throw you in that gods-damn machine."

"You won't let me play with him first?" Jinx pouted and rested her chin over Kayl's shoulder. Gods, the two of them possessed different forms—Vesper for Kayl, and Diviner for Jinx—but they were practically twins. It unnerved me.

My composure hung by a single thread, and I could barely meet Elijah's brass eyes. "Act as the lady commands, please."

Elijah's nostrils flared. "Quentin, this is madness—"

"Madness is creating a device which splits souls!" I wanted to destroy it, but with only two rounds left, I dared not waste any.

"The device was to end creatures like *her*!" His glare snapped to Jinx.

Jinx grinned with wicked viciousness.

I pressed the barrel of my pistol into Elijah's forehead. "Release the Godless. I won't ask again."

Elijah pursed his lips, but nodded at the Umber.

"Bring them alone," I ordered. "If you return with more Wardens, then his soul is forfeit, do you understand?"

The Umber stomped from the room, and the few remaining Wardens scurried after him.

Jinx sighed. "Now *that's* over with, can we have some real fun?"

"We're not maiming or killing anyone yet," Kayl said, her eyes wary as though not even she trusted her own twin.

"Look at me!" Jinx spun in a circle, twirling Gloria's dress. "I have a body. A mortal body! There's so much I want to see, to do, to eat, and to *fuck*. But that'll have to wait. You and I have work to do."

"If by work you mean protecting the Godless, then yes."

"No, silly. Don't you hear it?" Jinx put a hand to her ear. "The cries of our mother? She's calling for us. She wants us to free her."

Kayl suddenly screamed, and she sagged to the floor, her hands covering her ears.

"What did you do to her?" I snapped.

Jinx shrugged. "I didn't do anything."

"There's—There's screaming, in my head!" Kayl groaned between gritted teeth. "It's the aether—"

"It's not the aether, sister." Jinx crouched and took Kayl's head in her hands. "It's our mother. It's her screams you've been hearing all this time. I tried to block them out as best I could. One of us needed to stay sane." She let out a manic giggle. "But that's all Mother does. Day in, day out. Screaming, screaming, *screaming*. Now you know what it's like." She shoved Kayl aside and paced as Elijah and I both stared.

"Please, Jinx," Kayl moaned. "Make it stop."

Jinx came to a halt. "Oh. I will. We'll break her chains one by one. Who should we start with?" Her silvery-blue eyes turned to me. "Dor? Maybe." She tugged at her dress. "Golden girl Gildola? Eventually. But I promised I'd help you get your vengeance, sister. I didn't forget what pain Valeria put us through. Let's start with her."

"No, you can't!" Elijah spluttered.

"What are you talking about?" Kayl moaned.

Jinx grinned. "I'm going to take Valeria's soul. You hear that, Mother? I'll bring you a gift!" She laughed and then bolted from the room.

Elijah swatted my pistol aside. "Don't just stand there, you've got to stop her!"

My pistol shook in my grip. "I don't understand—"

"If that creature takes Valeria's soul, it won't just be her death! Every soul connected to Valeria will go with her! The entire domain of Eventide and *every* Vesper!"

"You can't be serious."

"Use your brain, Quentin! Why do you think we created these devices in the first place? To stop these aether creatures. It's not just Diviner souls at risk—"

"Are you saying they have the power to steal the soul of a *god*? An actual god?" I kept my pistol aimed at Elijah as I helped Kayl onto her feet.

"What am I?" Kayl demanded, her voice breaking. She leaned into my side, and I wrapped my spare arm around her waist to hold her steady. "Jinx and I—the *fuck* are we?"

"Did you never wonder how Chime could exist without a patron god when every other domain is powered by theirs?" Elijah said.

"You're saying that Chime is its own domain?" My mind raced through the possibilities. "A thirteenth domain?"

"*Yes!*" Elijah said, exasperated. "Chime is the thirteenth. If you don't stop that creature, she'll destroy everything we've built—"

"Then these aether creatures, they're mortals, and you knew—"

"Yes, they're mortals! But don't you understand? They are chaos! Destruction and madness. Their power goes beyond the control of time. They eat souls like Necro eat flesh. They cannot be allowed to exist!"

"How do you know this? Tell me the *truth*, Elijah!"

"Fine. You want the truth? This all started with *you*. On the day you fell. Not that you'll remember, Professor Burns wiped it from—"

"I remember."

"Quen?" Kayl prodded. "What do you remember?"

The memory shook through me, dislodged from the very depths of my darkest subconscious where I'd hoped it would remain. "Thirteen years ago, there was a freak accident. I somehow slipped between the Golden City elevator and platform and fell inside the clock tower. I should have died, but I landed on a service platform and survived. And I... I heard a voice." I rummaged inside my pocket and clasped my fob watch.

I'd broken it on that same fall.

On the day that'd I'd first kissed Elijah and witnessed a future yet to come to pass.

"Your screams awoke a god," Elijah said. "A god that had slept there since the dawn of time. And now she's trying to break free. These devices were Father's vision to stop the destruction He foresaw! Don't you understand? Sin is born from chaos!

"Father revealed this to me on that day you fell. He told me of my path, to serve as His mortal voice and stop these creatures. We thought if we could control sin, destroy it, then we could control chaos. Keep it locked away. But we didn't anticipate the aether we'd need to power the devices, or that chaos could force its way through them."

My hands were shaking. "You created these unholy devices to destroy sin when it has always existed? You're blind to your own sins! Creating this device likely gave rise to the aether creatures. This is a prophecy of your own damn making!"

"Corentine," Kayl gasped. "My god—she's in my head, she's called Corentine." Kayl's indigo skin turned a pale blue.

Corentine? That name felt ancient but familiar, though not even my restored memories could place it.

And I couldn't help but notice how it resembled my own name.

"Congratulations, you've found god," Elijah snapped. "Your god wants an end to existence, to life, to gain some petty revenge against the other domains. These aether leaks, these creatures—they're attacks by Corentine. But if the gods fall, then the domains fall with them. Even your Godless. They'll all fade into aether. Is that what you want?"

Elijah's words were utter lunacy. Yet I knew in the depths of my soul that he spoke true. It was no wonder the aether creatures targeted Diviner souls—we were their enemy. "I'm sorry," I said to Kayl. "I have to stop Jinx. If she threatens mortals—"

"Take me with you." Her nails dug into my arm. "If Jinx kills Valeria, then I'll lose—Malk will be lost forever."

The door burst open and the rest of the Godless tumbled inside—Harmony, Sinder, Vincent, and Miss Smith.

Thank the gods they were unharmed.

Miss Smith grabbed Kayl in a crushing hug as Harmony's gaze fell on the bodies littering the floor. "What happened here?"

"Never mind that," Sinder said, and pointed a flaming finger at Elijah. "What do we do with *him*?"

Elijah bristled. "A touching reunion, but you have far greater problems."

Sinder's fists flared with flame. "I'd say."

Kayl pushed between them. "Listen, he's right. I told you all I could change personas, but I left one detail out of my report. I was possessed by another soul, a twin who looks exactly like me, and thanks to Karendar's machine, my twin—Jinx, she's called—is now free. She has the same powers as I, and she's heading for Eventide. She's going to destroy it, and that'll mean every Vesper and Malk's soul, too. We need to stop her *now*."

"Destroy Eventide?" Harmony gasped.

"Everything she's described sounds insane, I know," I said. "I barely believe it myself, but she's speaking the truth. We'll need your help to save Eventide. Thousands of Vesper lives are at stake."

"But, it's only midday," Miss Smith said. "Eventide won't open for hours."

"Jinx is wearing a Diviner persona. She could fast-forward the Gate." I cringed as I said it because I knew that was exactly what she'd do. A being made of chaos would hold no regard for the laws of time.

"Please," Kayl pleaded. "There's still a chance we can save Malk."

"That settles it," Harmony said. "We lost Reve. I'm not losing any more of you. Are we all agreed?"

"Only if I get to destroy that machine, darling." Sinder pointed at the device.

"Done," I said.

"No!" Elijah yelled. "Destroy it, and we'll not be able to end the aether creatures!"

I holstered my pistol and patted Vincent on the shoulder. "Knock him out, will you?"

Vincent flashed me a fang. "With pleasure." He squared up with Elijah and punched him straight in the face. Elijah crumpled to the ground, unconscious. Honestly, I'd been expecting Vincent to use his Necro powers to place him in a coma, though I suppose this method was as effective.

Flame burst from Sinder's palms and we watched as Elijah's cursed device melted into molten metal. There were more waiting on Kronos. That would be an operation for another day.

"Are you one of us now?" Miss Smith asked, eyeing me cautiously.

Harmony huffed. "Corinth always has been. He's our benefactor."

I bowed my head.

How right she was.

From the moment I'd stepped foot out of that correctional facility, I'd sought to make amends. I'd not intended to inspire the Godless when I sent my notes off to Grayford, yet I'd assisted them from the shadows at every turn.

I'd scoured every file the Wardens owned on the Godless and rewrote them. Every scrap of intel, I misplaced or manipulated. Even Vincent's Warden record I'd destroyed. When I learned the Godless had made their base in Grayford, I diverted suspicion to Sinner's Row and contacted Varen to make myself useful. He'd been amenable then, and I'd been too naïve to realize he'd been using me for Elijah.

That was when I'd started wiping my memories. I couldn't afford to bring suspicion on myself, or on Varen and Grayford. That was when everything fell apart. I'd perform my song and dance for Varen, steal whatever intel I could for Harmony's Courier drop box, and then Walter would absolve me of my deeds. But each new wipe left gaps, and I slowly forgot the mission I'd tasked myself with.

And Eli... He'd taken advantage of my memory loss in so many depraved ways and forced Walter to wipe those so I'd be none the wiser.

Our entire relationship had been built on lies.

On the things he'd made me do.

I couldn't dwell on them—on the lives I'd taken, the body I'd offered behind closed doors on his command—for they brought me such shame and rage, and right now I needed a clear head.

My gaze fell on Walter. My dear friend. I'd fulfill his final wish—I'd find his daughter and ensure her safety.

Then I'd purge the Wardens, one way or another. I'd believed in them once. But under Elijah's leadership, the Wardens had allowed Chime's mortals to suffer. Had built infernal machines that split souls. Had almost ended the Godless.

I pulled my Warden badge out of my pocket and tossed it aside.

They no longer owned me.

Kayl was staring at me. "You—You're our benefactor?"

I forced a weak smile. "Chime needs Godless heathens."

Miss Smith plucked a golden flower from her brow and offered it to me. "Then thank you."

"Miss Smith, I couldn't possibly take—"

"It's not a marriage proposal, it's a gift. And my name's Dru."

I took the flower and placed it in my top shirt pocket in place of my Warden badge. "Quen, then."

Kayl wrapped her arm around mine. "We need to go."

"Yes, quite. I know these halls; I'll lead us out of HQ. We'll need to hurry; I suspect we'll face resistance. Can you manage?" My gaze moved to Harmony and then Sinder and Vincent. The Wardens had patched up the wound on Sinder's side at least, but too much exertion and his stitches were likely to burst open.

Sinder took Vincent's hand. "We'll manage."

"I'll carry Harmony," Dru offered.

Harmony balked. "You are *not* carrying me."

"Look," Kayl said, her voice agitated. "We don't have time—"

"Then cover your ears, girl," Harmony said. "I'll serenade us out of here."

Oh, dear gods.

We covered our ears as I led the march with Harmony by my side.

As I predicted, Wardens came rushing through the corridor armed to the teeth with pistols, batons, and tasers.

"Stop in the name of the Wardens!" a Leander roared and pointed a pistol at my chest.

Too late, their eyes landed on Harmony; a tiny lilac Seren with only one wing.

The leader of the Godless began to sing.

From between my fingers, her song sounded like an awful warble. I couldn't quite catch *what* she was singing, but her lyrics sounded something like *get down you fuckers*. While hardly poetic, her tone was enough to entice me.

The power of Seren song meant seduction and sedation. An irrational part of me wanted to throw myself at her feet and kiss them, and another wanted to roll over into sleep. Only the tight hold over my ears stopped those urges from taking me completely.

The Wardens, however, were lost to her dulcet charms. Some tossed their weapons aside and flung themselves to the floor, whereas others slumped to the wall, unconscious. It was comical. Instead of employing their own Seren, the Wardens had outlawed unlicensed singing in Chime and forced them into admin work. Their loss.

I led the Godless along an unmarked hall leading to a tram depot. "This is the service exit," I called. "We should be safer here."

Harmony stopped singing, and we collectively sighed with relief.

I drew my pistol. "Shadows, please."

Kayl obliged. Shadows crawled from her Vesper form and plunged the corridor into darkness.

"And light," I ordered Sinder.

Sinder's finger glowed like a candle, leading us out into a hangar. Really, I'd need to apologize for shooting him during the Grayford Incident, if he still remembered it as I now did, but this wasn't the time.

One tram remained stationed on the platform, ready to go.

"Everyone aboard," I ordered.

"A tram?" said Dru. "Are you serious? We're stealing a *tram*?"

I holstered my pistol and yanked the doors open. "The Wardens expect us to come through the main entrance and steal a carriage. They'll block off the roads. Nothing will block off a tram." And a tram would get us to the Gate a lot quicker.

Harmony climbed inside. "You heard the man, get in!"

The Godless scrambled inside the empty carriage as I headed for the driver's compartment. Shouts came from outside—maintenance staff who'd spotted us. Sinder leaned out of the door and shot warning flames to scare them off.

I swung into the driver's chair and flicked switches. The tram purred to life, the engine like a beating heart under my fingers.

Kayl leaned over my chair. "Can you drive this thing?"

"I told you; I always wanted to be a tram driver."

Steam hissed under the wheels and we lurched forward.

"Shit, Quen!" Kayl pointed ahead.

Blast it. The Wardens were closing the hangar doors, and we hadn't picked up enough speed to clear them. I glanced over my shoulder. "Sit down and grab hold of something! This'll be a bumpy ride."

The Godless scrambled into their seats. "You too, Kayl," I chided, as I reached for a lever.

Instead, she clung to my chair. "What are you going to do?"

"Play with time."

I slammed the lever up and the whole carriage jerked forward. I allowed a bubble of time to envelop the tram, but no further, and the platform blurred past us.

The hangar doors edged slowly together.

"We won't make it," Kayl gasped.

"Have a little faith." I chuckled at my own joke.

We burst past the doors, the sides of the tram scraping the metal with an almighty screech, and then we were free in the main train yard.

As soon as we cleared the yard and hurtled into Chime's streets, I slowed time to the present; going too fast down the tracks would only result in an unfortunate accident.

For a moment, I could breathe.

"Are you my Quen?" Kayl whispered. "Are you the Quen I—do you remember me?"

I reached over my shoulder and squeezed her hand. "Yes, I'm your Quen. Walter didn't remove my memories. He unlocked them. I remember everything." The first time we met in the Undercity elevator, when we dined in Sinner's Row, the bed we'd shared at the Mesmer's dream parlor, the kiss I'd so shamelessly stolen... and the harsh words I'd uttered to make her fear me, make her run. "I'm sorry I was such an utter bastard to you."

"You're forgiven. Just promise me you won't ever fuck with your memories again. Not even the bad ones."

"I promise. Not even the bad ones."

"I'm sorry we couldn't save your professor."

So was I. "How are you feeling? Is the aether affecting you?"

She rubbed her head. "It's... quiet. But I heard her before. My god. I'm not... I thought I'd escaped it, you know? I thought I was truly godless."

I knew nothing about Corentine, the supposed thirteenth god of chaos. But the Wardens had denied her mortals and tried to wipe away their existence. That alone was unconscionable.

YOU MUST STOP HER, QUENTIN.

Dor's voice yelled in my mind and I cringed. I held my head with one hand, while still controlling the tram with the other.

YOU STAND BY CHAOS AND YOU SIDE WITH OUR DESTRUCTION.

"Are you all right?" Kayl asked.

"It's Dor," I panted. "He's not pleased."

SHE WILL BE THE END OF EVERYTHING.

"What's He saying?"

"That we need to get a move on."

The tram clattered along the streets, past brick town houses and boutiques. I tugged on the horn as mortals leaped out of the way, cursing. Our track ran in a giant circle around the clock tower and the Gate; headed directly for Central Station.

We had no time to slow down.

The Gate came into view, its portal currently set to Memoria, just after one o'clock. Luckily for us, we'd missed the Kronos crossing—I didn't want Jinx to change her mind and head after Dor.

"There's a blockade," Kayl pointed out.

The Wardens of Central Station must have received word of us barging our way through the streets, and without Elijah to command them, we were Chime's greatest threat. They'd put up a whole metal barrier to stop us.

"We'll stop and run for the Gate," I called to the other Godless. "Do what you can to prevent the Wardens from chasing after us."

"Leave them to us, darling," Sinder yelled back.

I risked a glance over my shoulder. His head was dangling out the window, and he whooped a laugh as the air whistled past. Someone had wrapped a bandage around a wound on his arm. Poor Harmony was clinging to her seat with Dru. Only Vincent appeared calm and collected, a smear of blood on his lips as if he'd just fed.

"Can you stop Jinx?" I asked Kayl. "Will she listen?"

"I don't know. Do you trust me?"

I stole a glance at her silvery-blue eyes, and the depths of them reminded me of my most filthy thoughts. They brought warmth to my cheeks. "We're partners."

A smile tugged at her lips. "Apparently I am literal chaos."

"Well, I already knew that." I was overcome with the sudden urge to kiss her, despite hurtling in a tram to my likely death. Or perhaps because of it. I'd seen my death. I knew it came soon at Jinx's hands, and that thought should have terrified me.

After everything I'd done, the deaths I'd seen, the deeds I'd committed, losing one's soul was a different form of memory loss. A different absolution.

So long as I saved Eventide first. Saved Malkavaan. Protected Kayl.

The tram suddenly lurched forward as time sped up. I yanked on the brakes, but the tram ignored all resistance.

"Quen?"

"I'm not doing this!"

Aether rippled in the air as I tried to slow time, to battle against it, but whatever force was at work outmatched mine. Was it possible Jinx was *that* powerful?

Blood dripped from my nose. I couldn't stop time.

"Hold on, we're going to crash!" I yelled.

I swung out of the driver's chair and grabbed Kayl, shielding her as we dove to the carriage floor.

The tram smashed through the blockade.

Its wheels screeched as it tore along the tracks. The metal barrier scraped against the sides. The force of it flung me against the carriage wall, and I bashed my elbow with a sharp twinge. I glanced at the Godless.

They were frozen in time.

Kayl dragged me up. "We have to run."

Outside, the entirety of Central Station had stopped moving—the Wardens, the mortals running from us, the tick-tock of the clock tower.

I took Kayl's wrist and stumbled from the tram. The entire driver's cabin had folded in on itself. If Jinx hadn't stopped time, we may well have fared worse. We picked our way through the now-mangled barrier and ran for the Gate, past crowds of fearful mortals caught in mid-run.

And bodies. A whole collection of station staff and Wardens, all Diviner, littered the concourse. All without their eyes. I counted thirteen. Jinx had laid a path for us.

"Shit," Kayl mumbled.

If Jinx was this powerful, this crazy, then could I even stop her?

We raced to the Gate. Memoria stared back at us, and silhouetted in front stood Jinx. She turned to us, her silvery-blue eyes aglow with aether against the backdrop of Memoria's teal glass architecture. In Gloria's crimson dress, she looked formidable. Dangerous.

"I was worried you'd never make it in time," Jinx said with a smirk. "This'll be no fun without an audience."

"Jinx, stop this!" Kayl pleaded.

"Why? I thought you wanted to end the reign of gods? I thought we wanted the same things?"

"Not like this! If you take Valeria's soul, then you'll condemn Malk as well!"

"Isn't that better? To sleep for eternity rather than suffer at Valeria's hands day in and day out? To die once, rather than die every day?"

"No, Jinx, I don't want that!"

"No?" Jinx cocked her head. "Too bad. I didn't forget that he raped you, sister."

My eyes snapped to Kayl. "He did *what*?"

Kayl looked flustered. "He didn't—it wasn't like that! Please, Jinx. Listen to me—"

"I've been listening to your yammering my entire life. Frankly, I'm bored." Jinx raised her hands.

Time sped up around me.

The clock tower's bell clanged a distorted, harsh tone as the silvery lights of Memoria changed to the natural green of Juniper, the Fauna domain. Mortals rushed around me as they entered and came through the Gate, like blurred shadows. Behind me, more shadows and shapes whipped past, moving too fast for me to tell what they were.

I tried to halt time, but Jinx's power drowned me out, and all it did was send blood gushing out my nose. Kayl grabbed my hand, turning to Diviner, and she tried to help fight it. Even working together, Jinx outmatched us.

Kayl suddenly screamed and slumped into my arms. "Get out of my head!"

"This is what Mother wants!" Jinx cackled.

The Gate's portal switched from Juniper to Heartstone, and then began to cycle through the domains at an alarming rate—Solaris, Arcadia, Witheryn, Tempest, Obituary, Rapture. The sounds around me were a deafening mixture of metal clanging, screams, and the clock tower's bell struggling to keep up.

To the outside world, we were likely invisible, and I became aware of a barrier being set up behind us. Hours had passed in only a few short minutes. Elijah would know what was going on. He'd be trying to stop us.

The red glare of Rapture turned to Eventide's dusk, and time jolted to a stop. We had indeed been penned in by Wardens and Elijah stood there, staring at me.

At Eventide.

Jinx lowered her arms. "Now the fun begins." She leaped through the Gate.

Kayl shoved from my hold and ran after her.

Time resumed, and before the Wardens could grab me, I dove into Eventide.

33

The gods create mortal souls with their own energy, or aether, and these souls
therefore return to their god in death. Mortals are designed to obey the laws
of time; to age, wither, and die. Upon death, their body disintegrates, and
the soul merges with their god's energy.

What happens to a mortal soul then depends on one's god.

Many gods reanimate mortal souls to live out an external existence within
one's domain as officially recognized saints. Others allow their mortals to
enjoy an eternal sleep.

It is against the Covenant to reanimate a mortal and allow them back into
Chime. If singular mortals were to do so, Chime would be overrun.

Reincarnation into another mortal body, however, is an acceptable solution.
—E. Karendar, *On the Death of Mortals*

FOR THE SECOND TIME in my life, I passed through the Gate and entered
Eventide. Only this time I wanted—needed—to be here.

My lungs burned as I ran and screamed after Jinx, but she'd already
stolen a carriage and was riding up the road ahead of me. The skies darkened
with billowing storms, as though Valeria expected our arrival. I couldn't
forget this was the domain of a god, a vengeful vile god who'd tortured
Malk over and over, and would likely rip me to shreds.

Could Jinx actually take the soul of a god? A living god? Was that even
possible?

There'd been so many impossibilities these past few days, I felt certain
Jinx would be capable of conjuring more.

Quen stumbled behind me, a hand to his pistol. "There!" He pointed
to a spare carriage.

We shoved panicked Vesper out of the way as Quen threatened the
driver, making the poor man run. Then we wasted no time in climbing

aboard as Quen took the levers. The carriage sputtered to life with a puff of steam as I gripped the seat.

Then we were rattling up the dirt path to Valeria's castle.

WHY DO YOU SEEK TO STOP THIS?

I winced at the voice shouting inside me. Since Jinx had vacated my mind, I'd mourned her absence, mourned the quiet. She'd always been there, guiding me, listening to my fears. Now that she owned a body practically identical to mine, I honestly had no idea who Jinx was. My twin, yes, but what did that mean?

Gods, she'd taken lives without a shred of remorse. Ripped souls from their bodies. Would she rip mine if I stood in her way? Would she kill the Godless? My family? She certainly held no regard for Malk, and I'd loved him my entire life.

THEY DON'T UNDERSTAND YOU OR I.

Shit, Jinx may have left me, but another voice had taken her place—a loud, demanding one that I was trying my best to ignore. The first time it had spoken to me, I'd almost pissed myself.

YOU CANNOT IGNORE ME, DAUGHTER. I CREATED YOU.

"Quen," I said through clenched teeth. "Is there a way to block one's god from screaming at you?"

He glanced over to me, startled, his silver eyes laced with sympathy. "I'm afraid not. What's she saying?"

"Not a lot. Threats, complaints, the usual rantings of an all-powerful being with an ego the size of the glass elevator, I assume."

I COULD SNAP YOUR UNGRATEFUL ARSE OUT OF EXISTENCE.

Do it then! I yelled into my mind. *And be left with Jinx as your ambassador to Chime. When the Wardens finish splitting her soul and the rest of the aether creatures, they'll plug up your attempts to leak into the mortal world and you'll be left screaming alone. Good luck with that!*

SUCH DEFIANCE! THOSE CREATURES YOU SPEAK OF ARE YOUR BROTHERS AND SISTERS. WOULD YOU DENY YOUR FAMILY?

I already had a family, and it was those I chose to save. "Go faster, please."

Quen returned his attention to the road, though the carriage already huffed and puffed as fast as it could. He allowed time to speed up slightly, giving us a marginalized but controlled boost.

Blood stained his disheveled shirt, and his eyeglasses were smudged, but he was still Quen.

My Quen.

The Dark Warden who'd not only inspired the Godless, but had donated so much of his own bocs and intel to see us grow and flourish. Without Quen, we'd be nothing.

I'd be forever grateful for our partnership, even if our trust had faltered at times. But now I knew the *real* Quen. A part of me wanted to grab him and not let go. I'd almost lost him to Karendar's madness, and the thought of it opened a dark pit in my stomach.

We zipped past the mushroom houses of Vesper homes and the skies grew more ominous the closer we neared Valeria's castle. Startled Vesper farmers cried out while pointing to the rising clouds. They grabbed their children and ran for cover.

Their fears made my stomach lurch. They'd suffered Valeria's foul moods before.

I'd always thought of myself as a Vesper, had always resented what Valeria represented. For the past week, I'd believed I could be truly Godless. A free woman.

And then that freedom had been ripped from my hands.

YOU CRAVE YOUR FREEDOM WHEN I HAVE BEEN TRAPPED. MY DOMAIN TORN APART AND BUILT IN DIVINER IMAGERY.

You're a god, and I'm a mere mortal. Sort it out yourself.

Laughter rang in my head, and not my own. My god was just as mad as Jinx, it seemed, though I wasn't in on the joke. Poking the crazed temperament of a god would likely result in my death, but I'd lost my patience with beings who dangled power over me.

Why did my god turn out to be the crazy one?

Why couldn't I have been born as a gods-damn Umber?

SUCH WICKED BLASPHEMY. YOU SIN SO FREELY.

If you don't appreciate the quality of my thoughts, then you can politely fuck off out of my head. I hated having this being listening in to my mind, but I wasn't going to change who I was on Corentine's account.

She could either smite me or shut up.

We reached the road of Eventide where tithes and tributes were laid out, and then those dreadful cages. They blurred past as Quen sped up, likely on purpose so I couldn't linger on the faces trapped inside. Malk could have occupied one of them, but we didn't have time to stop and check.

The ground groaned beneath us, and the carriage spluttered to a halt.

Quen wrenched at the levers. "Blast it! Come on, you—no! It's Valeria!" He turned to me with wide eyes. "She's—"

A dark portal opened above us from out of nowhere. Gray hands reached through and swiped at me. I ducked under their reach, and they grabbed Quen.

With a single yank, they pulled Quen through, absorbing him whole.

"Quen!" I dove forward to grab him, but the portal imploded as though it had never existed, and Quen was gone.

Shit! If that bitch had killed Quen, I'd damn well take her soul myself!

I leaped off the carriage and ran for the castle. Lightning crackled above in a display of flashing purple against the now pure-black sky. Corentine's laughter echoed in my mind the farther I ran, as though she found the entire situation amusing.

Valeria's foreboding castle loomed ahead and figures stood outside in the courtyard—two stone Winged Twilights. Their massive bat wings flared open; their weapons pointed at the crimson figure approaching them.

"Jinx!" I yelled.

The Winged Twilights turned their confused growls to me and then back to Jinx.

"What in the world?" Varen called out.

Varen. My hands tightened into fists as the Winged Twilights parted and he emerged with a vicious obsidian knife in his hand. "How—There's *two* of you?" His eyes darted between me and Jinx. We were both Diviner—we looked alike. Only I still wore my cream blouse and black skirt, and Jinx was dolled up in an extravagant crimson dress.

"Where's Quen?" I demanded. "Your whore of a god took him—I want him back!"

Varen huffed a laugh. "You come into *our* domain and threaten us? Valeria is questioning Corinth, though I'm surprised to find you both here. I thought Karendar was more competent than this."

"And I thought you possessed more dignity and honor than to kiss Karendar's arse! Though I suppose you like bending over backwards and slobbering over whoever asks. Does Valeria own your will now? Or was everything you ever told me a damn lie?"

"I told you only what you wanted to hear." He sneered. "I'm Valeria's mortal voice. Her will is my will. Her desires are my desires. Though you forget where you are. If you were Valeria's, she'd be ripping you apart—"

"Then thank the gods I belong to neither of you."

"What god would want you?"

I swallowed a laugh. If only he knew.

Jinx examined her nails. "Can I maim this one, sister?"

I crossed my arms. "Go ahead."

She grinned and clenched her hands into claws.

Varen shuffled back. "Kill them!"

The Winged Twilights stalked toward us. They were humongous gargoyles made of solid black stone. I was taller than average, but these were twice my size! Even unarmed, they could crush us to death, and they each carried scepters curved into the shape of a moon's crescent. We, on the other hand, carried no weapons, save the ability to control time itself. But what effect would time have on stone?

Jinx bumped into me and took my hand. "Are you thinking what I'm thinking?"

"That we're about to die horrible deaths?"

"You have *no* imagination." She shot out her spare hand and a bubble of pulsing aether surrounded the two gargoyles. They didn't move. Didn't blink.

Gods, she'd trapped them in a pocket of time.

"How are you doing that?" I spluttered.

"Once you understand how aether is connected to all living things, it's quite easy." She twisted her wrist, as though turning a knob.

The gargoyle's shiny silver blades rusted, and then their bodies began to crumble. Dust fell from their skin in flakes as hundreds of years' worth of time passed by in the blink of an eye. Time eroded their bodies into a pile of rubble.

I'd never heard of a Diviner using their power in such a way, and I didn't know whether to be impressed or utterly terrified.

"Wha—What *are* you?" Varen spluttered, the knife in his grip shaking.

Jinx smirked. "We are the end of everything. The end of *you*. Ticktock!" She dove at him.

Varen thrust his knife, narrowly missing Jinx's arm as she twisted out of the way. She threw her hands open, as though scattering sand, and Varen stopped dead in his tracks, his body twitching, his eyes rapidly blinking.

Jinx wrenched the knife from his fist and offered it to me. "Your turn."

Varen's eyes only widened, but his mouth remained clenched shut. She'd frozen his body, somehow, but he could still comprehend his predicament.

The knife weighed heavy in my hands.

I'd never wanted to call myself a killer. That wasn't the Godless's style. We existed to help free mortals from tyrannical rule, not to step into the gods' shoes and dictate their fate ourselves. I'd always believed that Varen understood that, that he helped shelter us because he too wanted to be free of his god's shackles.

Valeria had enslaved him. Ripped off his wings. Forced him to act as her voice while throwing Vesper to the gutter.

Yet all the time he'd been willfully kissing her feet...

Jinx took my shoulders and steered me closer to Varen. "Go on. Remember what a conniving traitor he is? How he sold you and Malk to Karendar? And your Time Boy?"

"Why did you do it?" I asked him. "Why did you sell off Elvira? Why condemn her to a workhouse? I thought you loved her!"

Jinx snapped her fingers, and he sucked in a breath. He could move his head, but the rest of his body remained stuck. "My Queen!" he screamed. "Please, my Queen!"

"Pathetic," Jinx snarled. "Look at him. He's nothing more than a sniveling coward." She snatched the knife from my hand and pointed it an inch from his nose. "Renounce your god or I'll stab your eyes out and *then* steal your soul."

I stared at her, appalled. "For god's sake, Jinx—"

"Maybe if you Godless had spent less time stalking Glimmer and more time stabbing ambassadors, none of us would be in this mess!" she snapped.

I grabbed her wrist and tried to wrestle the knife free.

A thunderclap boomed in the sky above us, and the dark clouds suddenly grew larger. They descended in a thick fog and I gasped as we were swallowed in darkness. A gust of wind knocked me off my feet. I fell on my side, bruising my upper arm. From somewhere beside me, I heard Jinx curse as she was also thrown.

The fog lifted, and I found myself inside Valeria's castle. I scrambled to my feet and my heart sank at the sight before me.

Valeria sat on her obsidian throne, her long black nails scraping into the stone, her dark eyes lit by the many glittering treasures piled all around her. Varen stood by her side, a smug smirk on his lips.

And at the bottom of the dais were Malk and Quen. Both on their knees.

My gaze darted between them. Malk sat naked, blood dripping from scratches across his chest, his own gaze pinned on the floor. Quen's eyes met mine. He sported a nasty bruise under his left eye, but was otherwise unharmed.

Shit, we'd gone and pissed off a god.

Valeria snapped her fingers and six Winged Twilights appeared out of thin air, summoned with a single thought. They surrounded her throne, each wielding a sharp crescent-shaped scepter.

"Who are you to *dare* invade my domain?" Valeria bellowed. "On which god's behalf do you act? Gildola? Dor?" Fury burned in her dark eyes and they raked over Jinx's body, taking in her Glimmer dress and Diviner persona.

Jinx still held Varen's knife, and she ran a finger along the blade's edge. "Corentine."

The name of our god sent a howling wind rattling through the castle's rafters.

Valeria studied us both. "That's not possible."

Quen glanced over his shoulder. "You know of her?"

Valeria's eyes blazed. "What has Dor done? Speak truths to me, Quentin Corinth!"

"Dark lady, I assure you I have no knowledge of a thirteenth god—"

"No, because Corentine is supposed to be *gone*! Forgotten! How can she be awake? What does she want with me?"

Jinx giggled. "She wants your soul, silly."

VALERIA WAS ALWAYS A SELFISH BRAT, WANTING TO OWN THIS AND THAT. I GAVE HER AN ENTIRE DOMAIN AND THAT WASN'T ENOUGH.

I cringed at the voice. *You gave her a domain?*

DOR AND I CREATED THE GODS. HE IS THEIR FATHER. I, THEIR MOTHER. THEY ARE OUR CHILDREN, AS YOU ARE. UNRULY WHELPS WHO TURNED ON ME BECAUSE HE ORDERED THEM TO.

My mind reeled at the implication.

Greater gods that birthed lesser ones.

Gods who'd turned their family dispute into a battle for the domains.

Jinx winked at me, as though she'd been privy to our mental conversation. "Our dear mother wants what's hers. Your arse has been keeping her chair warm long enough."

Valeria rose from her throne in the slow, considered movements of a hunter. As she stepped from the dais, her height drew taller and her black nails elongated into deadly claws. "This is *my* domain, you impudent child. You have no power here." She placed a single claw under Quen's chin, forcing him to look up. "I grant you the single courtesy of leaving my domain forever. If not, I will destroy Dor's child."

Jinx shrugged. "I don't care for Dor's children."

"*Jinx!*" I hissed, but she ignored me.

Valeria turned to me then, a cruel smile splaying across her black lips. "You appear the same, but your souls are different. I remember when Quentin Corinth brought you here, and we traded in souls." She released Quen and instead her claws curled around Malk's shoulder, the sharp tips digging into his skin, drawing a trickle of blood. He didn't flinch. Gods, he didn't even make a sound. "You begged for this one, didn't you? I would offer another trade—I will release his soul if you forsake Corentine and kneel before me."

"Don't you dare!" Jinx snapped at me.

My heart thumped as my stare flicked between Varen and Malk. I couldn't trust Valeria's word—Malk's soul would always be hers. Could she even release him? What would he become then?

Malk's beautiful blue eyes lifted to mine, so full of exhaustion and pain. I could save him.

HE'LL NEVER BE FREE AND NEITHER WILL YOU.

Because gods like you enslave us! Serving you or Valeria—what difference does it make in the end?

WE WANT THE SAME THINGS. AN END TO THE GODS.

Could that be true?

"Fuck this!" Jinx yelled. She raised Varen's knife and charged at Valeria.

Shadows burst from the god, plunging me in darkness. Shit, I couldn't see a damn thing! I stumbled and was then blinded by silvery-blue light.

Jinx had returned to her aether form, her skin radiating with raw energy. Her light battled against Valeria's shadows, pushing the darkness back enough for me to see.

Quen was on his feet, pistol in hand and tracking both Valeria and Jinx as they fought each other in a flurry of swiping claws and the blade of Varen's knife.

Shit! What in god's name was Jinx thinking?

Varen had dug a silver knife out from the piles of treasures scattered around the throne and stalked behind Quen. Before I could shout a warning, Malk launched himself at Varen, tackling him to the ground. Coins flew in the air with a tinny *clink*.

The pair of them wrestled, but Varen didn't stand a chance against Malk's younger physique.

Malk grabbed Varen's neck and slammed his skull against the dais. Blood and teeth splattered the pristine piles of gold and silver as Malk raged with inhuman strength, slamming Varen's face over and over.

I stared, unsure what to do or whose side to fight for.

The six Winged Twilights flew after Malk. He scampered back while trying to fight them off, leaving Varen's unconscious form to bleed over the silver.

They ignored Quen altogether, deeming him the lesser threat. Instead, bats swooped from the rafters and flapped in a panicked whirlwind. They dove after Quen, attacking him with teeth and claws. He crouched into a protective stance, dropping his pistol as he covered his face against their relentless assault.

"Is that all you have?" Jinx broke from Valeria's hold and stood in a brawler's stance. Deep, bloody cuts lined her arms, staining her dress, and her chest rose in rapid panting. But she didn't back down, nor give up Varen's knife.

Valeria nursed a single cut on her arm. A lucky hit. The flesh knitted itself together with the skill of a Necro. "I offered you a courtesy, child of chaos. Now I offer you obliteration."

The god snarled, and her teeth lengthened into deadly fangs. Her dress tore in half, exposing her breasts, as her height grew and her legs fused together into shining black scales.

I covered my mouth and gagged as Valeria's lower body transformed into that of a snake's tail. Gods, her head almost reached the top of her castle.

What the fuck were we supposed to do now?

Jinx leaped at the tail and was promptly swatted aside. She flew through the air with a scream, dropping Varen's knife, and landed with a thump against the castle's walls.

I ran for Quen and snatched his pistol, taking aim at Valeria.

The Vesper god bared her fangs in a horrid hiss.

I squeezed the trigger.

A single shot pierced Valeria's stomach. Blood squirted from the wound, splattering the tiles in a rope of thick black blood. But the god merely laughed as her wound stitched itself together until not even a scar remained.

And then she came at me.

I turned and ran.

Her tail whipped under me, knocking me over. I fell onto nothing as Valeria scooped me into her embrace, her cold scaly tail wrapping around my torso, pinning my arms uselessly to my sides as she dangled me dangerously in midair. Shit!

Her face came close to mine, her fangs almost the entire length of my head. "Devouring you would be too easy," she hissed with the flick of a forked tongue. Her icy breath smelled rotten. "I want Corentine to feel the life I crush from your bones."

I glanced frantically at Jinx. She crawled to her feet, dazed. The fight had been literally knocked from her.

"Let her go, Valeria," Quen commanded. He'd escaped from the bats, though his face bore scratches and his eyeglasses had cracked. He pointed his pistol at the god. "Harm her, and you'll be breaking the Covenant!"

"You invaded *my* domain! The Covenant was already broken. I've seen Varen's mind, Quentin Corinth. Your Wardens care not for you, nor for Corentine's children."

Valeria's grip tightened, the scales of her snake form digging into my skin, and I sucked in a strangled breath.

I squirmed and kicked out, but Valeria's hold only constricted further, squeezing my limbs together until I couldn't swallow enough air to fill my lungs.

Something cracked in my chest. I let out an agonized howl.

"Dark lady, please!" Quen begged.

Fuck, it hurts! She's killing me! I need Jinx!

YOU CAN STOP THIS.

How?

TOUCH HER. TAKE WHAT IS OWED.

My palm rubbed against cold scales, and my form instantly changed from Diviner to Vesper. Shadows burst from my skin as Valeria squeezed them out, but all it did was hide the faces of those I loved—Malk, Jinx, Quen.

Then I felt the tug.

I'd never once followed that tug, not after Lady Mae. I didn't know what place it would lead me. But my breath now came in painful wheezes.

If I didn't do something, I'd have no breath left.

Tingles shot up my arm, and pure aether burned in my veins. It flooded my blood with a pleasurable warmth that masked the pain in my chest.

And then voices spoke in the back of my mind.

Thousands of voices came alive all at once. Men, women, children, alive and dead. Thousands of Vesper. I could sift apart the individual essences of each soul—their joys, their fears, the dreams which kept them alive. Their prayers. In them I found two I recognized intimately; Malk and Varen.

And then a feminine essence came to me. One that had once clothed me, fed me.

Elvira.

She'd entered my life for only a brief moment in my timeline, and yet in death, her soul found mine. It smiled at me.

I knew you were special, little one, Elvira's soft voice spoke. *When I took your hand and your skin changed to match mine. I thought I'd imagined it, that it was some trick of the Undercity lights, but I saw who you were then. I see who you are now. Free me,* Elvira begged. *Free us all.*

The Vesper gathered in my soul. With one final tug, I pulled the chain connecting us.

Valeria screeched. She dropped me like I'd burned her, and I fell to the ground with a painful thud.

Quen ran to my side and held me in his arms, his eyes scanning my broken body. "Where are you hurt? Kayl, please, talk to me."

I hacked a breath. Every movement pissing *hurt*. "I'm—I'm still alive, I think."

"I am darkness! I am *night*!" Valeria shrieked. "What have you done to me?" Her snake form writhed, and I stared in wonder as tiny flakes of shadow peeled away from her flesh.

"Holy saints," Quen whispered.

The Vesper god screamed. Shadows burst from her once more, but each one ripped a piece free—an ear, an arm, her hair, chunks from her flesh. One by one, the shadows ate away at her body until all that remained was dust.

Valeria was gone.

The Winged Twilights had faded with her.

I stared at my hands. They were no longer the indigo of Vesper, but glowed with the silvery-blue of aether, my fingertips a pastel pink.

There could be no denying what I was now.

I'd killed a god.

How—How had I killed a gods-damn fucking *god*?

Jinx whooped a laugh. "You did it! You sure showed that vile bitch!"

Dark purple dust fell from the ceiling as the castle began to crumble. The entire sky turned from black to gray, as though I'd literally drained the color from the world.

With Quen's help, I stood on unsteady legs, my gaze pinned on Malk.

Dust fell from his skin, too.

No. Gods, no. Not Malk.

"Malk!" I screamed and staggered forward, my lungs burning with every step.

The desperation in his blue eyes had lifted, and in his place the Malk I knew and loved had come back to me. He reached out. "Kay—"

And then he was gone.

His entire existence collapsed into dust.

"*No!*" I fell to my knees. My fingers dug through the pile of dust as though I could spark them back to life. "How do I fix this?" I turned to Jinx. "How do I pissing fix this?"

Her cool silvery-blue eyes met mine. "You just did. He's free."

I launched myself at Jinx, though I only made one step. The pain in my ribs tore another scream from me, and I would have collapsed if Quen hadn't caught me.

"We have to go," Quen urged. "Eventide is no longer stable."

"Time Boy's right," Jinx said. "We don't want to be trapped here when this place goes *pop*."

I spared one last glance at where Malk had stood.

I'd thought I could save him.

I'd loved him with everything I was.

Now he was truly gone.

XXXIV

Diviner children are created at an age when they possess an aptitude for time and the wisdom not to misuse it. Of all the elements in the universe, time is the most prominent and most delicate.

The rhythm of time flows like mortal blood. The many branches or capillaries can be amended or cut, but the arteries and veins are set.

Without them, time cannot flow at all.

Quite simply, time is a heartbeat.

The past and future rise and fall with one's pulse. Each beat corresponds to a moment in time. Once a beat is observed, so it is set. These laws must be obeyed by all mortals, otherwise the veins become blocked and the system suffers from cardiac arrest.

Without time, there would be no rhythm to mortal life.

There would be chaos.

—H. Bezel, *Horology and the Laws of Time*

EVENTIDE WAS FALLING APART all around us.

I didn't have time to dwell on what had just happened, or the implications. If we didn't get out of Eventide now, we could well be trapped here for eternity and fade with it. Kayl's look of horror and pain reflected my heart. Whatever happened next, I knew this wasn't her fault.

Though I knew exactly what would happen next.

I'd seen it in my visions.

I helped guide Kayl to the nearest carriage as Valeria's castle collapsed behind us in a miasma of purple dust, taking the remnants of Malkavaan, Varen, and their god with it. Kayl wheezed with each step. The rasps coming from her did not sound good—we needed to move fast, if only to get her to Vincent.

Jinx climbed in next to me with a spring in her step, and I couldn't help my flare of irritation. This was *her* fault. Her jovial energy made my teeth grind. This entire world was dying, its mortals wiped out in a single breath, and her sister could well be slowly suffocating from a punctured lung.

"Hurry it up, Time Boy," Jinx said with a leering grin. Her silvery-blue aether skin clashed with Gloria's crimson dress, though I noted the horrid scratches cut deep into her arms, still leaking with blood. They'd both taken the form of an aether creature—a fact I was still struggling to wrap my head around—but why hadn't their god healed their wounds?

"I'm twenty-eight years old, I'll have you know." I yanked at the lever and sent our carriage clattering along the dirt road.

The sky rippled ominously as more dark particles rained down, poisoning everything they touched with death. Ahead of us, mushroom trees still bloomed, though Vesper ran from their homes with panicked shrieks.

I glanced behind me. Valeria's castle was gone, and the road was disappearing at an alarming rate, leaving nothing behind but empty space. The gray nothingness rolled behind me in one great wave, and when I glanced back to the Vesper, they were gone.

Utterly gone.

"Faster, you idiot," Jinx snapped. "Use your time powers."

"Reality is literally collapsing around us. Speeding up the future may well have an adverse reaction."

"You're scared, is that it?"

"Of course I'm bloody scared."

"Leave him be," Kayl moaned. She leaned into my side and her breathing came out in shallow rattles. I didn't understand quite how her chaos powers worked—if she'd absorbed Valeria's soul, did she now possess the power of a god? Did she have the power to heal herself? To save Eventide?

I wouldn't mourn Valeria. Nor Varen. Not even Malkavaan, for the pain he'd put Kayl through, but every Vesper was now being subjected to the same fate. None of them deserved this. I tried not to linger on the piles of dust we passed inside the empty cages.

Perhaps Jinx had been right.

Was it better to not exist than to suffer the whims of a cruel god?

Color drained from Eventide. The fields we passed turned a dull gray. Even the bright purple mushrooms and the deadly red-and-white spotted caps along the roadside faded and then blew away as particles on the wind. Kayl buried her head in my shoulder, and her trembling wasn't just from her injuries.

Jinx bounced up and down in her seat. "Come on, we're almost there!"

"Hold still, for pity's sake!"

The Gate loomed ahead. The portal rippled with Chime's lanterns at night, and the sight of it made my heart soar. Though even from here I could make out the barrier erected on the other side through the shimmering aether. We weren't in for a welcoming return.

I wrenched the carriage's lever to a halt and quickly leaped down, swinging around to Kayl's side. "I'll catch you."

Kayl practically fell from the seat. She was heavier than she looked and sagged in my arms, but I didn't have time to be gentle. I hoisted her to her feet, and though she winced the entire way, I dragged her to the Gate, my feet kicking through piles of Vesper who had once breathed.

Jinx waited by the portal. "There's trouble ahead. Your friends, Corinth?"

I whipped out my pistol. "Former colleagues, I'll say. Take her." I passed Kayl into Jinx's arms. "I'll deal with them. Find the Godless and get her to Vincent."

"Quen," Kayl rasped. "Come with us—"

"If the Wardens catch you, they'll march you straight to Kronos—"

"What if they catch you?"

"They'll offer me a cup of tea at least." I glanced at the rolling gray skies headed straight for us. It was now or never. "Listen, Walter has a daughter named Ilona Burns. She studies mnemonics at Memoria University. Please find her and keep her safe. Remember, her name is *Ilona*."

Kayl broke from Jinx's hold and staggered to me, grabbing my arm. "Don't do this—"

"I promised Walter." I cupped her cheek. One last tender touch that wasn't mine to take, but in this moment, I needed her strength more than ever. "Follow after me and run."

I steeled myself for what was to come and stepped through the Gate.

And stopped dead in my tracks.

An entire line of Wardens had me penned in with my back to the Gate. They were a mix of Diviner, Ember, Leander, and Umber Wardens, all armed with either a pistol or taser pointed right at me.

Standing there in front of them was Elijah, a nasty bruise blackening the bridge of his nose.

His brass eyes widened at the Gate. "What have you *done*?"

Behind me, Jinx had dragged Kayl through, and the Gate sputtered. Aether sparks *snapped* and *popped* around it as the domain of Eventide turned into a blank gray canvas.

Then the Gate's power blipped out. The portal vanished completely, showing nothing but the back of Central Station.

Saints.

This had never happened, not *once*, during the entire history of Chime.

Even when I'd fallen from the glass elevator as a boy, the station staff had merely diverted the elevator's power to rescue me, leaving the Gate to flow uninterrupted.

The clock tower rang with the turn of the hour, but its call was distorted, wrong, and the hands turned with erratic abandon.

Once, twice, thrice it tolled, going through every hour. It should have stopped at eleven, for the domain that came after Eventide, but it ran straight past it to twelve.

And then the thirteenth bell tolled.

Just like in my visions.

The aether lanterns of Central Station flickered and burst, casting spots of shadow across the square. A tram careened across the street, completely out of control, as mortals screamed and dove from the carriage, and more ran out of the way.

"Oh shit," Kayl gasped. She pointed above us to the clock tower.

The glass elevator from the Golden City was falling down at an alarming rate. It must have lost control. "Eli!"

He followed my eye. "Diviners, go! Slow it down! Fetch any Zephyr you can!"

The Diviner ran for the clock tower, but they were held back by an invisible force. Aether rippled around us, and tears opened within the fabric of reality.

Silvery-blue creatures stepped onto Chime's streets. Dozens of them. More and more pouring through the aether in the air.

Jinx cackled. "Chaos is breaking free!"

The Diviner turned their powers on the aether creatures, but they had no effect. Neither did their pistols or tasers. The creatures were upon them in an instant, and they ripped the Wardens' souls clean from their bodies with a single touch.

Zephyr flew out of harm's way and their wings beat frantically as they raced to meet the falling elevator. Seren swooped to safety as Glimmer leaped from the open doors into waiting Zephyr arms, and my heart leaped with them.

But there weren't enough Zephyr to catch them all.

Glimmer fell like dying stars.

I shielded my eyes as the elevator came crashing down. Glass shattered with a deafening clatter, scattering deadly shards across Central Station. Mortals ran for their lives, though some unwittingly ran straight into the arms of the aether creatures.

It was chaos. Pure, unadulterated chaos.

Chime was my home.

But I could do nothing to save it.

"How do you like your city now, Ambassador Karendar?" Jinx taunted.

"Arrest them!" Elijah yelled, pointing a damning finger at me.

I aimed my pistol. "Go," I snapped, and my eyes met Kayl's. "Stop this, if you can. Please. Too many mortals will die."

Kayl's throat bobbed, and she nodded.

The Wardens marched toward us. I yanked time to a stop, pausing the Ember, Umber, and Leander Wardens, and allowing Jinx and Kayl to run through the empty portal and away to Central Station's maze of storage units, though I knew stopping time would allow the aether creatures to run rampant, too.

Elijah and the other Diviner Wardens fought against me, and our power butted heads, sending fluctuations of time around the station concourse.

"Stop fighting me, Quentin!" Elijah yelled. "You've seen what they're capable of! What they've done! Is this the future you want for Chime? For innocent mortals to die? You are a Warden!"

Was a Warden.

Though no, it wasn't the future I wanted, and that was the great joke; time couldn't be altered once set on its path, and I'd seen this moment over and over in my dreams. I'd wiped my memories just to be free of it.

Time never cared for what I wanted.

STOP THIS MADNESS, QUENTIN, Dor's voice rang inside my mind.

This is the flow of time, Father. If you didn't want this future, you should have corrected it yourself.

EVEN TIME CANNOT BEST CHAOS. MORTALS WILL DIE IF CORENTINE'S CHILDREN REMAIN FREE.

Ah, yes, the thirteenth god you failed to mention. Like it or not, these aether creatures are mortals. You denied their existence. Is it no wonder they despise us? That they fight for their freedom? You created these devices to split their souls. How could you?

TO END THEM. THEY ARE CHAOS—

And what is chaos?

THE SOURCE OF SIN AND DESTRUCTION. YOU HAVE SEEN IT. THE END OF VALERIA. MORE DOMAINS WILL FALL UNDER CORENTINE'S HAND. SHE WILL DESTROY EVERYTHING.

I didn't doubt Jinx's ambition; she was clearly insane, but I wouldn't let Kayl or the Godless fall because of her.

YOU FRATERNIZE WITH THE ENEMY. CORRECT YOUR PATH.

Correct my path? This *was* my path.

YOU ARE A WARDEN. YOU WILL PROTECT CHIME—

No.

You expect me to commit deeds in your name, Father, yet you did nothing to protect me from him—from the things he made me do. You must have been aware.

He locked me inside a correctional facility and tortured me. Beat me. Raped me. I killed innocent mortals and allowed more to suffer because he commanded me to. All to prove my loyalty, to purify my thoughts and cure my so-called sins.

What were my sins, Father? What were my sins compared to his?

Or yours?

WATCH YOUR THOUGHTS. ELIJAH ACTED TO PROTECT CHIME.

To protect Chime? I wanted to laugh. *All of this—this chaos—is because of his actions! Eventide would not have fallen if not for his meddling. And I was nothing more than a puppet to him. He pulled my strings this entire time. And you let it happen!*

I'd thought I loved him. Maybe I had, once, back when we studied at the Academy.

Elijah had used me. Abused me.

I'd willingly prostrated myself to him. He'd manipulated my mind, my memories, so I wouldn't know better, so I'd *want* it. Even in those darkest depths when I doubted, when I hurt, my own mind had convinced me otherwise.

But no more.

No more, Father.

STOP THIS PETULANCE, CHILD, OR I WILL TAKE BACK YOUR SOUL.

Then take it, damn you.

Blood ran from my nose and a sharp pain built in my head. I wouldn't be able to hold time for much longer. My pistol only contained one bullet, but I knew from my visions it would strike true.

Time rippled across the space between us, twisting and distorting with the aether.

The Wardens aimed their weapons.

"Don't," Elijah warned. "Think, Quentin, please *think!*"

Dor must have seen this moment coming.

Perhaps it had been one final test that I was about to fail.

"I remember what you made me do!" I yelled, my voice cracking. "You made me shoot her. I *killed* her!" The Vesper woman we'd recovered from Grayford five years ago. Elijah had forced Walter to block those memories. But I remembered her now.

I remembered her name.

Elvira.

The Wardens had dragged her to the same correctional facility as I. They'd tortured the confessed sins out of her. Both Elijah and Varen had sanctioned it—*watched* it.

Then they'd brought her to me.

She was an illegal, an unapologetic apostate who'd escaped from one of the Glimmer workhouses. I knew the Covenant, I knew Chime's law. She was sentenced by Varen to return to her god, and I was ordered to carry it out.

Not a trip to Eventide, but a bullet to her brain.

A test of my loyalty. To prove I was still a Warden.

There'd been many more tests since.

I deserved my name. Dark Warden. I welcomed the death it brought me.

For I would never be a saint.

"I tried to cure you of sin, Quentin! I tried to save your soul! No one will ever love you as I do!"

"You don't know what love is."

I squeezed the trigger, and my last bullet pierced Elijah's head.

For a moment, time hung around me, squeezing me with such familiar warmth, as though pleased fate had finally won out. My hand instinctively went into my pocket, to the broken fob watch I carried, and my thumb caressed the imperfect brass.

I glanced to my side. To Kayl, running ahead with Jinx. Our eyes met. Her beautiful aether eyes so full of horror yet so wonderful, even now.

We existed in different worlds, across eons that would never meet again. I shouldn't have kissed her, but I was glad for the memory, for the brief time we'd shared.

In her company, time had lost all meaning.

I only wished I could have been a man worthy of her respect. Godless and brilliant.

Time rushed back to the present. The Wardens were staring at Elijah as his body fell and then vanished into the aether. Returned to Dor.

Pain lanced through my spine, as though a spear had split me in half.

My lips twisted in a soundless scream.

I felt my own soul being yanked from existence.

And darkness found me once more.

35

*The clock tower pushes an immense amount of electrical energy from the
steamworks up to the Golden City while pumping waste down to the
Undercity through the pipeline. Leaks can be of an electrical or biochemical
nature and must be treated with the highest-level priority.*

*Faults which interrupt the flow of power can short-circuit and lead to
blackouts within the Golden City and Central or potentially disrupt the
elevators and Gate travel.*

*The Gate itself is a rotating mechanism invented by Diviner and Zephyr
engineering to keep the flow of power constant.*

*I've often wondered how the steamworks can generate such massive
quantities of energy to power Chime. Do the gods lend enough of their
power? Steam surely isn't enough.*

—Dr. Z. Finch, on Clock Tower Maintenance and Repair

"QUEN!" I SCREAMED.

JINX slammed her hand over my mouth, muffling my cries. But no one
would hear it over the mortals yelling and running from the aether
monsters.

I'd watched him shoot Karendar. Watched the ambassador's body fade
to nothing. Quen's silver eyes had met mine. So full of hope, it made my
heart break.

Then his back had arched in agony, as though struck by lightning. He'd
vanished into the aether, his clothes, eyeglasses, and pistol falling to the
ground. The golden flower Dru had gifted him fluttered to the station
gutter.

The Wardens hadn't even shot him. Dor must have taken his soul.

He'd been one of us.

A Godless.

And I'd barely gotten to know the real Quen, the Quen who'd defied his god, defied the Wardens to help a group of apostates. I'd never gotten a chance to thank him.

I'd lost him, too.

"He's gone, he's—" I stifled a sob.

"Are you really crying over a Diviner?" Jinx asked with such callous indifference. "You meant nothing to him; you know that, right?"

I shoved her away. "We were partners!" A sharp pain spasmed in my chest, and I bent over, clutching my abdomen. "I—I could have saved him!"

"Like you're in any state to save anyone."

"*You* could have!" I spat out.

Jinx's eyes flashed in irritation. "He did the pathetic chivalrous thing of protecting you. That was his choice to play hero. And if we don't get moving, the Wardens will find us, and then his pointless death will be even more pointless."

I wiped the tears running down my cheeks. I hated her. Hated her spiteful tongue. Hated that she was right.

Quen had asked me to help the Amnae professor's daughter. Ilona. I wouldn't forget her name. *Ilona*. I'd carve it into my arm if I had to. But first, I'd save this damn city.

I owed him that much.

Jinx took my hand, and I staggered onward to wherever she led me, though I could barely walk. Any movement felt like grinding agony in my chest. Even to breathe and talk.

We moved away from Central Station, around the warehouses to the back. There were no station staff here, though we passed the occasional pile of dust. These couldn't have been taken by aether creatures. No. These were once Vesper.

Shit. Not even the Vesper of Chime had escaped.

I sagged against a crate and wheezed. "I can't—I can't go on." Cold sweat poured from my brow from the exertion of living. I couldn't even close my eyes to rest, because all I saw in my own darkest depths was Malk's body turning to dust. Not just him.

Every Vesper in existence had been wiped out because of me.

Because of Corentine.

I'd lived my entire life believing myself to be a Vesper. I should have died with them.

And now aether creatures were stalking the city I loved, ripping souls from innocent mortals, and I had no idea how to stop it.

Jinx leaned her arm against the crate. She'd transformed into a Diviner again—she must have brushed against Quen at some point, for I hadn't noticed, and that thought sent a rush of anger in my stomach. "Wardens are looking for us. Gotta keep moving."

"I can't. It's too far."

"Get a grip. We only need to get around the clock tower."

"What? I thought—the Godless safe house," I rasped.

Jinx scrunched her nose. "Why would we go there?"

"Why wouldn't we? I need—I need Vincent!"

"Forget the Godless." Jinx placed a hand on my shoulder. "We don't need them."

"They're my family—"

"*We're* family. We have a mother. Don't you want to meet her?"

Not particularly, no. "How?" Come to think of it, *where* was Corentine trapped? The steamworks? Perhaps if I could meet her, as much as I really didn't want to, I could find a way to stop aether creatures from ripping Chime apart. I could fulfill my promise to Quen.

"I told you. The clock tower."

I gawked at her. "A god has been hiding inside the clock tower all this time?"

"Where else would she be? Though, with all these Wardens stalking around, I don't know how we're gonna get up there. And you're useless—"

"It *hurts*, Jinx—"

"Yeah, I know. You're probably bleeding internally. The quickest way to return to our god is through death. Maybe I should speed up the process." The glint in her eye turned predatory.

"*What?*"

She tapped her chin. "Oh, wait, no—Mother says I can't kill you. Sadly, she doesn't have her full powers to yank you outta your body or find you among our siblings—and you're carrying Valeria's soul, so we can't risk losing you. Guess we'll need to do this the hard way."

"Thank you for not killing me, I suppose."

"You're welcome." Jinx placed her arm around my waist. "Now quit whining and get moving."

I leaned into Jinx as she led me around stacked crates behind the clock tower where the elevator to the Golden City awaited. I'd watched the whole elevator come crashing down, tossing aside mortals. Diviner and Glimmer had fallen to their doom.

Those the Zephyr couldn't save had faced a quick death and left behind their clothes as their souls returned to their god. The bodies which remained had been taken by the aether creatures—by my own siblings. *Gods.*

Those who survived had limped away, joining the throng of mortals running for their lives. The screams had quieted as Central Station emptied, leaving the Wardens to battle with my aether relatives.

I could only hope the Godless had escaped. There was nothing they could do against soul-sucking creatures. Nothing I could do, either.

Only Corentine could stop this madness.

That was the reason I allowed Jinx to drag me onwards. I was in no fit state to fight her off and run regardless, but my twin was withholding information from me, and I needed answers. I needed to learn Corentine's measure for myself, to discover exactly what fate she planned for Chime, and put an end to it. I needed to know if her promise of a Godless world was worth destroying the entirety of the Vesper.

If it was worth sacrificing Malk and Quen.

Three Diviner Warden males stood on guard outside the service entrance to the elevator. Bodies were scattered around them—Diviner, I realized. Their eye sockets empty, their mouths slack. I pulled on Jinx's arm.

"Relax," she said. "They're family."

As I neared, their eyes turned to us. The silvery-blue of aether.

Shit.

The three males said nothing as their form rippled from the chrome skin of Diviner to the silvery-blue of the aether creatures.

Jinx released my arm and her skin too changed from Diviner to match. The same silvery-blue skin, pure white hair, though a pastel-pink shade highlighted the tips of her elongated ears.

"How are you doing that?" I gasped.

"It's easy to swap forms once you've taken a soul." Her skin rippled to Diviner and then back again to prove it. "You don't let yourself go that far, so you don't see how it's done. You *should* learn, you know. Can't have you walking around Chime looking like aether. Bit suspect."

One of the aether creatures stepped forward and their form changed to that of a Necro.

"He's offering to heal your ribs," Jinx said.

I eyed the Necro. "He can't make the offer himself?"

"They don't trust you yet."

The feeling was mutual, though I couldn't help but feel unnerved to be left out of these private conversations when we were supposedly family. Though what unnerved me more was how easily Jinx had taken command of this entire situation.

These beings were my siblings. I shared a god with psychopathic creatures made of chaotic energy. Maybe I was still in that Mesmer dream parlor with Quen and I'd wake up to discover this had all been some terrible nightmare.

Still, I didn't have the luxury of snubbing them. I nodded at the Necro, and his hand went to my neck. His icy touch was a shock, though that didn't compare to the burning sensation that flooded my blood. Something cracked inside me, and I bit down on my fist to keep myself from screaming. And then the pain vanished with one last aching throb.

I sucked in a deep breath. "Thank you."

The Necro ignored me and turned to Jinx. With a single touch, her cuts and scratches were wiped clean.

"What now?" I asked, my breathing finally returning to normal. "Thanks to your attacks, the elevator is smashed to pieces. How do you expect to get up the tower? Climb?"

The Necro bristled at my tone. The other two shrugged off their jackets and sprouted massive silvery wings as their forms changed to Zephyr.

"Oh, come on," I moaned. "We're not flying up the shaft?"

"They're flying," Jinx said. "We're gonna hold on and hope they don't drop us. Though it'd be funny if they did. Splat!" Jinx clapped her hands and giggled.

Yes, falling to my death would be the cherry on top of this shit cake.

The taller of the two Zephyr approached me and his height dwarfed my own, which was a rarity. "Don't like heights, miss? I promise I'll keep a tight hold, though don't be offended if my hand slips."

"So you do talk?" And with surprising clarity.

"We're rather chatty, actually, miss. Just not with outsiders."

"I'm one of you, aren't I?"

"Are you though?" His beak peered closer, as though examining my face. "We spent our entire lives trying to free ourselves from that accursed clock tower while you skipped merrily around Chime, completely oblivious. Forgive us for feeling a little resentful."

"The clue there is *oblivious*—I had no idea you existed." I glared at Jinx.

"You try being stuck inside someone's inane thoughts," Jinx muttered.

The Zephyr chuckled and opened his arms as though welcoming me into his embrace.

I lifted my nose and turned to Jinx. "Surely there must be some other way?"

But she'd already climbed into the arms of her Zephyr. "Nope," she said, the word coming out with a *pop*.

Shit. They left me with little choice. "Do you have a name?" I asked my Zephyr. "We're about to become well acquainted."

"Chance." Light danced in his aether eyes. "I hope you'll take a *chance* on me, miss."

His leering grin was just as troublesome as Jinx's, and I scowled at them both for making light of this situation. Thousands of Vesper were gone, many more were dead across Central Station, and they were making *jokes*?

Gods knew what chaos I was about to walk—or fly—into, but I allowed his talons to grip my waist as I wrapped my arms around his neck.

I didn't want to be *this* intimate with another male, a stranger, but at least this one was hugging me instead of killing me. His mighty wings flapped. My stomach lurched, and I bit back a scream.

We were flying up.

Chance swerved into the clock tower's shaft with practiced finesse and my nails dug into his shoulders, holding on for dear life. The darkness of the clock tower swallowed us whole, with only the silvery-blue aether lights flashing by every so often. I no longer possessed the Vesper vision to see just how high we were going.

A bluster of air wafted from the other flapping Zephyr beside me, ruffling my hair and skirt. Jinx whooped a laugh as I tried not to bloody piss myself.

Were we headed for the Golden City? Though a few heartbeats later, we slowed. Chance's wings flapped to a halt, hanging us precariously in midair, and then he maneuvered toward some sort of platform covered by a hatch in the wall. Reds signs warned of electrical danger ahead, but Chance ignored them as the hatch opened, and we landed inside a metal tunnel.

I staggered inside, my steps dizzy and unsteady from flight. "What is this?" Dim aether lights highlighted what appeared to be some rusty old maintenance tunnel. Thick bronze pipes lined the walls and ceiling, creating a passageway of glittering gold.

"Keep going and you'll see," Chance said.

The others landed behind me. I placed one careful foot in front of the other. The tunnel eventually opened out into a chamber with a large round hatch twice my size. More piping and wires covered the walls, and though nothing seemed powered other than the odd emergency light, I could hear—no, feel—the hum of aether.

"Corentine—she's not hiding behind that thing?" I huffed a laugh. "It's hardly the most secure location, is it?"

"Maintenance staff are forbidden from entering," Chance explained. "Not even Diviner engineers come here. See those wires?" He pointed to the walls around us. "They direct power to the Gate. And when the Gate is churning, the amount of aether in this room is enough to melt skin from bone."

Jinx slapped my shoulder. "Why do you think we needed to break the Gate first? With that thing powered down, we can get inside."

In all the commotion, I'd forgotten that Eventide's destruction had effectively broken the Gate. "Will the Gate power back on?" Without it, there'd be no traffic from Chime to the other domains, or vice versa. Though given what had befallen Eventide, maybe that was a good thing.

"The Wardens will get it working again. We'll be long gone by then." Jinx stepped up to the hatch and wrenched up a handle. It opened with an ominous creak and a flash of bright silvery light spread across the floor. "It's time to meet our maker." Jinx grinned. "Welcome to Babel!"

I stepped into disaster.

I don't know what I'd expected—a room full of bronze metal and steaming pipes? A cage made of bleeding spikes? A pit of lava full of hissing obsidian snakes? What I stood in felt completely impossible.

The sky wasn't a gorgeous blue with wispy clouds, but a swirling mess of bright pink and blue dotted with silvery stars, each rotating in maddening circles and their tails fading into some never-ending black hole. It was aether on a grand cosmic scale.

And we—Jinx, Chance, and the other Zephyr—stood on a floating barren rock in the middle of it. More rocks floated around us, but not all were barren. Some were made from buildings, like the brick homes of Chime's Central square. Most were intact, though others crumbled, as though they'd been blasted in half. An assortment of other random objects floated by in the aether—a tram carriage, a bench, a lamppost, a printing press, a single sloshing cup of tea. The order of it made no sense.

Babel resembled the end of time—like Chime had exploded, and this was all that remained.

"What is this?" I asked.

AN ILLUSION.

The voice rang in my head, though I couldn't tell from what direction. Judging by the reactions of Jinx and the others, they'd heard it too.

"An illusion of what? The future?"

THE PAST. THIS IS WHAT OUR DOMAIN ONCE RESEMBLED. WHAT BABEL ONCE LOOKED LIKE BEFORE THE TWELVE GODS FORGED IT INTO CHIME. THIS WAS MY DOMAIN. OUR HOME.

"No offense, but it's not much. No cafés for a start?"

Jinx scowled at me, but Corentine laughed, and her laughter echoed in the depths of my mind.

The world seemed to shift, and I gasped as a brilliant blue sky replaced the oppressive pink aether, as though plucked from my imagination. The floating amalgamation of rocks and buildings formed tiny floating paradises of palm trees and cascading waterfalls that ran off the cliffs and splashed into nothing, casting rainbows instead of chaos.

IS THIS THE WORLD YOU SEEK? BABEL WAS A PLAYGROUND. EACH OF MY CHILDREN CREATED THEIR OWN WORLD. THEY PLAYED WITH REALITY, SCULPTED THE COSMOS TO WHATEVER THEY DESIRED. MILLIONS OF DOMAINS ALL BOUND TO ONE.

"Millions? But there's only twelve—thirteen domains?"

THE VASTNESS OF INFINITY IS ONLY LIMITED BY IMAGINATION, BUT EVEN CREATION NEEDS RULES. YOU ARE MY CHILDREN, BUT THE ELEVEN WERE THE FIRST. DOR AND I BIRTHED THEM AND THEY IN TURN MADE THEIR OWN DOMAINS SEPARATE FROM OURS. THEY WANTED THEIR FREEDOM. I GRANTED IT. AND THEN THEY LOCKED ME HERE, STOLE MY DOMAIN, AND MADE IT THEIR OWN. CHIME IS NOT MY CREATION. IT IS THEIRS.

I glanced toward Jinx and the others, who were staring in awe. "So you and Dor were a thing?" Could gods even love as mortals did?

"That's your question?" Jinx said with a raised eyebrow.

"Well, no, but I don't understand why I'm here—and how an all-powerful god of the cosmos found themselves being imprisoned by their own children. This is your domain, isn't it? How could they steal it?"

THEY CONSPIRED AGAINST ME. DOR BETRAYED ME. HE TRICKED ME INTO ENTERING MY OWN SUBMISSION. FOR THOUSANDS OF YEARS, I HAVE REMAINED HERE AS THEY LEECHED MY LIFE FORCE AND USED IT TO POWER THEIR GREAT GATE. IT IS MY ENERGY, MY AETHER, WHICH LIGHTS YOUR LANTERNS. WHICH TRAPS ME. FOR AN ETERNITY, I SLEPT.

AND THEN DOR'S CHILD AWOKE ME.

"Quen," I whispered.

The floating waterfalls vanished, replaced with a vision of the same platform inside the clock tower shaft I'd landed on. And there, screaming in pain, lay a young Diviner boy.

A younger Quen.

He appeared so much smaller and innocent, and his face lacked the eyeglasses I'd become accustomed to, but it was undoubtedly Quen.

SPEAK OF YOUR VISION, Corentine's voice boomed. *AND I WILL SAVE YOU.*

I watched as the younger Quen dragged himself through the maintenance tunnel. The *snap* and *crackle* of aether danced around him, but in this vision, Quen wasn't perturbed, and he followed Corentine's commands to a panel with a series of buttons.

All the while he described the aether attack on Chime. The visions he and I had both shared. He'd spent his life wiping these memories, running from inevitability.

But he always knew it would end this way.

The younger Quen flipped a lever. Then he screamed as the tower, and the vision, went dark.

"What did you do to him?" I demanded.

THIRTEEN YEARS AGO, DOR'S CHILD PAUSED THE FLOW OF AETHER TO MY PRISON. I SENT YOU AND YOUR SISTER THROUGH THEIR MACHINES.

"No way!" Jinx was shaking her head. "We exist because of *Corinth*?"

Gods. I owed my entire existence to Quen. "Then how did we end up in the Undercity? Why don't I remember?"

I HAD ONLY ONE CHANCE, BUT I WAS EXHAUSTED AND FULL OF PAIN. I MISCALCULATED THE AETHER REQUIRED, AND YOUR SOULS MERGED INTO ONE BODY. YOU DO NOT REMEMBER. BUT SHE DOES.

I SPOKE TO HER. YOU NEVER ANSWERED.

Jinx had always described herself as my brain, and her presence inside my head had effectively blocked my connection to Corentine. To keep me sane, she'd said. With all the mental screaming I'd endured, perhaps Jinx had done me a favor.

Though I... I'd never been quite right, myself. Foolish. Clumsy. Forgetful. Prone to wanton acts of self-destruction and pure idiocy.

Perhaps I existed in my own sphere of madness.

"Why?" I demanded. "Why blast us out of the aether?"

Jinx rolled her eyes. "To free her, idiot."

"And how are we supposed to do that?"

The world of Babel shifted once more, shimmering through the haze of heat. And then it vanished altogether.

I blinked as my eyes adjusted to the dark. All I could make out were wispy strands of multi-colored energy floating through the air like smoke.

"Please don't kill me," mumbled a voice by the giant window that took up the entire length of the far wall. No, it wasn't a window, it was the clockface of the tower. The numerals were taller than I, though through the white stained glass, I could see the city below. And huddled against it was a familiar Zephyr in a white lab coat.

"Doctor Zachery Finch," Jinx confirmed.

I crouched by his side. He flinched from me, burying his head in his hands as he ruffled his feathers in defense.

"Why is he here?" I snapped to Chance.

"We needed a Zephyr. And he worked on these machines. We wanted his knowledge."

"What machines?" I asked as the aether lights hummed into life. Bright silver shone on the rusted metal that covered the entire room.

"Mother," Jinx gasped.

My gaze followed Jinx's hurried steps across the bronze-plated room to what appeared to be a large reactor like the one in the steamworks.

I swallowed bile.

A woman sat in the heart of it, on a similar chair to the god-splitting machine, her naked body strapped in and unable to even wiggle, though her skin was so taut, the bones pressed prominently against it. Various black wires and pipes were plugged into the veins of her arms, legs, and neck, and they fed back into the machine. The skin around each entry point was a necrotic black rot against the silvery-blue of her skin.

I looked up into her face and swallowed a scream.

She wore Jinx's face—*my* face—and her mouth contorted in agony; her blackened teeth grinding, her eyes rolling to their whites. Her head had been shaved completely bare and she wore the same headpiece the Wardens had forced on me.

Jinx ran to the machine and tried to reach out, to grab the woman, but a bolt of aether rippled like a shield, knocking her back. She stared at me over her shoulder, her eyes lit with blazing fury. "You see what your precious Diviner have *done*?"

DON'T BE SO HARSH, DAUGHTER, Corentine's voice rattled in the room without moving her lips. *I ONCE FELL FOR A DIVINER'S CHARMS. IT'S WHAT LED TO MY IMPRISONMENT.*

I'd never been known to pity a god, but this... Corentine had been reduced to a wretched mortal. How long had she been trapped here? Truly thousands of years, as she'd said?

No wonder she'd been screaming.

No wonder Jinx hated the Diviner.

If the Diviner were capable of this, of imprisoning a god within their own domain and turning them into some glorified power source, then what else were they capable of?

They'd split their own mortals' souls to keep this hideous secret private. And the Wardens were completely in their pocket.

"Why would Dor do this? Why not kill you?" If killing a god was even possible, though... It must be. I'd taken Valeria's soul.

FOR AS LONG AS CHAOS HAS EXISTED, SO HAS TIME. THE COSMOS IS FORMED FROM THE BUILDING BLOCKS OF AETHER. ALL THAT EXISTS SHARES THIS ENERGY, AND THE AETHER IS INTERCONNECTED LIKE VEINS. IT CANNOT EXIST ALONE.

THE GODS ARE ORGANS, VITAL SYSTEMS WHICH KEEP THE AETHER HEALTHY AND WHOLE. TIME IS THE BRAIN. NO BODY, NO SYSTEM, CAN FUNCTION WITHOUT IT. BUT IT IS THE HEART WHICH HOLDS EVERYTHING TOGETHER, WHICH PUMPS THE AETHER THROUGH THE ORGANS, THE BODY. NONE OF THE GODS, NOT EVEN TIME, CAN EXIST WITHOUT THE HEART.

WE ARE THE HEART.

"All to power this shit heap of a city," Jinx said, and waved her hand at the clockface.

I stared out at the glittering lights. I'd always paid attention to the aether lamps because they hurt, but from this high I could see a whole pulsing ocean of them. And directly opposite me stood the Silver Suite. Quen's apartment.

From inside his home, I'd stared right into this room without ever knowing what lay trapped inside it.

Jinx took my hand and dragged me to the machine. "We can free her. Look." She brought my hand up against the invisible barrier surrounding the machine and a ripple of static tickled my palm. Then the colors flashed individually, enough for me to make out patterns layered over one another.

These were chains. Twelve chains, each representing the gods and their domains. My palm snagged on a dark purple one. Valeria's energy. It tugged at my hand, wanting to draw me in. Wanting me to break it.

"It's the gods' own aether which keeps Mother trapped," Jinx said with sudden eagerness. "With Valeria's soul, you can break her chain. But we need the others to fully drop the barrier. Destroy the gods, and we can free our mother."

I withdrew my hand. "Destroy them?"

"Take their souls." Jinx's aether eyes came alive. "Fucking up Eventide stopped the Gate and allowed our siblings to escape this room, but the Wardens will soon patch those leaks and get the Gate running again. Then Mother will remain trapped here with no way of sending more of our siblings through the aether.

"But you have Valeria's soul, don't you see? You can break her chain—and then Mother will have enough energy to create more souls—to invade the other domains and take back what's ours. We could end the reign of gods!"

"But—you saw what happened to Eventide. To the Vesper. If we did that to every god..." Then the domains would fall. All of them. And their mortals would go with them.

Jinx shrugged. "The gods trapped our mother. They deserve what they get."

I took a step back. "The gods may deserve it, but their mortals don't! You're talking about killing thousands of mortals—of mass genocide—"

"You weren't so bothered when you took Valeria's soul."

"I lost Malk! I will *never* see him again. Do you hear me? I—I—" I covered my mouth. I'd wiped Malk from existence.

Gods. I loved him. I loved everything he was.

Once, after we'd first confessed our feelings for one another, he'd shared his fears of losing his soul to his god, of being at the mercy of an entity who could wipe him away in an instant without a second thought. He'd lived his life taking risks because to Malk, life was so precious, so fragile, that he could lose it all—lose me—in a single breath.

But I'd done that. I loved him, and I'd been the one to rip him from reality.

To send him to a void beyond death.

And not just him. I'd condemned all Vesper to the same fate. I'd completely obliterated them. Thousands of mortal souls wiped away in a heartbeat.

And Jinx wanted me to do that to *every* domain?

Take the soul of Serenity, and I lost Harmony.

Take Edana, and I lost Sinder.

Take The Nameless One, and I lost Vincent.

And Dru too, my dearest friend... I couldn't lose her. None of the Godless deserved that fate. No mortal in Chime did.

"And what then?" I tried to keep my voice steady, but it cracked. "You destroy all the domains, what are you left with?"

WE WILL REMAKE THE UNIVERSE.

"Remake it out of Chime's ashes?"

YOU WANTED A GODLESS WORLD. I'LL OFFER YOU ONE.

Except that would be a lie. There'd still be a god. A crazed, tortured one that I would be bound to. That wasn't freedom.

"Kayl." Jinx forced a smile, though I could see her irritation flare again, as though she thought me some simpleton who couldn't understand the basic mechanics of the pissing cosmos. "If you're so scared, you can stay here. Keep Mother company. Chance and I will do the dirty work and you can sit in your happy little bubble. All we need is Valeria's soul." Her eyes flared. "Break the chain, sister."

If I did that, I'd be giving Corentine more power to steal the souls of innocent mortals. If I didn't, the Wardens would regain control—they'd attempt to split the souls of my siblings, and then their grand clock tower reinforcements would go ahead.

There could be no doubt the Diviner's actions were reprehensible, that Dor had condemned an entire domain and its mortals to torture and imprisonment.

I held no love for the gods. Of course I didn't. But damning the remaining eleven domains was no answer.

SHE HAS DOUBTS, Corentine's voice rang in the room.

Shit!

Jinx lunged at me.

I slid from her reach and ducked under Chance, who also dove forward to grab me. The three Chaos in the room formed a semicircle, penning me in against the clockface and the darkened corner where Doctor Finch had curled into a whimpering ball.

"Stop being a selfish brat!" Jinx snapped. She and Chance stalked toward me with their hands stretched out, ready to tackle me to the ground. "Mother needs us and you won't even help? We're family!"

I shuffled back against the window, my palms pressing against cold metal. I should have known the glass would be too thick to break. "Family doesn't force you into committing mass genocide."

"Come on, Kayl." Jinx smirked. "I spent my entire life doing what you wanted. You can't let me have this one thing?"

"These situations are hardly comparable." Gods, they spoke of genocide as if it were some family picnic in Meridian Park.

From the corner of my eye, I spied a door cut into the glass by Doctor Finch's side. If I could take his form, I could glide down to Central. The thought didn't fill me with joy, but my twin had me trapped. And if I left him here, he'd likely lose his soul, too.

"It won't hurt," Chance said, his voice some parody of sympathy. "We just want the power that's inside you."

The power of a god.

They thought I was nothing more than some incompetent idiot. Even the Godless hadn't trusted me to make my own decisions, to run my own operations. Sure, I'd made mistakes—but how many of those mistakes were mine? How many were Jinx's? She and Corentine had manipulated me into taking Valeria's power, into damning an entire domain of mortals. Into leaving Quen behind.

He hadn't doubted me. He'd believed I could stop this madness.

Jinx had said it herself; we were all made of aether, and if I possessed the soul of a god, I could manipulate it. I could keep it from Corentine.

And Chime would be safe. At least for now.

Deep inside, I felt it. Not the hum of aether, but the warmth of a soul that wasn't mine. Valeria's soul. And I could reach it. Touch it. Use it. Her power now belonged to me.

Through me, the Vesper would live on.

STOP HER.

My body switched to Vesper, as easily as though I'd touched another Vesper—though what I'd touched was Valeria's power—and I plunged the entire room in darkness. Jinx swiped the air, missing me by an inch, and she stumbled into the window.

"You bitch!" Jinx yelled.

Chance tried to find me, and his desperate attempts at catching me sent him careening into the other Zephyr. Silver light battled against my shadows, but couldn't penetrate the darkness of a Vesper. Hah! They couldn't see a damn thing!

COME TO ME, DAUGHTER.

No, thank you.

I grabbed Doctor Finch's arm with one hand and covered his beak with another. "I'm getting you out of here," I whispered. "Don't scream, and follow me."

He sucked in air around my palm as I yanked him up.

I kicked the door to the clockface open, though in opening it, I sent a beam of light into the room which highlighted my position.

"Grab her!" Jinx screeched.

Chance ran for me, but I shoved Doctor Finch out onto some sort of platform and slammed the door in Chance's face, making him fall with a howl. The whoosh of air fluttered my skirt. My foot slipped, and I almost stumbled off the dangerously thin platform.

Shit. We were hundreds of meters up in the air. One false step, and my soul would be floating in the aether.

"Are you *crazy*?" Doctor Finch squawked as he clung to a fragile-looking railing. "Do you think I can *fly*? You may not have noticed, but I *don't have wings*!"

I clutched the railing and edged slowly to his side. My heart pounded with each miniscule movement. *Don't look down, don't look down.* I grasped onto Doctor Finch's wrist. Wings burst from my back and almost blew me away like a kite, but the doctor grabbed my flapping blouse and pulled me onto the platform.

The door to the clock tower swung open. "Kayl!" Jinx screamed, and this time her eyes were full of horror. "Stop it! Fuck's sake, you're going to fall!"

"Tie your lab coat around me," I said to Doctor Finch. "And hang on like your life depends on it." I wrapped my arms around him.

"Oh god, I never asked for this," he whimpered as he clung to my waist.

"Why are you doing this?" Jinx stepped onto the platform and it lurched beneath us. "You're my sister! My twin, my heart! I've loved you my entire *life*! Why don't you love me? Why are you rejecting our mother?" Her voice broke, and even in the wind, I could feel her despair as though she were still in my mind.

Tears burned in my eyes. "I'm sorry, Jinx."

I stepped off the platform and plummeted through the air.

36

Who owns your thoughts?
Who is making your decisions?
Who is responsible for the consequences of your actions?
Think for yourself.
Or the gods and their Wardens will think for you.
—Anonymous, *Godless flier*

THE AIR BILLOWED AROUND me and Doctor Finch as we fell from the clock tower. Shit, we fell so fast, I could make out no details of the tower or the city beneath us. They merged into one terrifying blur.

"Open your wings!" Doctor Finch screeched.

Oh right, that was what I was supposed to do.

My wings flared wide, and I jerked backwards as the air current whipped us wherever it pleased. Doctor Finch was shorter than I, but his weight dragged me down. Even though he clung with a rib-crushing squeeze, I could feel him slipping from my grip.

We wouldn't make it to Central in one piece.

Jinx had helped me fly the first time, and I tried to remember how she'd manipulated my wings. I stretched them out as far as it felt comfortable to do so, and the heart-stopping plummet steadied into a smoother glide, though we were still descending with impossible speed. How in god's name did Zephyr live like this?

"Aim for the towers!" Doctor Finch yelled.

I quickly scanned the horizon. Directly ahead of us were the tower blocks of Central, including the Silver Suite. The tallest of the towers was a Zephyr-owned one, Sky Loft, and I knew from passing gossip that it contained its own landing pad specially made for Chime's Zephyr mortals.

That would be the obvious place to land, given how close it was to Harmony's safe house. Perhaps too obvious.

Though my biggest problem was that I didn't know how to steer or land. Chances were, I'd fly us straight into someone's window and we'd leave a bloody smear.

The wind, it seemed, agreed with me as it steered me away from the towers altogether.

"Oh my god! We're going to die!" Doctor Finch dug his claws into my hip to stop himself from slipping further. "Zyclone, *please*—"

"Don't start praying, you idiot!" I yelled back. Sure, if his god snapped him out of existence, I wouldn't need to worry about carrying his ungrateful arse, but he'd be dead, regardless. If his god hadn't bothered to birth the doctor wings, then I doubted Zyclone cared for his life at this point.

Honestly, you'd think a Zephyr with no wings would be happy to fly.

Sprawling patches of dark green spread beneath me. Meridian Park. I tried to steer toward it. At least crashing into a tree would be safer than trying to land between buildings.

My flight pattern spun in a circle as the ground raced to meet us. And then a dark blue mass appeared between the green. Of course, the lake! I pressed my legs together and dove for it. "Can you swim?"

"*What?* No!"

"Then try not to drown. I'm going to drop you!"

Doctor Finch screamed the entire way down and for a moment, I thought he'd pull me with him and we'd become tangled underwater. But then he slipped from my grasp.

I didn't see him land, but his screams cut off with a satisfying splash. He'd survive, I hoped.

I steered to the embankment and aimed to take a running landing like I'd done in the steamworks, but the ground appeared far too soon. I braced my knees for the impact.

My right foot slipped on the dirt with a painful twist.

"Shit!" I fell face forward and my palms scraped pebbles as I landed on my knees.

Fuck, I'd landed. I'd actually landed!

But now I was stuck in the middle of Meridian Park.

I tried to stand. Pain cracked through my right ankle and sent a rush of nausea through me. Nope, that wasn't happening.

My persona quickly switched to Vesper, and I used a cloak of shadow to crawl into the nearest bush. I sat back on my arse and stretched out my foot. I couldn't bend it and trying to do so sent spasms of pain up the joint. Walking would be impossible for a time, and I was still out here in the open. I let my breathing relax as I stared at the evening skyline.

The clock tower's face was still stuck between twelve and one, though I knew it must be later by now. Aether lamps dotted within Meridian Park hummed with an irritated buzz, as though trying to find me.

Maybe my new siblings could locate me that way; I possessed a soul Corentine needed. Both Jinx and the Wardens would likely be looking for me. My graceful fall from the sky wouldn't have gone unnoticed.

Though I was in no state to run for my life just yet. The Godless safe house was a fair distance for me to crawl to. Doctor Finch might be able to splint my leg if he'd survived. I couldn't hear any screaming coming from the lake, which meant he'd either managed to swim to safety, or he'd drowned. But I didn't think he was that sort of doctor anyhow. Healing was a Necro's business.

The bushes rustled. I grabbed a stone and aimed it to defend myself in case Doctor Finch hadn't found me, but the dark face peering at me was the last I expected.

A Mesmer woman.

"Uh, Lady Nala? Nora?" I couldn't remember the name of the Mesmer from the dream parlor in Sinner's Row, and this Mesmer looked suspiciously like her.

The Mesmer reached for me. "Hush. Sleep now."

"What are you—"

Her fingers pressed into my forehead.

Tiny black dots swallowed my vision, and I felt myself fall once more.

I woke buried among a sea of pillows. Relaxing puffs of lavender incense enticed me back to slumber, but I sat up and rubbed my eyes.

It was like being inside a Mesmer dream parlor, only the entire domed room was filled with pillows like one gigantic bed. I rolled my right ankle. It no longer hurt, as though I'd never injured it at all, and my skin was still the indigo of a Vesper.

This had to be a dream. A silly jaunt to Sinner's Row. I stifled a giggle.

Any minute now, Malk would waltz through those doors and snuggle beside me. There was no thirteenth god, no crazy twin sister. Eventide still existed. Reve slept in Grayford. Varen awaited tales of my latest exploits. Harmony would ask for my help with the printer. Dru would chide me for my appetite, but split a cream cake with me. Sinder and Vincent would be sitting in the tram playing a heated game of cards.

I'd never befriended the Dark Warden, a Diviner named Quentin Corinth. Hadn't kissed him or missed his comforting touch. How absurd would *that* have been?

No, I'd consumed some fabulous Vesper mushroom and dreamed the whole thing. Of course I had. Dru was always saying my imagination was out of control, and that was what these dream parlors were for; to live your wildest dreams. Though why my dreams held so much misery and death, I didn't understand.

YOU HAVE ABANDONED ME.

I screamed and leaped up. "You're not real! You can't be!"

The door swung open, and Vincent bounded inside. "You're safe, Kayl. It's okay."

"Where's Malk? Is he out there?" I crawled over the cushions and grabbed his jacket. "Please tell me this has all been a dream, some terrible nightmare, *please.*"

Vincent held my shoulders and offered a pitying smile. "I'm sorry."

Tears ran down my cheeks. "But it—it can't be real. They're gone. The Vesper. They're all gone?" I scrunched my eyes closed to fight the wave of sobs crushing through me.

They'd faded into dust. Every single one of them. And *I'd* been responsible for it.

I'd watched the love of my life fade into oblivion.

Images of the Vesper disintegrating into nothing burned in my mind's eye. They squeezed my chest until I couldn't breathe, until I thought they'd burst from my lungs and leave a bleeding wound where my heart should be.

Now I understood why Quen wiped his damn memories.

Vincent put an arm around my back, allowing me to burrow my face into his shoulder and lose myself to the cold numbness of his body. I didn't deserve his comfort.

He offered me a handkerchief from his inner jacket pocket, and I withdrew from his embrace to blow my nose. "Dru, and the others?"

"They're safe and unharmed."

"Where are we? This looks like a dream parlor."

"Because it is. Our safe houses are compromised. The Wardens knew we'd be there, but a Mesmer came to us and offered shelter. She witnessed a vision of you falling from the clock tower, and so she gathered us here. We... saw the Gate stop."

"The Vesper, I... I need to explain what happened in Eventide—"

"You need to rest."

"I'm fine," I lied, and wiped my eyes clear. "Get me a drink, something strong, and I'll explain everything. Harmony, you... You need to know."

Vincent helped me up and offered me his jacket in place of my torn blouse that had ripped to shreds, thanks to my Zephyr wings. I buttoned the jacket up and straightened my skirt as best I could. He led me out into a hallway and we entered another domed room—a planetarium.

Figures sat by a round table which took up space instead of a bed. Harmony, Sinder, and Dru. They were all here.

All except Malk, Reve, and Quen.

"Kayl!" Dru leaped from her chair and tackled me with a crushing hug, the vines of her hair tickling my neck. "You're okay."

I bit back tears as the rest of my family came to me. Sinder placed his warm hands on my shoulders, and then I was hugging him, too.

"We were worried sick, girl!" Harmony chided. "Is it true? Is Eventide gone?"

Sinder shot her a scowl. "She needs rest, Harm."

I patted his arm. "No, it's fine. I—"

"Chaos has awakened," came a dreamy voice from the door. The Mesmer who found me in Meridian Park.

We all turned to watch as the Mesmer female seemed to glide inside the room as though cut from silk. Her dark skin merged with the painted night sky, and the freckles of her cheeks glowed like silvery stars. She wore a flowing black dress and a glittering diamond necklace as though she'd just returned from a night on the town.

"She's the ambassador for the Mesmer here on Chime," Harmony said, her brows raising as though she couldn't quite believe what she'd said.

Neither could I. Why would the Mesmer ambassador be helping us? "I have, uh, a lot of questions, Your Excellency."

"They call me Reverie."

"Reverie? Like Reve? You Mesmer are connected, right? Is Reve with you?"

"We are connected, yes. We dreamed of Reve's journey. But he is no longer with us. Please, sit and make yourselves comfortable."

Dru pulled up two chairs close together as the other Godless sat by the round table and helped themselves to the pitchers of water and fruit juice waiting for us. I slid onto a chair beside Dru and stared at the ceiling. Splotches of sparkling stars glowed within the black paint, and round pink orbs dangled above us, moving in a slow circular pattern.

It reminded me too much of Corentine's visions; of Babel.

Reverie took her place by the table. "We are aware that Corentine awakens."

"You know of her?"

"Mesmorpheus does. We witnessed visions of Chime's destruction through the dreams of Quentin Corinth. We saw that you would play a part."

I exhaled one large breath. They'd stolen these visions from Quen's subconscious when we'd visited the dream parlor only days ago. "And you did nothing with this information? Nothing to help save Chime?"

"We thought Corentine asleep—"

"Corentine has been awake and screaming through the aether for years!"

"So there truly is a thirteenth god here on Chime?" Harmony asked, her eyes darting between me and Reverie. "And she's the reason Eventide is gone?"

"Indeed," the Mesmer said. "The other gods will be aware of her presence, and her threat. Corentine wants an end to the gods, much as you Godless do, but your goals do not align. She will destroy the domains, as she has destroyed Eventide. And the mortals of those domains will fade with them."

"The Vesper—they're really gone? All of them?" Harmony glanced to my Vesper form in disbelief, and I suddenly found the words stuck in my throat.

"They are gone," Reverie confirmed for me. "Mortals are but a dream of the gods, and Valeria's dream has now ended."

A heavy silence hung in the planetarium.

"Malk—he's gone forever?" Dru whispered. "And Reve?"

I wanted to wrap my arm around her shoulder, but shame made my limbs useless. Their deaths had been my fault. Quen's, too. Knowing I'd never see them again hurt my soul more than any god-splitting machine ever could.

If I hadn't helped the Glimmer with that cursed machine, none of this would have happened. That had been my operation, and I'd fucked it up in the most unimaginable way.

For years we'd served Grayford's poorest. Now, there'd be no mushroom stalls. No hurdy-gurdy players. No shadow puppet theaters. No tithe donations to dole out. No Varen to watch over them.

"I'd understand if—if you didn't trust me." The words caught in my throat. "It's because of me we no longer have Reve." I couldn't meet Dru's eyes. "No longer have Malk. Nor Quen to help us."

Harmony grabbed the back of her chair and stood on it with a shaky balance.

"That isn't safe, dearest," Sinder warned.

499

Harmony waved him off as she stood over us. "This is on me. Malk, Reve, and Corinth—their deaths—"

"No, Harm," I interrupted. "None of that is on you—"

"I'm responsible for you heathens." She shot me a glare. "But you're right, girl. Five years ago, you, Malk, Sinder, and Vincent set up the Godless thanks to our anonymous benefactor, the Dark Warden. You did it to serve the mortals of Chime, to protect them from their own gods. Corinth helped us because he knew, deep in his soul, what the gods and his Wardens were. Malk and Corinth, and yes, even Reve, all shared that same vision of a world where mortals could be free. None of that changed. They took fate into their own hands. They chose to be free. We'll honor them not as saints, but as the Godless they were."

"We'll honor them," Sinder repeated.

"We'll not forget them," Vincent added.

Dru placed her hand on my knee under the table. I had no words of gratitude for that small comfort, and could only pat her hand.

Harmony was right. Malk, Reve, and Quen; they'd all made their choice.

As I would make mine. Not on the side of the Wardens, and not on the side of Corentine and Jinx and the rest of those lunatics who called themselves my family.

No, I stood where I always had. With my real family.

"We'll honor them the only way a group of depraved heathens can," Harmony continued. "We move forward. But if the gods and the domains know of Corentine, surely they'll protect themselves?" She turned to Reverie. "The Wardens will step up to fix this?"

"They will," Reverie conceded. "But we see a future of much uncertainty. The children of Chaos will fight for our souls." Her dark eyes bore into mine. "And more domains will fade after Eventide unless you prevent it."

Jinx had taken the stage and won the first act, but the play was only beginning. Who knew where the curtain would fall? "I don't care for what the gods want. I don't care to protect them either. But you saw what happened to the Vesper—if the gods die, then their mortals die with them.

Our organization exists to protect them from their gods, but now... now we need to find a way to balance both."

Harmony flumped back into her seat. "This... complicates matters."

"The understatement of the century, darling," Sinder muttered.

"This goes beyond our conflict with the Glimmer. Shit, it goes beyond the Wardens and their soul-ripping machine. *This* is the story that'll break Chime, that'll pit the Wardens against the gods."

"And I have a crazy god shouting inside my head who wants to kill you all," I added. "As well as a crazy twin sister who wants the same. Just to keep us on our toes."

"Never a dull moment," Vincent said with a slight grimace.

"Corentine may be my god, but I will *not* stand by and let her destroy Chime or the other domains. I won't allow her or any of them to hurt more mortals."

Harmony smirked at me. "You've always been a liability, girl. But now I think you're truly Godless. We'll act as we've always acted, in the interests of Chime's mortals. Even if that means going up against both Wardens and this new god. If none of you can stomach that, then leave this room."

I glanced around the table, but no one moved. No one twitched.

"Dru?" I asked.

She'd always been close to her god, despite knowing our agenda, and I expected this to be too much even for her. But Dru glanced at me with a defiant anger, her golden flowers standing on end and quivering slightly. "I'm in."

"Are—Are you sure?"

"I'm cursed, aren't I? I gave Reve my flower, and he died. I gave Corinth my flower, and he died too. Maybe I should start handing them out to bloody Wardens—"

"Easy now, Dru," Harmony said. "You're not cursed."

Dru sucked in a breath and her flowers wilted. "No, but I'm pissed off, so I'm in, okay?"

I'd never seen her so angry. "Thank you, Dru. You're a true friend," I whispered.

She nudged me with her elbow.

Sinder slapped both hands onto the table's surface. "You know I enjoy endangering my life, dear ones. I'm in."

Vincent took one of Sinder's hands. "As am I."

"And what of you, Your Excellency?" I asked Reverie. "What's your stake in this? Why help us at all?" We Godless didn't care for Mesmorpheus either, and I didn't like the idea of being trapped inside an ambassador's home after Varen had betrayed us.

"Mesmorpheus enjoys your apostasy," Reverie said with the voice of one contemplating the weather.

"He... enjoys it?"

"They enjoy it. To Mesmorpheus, apostasy is another blueprint of mortal existence, a series of emotions which are worth exploring, not punishing. We will offer you sanctuary and resources in exchange for your nightmares, child of Chaos."

"My what?"

"Your nightmares," Reverie repeated, as though she'd just offered me a pissing cup of tea. "They are bound to be delicious."

Quite what the Mesmer wanted with my nightmares, I didn't know, but after everything that had happened, I was sure I'd be drowning in them. "Fine, they're yours. So what now?"

"Does this parlor have a printing press? Or room for one?" Harmony asked Reverie. "We're going to need to make more fliers. Thousands of them."

"What are you thinking?" Sinder asked with a shrewd smile.

"The five of us aren't enough to save Chime, even with Kayl and her special powers." Harmony winked at me. "No, it's time the Godless stopped living in the dark. No doubt the Wardens will cover up the real reasons for the Gate crashing and Eventide's disappearance, though they and the ambassadors have a task on their hands if they think they can cover up this many deaths. We need to show Chime's mortals the real monsters living in this city."

The Wardens had wanted to snuff us out. Neither they nor the gods listened to what their mortals had to say. We'd make them listen.

Chime needed godless heathens.

May the gods leave us to our fate.

For the first time in Chime's history, the Gate was closed.

I'd taken on an Umber form thanks to Dru and returned to Central Station to gather intel the next morning. The Godless hadn't wanted to let me leave on my own at first, but I assured them that no one would recognize me or care for an Umber wandering the streets, and honestly, I needed air.

Even with the plans Harmony had devised, I still felt restless. Useless.

Panicked whispers followed my stroll along the cobblestone streets. No trams cut through the morning throng of workers. No mortals hurried to grab a cup of tea or a bite to eat from their favorite café as all shops and boutiques were closed—boarded up in some cases. Even the delightful Lady Mae's. No Seren paperboys rushed by with their early editions of the Chime Courier. No lines of mortals formed queues beside the elevators leading up to the Golden City or down to the Undercity.

Though curious and angry travelers waited by Central Station, turned away by Wardens wielding batons and tasers.

They'd done a good job of cleaning up the devastation, however. The glass from the Golden City elevator had been swept up, the bodies removed. Posters lined the station walls and dominated the headlines of the Chime Courier, telling us to keep calm and carry on. The aether lamps no longer hummed—many had either exploded or been switched off, replaced by orange oil lamps.

I'd always loved the energy that sparked this city, but now that energy had been choked off and felt wrong. The clock should have struck nine, but the clock tower's hands were still stuck between twelve and one.

At the thirteenth hour.

Rapture should have opened, casting its glowing red light across the station, but instead the Gate's emptiness lingered like a gaping hole.

I'd no doubt the Wardens would fix it soon, though by then every domain would have suffered disruption. There'd be more angry voices asking questions and demanding answers.

Until then, Chime no longer ran like clockwork.

I wandered to the bench where Dru and I would wait for Malk after our shifts at Lady Mae's. Valeria's energy hummed inside me, buried somewhere in my subconscious. At times, I thought I could hear the voices of a thousand Vesper whispering feverishly in my brain. I thought I could hear Malk among them.

But that may have been wishful thinking.

WE COULD REMAKE EVENTIDE. YOU COULD HAVE YOUR VESPER BACK.

My heart caught in my throat. I knew Corentine's words were likely a trap, but I had to ask. *How?*

AETHER CAN BE RESHAPED. BRING ME VALERIA'S SOUL AND I WILL REMAKE YOUR LOVER.

And the rest of the Godless? You'd remake them? And Quen?

FOR YOU, DAUGHTER.

I didn't believe a word of it. Perhaps Corentine would bring back the Godless, but certainly not a Diviner.

The gods were made of aether, but could I, as a being of chaos, reshape that energy? Could I find a way to break the bond between mortal and god without the use of a god-splitting machine? Without tearing a soul apart?

Without my own god?

WHAT INTOXICATING INNOCENCE. Corentine's laughter rattled inside my head. *A MORTAL CANNOT EXIST WITHOUT THEIR GOD.*

You need me more than I need you, so I beg to differ.

YOUR SOUL BELONGS TO ME, DAUGHTER.

And yet you lack the power to take it, don't you?

YOUR ARROGANCE BLINDS YOU. YOU POSSESS ONE GOD'S SOUL, BUT YOUR SIBLINGS WILL TAKE THE REST, AND THEN THEY WILL COME FOR YOU.

Good luck to them.

So long as the Gate remained closed, not even Corentine's children could reach the other gods. Hopefully, the Wardens had the sense to reinforce the clock tower before powering up the Gate again, and the sense to at least inform the domains' ambassadors of the danger waiting to pounce. The Glimmer and Mesmer at least knew to protect themselves.

The Diviner most certainly.

It disgusted me that I now needed to worry for them, for god's sake.

But they also needed to worry about *me*.

I possessed the power to bring the gods down to my level.

Could a god feel fear? I'd soon find out.

Something bronze caught my eye in the trash can beside me, and I peered inside. A fob watch.

Not just any fob watch—I recognized the intricate pattern engraved into the brass. Quen had carried this beauty around with him everywhere. I scooped it out and cradled it in my palms. It popped open with a *click*. The glass had cracked in the middle and the hands were also caught between twelve and one. It must have broken during the scuffle.

A Diviner could fix this. I wound the crown, and it began to tick, though even I knew it wouldn't keep time. A bit like me.

"You've really chosen your side, huh?"

My eyes snapped up to Jinx leaning on a lamppost, still in her Diviner form and wearing that ridiculous crimson dress. Shit, Corentine must have guided her here.

"I'm on the side of the Godless. You know that."

"The gods don't care for the Godless. Your so-called 'family' will be swept aside when we do battle with the real powers of this universe. Why waste your time?"

I slowly rose from the bench, shoving the fob watch into my pocket. "I could ask you the same. You're fighting Corentine's battles, not your own. Do you need someone to be in charge of your fate, Jinx? Some higher authority to tell you what to do, what to think?"

Jinx pushed from the lamppost with a smirk. "You jabber on about freedom, but who will you blame next when you fuck up again? You've made quite a few fuckups, haven't you, sister?" She stepped forward. "Do you trust yourself? You haven't got me to bail you out anymore. Nor Malk, or Varen, or your Time Boy. Admit it. You need me."

"That's where you're wrong."

I switched to my Vesper form and faded into the shadows.

Jinx dove into the shade and swiped for me, but each frantic motion swept through nothing until her frustration grew and she kicked over the trash can.

"I'm going to find you, Kayl! And when I do, I'll rip your goddamn soul from your useless-arse body and trap you in mine! We'll see how *you* like it!"

I left her raging and stalked my way out of Central.

The Godless had enough enemies; throwing a crazed god and my own twin sister into the mix would liven things up, I supposed.

My thumb ran over the fob watch's brass in my pocket.

I only wished my partner were still here to help me face the chaos to come.

XXXVII

Is time never-ending? Do gods age and die as mortals do?
Only the gods can answer these questions.
The mortal mind is too limited for infinite concepts, and this itself is by
design. Our Father creates each of His sons with a specific path in mind. It is
our duty as His children to walk this path while honoring Him for our
existence. We do this by abstaining from sin—from distractions that
deviate from our designated path.
Our mortal minds have the capacity for thought and logic, which enables us
to fulfill the path our Father sets for us. But we do not have the capacity to
understand why. Such machinations belong to our Father, and it is sinful to
question it. Instead, meditate on your path. Seek guidance from Father and
your fellow Diviner.
In all we do, we must honor His will.
—H. Bezel, Philosophy for the Young Diviner

I SWAM IN A river of aether.

It was pleasantly warm, like the correct temperature to enjoy a good cup of tea, though now *I* was the tea leaves steeping among the milk and sugar of the universe. Thoughts and emotions floated past me on currents too fast for me to grasp, but I didn't concern myself with their existence, nor my own. Here, in the nothingness of the cosmos, I didn't need to think or breathe.

I simply was.

Moments splashed into the aether, sending ripples of time underneath me. They were my moments. Memories from my timeline. Points from my past. Visions of the future. It was remarkable, really. From all I'd studied of horology, I knew that time could not be altered. Once it had been observed, it was a fixed event, a point that could not be stopped. And yet I had altered my own timeline, somehow.

I'd witnessed the same death so many times in my visions. But the death which had found me was not the one I'd seen. It had been a far kinder death, in retrospect; to be yanked by one's god and tossed into the aether. Only a god of time could command the sort of power to ruin one's destiny.

The ripples grew stronger, and the rivers of time became choppy.

QUENTIN, my Father called. *WE WILL CORRECT YOUR PATH.*

A storm whipped time's foam into a frenzy. I cried out as it tossed me in the tumult.

And then I inhaled a breath. A real breath.

The tempest dumped me unceremoniously into the cold, harsh physicality of reality. I stood on shaking legs, the hairs across my body fighting off the aether static all around me, and I rubbed my arms. My very skin felt too tight, wrapped around my freshly made bones, and even my blood itched, as though my pulse pumped glass instead of life.

Without my spectacles, the world looked a blur, and my eyes squinted at the too-harsh glare of sunlight.

Then I heard it.

The *tick-tock* of time.

I slapped hands over my ears and winced. The *ticks* and *tocks* sounded like a thunderclap in my brain, the noise so sharp it made my teeth rattle. A second *tick* and *tock* joined it, and then many more, different pitches and tones that formed a deafening chorus of clocks and bells.

"Stop!" I yelled, but my dry voice died on my lips and could do nothing against the thousands of clocks chiming in and out of time.

If this was life, then take me back, let me bathe in nothing!

QUENTIN. MY SON.

His voice clapped against the cacophony.

The world adjusted itself to my eyesight, and I swallowed a scream.

Thousands of clocks hung suspended in the air, as though the world was made from the tapestry of clockwork mechanics. Each clock was a completely unique design or mechanism, ranging from wooden and brass regulators to swinging pendulums to screeching cuckoo clocks and hourglasses.

And my god floated in the heart of it.

"Father," I gasped, and glanced down. I stood on the line that traveled across His palm. I couldn't see the entirety of His being, for He dominated this dimension with His presence, and I was merely a speck of dust in His grasp, the height of His thumbnail.

This incarnation of Dor held the infinite age of an older mortal. A pure white beard cloaked His body and dangled into nothingness, though His skin was the same pearly shade as mine. His eyes the same startling silver, like gigantic moons.

YOU DISAPPOINT ME, QUENTIN, He said without once moving His lips. The ringing of the clocks faded from my mind in reverence to our maker.

I suddenly became aware of my own nakedness and tried to conceal myself with my hands. Tears ran down my cheeks, and my entire being burned with shame. "I'm sorry, Father." I blinked my eyes clear. "Why do I exist? Why bring me here?"

YOU EXIST BECAUSE I WILL IT. THOUGH YOU HAVE STRAYED FROM THE PATH I SET YOU, AND NOT FOR THE FIRST TIME.

"You forced me onto that path. I never wanted it." The words sounded so childish.

YOU MUST PUSH YOUR FANTASTICAL NOTIONS ASIDE. CHIME NEEDS WARDENS. THOSE WHO WILL PROTECT THE MORTALS FROM THEMSELVES.

"Why us? Why Diviner? We broke our own Covenant! The Wardens are meant to be controlled by all twelve ambassadors, and we let mortals like Varen and Gloria corrupt it!" And Elijah, but I couldn't bring myself to utter his name. To utter his betrayal.

YOU UNDERSTAND THAT MORTALS ARE FALLIBLE. EVEN OUR MORTAL VOICES FALL TO THE SAME MORTAL SINS. BUT WE ARE THE LOGIC WHICH HOLDS CHIME TOGETHER. WITHOUT US, THERE IS CHAOS.

"Eli—" I sucked in a breath. "He wasn't your perfect son." Though neither was I. "Chaos cannot be controlled. To even attempt so is illogical."

YOU HAVE SEEN CHAOS. YOU'VE SEEN WHAT WILL BECOME OF US IF WE DO NOT STOP IT.

"What would you have me do? One cannot stop the future in motion. If you couldn't prevent the destruction of Chime, then what hope did I have?"

YOU COVET CHAOS.

My cheeks burned. Perhaps I did. Sin and shame came to me too readily, no matter how much Father and Elijah had tried to correct my behavior. There was some flaw in my design that drew me to sin...

That wanted chaos.

YOU WERE MADE IN MY IMAGE, QUENTIN CORINTH. THOUGH I DESIGNED YOU TO BE HER MIRROR. CORENTINE.

"Then how can I beg forgiveness for acting as the man you designed, Father? I am your son! You let me suffer, you let me hurt!"

HOW CAN I HELP YOU WHEN YOU DO NOT HELP YOURSELF? WHEN YOU LIE TO ME, WHEN YOU ATTEMPT TO MANIPULATE YOUR OWN THOUGHTS AND MEMORIES? I OWN YOUR THOUGHTS, QUENTIN.

I'd tried to hide my mortal failings, but Father had seen them all, regardless.

But I was a mere mortal. I couldn't switch off my emotions.

DO YOU BELIEVE LOVE AND LUST TO BE UNIQUELY MORTAL CONCEPTS? OUR EMOTIONS SIRED MORTAL EXISTENCE, DESIRE, AND BLASPHEMY. YOU WERE CREATED WITH THESE SAME WEAKNESSES SO THAT YOU MAY UNDERSTAND THEM. YOUR EMPATHY FOR THE HEATHENS WAS DEVISED TO TEACH YOU THEIR THINKING AND DESTROY THEM.

Could that be true? That my entire existence had been orchestrated to infiltrate the Godless and the sinners of the world for so terrible a reason?

Then Father had made me wrong. I wasn't that bloodthirsty. I wasn't Elijah.

YOU MUST TAKE ELIJAH'S PLACE.

"No! Send me to the aether and bring back Elijah to mop up the mess he created—"

THIS IS YOUR MESS, QUENTIN. YOU KILLED ELIJAH. I WILL NOT RETURN HIM. YOU WILL TAKE HIS PLACE, AMBASSADOR CORINTH.

"You can't! To bring a mortal back to life goes against the Covenant—"

CHAOS BROKE THE COVENANT. WE MUST PLAY BY THEIR RULES.

Because to a god, the Covenant was simply an inconvenient guideline rather than a set of laws the rest of us mortals abided by. "Why me?" Why not someone—*anyone*—more competent?

BECAUSE SOON THE CHILDREN OF CHAOS WILL WAGE WAR AGAINST THE DOMAINS AND THE GODS WILL FACE THE SAME FATE AS VALERIA. AS WILL I.

"You imprisoned Corentine, you started this! She was one of the twelve—the thirteenth—and you condemned her and her mortals! Give them their freedom, their own domain, and they may well leave the others alone."

CORENTINE DESIRES REVENGE MORE THAN FREEDOM.

I couldn't say I blamed her.

YOU DO NOT UNDERSTAND. I WITNESSED A FUTURE WHERE SHE DESTROYS EVERYTHING WE BUILT. NOT JUST THE DOMAINS. NOT JUST THE GODS. BUT EXISTENCE ITSELF. EVEN HER OWN MORTALS. EVEN CHIME. SHE DESTROYS IT ALL IN HER MADNESS. IT HURT ME TO IMPRISON HER, BUT TO SAVE MILLIONS OF LIVES, PAST AND FUTURE... I HAD NO CHOICE.

That madness, that violence... I'd witnessed it in Jinx's eyes enough to know my Father wasn't simply speaking lies. Hadn't I been haunted by my own visions of destruction? I'd done nothing but watch as Chime had descended into chaos.

I'd watched Eventide and its Vesper fade into nothing.

But if time itself couldn't prevent it, then... "How can we stop chaos?"

YOU WALK THE PATH I SET FOR YOU.

To befriend the Godless? Kayl and Jinx? To infiltrate them, and what, kill them?

EVISCERATE THEIR SOULS. IT IS THE ONLY WAY.

"I can't," I whispered.

YOU CAN AND YOU WILL. I DESIGNED YOU TO CARRY THIS BURDEN.

"Is this why you make me suffer visions of death and destruction? Knowing how futile it is?" I'd not saved a single life. Not a single sodding one.

Those visions of death had destroyed *me*. I'd wiped them from my memories because I wasn't strong enough to carry those burdens.

How could I carry this?

YOU ARE STRONG, MY SON. THIS PATH WILL HURT YOU. BUT YOU WILL WALK IT. YOU ARE A WARDEN. IF YOU DO NOT ACT, THEN TIME ITSELF WILL END.

I knew, deep in my heart, that I couldn't.

Because the visions of my death haunted my dreams. The same dream, over and over. It had taken Jinx's true form to make me realize what those dreams were. I'd always thought a random aether creature would snatch my soul away. Maybe even Jinx.

But no. It was Kayl. It would always be her.

In my most wondrous dreams, I sagged to my knees, tears streaming down my face. I hugged her legs and pleaded not for mercy, but for her to do it.

She'll one day reach down and kiss me with such sweet lips, her silvery-blue eyes burning with determination, and her palm will rest on my neck.

Kayl will rip my soul apart.

And I'll thank her for it.

Author's Note

Thank you for reading! If you enjoyed THE THIRTEENTH HOUR, then please consider leaving an honest review on Amazon or Goodreads. Reviews mean the world to me and help support your favorite authors.

Kayl, Quen, and Jinx will return in 2022 for:

THE CRUEL GODS BOOK TWO

THE CHILDREN OF CHAOS

WANT MORE FROM CHIME?

Want updates on my next book or to sign up for advanced reader copies? Then join my monthly newsletter and you'll also receive a copy of THE TRAVELER'S HANDBOOK TO CHIME AND BEYOND, your guide to the domains of the gods:

TrudieSkies.com/Newsletter

Visit my website for a full color version of the domain map, character art, appendices, pronunciation guides, and other extra goodies:

TrudieSkies.com

Domain Glossary

A list of the twelve domains in order of their designated crossing time:

Memoria
Home to the Amnae.

An underwater city. Ruled by Anima, the god of academia, books, history, memories, and water.

Juniper
Home to the Fauna.

A treacherous jungle. Ruled by Faen, the god of animals, creatures, metamorphosis, and sacrifice.

Heartstone
Home to the Umber.

A mountainous region with valleys. Ruled by Unghard, the god of craft, discipline, earth, nature, servitude, and trade.

Solaris
Home to the Glimmer.

A golden city of cathedrals. Ruled by Gildola, the god of birth, dawn, femininity, piety, spring, and sunlight.

Arcadia
Home to the Seren.

A series of tropical islands. Ruled by Serenity, the god of art, beauty, creativity, song, and summer.

WITHERYN

Home to the Necro.

A frozen wasteland. Ruled by The Nameless One, the god of blood, disease, flesh, healing, and winter.

TEMPEST

Home to the Zephyr.

A sky world made from floating airships. Ruled by Zyclone, the god of air, machines, science, and technology.

OBITUARY

Home to the Leander.

A desert plain. Ruled by Lionheart, the god of battle, challenge, domination, legacy, masculinity, strength, and trials.

RAPTURE

Home to the Ember.

A volcanic strip of casinos. Ruled by Edana, the god of depravity, flame, pleasure, and sensuality.

EVENTIDE

Home to the Vesper.

A land of glowing mushrooms. Ruled by Valeria, the god of autumn, dusk, moonlight, and shadow.

PHANTASY

Home to the Mesmer.

An observatory of stars. Ruled by Mesmorpheus, the god of dreams, nightmares, stars, and visions.

KRONOS

Home to the Diviner.

A clockwork city. Ruled by Dor, the god of bureaucracy, justice, law, logic, order, and time.

Acknowledgments

Writing a book is always an emotionally adventurous endeavor. When I started writing THE CRUEL GODS, I knew I was creating an obnoxiously ambitious world and chaotically ridiculous story. Yet I fell in love with Chime, Kayl, and Quen, and I needed to write this book, even if I feared I'd written the most confusing book ever.

So, THANK YOU to my beta readers for attempting to make sense of this story and helping me to smooth out the confusing parts. Thanks to Catherine Bloom, Maria Z. Medina, and Olivia Hofer for reading the worst version of this book. Your sacrifice led to a much better book.

Thank you to Nia Quinn for your fantastic edits and support, Belinda Williams for your help with the blurb, Nathan Hansen for your lovely image headers, Seraphim for bringing my characters to life, Rey Morfin for your guidance in navigating the land of self-publishing, the amazing Soraya Corcoran for your absolutely gorgeous map of the domains which is just the best damn thing ever, and James T. Egan of Bookfly Design for the stunning and magical cover. It has been a pleasure working with you all.

Thank you to all the bloggers who continue to support indie authors!

Thank you to all the indie authors I have met and learned from over the years, especially those of you over at the Indie Authors Discord Server!

Thanks also to my dogs, Ben and Butch, for being a constant source of distraction.

Though the biggest thanks must go to Jack Roots. If not for you, the housework would never get done.

And THANK YOU, dear reader, for joining Kayl and Quen on this adventure of cruel gods and tea.

ABOUT THE AUTHOR

Trudie Skies is a British author based in North East England where she daydreams about clouds and fantasy worlds. Her debut novel, *Sand Dancer*, is a young adult fantasy adventure published by Uproar Books.

Follow the Author:

www.Facebook.com/AuthorTrudieSkies
www.Bookbub.com/Authors/Trudie-Skies
On Twitter @TrudieSkies

ALSO BY TRUDIE SKIES

The Sand Dancer Series

(Young Adult Fantasy)

Sand Dancer
Fire Walker
Wraith Maker: Coming Soon!

When her father's murder reveals a lifetime of lies, a half-starved peasant girl must disguise herself as a young nobleman if she hopes to make her way into the heart of her enemies. But what is she truly after—the truth or revenge?

Made in the USA
Las Vegas, NV
04 November 2021